Honeymoon to Die For

Honeymoon to Die For

A novel by
Don L. Searle

WAKING LION PRESS

ISBN 978-1-4341-0493-9

Published by Waking Lion Press, an imprint of the Editorium

Waking Lion Press™ and Editorium™ are trademarks of:

The Editorium, LLC
West Jordan, UT 84081-6132
www.editorium.com

The views expressed in this book are the responsibility of the author and do not necessarily represent the position of Waking Lion Press. The reader alone is responsible for the use of any ideas or information provided by this book.

This book is a work of fiction. The characters, places, and incidents in it are the products of the author's imagination or are represented fictitiously. Any resemblance of characters to actual persons is coincidental.

1

The telephone in their room was making its warbling ring tone when Matt opened the door.

"Who would be calling us here?" Jane said as he stood back to let her enter. Only a week before the wedding, Matt had surprised her with the news that they were going to honeymoon in San Francisco, after he figured out how to make the trip fit into their limited budget. Only a few close friends and their parents knew where they were. Was there some problem at home?

"Hello?" she said as she picked up the handset of the phone on the desk. She looked at Matt quizzically as she turned to hold the phone out to him. "For you."

He put the phone to his ear tentatively. "This is Matt."

A raspy male voice obviously not at its normal timbre said huskily: "You have something that doesn't belong to you. You have to give it back."

Matt was silent for a moment, unsure how to answer. "What? What are you talking about?"

"You have something that belongs to us. We want it—and you're going to give it back. I'll tell you where—"

"You've got the wrong number." Matt hung up the phone.

"That sounded like someone trying to disguise his voice," Jane said.

"Someone who wasn't making any sense." Matt put the call out of his mind as he picked up the San Francisco tourist brochure lying next to the telephone and began leafing through it. "Today we did Fisherman's Wharf, Alcatraz, and Ghirardelli Square. What do you want to see tomorrow?"

Jane put her arms around him and kissed him, letting her lips linger on his mouth. "I'm looking forward to seeing more of my thoughtful, handsome, loving husband." She let go of him and walked toward the bathroom. "But you can read me more sightseeing choices while I brush my hair."

"There's Chinatown. Golden Gate Park, the zoo, and—" He stopped to stare as the telephone warbled again. He let it sound four times before he picked it up. "Hello?"

"Matt Randall?" the same raspy voice asked.

"Who's calling?"

"You have something that doesn't belong to you. We want it."

"I don't know what you're talking about."

"Yes, you do. He shouldn't have given it to you. And you're going to turn it over to us."

"Who is 'he'? And if this is some kind of sick joke, you've got the wrong guy, so—"

There was an angry curse on the other end. "Stop trying to play games, big man, and listen up! You know what this is about, and if you don't give it back to us, you're not going to like what happens. Now pay attention while I tell you where we're going to meet."

"I don't know what it is you want, and we're not going to meet anywhere. Don't call again."

Matt dropped the phone into its cradle. Jane, watching him from the bathroom doorway, raised her eyebrows in a question. Matt frowned and shook his head. "I don't know. He says I have something that belongs to them, whoever *they* are, and they want me to give it back. I have no idea what he's talking about." He couldn't put the call out of his mind this time. It was unsettling.

Jane glanced into the bathroom, then turned back to him looking puzzled. "Come here."

He walked to the bathroom door and she pointed at the counter by the sink. Her lipstick, mascara, body lotion, toothbrush, toothpaste, comb, and hairbrush were spread out around her makeup case. "I didn't leave those out. I think someone's gone through my things."

He looked at her uncertainly. "Who would do that?"

"I don't know." She walked to the closet and looked down at their luggage where they had stowed it. "Someone's moved my suitcase, and the zipper's partly open. I didn't leave it that way."

Jane put the suitcase on the bed, opened it, and examined its contents.

"They've been through my clothes." A red flush spread over her cheeks. "*All* my clothes." She smoothed out a pile of underwear.

"Are you sure? Maybe things got messed up when you dropped your suitcase into the closet."

"My blouses and my shirts are in a wad underneath everything else. Somebody took things out of here and just shoved them back in! Yes, I'm sure!"

"Easy, J, I believe you," Matt said. "I'm just trying to understand what's going on." He hauled his own suitcase out of the closet, opened it on the bed, and looked at the jumble of clothing and personal items. "They looked through mine, too." He moved his shirts aside and held up his other pair of shoes to show that the laces had been loosened and the tongues pulled up. "Wonder what they were looking for in here?" He was trying to stay calm for Jane, but alarm bells were going off in his mind. Why had this happened to *them*?

Jane was examining her carry-on bag she had taken out of the closet. She held up the leather case that contained her small tablet computer. "If they were looking for valuable things, why wouldn't they take this?"

Matt opened his own carry-on bag. "Or this?" he asked, pulling out the small video camera he had bought to document the beginning of their life together. He turned the camera over in his hands, then opened its swing-out display screen. As the camera turned itself on, his eyebrows knitted in a frown. "It looks like they may have played what I recorded." He set the camera aside and pulled out his shaving kit bag, which had been dumped back into his carry-on unzipped. "They went through this too." He held it up to show where the plastic lining had been sliced open and pulled away from the leather inside the bag.

"This doesn't make any sense." The initial shock of realizing that some-one had searched their room was giving way to anger. It felt like something important had been stolen from them even though it appeared nothing had actually been taken. He picked up the room telephone again and di-aled the front desk. "This is Matt Randall in room 421. We need hotel Se-curity up here," he said. "Right now. There's been a break-in." The phone made a loud *whack* as he slammed it back into its cradle.

Jane stepped into the bathroom and came out holding a travel-sized tube of lotion and her long-tailed comb. The top was off the tube and the comb's tail was covered with vanilla-scented lotion where it had been pushed down into the tube. "This is crazy! What could they have been looking for?"

A man in a dark sport jacket, white shirt, and tie was at their door in less than three minutes. The plastic badge on the pocket of his jacket bore the hotel logo and the word SECURITY. Underneath that word was his last name: *Wong.* "Mr. and Mrs. Randall? You folks had some trouble here?"

"Somebody got into our room and went through our things while we were at dinner." Matt pointed at the bags on the bed. The man stepped inside and Matt shut the door behind him.

Wong was just over six feet tall, broad-shouldered, and well-muscled, but this hotel guest was even more broad-shouldered and muscular, and six or seven inches taller, the security man noted. No thief would have wanted to confront Mr. Randall in a small room.

Wong glanced at the suitcases open on the bed. "What did they take?"

"Well, ah . . . I can't see that anything's missing. J?"

She shook her head. "I don't see anything missing—yet."

Wong's bushy eyebrows knitted in a frown. "Do you think maybe your things could have been jumbled up when your luggage was stowed on the plane, or when you put it away? You're sure somebody here really—"

"Yes," both of them answered, cutting him off.

"My wife and I had that conversation already," Matt said. "Someone moved stuff around in our bags and put it back in a different way. They played what I had recorded on the video camera. They cut open the lining of my shaving kit." He held it out to show the damage.

"They searched through my makeup and left it all out," Jane added, gesturing toward the bathroom.

"But—they didn't take anything?" Wong scanned the room slowly, then focused on their bags once more. "Do you mind if I look inside?"

"Help yourself," Matt answered.

Wong peered into Matt's carry-on bag first, then Jane's. "Mind if I look at your tablet?" he asked her.

"Go ahead."

Wong picked it up off the bed, grasping it carefully by its edges with his fingers, then walked over to hold it under a lamp, turning it at different angles and examining its shiny touchscreen.

"Do you see something on there?" Matt asked, frowning.

"It's what I *don't* see that makes me curious. The screen is smooth and shiny, and there's *nothing* on here—not a fingerprint, not a smudge, nothing." He looked at Jane. "Like whoever held it last wiped it clean. Did you . . . "

She shook her head slightly.

Wong put the tablet back into her bag.

Matt looked speculatively at his video camera, picked it up by the strap, and opened its swing-out display screen carefully with one finger. Wong watched as Matt turned the camera into different positions under the light. "You have to touch the screen to operate this," Matt explained. "My fingerprints were all over it, and Jane's too. Now *nobody's* fingerprints are on it. It's been wiped clean." He held the camera so the other man could see for himself.

Wong nodded. He glanced at the two open suitcases. "If they just dumped things back into your bags, they must have been in a hurry to leave." He pointed at the closet. "Were the bags stowed in there?"

"Yes," Jane answered as she carefully rearranged things in her suitcase. "Why?"

"I'm guessing they didn't want you to see as soon as you came in that they'd been here, so they put the bags back. That gave them extra time to get farther away before you realized what had happened."

Matt looked at him thoughtfully. "You believe they knew we were on our way back to the room?"

"You mean we might have caught them here?" Jane asked, alarm in her voice.

Wong had noticed when he entered the room that this woman was as tall as he, trim, but like her husband, solid and athletic. He imagined the average thief would not want to confront her either. She might scream, but she could certainly fight back. "I'm wondering if they could have arranged a way to be sure you *wouldn't* catch them," he said. "Maybe, they, ah. . . . " He looked away and left the thought hanging, realizing that he might have said too much.

Matt followed up on the thought. "You're suggesting that somehow they knew we were out—and maybe when we were on our way back. How could they have known that?"

Wong looked away, gazing at the items on the bed. Matt and Jane looked at each other questioningly. The security man cleared his throat. "I'll make a report on this incident and start an investigation tonight," he said. "I'm going to—"

Matt interrupted. "What you're *not* saying is that they could only have known we were on our way back up to our room if somebody here in the hotel told them. Is that right?"

Again, the security man did not answer directly. "I promise you," he said, "if someone in the hotel was involved, that person has worked his or her last day here."

Matt raised his eyebrows. "You haven't said anything about calling the police."

"I'll do that if you want. They'll come sometime tonight. They'll take your statements, and their reports will go into a file somewhere in a database. But since nothing was stolen . . . "

"At least the police could look around for other fingerprints, or . . . or *something*," Jane said, frowning.

"They could. But this *is* a hotel. Fingerprints in this room might belong to any of dozens of people who stayed here before you." Wong shrugged.

"I'd think a reputable hotel would take something like this more seriously," Matt said. It was more than a statement; it was an accusation.

"Oh, we will," Wong said hastily. "We'll—"

"And I'd like to know why someone picked on *us*." He moved close to Jane and put his arm around her.

Wong looked both of them up and down. "Just married, right?"

Jane and Matt looked at each other. "It shows?" she asked.

"Sometimes it's not hard to tell," Wong answered, smiling slightly. "Was there a lot of publicity about the wedding back home? We've had people targeted by thieves who read the society pages in Sacramento or Fresno or Palo Alto. Did you let everybody know where you'd be going on your honeymoon?"

Matt shook his head. "Just our parents and a few close friends. I even kept it as a surprise for Jane until about a week before we were married. And we're from Phoenix."

"You're sure no one else could have found out?"

Matt shrugged. "I don't see how."

Wong shrugged. "Sometimes thieves will prowl through a hotel looking for any doors that didn't shut all the way when people walked out of the room. We have security cameras in the lobby, and the staff tries to watch for people who just walk in off the street. But if they get past us, it's possible they could find their way to guest room floors."

"I'd like to know how they got into *this* room," Jane said. "Our door was locked."

Wong opened the door and bent down to look at the key card slot on the outside. He peered at it intently for several seconds. "No damage here. Your card worked okay?"

"Yes," Matt answered. "So whoever got into our room must have had a key card too?"

There was a flush in the security man's face as he straightened up. "We try to keep tight control on those. Housekeeping, Engineering—we hold them responsible for all the cards they have. We drill them constantly on not letting those out of their sight. There's supposed to be no way anyone from outside the hotel could get one." He frowned, gazing off down the hallway. "But I keep telling the manager we need to do more careful back-ground checks. A few workers with phony documents have been hired here. Those people are vulnerable. If somebody threatens to report them or call immigration, they can be pushed into—"

Wong stopped suddenly, realizing how much he had said, and the flush faded from his face. He had argued for tighter security again and again with management, and gotten nowhere, but this wasn't something to hash out with guests.

. He manipulated the deadbolt in the door to be sure it worked. "Keep the security chain on your door tonight. Don't open it for any-body unless they have identification. And I promise you that lock will be reprogrammed—tonight, if possible. I'll get someone from Engineering up here right away." He stopped examining the door and turned to face them. "On behalf of the hotel, I apologize. We'll do anything we can to make your stay more pleasant and to make this up to you."

Matt glanced at Jane. She was frowning again. "J?"

"I don't like this—this feeling. I feel like . . . " She gestured toward her bag, open on the bed. "Someone I don't know has been pawing through my things and my clothes, looking for I don't know what. That's way too personal." She looked at Wong. "Another room would be nice. I don't think anything could make me feel really safe in this one now."

"Done. I'll take care of that immediately." He started to walk down the hall toward the elevator, then turned back to say, "And if anything else out of the ordinary happens tonight, or if you find that anything is missing, please feel free to call me."

Matt and Jane watched him walk toward the elevator. "We didn't tell him anything about the phone calls," Jane said. "Do you think we should let them know about those too?"

"Maybe. But you heard what he said about the police. If a possible burglary isn't a serious issue for *them*, I don't think they'd care about a couple of phone calls." He stood frowning in the direction the security man had gone. "And I didn't get the impression the hotel's going to do much more."

Matt closed the door, slipped the security chain into place, and jiggled the handle to be sure the door was locked. Then he turned to find Jane standing very close behind him.

She stepped closer and leaned her head against his chest. "Hold me." Matt wrapped his arms around her tightly. He was the only man she had ever cared about or dated who was big enough to enfold her in his arms. But he was more than that; he offered a kind of emotional security she had never felt before.

Jane looked up into his eyes. "You're angry, aren't you? You don't show it a lot, but I can tell when you are."

"Yeah." He pressed her tightly to him. "I'm mad that somebody's messing with our time together. It was supposed to be just for us."

Within half an hour, they had been moved to a different room in the hotel, one floor down. Wong had sent a bellhop and a maid to help with their luggage.

As soon as they were alone, Matt locked the door, put on the security chain, then wedged the back of the desk chair under the inside door handle so the door could not be opened from the outside.

Jane studied the door as though she were uncertain about its security.

Matt sat on the edge of the bed and pulled her down onto his lap. "I'm sorry. Tomorrow we'll look for another place."

"No, it's okay." She looked again at the chair wedged under the door handle. "We should be all right."

He took out his cell phone. "I'm going to call home and find out if Mom and Dad let it slip to anyone where we are."

No, his mother said, they had not shared the honeymoon plans, and no one had asked about where Matt and Jane were. Why did he want to know? When Matt told her about the strange phone calls, he could almost feel her anxiety rise. She was the kind of mother who had always worried about her little boy even when he grew big enough to tower over her. He didn't want to worry her more, so he said nothing about the break-in. He promised to call home again in a couple of days.

Jane used her own phone to call her mother and ask whether her parents had told anyone the honeymoon destination, explaining as briefly as possible about the phone calls. Marilyn McDougal's finely tuned mom radar was immediately on alert. "What's going on?" she asked.

"Everything's all right, Mom," Jane soothed. "We're really enjoying the sightseeing." She too finished her call without bringing up the search of their room. Her brow furrowed. "I try not to hold anything back from Mom, but there's no point in getting her upset."

Her eyes went to the chain on the door again. Then she looked at Matt and smiled weakly. "I feel like I need a bath—a nice, warm soak." She picked carefully through the clothes in her suitcase, selected what she needed, and then gave her husband a peck on the cheek before walking into the bathroom.

Matt and Jane had known each other for about seven months, and she was learning to read his feelings well. He hoped she had not sensed his level of concern about this. To the hotel security man, it might seem like a random burglary, but Matt knew they had been *targeted*. Someone had gone through everything here, but had not taken anything. Did that mean the burglar had given up? Or that he had just run out of time to find what he was looking for?

This room was on the corner of the building—better view, the bellhop had said. Matt walked to the front window and pulled back the curtain. Out the window to the right was the junction of Powell and Market Streets, with its end-of-the-line cable car stop. The colorful crowds moving by on the street during the day and the clanging of the cable car bells added to the flavor of San Francisco. This area was picturesque, but the hotel was older, without some of the amenities of newer places. It had fit his budget perfectly. Now Matt wondered if he should have worried less about cost. Security was undoubtedly tighter in some of the newer, more upscale places.

Tomorrow they could change hotels. It would be worth the additional cost to protect themselves—to protect the woman he loved.

Matt looked at the building directly across the street. A few of the office windows on the upper floors were still lighted. Through the evening fog, he could see the silhouette of a man in one of the windows staring across the street at their hotel—looking in the direction of the room where Matt and Jane had been. From that vantage point, the man could easily see this third-floor window too. The man slowly lowered his gaze—and realized someone was watching *him*. He quickly dropped the blinds into place at his window.

Did this man make a habit of staring into windows of the hotel rooms across the street? What was he watching?

Or was the man watching anything at all? Matt wondered if he was simply being paranoid after what had happened.

One of the slats of the blinds in that office window across the street was raised slightly, so that someone could be peering out. As Matt watched, the slat dropped into place and the opening in the blind closed. He carefully drew the heavy drapes over their own window before turning away.

Matt was checking his video camera again, trying to be sure he was right about somebody reviewing the recordings in it, when there was a knock at the door.

Was it Wong with some information?

No. The man Matt saw through the peephole was a waiter holding a tray. His voice was muffled by the door. "Mr. and Mrs. Randall?" He raised the cloth covering the tray to show a wine bottle.

Matt moved the chair out from under the door handle and opened the door as far as the security chain would permit. "Yes?"

The waiter was no more than five foot eight; he seemed momentarily surprised as he took in Matt's full height. He held out the tray. "Compliments of the hotel. Can I bring it in?"

Matt did not remove the chain from the door. "Mr. Wong arranged this?"

"Who?" The waiter looked at him blankly for a moment before his thoughts seemed to fall into place. "Oh. Yeah—Wong. With Security? I guess you had some trouble here?"

"Tell him thank you very much, we appreciate his generosity, but not tonight."

The waiter was obviously surprised. "It's a good wine."

"That's generous—but we wouldn't drink it. I'm sure the hotel will be able to sell it to another guest."

The waiter looked at him strangely. He seemed surprised to hear no for an answer. "You're, uh . . . you're sure?"

"Thanks anyway." Slowly, Matt closed the door, leaving the waiter looking at him uncertainly. Matt made sure the deadbolt was locked, fastened the chain in its track on the back of the door, then wedged the chair under the door handle again.

Jane came out of the bathroom in her pajamas, a towel wrapped around her hair. "Did I hear you talking to someone?"

"A waiter. Mr. Wong had some wine sent up, compliments of the hotel. I told the man thanks, but no thanks."

She smiled as she came to put her arms around him. "I'm feeling a *lot* better after my bath. But I'm exhausted. I'm sorry. I'll probably be asleep as soon as my head touches the pillow."

Matt forced a smile. "Me too."

It wasn't true. An hour later, with Jane curled up sleeping against his side, he lay in bed still staring up at the ceiling.

His mind went through every recording in the video camera's memory. There was nothing but tourist stuff—shots of Jane looking at the sea lions off Pier 39, of him striking a heroic pose behind the wheel of a sailing ship in the maritime museum, of her behind bars in a cell on Alcatraz.

What were they looking for? . . . Did they really go through every clip in the memory? . . . Or did I just rewind the camera and forget I did it?

No. Someone had wiped the display screen clean of fingerprints.

Maybe the intruder or intruders had simply been looking for untraceable cash or jewels.

In this hotel? No. The kind of guests who could leave money or jewels lying around stayed in hotels farther up the cable car line, or in other parts of town.

Matt drifted off to sleep still wondering what they could possibly have been seeking.

He was not sure what brought him awake suddenly. A small sound at the door? Or had he only dreamed it?

He raised himself up on one elbow. The clock on the desk read 1:20. He looked at the door of the room. It did not meet the carpet at the bottom, and a faint band of light from the hallway shone under the door. Two narrow bars of shadow interrupted that band of light—two shoes. Someone was standing just outside the room.

Matt slipped out from under the covers as soundlessly as possible and padded quietly across the carpet. He was startled to hear a small click and see the lever that opened the door move slowly downward. Carefully, he grasped the chair he had wedged under the door handle, planning to move it out of place quickly so he could yank the door open and confront who-ever was there. But the back of the chair made a scraping sound on the door as he moved it. Instantly, the two narrow bars of shadow disappeared from the band of light on the floor and he heard footsteps moving quickly away from the door.

He snatched the chair away, flipped the tabbed end of the security chain out of its track, and pulled the door open.

The hallway in front of him was completely empty. No one was waiting by the elevators. To his left, a hallway ran from their front corner room to-ward the back of the hotel. The stairwell exit door at the end of the hallway was just easing shut against the resistance of the piston mechanism that kept it from slamming. Matt could hear no footsteps from the stairwell. Whoever had just used that door was already gone. Or the person might be waiting silently in the darkened stairwell—waiting for Matt to charge through the door. Waiting with a weapon?

Matt felt something in his gut that he wasn't used to—anxiety, fear. Whatever someone was looking for, that person wanted it badly enough to risk confronting him in the middle of the night in this hotel room. Maybe the intruder even wanted Matt to come after him. But confrontation didn't seem like a good idea right now. Matt shut the door to their room quietly, then carefully locked it and replaced the chain and the chair.

Whoever tried that door handle must have had a key card. And if it was the same person who searched their room on the fourth floor earlier, somehow that person knew they had been moved—and where.

Matt turned to look at Jane, sleeping peacefully in the bed.

Tomorrow morning hotel security would hear about this, and the phone calls. And tomorrow before noon, he and Jane would definitely be out of here.

2

He stood in the bathroom doorway watching as she applied mascara to her eyelashes. Jane wore little makeup. She didn't need it. Her beauty was natural. She probably could have been a fashion model—her long auburn hair, her face, her build were a winning combination—but she would never have tolerated the lifestyle. She was not a woman who enjoyed primping. She didn't believe she was good-looking; her mouth was too wide, she said, and her nose too sharp. But she was the most beautiful woman Matt had ever known.

She glanced at him in the mirror and smiled.

He had loved that smile since the first time he saw it, at the party where they met.

"Pour one for me?" she asked.

"Sure," he said, moving the spout of the soft drink bottle over the cup she held out to him. He looked into her eyes, she smiled at him, and he forgot what he was doing. He managed to stop pouring just before the soft drink overflowed on her hand.

Their eyes had met earlier, over the heads of a small group talking by the pool. But the two of them had drifted away in opposite directions when the talk turned to local politics.

She sipped from her soft drink so it didn't spill. "Thanks," she said, looking at him over the top of her cup, and he got lost again in those deep green eyes.

The feeling was magnetic—warm and exciting, and yet a bit alarming because nothing like it had ever happened to him before. He didn't want to look away from those eyes. "Would you like to sit down?" he asked.

She walked with him toward a pair of empty chaise lounges at the end of the pool. "Are you a friend of Cole Brewster?"

"He's my boss."

She laughed lightly.

"What?" he asked, looking at her curiously.

"His name. He sounds like a law firm—Coleman-Brewster, Coleman and Brewster, Brewster and Coleman."

Matt laughed too. "And then you add in his middle name: Coleman Thurgood Brewster."

They sat opposite each other on the chaise lounges balancing plates of barbecue and potato salad on their knees. The rest of the people at the party faded away for them. Over the next hour, they learned a lot about each other. He learned that she taught physical education and dance to elementary school students. She had attended Arizona State on a volleyball scholarship. She had turned down three offers to go pro in beach volleyball after college. Full-time dedication to sports would have blocked too many other things out of her life, she explained—probably no time for social life and no Sundays. Her faith was important to her, she said. And besides, she wasn't comfortable putting herself on public display. "I think it's as much about bikinis as about volleyball."

"What was the attraction of volleyball for you?" he asked. "I'll bet you'd be good at basketball."

She thought for a moment. "I am *good at basketball. But there was always something about volleyball—about looking somebody in the eyes across the net, one on one, and knowing I could handle anything they threw at me." She smiled her smile that caught him again.*

Her name, she had told him, was Jane McDougal—Jane for her great-great-grandmother, who stood out in the history of early settlers in Arizona. The first Jane McDougal had been a determined woman known for her strength in facing the challenges of pioneering. Jane the great-great-granddaughter hoped to live up to her ancestor's example of strength and stamina.

On the volleyball court, at least, she had done it, Matt would learn later. Her physical ability and her refusal to give less than her best had made her a leader. Her teammates, who knew her as Big J or just J, had come to rely on her, on the court—and off. Jane had attended Cole's party that night only because a former teammate didn't want to go alone and had invited her to come along.

"Usually on a Friday night like this, I'd be sitting at home watching old movies," she said. "This is a big event in my social life."

"No! I can't believe you don't get out a lot. You must have guys . . . " *He stopped, realizing there were pitfalls almost anywhere he might go with that comment. He felt heat rising in his cheeks. Could she tell he was embarrassed? Time to redirect the conversation.* "Do you like old movies?"

"Mostly the romantic ones." *Jane felt as though she might be blushing a bit. Would she have been this open about her social life with any other guy she had just met? But she felt . . .* safe *talking to this man.*

He kept his eyes on hers as he raised his cup. "'Here's looking at you, kid,'" *and he sipped from his drink.*

Jane laughed. "'We'll always have . . . '"—*she looked around them*— "Cole's party?"

"You knew!" *he exclaimed.*

"The line from Casablanca? *That movie's one of my favorite oldies." She smiled. "You must be an oldies fan too. But I'll bet you go for all the action classics.* The Dirty Dozen? Indiana Jones? *Or maybe newer ones.* Captain America?" *The smile faded from her face as she realized she'd just thrown a standard guy stereotype at him. A mistake? But he didn't seem to notice.*

"I like all of them, really—including the romantic ones. My senior project, for my degree, showed how technology has changed the movie business over time—how computer-generated images can bring the actors back to life or change some of those old stories. Some of the newer ones wouldn't have been possible without CGI."

"You're in computers?" *She looked at him quizzically for a moment.* "I don't know many tech people, but your name sounds familiar somehow. I just can't place it."

It was a question, he knew. "I went to that 'other' university up here to the north—you know, the University of Arizona," *he said, smiling.* "Played football. Fullback. Had a good game the last time my team played your school."

Jane laughed. "Now I remember! You ruined *our homecoming game when I was a junior."*

"Not all by myself. But I got in on a couple of touchdowns—one by accident." *The accidental one had been a broken play. The fullback wasn't supposed to end up with the ball, but he was the last option for a desper-*

ate quarterback about to be sacked. Matt finished a 27-yard run dragging a defender across the goal line with him. It was the winning touchdown.

"Don't be so modest! You were in the news—you and a couple of our play- ers. They said the NFL scouts were there especially to watch you, and they were impressed. You were an NFL prospect for sure." She paused. "Did you try out?"

"I got an invite." He was silent for a moment. "I almost went. I. . . . " He never knew how to explain his choice. People told him he had been crazy to pass up the opportunity. "The scout and my coach told me I had a shot. I could play football for a few years, make a lot of money, enjoy all the perks." He paused again. "But careers in the NFL can be pretty short, especially if you get hurt. I had a broken collarbone my sophomore year, after I came back from being a missionary, and that ended my season early. It made me think about the future. What if I were lucky enough to get drafted into the pros and then in a few years it was all over? And what if life on the road kept me from finding other things I really wanted in my life . . . family, maybe, and, uh . . . " He shrugged. "While I was thinking about it, Cole found me through one of the sites where I posted my resume. He said he'd been looking hard for someone with my computer skills. He needed to be able to guaran- tee his clients digital security. He told me he could show me how to make all the money I'd ever want over the steady, long term." Matt grinned. "I just paid off my student loans with the first-year bonus he gave me, but the part with the big bucks hasn't started yet."

"So here we are now—me teaching PE and dance to elementary kids while you help other *people get more out of their money."*

"Well, supporting the guy who helps them."

She sipped from her drink and sat looking at him for a moment. "We both passed up the big bucks for things we wanted more."

What they both wanted more, they had decided after only a few weeks of dating, was life together, life with all that could happen to two people committed to each other—trouble and triumph, children, the challenges of a marriage, living and growing together for a lifetime. They felt like the wedding date that fit into their plans best was a lucky day—7/17/17. They had been married in the temple of The Church of Jesus Christ of Latter-day Saints in Mesa, Arizona, where they promised each other eternity together. Matt had vowed to her and to himself that he would invest the rest of his life on earth in trying to become the kind of man she deserved. Jane meant everything to him now.

He moved behind her and wrapped his arms around her, watching in the mirror while she put on her lip gloss. She blew him a kiss.

The phone on the desk in their room warbled again. He frowned as he glanced at his watch; most people might assume that hotel guests would be out of their rooms by this time of morning. He had slept late after last night's stress, and Jane had let him do it. But who would be expecting to find them here now?

"I hope it's not another one of those calls you got last night," Jane said warily as he crossed the room.

He answered "Hello?" and then a red flush began to creep up his neck. "You didn't find what you were looking for last night? That's not my problem. And you'd better—" He listened for a few seconds longer, then slammed the phone down. "He *threatened* me. My last chance, he said. If I don't meet them to hand it over, they'll get it anyway, and I'll be sorry."

"Did he say what 'it' is?"

Matt shook his head. He took his jacket off the hanger in the closet and yanked the chair out from under the door handle. "I'm going down to report the calls to Security right now. Maybe they'll have a record of the numbers so we can find out who's calling. And then we're going to look for another place to stay," he said, shrugging the jacket on as he walked to the door.

"Matt?"

He turned to look at her.

"We decided we wanted to pray together every day. We haven't done that yet today."

He walked back to take her by the hand. "You're right, and I'm sorry I forgot." They knelt by the bed, and he prayed that they would be able to enjoy their time together and that they would be protected. That last part seemed especially important somehow.

When they stood after the prayer, he said, "Thanks for that. I'm better now." He kissed her lightly. "But I'm still going to report those calls. I won't be long. Be sure to lock the door and put the chair back in place." He grinned. "When I come back, we can go to breakfast, and then we'll find a new hotel."

Jane gave him another of those smiles that crowded everything else out of his mind. "You mean brunch. It's almost halfway to lunchtime."

* * *

The chief of security for the hotel, Ed Bills, was an ex-policeman, average height, stocky and muscular. His biceps strained at the sleeves of his blazer—but the blazer was tight over his belly. Obviously, it had been some time since he had worried about passing a physical fitness test.

"Mr. Randall, the kind of experience you've had here is very rare," he said. "I don't even remember a case like yours before. It will help if I can get more information from you, and also a statement from your wife." Bills looked at the report in front of him. "Help me understand this. There were some calls, anonymous—maybe pranks. And you told Wong—"

"They didn't sound like pranks!"

"And you said nothing was taken from your room?" Bills continued resolutely.

"Yes, but—"

"Someone broke into your room but didn't take *anything*?"

"No, they didn't take anything, they only—"

"There was damage to your . . . " Bills glanced down at the report. "Shaving kit. Was that a new item—or maybe something you've had for a while?"

"I've had it for three weeks! Someone sliced open the lining."

"Just trying to be sure I understand," Bills said. He looked into Matt's eyes for a long moment, seemingly assessing him. "The hotel would be willing to replace that for you. And pay any other damage to your property. Would that make things right for you and the missus?"

It took effort for Matt to control his words "Mr. Bills, I don't understand why the hotel isn't more concerned about the fact that two of your guests have been threatened and victimized. What would it take for you to get the police here to investigate?"

Bills reddened. He also seemed to be straining to keep his patience. "They'd have to see some solid evidence that a crime was committed—something solid. Nothing was taken, and there's no physical evidence of a break-in. So what do you want them to investigate?"

"How about the calls?"

Bills glanced at his notes. "Right." He looked into Matt's eyes again. "You didn't tell Wong about those last night." He paused as though waiting for an explanation. When none came, he asked: "Did the caller talk to your wife, or just you?"

"My wife answered the phone the first time. She heard the guy. He was disguising his voice."

"You *know* the voice was disguised?"

"It wasn't natural. Nobody talks like that."

"So did he threaten your wife?"

"No. I'm the only one he threatened—but I told her what he said to me." It sounded weak, Matt realized. "All right, I should have told Wong about the calls last night. At least he seemed willing to listen."

Bills looked up from the report with anger in his eyes, and then his face settled into a look that suggested this conversation was probably a waste of time, but he was obligated to carry on anyway. "All right, Mr. Randall, what did the caller say to you?" He poised his pen over the form that contained Wong's report.

"He knew my name. I don't know how he knew we're at this hotel, because we only told our parents where we'd be staying. The guy who called said I needed to bring them something. And I don't know who 'they' are."

Bills looked at him expectantly once more. When Matt did not go on, the security man asked, "What was it they wanted?"

"I don't know. He wouldn't tell me. All he said was, 'He shouldn't have given it to you.'"

"Who is 'he'?"

"I don't know. He didn't tell me that either. It's like some sick game."

Bills looked even more skeptical. "So how was it exactly that he threatened you?"

"This morning he said that if I won't give them what they want, they'll get it anyway and I'll be sorry."

"And did he say what they're going to do to make you sorry?"

"No."

The security man made more notes on the report below what Wong had written last night. Matt was able to read part of Bills' writing, even though it was upside down: " . . . threatened to make guest 'sorry'—nothing specific."

Bills frowned at what he had written, glanced back over the report briefly, then looked up at Matt again. He spread his hands in a gesture of helplessness. "Mr. Randall, you can see we really have nothing to go on with the break-in. And the calls? Well, a vague threat. It could be somebody just playing a prank."

"A *prank?* Why *our* room? And how would they know my name? How did they know we changed rooms? Have you got some kind of leak here in the hotel?"

Anger flared in Bills' eyes. "Look, Mr. Randall, you need to understand. . . . " Bills left the words hanging as he seemed to gain control. The flush faded from his face as he stood looking at Matt coldly.

Matt looked up at the ceiling and blew out a breath, then looked into Bills' eyes again. "Is this what you call security? I came to tell you your hotel has a problem. That's why we're leaving." He thought what he said next might get some action from the security man. "I'm going to call the police and report this. Maybe *they'll* follow up here."

Bills sighed. "When I was with the police, I used to take calls like that. They'll listen to you, they'll make an incident report, it will go into a computer file somewhere, and—"

"Never mind. Wong went through this last night," Matt said impatiently. "Before I go, I just want to know if you've got the number of the guy who called us."

"That I can find out." Bills held the door open for Matt to exit the office. "I may not be able to give you his number—privacy laws. But I could report him for harassment."

In the hallway, the security man glanced at the nearby EXIT door, standing partially open, and frowned. "Door to the loading dock," he muttered as he walked over to shut it. "I've asked Engineering to fix it so it stays closed. Wastes AC and heat."

"What about the problem with our room doors last night?" Matt asked. "Wong was going to have Engineering check it out. Someone had to have a key card to get into 421. What about the person who tried to open the door to 317 in the middle of the night? Can you tell me how someone could open that door?"

Bills glanced sideways at him. "I'm on that, as soon as we're finished here. But you don't know that whoever tried the door of 317 had a key card. Anyone can turn a handle to see if it opens."

"I *heard* the lock click open. That's what woke me."

Bills pursed his lips and gave no answer. He led Matt up the hallway toward the front of the hotel, then stopped a few feet short of the lobby and opened a door that was flush with the wall. The room they entered was small, with another door that evidently led out to the registration desk. Two women wearing headsets were seated at computer terminals. Just beyond them was a video monitor that showed the security camera's view of the front desk and lobby. The hotel's telephone and video monitoring systems appeared up-to-date, Matt thought. That was a good sign.

The two women took their eyes off their monitors to look up at Matt and the hotel security chief. Bills nodded to them. "Irina, Trudy, this is Mr. Randall. He's been receiving harassing phone calls in his room—421 last night, and 317 this morning. We want to check the log to see if there's a record of the number they came from."

Trudy frowned at the mention of harassing calls. She was an older woman with dyed blonde hair showing gray roots. Her bright red lipstick more or less matched the bright red blouse she wore above nondescript brown pants. She reached for her keyboard and tapped a couple of keys, but a call came in on her line that she had to answer.

With Trudy busy, Bills turned to the other operator. Irina was a slim, dark-eyed woman wearing a crisp white blouse above a tailored gray skirt. The hotel badge she wore said "Assistant Manager" in small letters below her name. She kept her cool, professional demeanor as she tapped on her keyboard and brought up a log of calls that had come into the hotel in the past 24 hours. "Mr. Randall can give you the time of the call this morning," Bills said.

"Yes, of course." Irina smiled at Matt. "I'll be happy to help." Her English, he noted, was very good, but a bit formal and tinged with something that sounded European. Her smile was courteous, but mechanical, like the smiles that people who meet the public give to customers because it is their job.

"About nine twenty this morning," Matt said.

* * *

Jane had not wanted Matt to know how upset she was about last night. He had worked hard and spent a lot of money to arrange this trip as a surprise for her. She had told him once while they were dating about a family trip to San Francisco when she was 12, and how much she had enjoyed the place. He was trying to make everything perfect for her here. She didn't want the man she loved to think she was disappointed with anything he had done. One of the reasons she loved him was his thoughtfulness in showing how he cared for her.

But someone had been spying on them in this hotel—someone who violated their privacy and threatened her husband—and now the place felt creepy.

She was not a fearful person. Her approach to challenges in life was to face them directly and move ahead. She was usually confident in her own ability to do that. Matt was strong and smart, and she had confidence in him too. But she was having a hard time convincing herself that last night was just a fluke, no real threat. This wasn't like the challenges she was used to facing.

Jane had just finished putting a French braid in her hair when there was a knock at the door. Matt had been gone less than fifteen minutes. That hadn't taken very long.

But it wasn't Matt she saw when she looked through the peephole. It was a sandy-haired man wearing a dark blazer. He flipped open a small case in his hand and held up a badge so she could see it. "Mrs. Randall?" His voice was muffled through the door. "Lee Waters, hotel security." She moved the chair aside and opened the door a crack with the security chain still in place.

The man had to look up at her. "I've been asked to bring you down to the security office to give us some information." He pointed to the plastic placard pinned on his blazer. It read: "L. Waters," and below that, "SECURITY."

"Where's Mr. Wong?"

"Wong works nights."

"Oh, of course."

"He should have taken a statement from you last night. This won't take long."

"My husband just went down to your office a few minutes ago to report some threatening phone calls he received."

"Yes, ma'am. The switchboard got the number from one of the calls, but your husband didn't recognize it. He thought you might. Mr. Bills, the head of security, asked to have you come down." He smiled reassuringly. "This will only take a few minutes, and then you'll be on your way to see the sights."

Jane thought for a moment. "All right. Let me get my jacket. We may be going out after we finish." She got her windbreaker from the closet, put it on, and slipped her cell phone into the pocket of her pants. Then she took the security chain out of its track so she could open the door.

"This way," the man said, smiling broadly and pointing down the hallway to her left. "The stairs are faster. The door to our office is right at the bottom."

* * *

Irina finished scrolling through the file, then reversed the direction and scrolled backward more slowly. She put a finger on the screen as she stopped scrolling and turned to look at Bills. "It should be right here—but no. There is nothing."

"What do you mean, 'nothing'?" Matt responded. "There *was* a call this morning. There has to be a record."

Irina looked at Bills intently as though trying to read his feelings about this guest and his problem, then smiled apologetically at Matt. "But there is nothing. You can see for yourself." She gestured toward the monitor.

Bills leaned over to look closely. Matt looked too. He probably shouldn't have been allowed to see it, but he scanned the list of calls that had come to rooms in the hotel this morning. There were none at 9:20—and none to room 317. "That can't be!" Matt exclaimed. "I talked to him on the phone in our room."

Irina shrugged helplessly. "But—nothing."

"Check last night," Matt demanded.

"I was not here on the phones," Irina said, "I was helping at the front desk. But I will check." She opened another file on the monitor and began scrolling through it. "Can you tell me the time?"

"Um—between 8:30 and 9:00," Matt said. "Room 421."

Irina scrolled slowly through the call log for the previous evening. Then she turned to look pleadingly at Bills, as though she were afraid she might be criticized for not being more cooperative. "I'm sorry. Nothing."

"That's impossible," Matt protested. "There's got to be something wrong with your system."

"You can see there's nothing there for 421," Bills said, nodding toward the list on the monitor.

"Well, my wife and I both talked to him. She can tell you."

"Why don't you bring her down?" Bills suggested.

Matt spent the elevator ride to the third floor thinking that most of the hotels he had checked around here were pricier, but he was more than ready to pay the cost.

He knocked on the door of their room and waited. When Jane did not answer, he wondered if she might not be able to come to the door for the moment, or if she simply had not heard him. He unlocked the door with his card and pushed. It opened easily; the chair he had used to block the door was sitting just to the side. Matt frowned. Why hadn't she locked the door after he left?

"I'm sorry that took so long, J," he said as he walked across the room. "They couldn't—"

He stood in the bathroom doorway staring at—nothing. She was not here.

* * *

Lee Waters led the way down six flights of stairs to the ground floor and stood holding the stairwell door open for her. He put his hand on the handle of a door in the wall next to the stairwell exit. A sign on the door read: DOCK. When Jane reached the bottom, she glanced at a door in the wall behind him, with a sign that read SECURITY. Instead of turning to the door behind him, Lee Waters threw the DOCK door open quickly, took her arm and pushed her through it. He crowded through it quickly behind her.

She looked around at the empty loading dock behind the hotel, then spun angrily to face him. "What do you think you're—"

He was holding an automatic pistol pointed at her. Too late she noticed that the placard on his jacket did not have the hotel logo on it like Wong's, and she realized that he had simply flashed the badge without giving her a good look at it. He grinned. With the muzzle of the pistol, he pointed toward a nondescript Ford sedan parked next to the dock. "Go. Get in."

She glanced at the door they had just come through. But he was standing between her and the door.

He shook his head. "And don't even think about screaming. Probably no one would hear you, but I'd just leave you here bleeding and come back for your husband later. So if you don't want anyone to get hurt . . . " He gestured once more with his pistol. "The car. *Now.*"

* * *

Her comb and brush and makeup were put away neatly in their case as though she had just left.

Matt glanced around the room in alarm. Nothing was different, really—except that the folding door of the small closet was half open. He walked around the bed quickly and opened the closet all the way.

Nothing. Nothing was different here either.

No—one thing was different. Jane's jacket was not hanging in the closet.

Maybe she had misunderstood because he had taken his jacket with him. Maybe she had gone down to the lobby to meet him. He quickly checked the room to see if there might be a note for him somewhere, but there wasn't. He left the room and took the elevator to the ground floor, punching the OPEN button impatiently as the elevator stopped.

He walked through the lobby slowly, checking to be sure Jane wasn't sitting in a chair behind one of the pillars, waiting. He walked to the entrance of the hotel restaurant. A sign on the door read: "Open at 11:30." It was just now 10:09 by his watch.

He stepped out onto the street. But why would she have come out here?

Maybe she thought he would go to the fast food restaurant around the corner where they had eaten last night.

He almost jogged around the corner and across the street. But he knew before he reached the doors of the restaurant that she wasn't there. Through the front window, he could see three people sitting in the booths, and none of them his wife. He stepped inside anyway and looked around, then walked slowly back outside.

Where would she have gone?

He tried to ignore the memory of the voice on the phone this morning saying he would be sorry if he did not cooperate.

What would Jane do if she went looking for him and could not find him?

She would go back to their hotel room. He picked up his pace as he walked back toward the building.

It was not a large hotel, with shops or other services. How could she have vanished so quickly?

Hotel Security! Bills would believe him now. The man would *have* to help him.

Matt threw the front door of the hotel all the way back on its hinges and strode through the lobby toward Bills' office, down the hallway at the back of the building. He shoved the office door open without knocking. Bills looked up from his desk, startled. Matt wondered momentarily if the man spent time anywhere but here. "My wife is gone," he said. "You've got to help me find her."

"What do you mean, 'gone'?"

"Missing. I can't find her anywhere."

Bills looked at his watch. "You were in here less than 15 minutes ago. How could she be missing?"

"She wasn't in our room when I went back upstairs. She was going to wait for me there. Now I can't find her anywhere."

"Not anywhere? Have you checked—"

"Let's cut to the chase this time. I've checked the places she might be, and she isn't there."

The security man smiled indulgently. "*All* the places? Some of our guests like to spend time in the stores around here—that shopping center across the street. It takes some women half an hour just to decide what dress to try on, so maybe—"

"She wouldn't leave here without telling me! And we saw the shopping center last night. She's not a shopper!" Matt exploded. "Are you going to help me, or not?"

A flush appeared in Bills' face. When he spoke, his words were even and deliberate. "Help you how? Is there any evidence that anything has actually happened to your wife?"

"Are you going to call the police?"

"If I call the police, they'll only—"

"Then I will."

Bills stood up from his desk trying to look Matt in the eye, but he was several inches too short. "If a mature woman has only been gone for half an hour and there's no physical evidence that any harm came to her, they'll take your name, send someone when they can, and suggest that in the meantime you keep looking."

Matt turned, yanked the door open, and walked out of the security office. He wanted to back Bills up against a wall and demand that the man
do something, but obviously that wouldn't accomplish anything. And the
man might be right about the police reaction.

He would check their room one more time before calling the police.
Maybe there was something he had hastily overlooked, something to indicate where she could have gone. Or maybe she had gone to find him
and had returned to the room when she had not been successful. He tried
to hold that thought as he rode up in the elevator.

3

The room was still empty when he opened the door, but the message light on the telephone on the desk was blinking. Had she called looking for him? Why didn't she just call his cell phone? But they had found a few dead zones in phone service here. He picked up the phone on the desk and quickly punched the number to retrieve messages.

For an instant he thought it was Jane's voice speaking. But, no—it was her mother's. "I hope the two of you are having a good time in San Francisco." Matt could tell immediately by her tone that Marilyn McDougal was concerned about something. "I have to share a little bit of bad news. But don't let it upset you, everything is all right," she added quickly. "After your call last night, we were a little worried, so your father went over to your new apartment this morning to have a look around." She paused. "Someone had broken in and gone through all your things—all the wedding gifts we left there. But don't worry, they didn't take anything. We checked against the list from the reception. The police came, but they said since nothing is missing, there's not a lot they can do. The landlord changed the lock, and we've got the new key. We've cleaned everything up, so—well, anyway, I thought we ought to tell you, but I really don't want you to be worried." It was clear that Jane's mother was worried. "We know you're probably busy, but call us when you . . . well, call us."

So there *was* a connection with Phoenix. Maybe someone *had* followed them here, Matt thought. And if that person had come looking for him and found Jane alone in the room. . . .

The knot in his stomach grew larger. He tried to believe there was some ordinary explanation for her absence. He walked around the room hoping for any sign, some clue that she might simply have gone out looking for him. But he knew he was not going to find anything; he had already done this once. He sat down at the desk to call the police.

He was startled when the telephone rang before his hand touched it. *J!* She was calling from somewhere, wondering where he was. He picked it up quickly and said, "Hello?"

The voice that he already hated rasped in his ear, "Missing something? Feeling a little lonely right now?" There was a laugh—a forced, phony, cackling laugh—and the call ended abruptly.

Matt stared at the telephone receiver in his hand. *They have Jane!*

Slowly he sat down on the bed and hung up the phone.

They have Jane!

What could he do?

Nothing. There was not a single thing he could do to change the fact.

They took her.

He didn't know who, or where, or how. The only thing left for him to do was make the call to the police that he had told Bills he was going to make—*right now.*

His hand was on the telephone when it rang again. He snatched it up immediately.

Same voice. "Mommy and Daddy in Phoenix are worried about their little girl. They should be," the voice rasped.

"Mommy and Daddy in Phoenix"? Do they know about the call from Jane's mother?

"Don't call the police, and don't talk to hotel security again if you want her back," the voice added. The line went dead once more.

"Again"? They knew he had talked to Bills?

They know!

How?

He sat stunned—too stunned to think. The only thing fixed in his mind was Jane. They had the woman he loved!

Panic flooded his mind instantly with fear. He couldn't leave her in their hands. He had to do something—now!

But what?

He needed to turn this problem over to people who knew how to handle situations like this. It would be important to get the police or FBI involved as soon as possible. He reached for the telephone, but his hand stopped before he touched it. His mind raced through the possibilities. The voice on the phone had warned him not to call the police. If he called, would they somehow know about that call too? If they knew, what would they do to Jane?

He drew his hand back.

Whenever he had watched suspense movies or shows involving kidnappings, he had always wondered why families were too dumb to ask for help from law enforcement immediately. He had always thought it was the only way they had any real chance of getting their loved ones back. Why did they always let themselves be manipulated by the kidnappers?

He reached for the telephone again. His palm was clammy when he touched it. He sat with his hand on top of the phone for a minute or more.

Back when he had watched those movies and TV shows about kidnappings, he had not known Jane. He had never loved someone whose life was at risk—someone whose life meant more to him now than his own. In one part of his mind—some calm, rational place—he knew that he was letting emotion control him, but he could not bring himself to lift the receiver and risk making a call that could get the woman he loved hurt or killed. He was afraid—scared in a way he had never felt before.

He had been in dangerous situations. Once in Colombia he and another American missionary, also a big man, had been confronted by four teenage toughs looking for a fight. One of them had a club and one had a knife. The boys seemed to want to attack, but they were wary because the two missionaries towered over them. Matt had been scared on the inside—*very* scared—and yet calm. As missionaries, they had been instructed about what to do in situations like this, and Matt believed if they followed those instructions, they would be protected. They did not resist or offer to fight, but they stood together, ready. There had been nothing else to do because their would-be assailants were blocking any escape route.

The one with the club—maybe 17, Matt thought—had edged close enough to him to take a swing. He had underestimated Matt's long reach. Matt caught the club, yanked it away, and in the process spun the teenager off his feet, leaving him laying dazed. The one with the knife wanted to advance, but now it was three against two and Matt held the club. His reach with it would be formidable.

In the end it was the four gang members who had backed down and walked away, breathing out threats as they went.

Talking about it later, the two missionaries agreed that the four attackers had wanted them to cower or plead, had hoped to provoke them, creating a rationale for the beating they wanted to give to two foreigners. When the two missionaries did not react in the way they desired, the four bullies had begun to doubt and lost their nerve. They needed to see fear from their victims. Matt had hurled the club into a vacant lot as he and his companion walked home that night, hoping to put the incident behind him, trying to focus on the many good people he had already met in the country. Still, he had not forgotten the lesson about facing down evil when there was no other choice.

But the fear he had felt back then was nothing like this—nothing like the paralyzing knowledge that there was not a single thing he could do for Jane. Where was the evil to face? At any other time when he was afraid, he had always been able to see some course of action—try to apply reason, seek help, flee, or fight back. Now each of those avenues was closed. Reason did not apply here; the situation he was in made no sense. There was nothing or no one he could get his hands on, no information he could get his head around, nothing tangible—*nothing*! This was some kind of unexplainable . . . what? Nightmare? He was sweating in this over-air-conditioned hotel room. He could feel the adrenalin flowing, and there was nothing to spend it on. He realized he was gripping the telephone receiver so hard his fingers were turning white.

Never had he thought about dealing with a situation like this, where the life of someone he loved might depend on what he did next. Never had there been a decision he needed to make more thoughtfully—and yet the empty room seemed to scream at him, "Do something *now!*"

Slowly he took his hand off the telephone. He sat on the edge of the bed trying to get control of his thoughts. He had to keep fear and anger in check.

Somehow he had to make the people who took Jane understand that they could not hurt her—that her safety was in their best interest. But he couldn't talk to them because he did not know how to contact them. He could only wait for them to call again.

What might they do to her? He could not bear to think about the question. If they did anything—anything at all. . . . He felt anger and fear rising in him at the same time.

Focus!

What did he know about the situation right now?

There was at least one man holding Jane. That man knew his name.

There was more than one person involved; whatever they were after, the voice had said, "*We* want it back."

They could get into this room if they wanted, and apparently they had some way of knowing about his phone calls—maybe even listening in on them.

Whatever they were looking for, they had come after it in two different states. They believed that if they held Jane, he would be forced to give it to them. He could not let them know he did not have it; if they knew, then Jane would be useless—even dangerous—to them.

So, what did he *not* know right now?

If they've done something to her already—if she's hurt, if she's . . . that man is evil. He enjoys trying to make me afraid. What would he do to Jane?

No! No, focus on what you know.

Matt replayed the last phone call in his mind.

"Mommy and Daddy in Phoenix are worried," the voice had said. How could they know her parents were worried unless they had somehow heard the phone message from Jane's mother? He looked at the telephone set on the desk. It looked ordinary—standard wiring. But would it look any different if it were bugged somehow?

"Don't talk to hotel security *again*," the voice had said. *They knew.*

He went over the call once more in his mind, starting from the beginning.

There had been noise in the background, but he hadn't paid much attention to it. Street noise—traffic.

There was a *bell!* A bell—a cable car bell—had clanged in the background while the man was warning him not to call the police.

Matt sat up straight on the bed. The man could have been calling from somewhere close by. Would the kidnappers stay close? If he had something they wanted, would they stay near enough to keep an eye on him?

He walked to the window, pulled back the sheer drape, and looked out at the cable car stop below. From out there, could someone see into this window? No.

He raised his eyes to the fourth floor window across the street. The blinds were still closed over there—except for that one small slit. Someone with binoculars could easily see through that slit. And he knew there were electronic devices that could pick up telephone and other audio signals from a distance. Could they aim one of those through that small opening in the blinds? Would it work when the telephone was not wireless?

He looked down at the ground floor of that building across the street. In front at street level it was a clothing store. What was on the floors above? Offices? Apartments?

Matt glanced quickly around the hotel room. He wasn't accomplishing anything in here. There was sweat at his hairline, and he realized his feet were moving, taking small steps back and forth even though he was hold-ing his place at the window. It was almost as though his mind were willing him to move, act, do *something*. He wanted to run out into the street, to run after Jane.

But what direction would he run?

If he could just get a look at the building directory across the street to find out what was on the fourth floor facing their room. . . .

But if he went out, *they* might call.

Maybe if he just stepped outside long enough to get the lay of the land again, to see how they might have taken her out of this hotel. . . .

But *had* they taken her out of the hotel? She had disappeared so sud-denly. What if they were holding Jane somewhere here in the building—in the room just above, or below, or next door?

The thought that she could be so near tormented him. He paced back and forth by the window.

He looked outside once more, wondering who was behind the gap in those blinds across the street, wondering about the distant clanging he had heard during the last call. Could it have come from out there on Pow-ell Street?

He glanced at the telephone, then snatched up his jacket from the bed and walked out of the room, locking the door behind him. He ran to the EXIT sign at the end of the hall and ran down the stairs. He burst through the door at the bottom, turned right, and jogged up the hallway toward the lobby. He almost collided with Trudy, the telephone operator, as she opened the door of the telephone office; she and Irina stared at him in surprise as he veered around Trudy and kept jogging. When he reached the reception desk, he slowed to a walk and tried to cross the lobby rapidly without drawing attention to himself.

He stepped out onto the street and looked around him. The morning fog had burned off. With the sun approaching its highest point in the sky, both the cable car stop and Powell Street running uphill from it were bathed in light. At first glance, nothing seemed mysterious here.

He looked up at the building across the street. The gap in those fourth-floor blinds could not be seen from this angle. If someone up there were looking out, they could not see him.

He started across the street, waited for one car that honked at him, then dashed to the entrance of the other building. He was just stepping through the doorway when he heard the ringing from his jacket pocket. He had a bad feeling even before he could get his cell phone out to answer it. "Hello?"

"Naughty, naughty," the raspy voice said. "You went outside without asking." The man's laughter cackled in his ear again. "Now go back to your room and stay there until I say you can leave." The line went dead.

My cell phone!

They could reach out and touch him there too. It was a new number; only Jane and a few family members had it. *How can* they *know?*

No matter what he did, they seemed to know somehow. He stood on the curb momentarily wondering about that, and then he remembered that he needed to get back to the hotel room. Jane's safety might depend on it.

He had not even had a chance to try to tell them not to hurt her—had been too shocked to even think about it.

He looked to his right before crossing the street again. About a block and a half up Powell, a cable car was heading down the hill. Matt heard the distant clanging of its bell as it approached an intersection, and he realized as the sound came to his ears that if the cable car he heard during the telephone call had been near their hotel, he would have heard its sound not only through the phone but from outside the window. And one more thing registered in his mind about the traffic sounds in the earlier call: the caller had been *moving* when he passed that clanging bell. The man had been driving somewhere. He could have been calling from anywhere in San Francisco along a cable car line.

Crossing the street, Matt glanced over his shoulder at the building facing their hotel. He could see blinds in most of its windows, and more than one window had blinds that were closed or partially closed. That might be simply normal, keeping out daytime glare.

He shook his head as he walked into the hotel lobby. *Dumb, Matt! Dumb.*

He had wanted so much to believe Jane was nearby that he had let his imagination run away with him.

He could not make a mistake like that again if he were going to have any hope of getting her back. He could not let fear manipulate him. The kidnappers could use it against him.

* * *

Something hard hit her in the small of her back. It felt like his fist. "Hey! Keep your head down back there," said the man who had called himself Lee Waters.

"I *am*," she muttered. Her voice was muffled by the blanket that covered her.

He had forced her to lie down in the back seat of his car, face down; she had to bend her legs at the knees and lie partly on her side to do it. Then he had handcuffed her hands behind her back and covered her with a dirty olive drab blanket. It felt rough against her face, and it smelled of mildew.

Just before shutting the car door, he had put something against her head—it felt like the barrel of his pistol—and said, "You're going to stay down and be quiet. Do you understand?"

"Yes," she had answered.

He had prodded her in the back, emphasizing each word this time. "*Do . . . you . . . understand?*"

"Yes!"

He had been driving since they left the hotel. She had no idea how far they might have come, but she had told herself to pay attention to all the cues of sound or smell or motion. All she could smell was a mingling of mildew and the kind of sweet air freshener scent that used car dealers put into vehicles to mask other odors. This man had driven up and down hills and turned corners so many times she had lost track. But she had captured some of the aural cues. Twice they had passed cable cars with their clanging bells. They had stopped more than once at intersections, apparently; there was the noise of idling vehicles next to them and of pedestrian chatter close by. The front windows of this vehicle were open; she could feel a small breeze, and she could hear the noise from the wind when he sped up.

She had been forced to listen to him taunt Matt on the phone. He deliberately deepened his whiny voice to a throaty rasp when he called, as though it mattered that Matt might hear his normal tone. She had never seen nor heard this man before, and she didn't know how Matt could possibly recognize his voice.

What he had said to Matt about "Mommy and Daddy in Phoenix" had heightened her level of anxiety by several degrees. What could this man know of her family? How did he know where they lived? She wanted to find out—but she was almost afraid to know the answers.

She had heard him tell Matt not to go to the police. She heard the instruction for Matt to stay in his room and wait. Matt must be struggling not to go crazy. He was a person who acted when he saw a need; he could not bear to sit and do nothing. He let her know often how deeply he cared about her. What would he be feeling right now?

She struggled to keep her own emotions in check. She felt anger, at this man and at herself. Why had she let him do this? Would it have been better to scream and fight him back on that loading dock, even though he had a gun? She had never faced a choice like that before—never even thought about it. Had she done the wrong thing?

She was afraid at the same time. What was going to happen to her?

She tried to keep fear and panic at bay. Those reactions would keep her from thinking clearly, and thinking clearly might mean the difference between being a victim or surviving. She meant to survive.

This man with the gun had control of the situation—at least for now. But she did not have to accept the situation passively. She did not have to let him control her thinking or her emotions.

His fist hit her in the back again.

"Ow!" Her response was almost involuntary.

He chuckled. "Just wanted to see if you were awake."

She felt the car slowing. It stopped, but the engine continued to idle. She heard the tones of the keypad on his phone again. There was a pause, and then he said, "Room 317." There was another pause, and when he spoke again, it was in his raspy disguised voice. "How are things, cowboy? Lonesome this afternoon?" He laughed again.

Faintly, Jane could hear a voice from his telephone receiver. Matt must have been nearly yelling at him. When the man answered, he was mad enough to forget his vocal disguise for a moment. "Shut up!" he snapped. He remembered to rasp out the next words. "Don't talk unless I say so. You're not going to talk to your wife unless we feel like letting you. When *we're* ready, you'll get a call telling you where to bring what we want. Stay by that phone and wait."

The car began to roll, and gravel spun out from under its tires as the man in the driver's seat hit the accelerator pulling into traffic.

When he spoke to her, he was almost yelling. "Your husband's got a big mouth to go with his big muscles. Too bad he's not smarter." The man paused. When he spoke again, he sounded as if he were making an effort to control himself. "I hope I get a chance to meet him again. I have a few things I want to teach him."

Again? This man had met Matt before? Was that why he was trying to disguise his voice? But where could they have met him?

The man kept driving, turning occasionally, going uphill, then downhill again. Jane had no idea how long they had been in this car since they left the hotel. She was fairly certain it was close to an hour. More? She could not be sure.

Where was he taking her?

4

The car began to slow again. Jane wondered if the driver might be preparing to make another call to Matt. There was the crunch of gravel as he let the car roll to a stop.

This time he turned off the engine and opened his door.

She could follow the crunching sound made by his feet on the surface outside as he walked around the back of the car and stopped at the right rear passenger door. The hinges of the door squeaked as he opened it. She felt him grasp the bottom end of the blanket covering her. He yanked it off.

She blinked against the light as she turned to look at him. He grinned at her. "Did we have a nice ride?"

He reached in to grab the short chain on the handcuffs behind her back and began to pull, hurting her wrists and arms. His sharp tugging at the handcuffs forced her to sit up on the edge of the seat and scoot across it sideways as he pulled. "Keep coming," he said, "this is your stop." She put her right foot out of the car and then turned, his hand still on the chain behind her, so she could put the other foot on the pavement too.

When she stood and gained her balance, she was facing toward the front of the car. They were on a narrow side street that ended on what looked like a major thoroughfare. Directly across that street, she could see a small storefront rescue mission with a neon sign in the form of a cross bearing the words "Jesus Saves." The car was parked beside a building that extended perhaps thirty yards to the busy street. For the last fifty feet or so, the white wall of the building was decorated with a colorful street mural, but her view of the painting was partially blocked by a large garbage container about two car lengths ahead of the car.

To their left across the side street was an old brick building with a rusty metal fire escape zigzagging down its side. The fire escape ended in a counter-weighted ladder that hung above the sidewalk but would, in theory, dip down to street level if someone descending the stairs from above put weight on it. The ladder looked like it might be too rusty to move.

Jane had little time to study the scene. The man behind her threw the blanket back in the car, then grabbed her arm and spun her around. "Close your eyes!" he commanded, and slapped her hard across the face. Her eyes went wide as she looked down at him in shock. He raised his hand again, and she shut her eyes obediently.

He led her around the back of the car. Their feet made crunching noises and then the noises stopped. He seemed to be leading her across the street. She had to know more about her surroundings, so she opened her eyes just a slit—enough to see that he was leading her toward a door in the side of the building, about thirty feet to the left of where the fire escape ended.

The man must have seen her eyelids flutter. He spun her to the left, toward him. "*Closed!*" He gave her another stinging slap across the face. "I told you to keep them closed!"

She squeezed her eyes tightly shut. He turned her and drew her forward again by her arm. A few steps later she stumbled over something and would have fallen except for his support. "Stupid," he muttered, followed by a filthy name. "Don't you know enough to step up on a sidewalk?"

"How could I? I couldn't see it," she answered angrily.

"You saw it!" He pulled her roughly up on the sidewalk, then pushed her forward. Two steps more and he halted her again. She heard a small creak as the door in the side of the building opened on its hinges. He put his hand on the small of her back and pushed her forward. The light she could see through her eyelids diminished as they stepped inside.

The place smelled dank and musty. There was a faint odor also of something unpleasant from long past. Vomit?

The man took hold of her arm again and drew her forward until her foot hit another obstacle and she almost stumbled. "Up," he said curtly. "Stairs.'

She stepped up with her right foot, then with her left. She moved her right foot up on the next stair tread, then stepped up again with the left.

The man moved up one ahead of her. "Faster," he said, yanking her arm.

Jane opened her eyes and looked angrily into his. Immediately he swung his hand at her face, but she ducked away and he missed. He had to put his hand on her shoulder to keep from losing his balance. Then he cocked his arm back, threatening to swing again.

"Stop it!" Jane said. She looked around the narrow, dimly lighted stairwell. "What's so secret about stairs?" She paused. He glowered at her, his arm cocked back. "If you want me to go up, just let me do it," she said.

Slowly he smiled. "That's better. That's the spirit of cooperation we're looking for." He reached into his jacket pocket and pulled out the gun he had shown her earlier. "Up. And don't be stupid enough to try anything."

She climbed the two flights to a landing with a door and stopped. "Up," the man said, motioning with the pistol. She climbed two more flights, to the next door, and halted again. "Don't stop," the man said, "keep going." She kept climbing until the stairs ran out. Five floors.

The man stepped up beside her and raised the gun in his right hand as though he would hit her across the face with it. "Close your eyes and don't open them until I tell you. Understand?"

Jane said nothing, but she closed her eyes. She heard the door open and he pushed her through, then took her arm again and guided her forward. They were walking on something softer. Carpet? His shoes made small scuffing sounds. There was no sound from the athletic shoes she had put on this morning. After several seconds, he stopped her again. "Keep your eyes shut and don't move." She heard him insert a key in a lock, heard a small scraping noise that sounded like a lock lever turning, and then felt a brief movement of air.

She had to know where she was. As he stepped back to her side, she risked opening her eyes just a slit for a momentary glimpse. She was looking down at the floor. Her gray and white shoes stood out against a section of threadbare brownish carpet that looked like it had last been vacuumed before she was born. Inside the room was carpet that looked like it might have been light blue or grey at one time, but in the entryway it had long since turned black.

The man took her arm and pushed her into the room. He closed the door behind them. She heard him locking it. Then he took her arm, turned her ninety degrees to the right toward him, and made her step back three steps. He let go of her arm and stepped away from her.

"You can open your eyes now," he said.

The room was small. He was four or five steps away and he was almost against the far wall. The wood panel door they had entered was painted a drab gray, but the paint was peeling off the back. The walls might have been institutional tan at one time, but the color was faded now, except for a couple of places where patches in the wall had been painted over. There was a door in the corner of the room that might lead to a bathroom. On her left, between that door and the window in the other corner of the room, was the bed, a standard double that sagged in the middle. The faded brown bedspread looked grimy. It had snags hanging toward the floor at the bottom.

The man had obviously positioned himself so he could watch her face when she got the first look at her surroundings. He grinned at her again. "Homey, isn't it? Almost as nice as the place you've been staying." He laughed his cackling laugh.

He obviously hoped for some reaction from her—disgust or horror. Jane tried hard to keep her face expressionless.

His grin faded. He walked around behind her. There was a scraping noise, and then something touched her calves. "Sit," he commanded.

She turned to glance behind her. There was a cheap metal-frame chair whose vinyl seat cover was split open. Slowly she started to sit. He grabbed the chain on the handcuffs and jerked her arms out in back so she was forced to sit down suddenly with her arms behind the arched frame of the chair. She wondered if he would have been gentler had she given him the reaction he wanted when she first glimpsed this room.

The man walked around in front of her again. He crossed the room to the door with the peeling paint, leaned against the wall, and stood watching her.

She hated the way he looked at her—like she was some delicacy he was planning to savor later. She tried not to let him unnerve her. She had seen players on the volleyball court try to intimidate opponents and establish dominance. She was determined not to give this man that edge. She was watching him too; if he had weaknesses, she would learn them.

He stared at her, letting her wait before he spoke. It was part of his game.

Finally, he said, "So, Mrs. Randall, maybe we ought to get to know each other. Tell me all about yourself."

When she said nothing, he chuckled, and walked slowly around behind her again. She didn't like having him behind her either. She could feel him looking at her. Finally he leaned close to her ear.

"Everything could have been so much easier for all of us if the two of you had just drunk the wine last night."

The wine? That waiter last night . . . Jane gave a small involuntary shiver as she recognized the meaning in what he had said—the wine had been drugged. Or poisoned? She started to turn to look at the expression on his face, then stopped herself.

The man behind her chuckled again.

A flush of embarrassment spread in her face. Jane wished she could will it away. The thought of being drugged and unconscious in their room while he searched it revolted her, but she did not want to let him see that.

* * *

Matt looked over the items spread out in front of him on the bed.

Which one of them might be hiding a secret?

He had been kneeling beside the bed for most of the past hour. After the telephone call down in the street, he had walked back to this room mechanically and stretched out on the bed, numb. But after a few minutes of staring up at the ceiling, he had forced himself to take control of his thoughts, to go over everything he knew about the situation once more. Thinking was the only thing he could do for Jane right now.

Well, not the only thing. During the past hour, he had prayed fervently more than once for Jane's safety. There were few words to say beyond, "Please protect her." But he had said those prayers more meaningfully than ever before in his life. He was beginning to understand now what pleading meant.

He had risen from his knees and paced for a while. It didn't help. He had to act somehow.

The kidnappers were looking for something, they seemed willing to do anything to get it, they seemed certain he had it—and he had no idea what it could be. So he had gone to the closet, pulled out the bags he and Jane had brought, and begun to examine the contents again.

First he had gone through the clothing in his suitcase, then Jane's. But no. What would they want with an item of clothing? And why wouldn't they have just taken it?

He had put their suitcases back in the closet and pulled out their carry-on bags, spreading the contents out on the bed. The waist pack Jane had left in her bag was empty, and the items in her small purse could have been bought in any drugstore. She carried her phone with her in a small wallet that also held her driver's license and a credit card. Her tablet computer was the only thing of any monetary value in her bag, and they had not taken it when they had the chance.

And the voice on the phone had said, "He shouldn't have given it to *you.*" Whatever they wanted, they were sure *he* had it.

Matt turned to the contents of his own carry-on bag. Whoever searched his things had found nothing in his damaged shaving kit except standard men's toiletries. His video camera had received special attention, but they had not taken it either. Was the thing they wanted something that might be seen on a video recording? Apparently, they had not found what they were looking for on any of his recorded video clips. Maybe they had not had time to watch all the clips. Would the camera still be of interest to them? Matt was sure it would be a blind alley. He liked putting together videos, so he had purchased the camera before the trip to record the beginning of his and Jane's life together. No "he" had given the camera to him, and all of the clips in it had been shot here in San Francisco.

He scanned their other personal items again and shook his head. There seemed to be nothing here that could hold any secrets the kidnappers might be seeking.

Whatever they were looking for, it must be small. They had even opened the small packages of makeup in Jane's case.

Matt sat back against the wall, stretched his legs out in front of him, and looked at his watch. *I wonder when he's going to call again. It's been more than an hour. I wish he'd call. I need to know if she's . . . if he's hurt her, if . . .*

No! Focus. Focus on the problem. He had to shut down fear and panic.

He surveyed the things on the bed once more. If there was nothing hidden in these, then where?

What were the things that any "he" had given to him recently?

There could have been something among the wedding presents. Matt wouldn't know about those. Their parents and siblings had taken charge of the gifts after the reception—unwrapped them, tagged them, left them in the apartment where Matt and Jane would be living after the honeymoon. The caller or his friends apparently had not found what they were looking for among those gifts.

Doug.

Matt's younger brother had given them an early wedding present two days before they got married. He had waited until Jane and Matt were together at his parents' house, then brought out a gift-wrapped package and insisted that they open it while he could watch. It was a collection of some of their favorite movies and music on a small hard drive. "All suitable for loading on your phone or computer whenever you want," he had explained, grinning.

They had thanked him delightedly, appreciative of his thoughtfulness, but Matt had made a mental note at the time to talk to Doug about how he had obtained the recordings. Doug was good at mining a wide variety of Internet sources, as well as the private collections of friends, for copies of movies or music. He was one who didn't see any reason why there should be boundaries or restrictions on material from the Internet; he didn't yet know some of what Matt had learned in his work about the darker side of the web. While Doug was gathering the items on that hard drive, had he accidentally downloaded or copied something he wasn't supposed to have? Could there be a secret buried in that collection somewhere?

Then there was the new phone. Matt reached for his jacket, lying across the foot of the bed, and fished his mobile phone out of its inside pocket. The device was the newest large-screen smartphone with a collection of apps useful in business. It could easily download documents or files from his office computer or access cloud files so he could have business information at hand whenever or wherever he might need it. It had a top-of-the-line camera and room for all the tunes he could ever want to carry. Cole Brewster had given him this new phone just three days before the wedding. "It's not sheets or towels for the home, but it really is for both of you," his boss had said, winking. "You'll want to keep in close contact with that beautiful wife of yours, so I'm paying the tab for personal calls too. You've got all the minutes and data you'll ever need. Enjoy."

Matt had protested that the phone was too generous a gift, and that he already had a smartphone of his own. Cole replied, "You've turned out to be all I could have hoped for. This is an investment in a trusted employee who's a key to some of my future plans. I want you to have certain information and documents at your fingertips anytime I need you to access it—maybe even when you're out of the office. This is an insurance policy for me."

Matt had not resisted because his own phone was a basic model more than a year out of date. Smartphones had been introduced to the world when he was a teenager, just getting deeply involved in computers. He had ignored the new phones at first because they didn't seem to offer much he needed. But as their capability had grown, he had become intrigued with the idea of experimenting to see how much could be done with them. He had been thinking about buying a new one but had put it off because he was saving for marriage.

He activated the phone Cole had given him and studied the icons on its touch screen. He had been too busy before the wedding to download any office business files for these apps, and Cole had never indicated exactly what information he had in mind. Matt had entered only a handful of personal phone numbers. If the kidnappers were looking for phone numbers, why would they cut out the lining of his shaving kit, or look in Jane's makeup? It couldn't be the cell phone itself they wanted. Phones like this one were available in any upscale phone store and a lot of big box consumer outlets. The people who had kidnapped Jane obviously knew about this phone—they had called his number—but they had not mentioned the device. He slid the phone back into his jacket pocket.

He saw nothing among their things that anyone could want badly enough to carry out a kidnapping.

If he could just look again at the collection his brother had recorded on that hard drive. Doug was *too* good at finding his way around the worldwide web. His kind of curiosity could get a person in trouble—a lesson Matt had learned for himself a few years ago. He had tried to warn his younger brother to be more careful.

Matt tried to visualize in his mind what had been listed in that movie and music collection. He could remember exactly where he had left the hard drive in his parents' house.

Mom and Dad's house! He sat up straight and looked at the things on the bed again. His and Jane's apartment in Phoenix had been searched, then the hotel room here, and still the people behind this had not found what they wanted. Would they turn next to his parents' house, or to Jane's parents' home? He had to warn them somehow—his parents and hers.

But how? Would the people holding Jane know if he called home—maybe even know what he said? If he shared any information with their parents, what would the kidnappers do to Jane? And could he say anything to his parents or hers without putting them in danger too?

Maybe they're already in danger, and they don't know it. I have to warn them.

His thoughts tried to go in several different directions at once. Panic prowled around the shadows in his mind. He forced himself to focus once more, to think clearly.

Was there a way to say something to caution his parents without really saying anything?

Maybe. He had to try. If he could talk to Doug and steer the conversation just right, maybe he could casually suggest that his brother take the hard drive over to his and Jane's apartment. That would remove the danger from his parents' home, and if the people behind this kidnapping were somehow listening, maybe that would point them away from his family.

He called from the phone on the desk in the hotel room. He wasn't sure whether the kidnappers would be able to intercept his cell phone conversations; it seemed more likely they could know what he said on the hotel phone. He *wanted* them to know this time.

"Hi, Mom," he said when she answered the phone, trying to sound cheerful. "How are you?"

"We're fine!" She sounded surprised, and pleased to hear from him. "How are you? Are the two of you having fun?"

He didn't answer her question directly. "It's . . . interesting here. I just have a couple of minutes, and I needed to talk to Doug about something. Can you put him on?"

"Oh, I'm sorry, dear, he's left for work already."

Matt glanced at his watch. Of course. Doug's shift at the electronics store started at 1:00 P.M. and ended after the store closed at night.

"Matt,' his mother continued, "I'm sorry about the break-in at your apartment. The McDougals called to let us know, so I went over and helped clean up. We don't want you to worry about it. Nothing was stolen so far as we can tell."

Way to go, Mom! She had given him the opening he needed. "I hope nothing's gone. *Everything* the two of us own is in that apartment. We'll check it out when we get home."

"What have you been seeing?"

He briefly reviewed their itinerary from the day before, trying not to sound nervous or worried. She was good at reading his moods.

'Wow, you were busy. What are you doing today?" she asked.

"Just, uh . . . learning more about San Francisco. I'll tell you all about it when we get back."

"We'll be looking forward to that. Have a good time."

Matt said good-bye, hung up the phone, and reviewed the conversation in his mind. He hoped he had made it plain to anyone who might be listening that he had left nothing worth looking for at his parents' house or anywhere else.

* * *

The man was standing behind her looking out of the window, the only source of light in the room right now. Jane glanced over her shoulder occasionally to check on what he was doing. He had opened the window to let in some air. The room had become stifling in the midday heat. She was sweating inside her jacket, but in one way she was grateful for it; the jacket felt like protection somehow.

The man's cell phone rang. He turned back toward her as he answered it. "Yeah? When?" He listened for a moment, and Jane could faintly hear a voice on the other end of the phone. "That number is . . . yeah," the man responded. Jane heard a beep indicating that he had ended the call.

The man walked around in front of her so he could see her face. "Sounds like it's time to give the lonely hubby another little reminder of what he's missing." He stood looking her up and down, and then his eyes went to the bulge in her pants pocket. "That your cell phone?" he asked, pointing.

Jane did not answer. He knelt beside her, put his hand on the bulge, and began to work the phone out of her pocket. She hated having him touch her, even though his hand was on her phone. His right hand lingered on her hip for a second as the phone fell into his left. He pushed the *On* button. "Does it have a good camera?"

He stood in front of her studying the icons on the phone's touchscreen and tapping at them until he figured out how the camera worked. Then he pointed it at her. "Smile."

She sat looking at him without responding.

He scowled at her. "Smile for your husband, Mrs. Randall. Show him you miss him. Let him know you're all right—so far."

Jane managed a weak smile.

The man chuckled as he snapped a photo. He studied it on the display for a moment and began to tap at the screen, smiling to himself. Then he read her what he had written.

* * *

Matt jumped at the musical tone from his jacket pocket. He had been gazing out the window, thinking, wondering what the kidnappers' next move would be. He tried to remember what that tone meant as he retrieved the phone from his pocket. The words on its display reminded him: NEW MESSAGE.

His heart jumped momentarily when he checked the sender's number. It was Jane's! She had sent him a message. And there was a photo with it!

His heart sank again when he opened the photo. It showed Jane sitting in a chair in a bare room, her hands behind her back. Her smile was weak—forced. The message with the photo was obviously not from her. It was an attempt at a clever taunt. "How are things with Mom and Dad back home in Phoenix? Too bad the wife can't call right now. All tied up. But we'll all get together soon. Meantime, I'll be taking good care of her."

Matt realized his fingers were turning white as he gripped his phone. He tried to relax.

The man holding his wife was baiting him. Matt knew it. He could not let anger cloud his thinking. He could not afford to let his mind be focused on what he would do if he could find that man right now—or if they hurt Jane.

The message offered no proof that someone had actually listened to the conversation with his mother, but they apparently knew at least what number he had called.

This man who sent the photo and the message obviously enjoyed tormenting people. Let him enjoy his little taunts long enough and he might give away more.

He *had* given something away in the photo, Matt realized. In the background, to Jane's left, there was a window, and outside the window was a building. The white wall of the building was overexposed, but Matt could see part of a colorful mural on it. He wondered if there would be any way to locate that mural.

And maybe the man had given away something in the message too.

"We'll all get together soon," he had said. Was that some indication of what they were planning? What kind of get-together would it be?

5

No words had passed between them in more than half an hour. The man spent much of his time behind her, looking out the window—or at least that was what Jane hoped he was doing. Sometimes she thought she could feel him watching her. But the few times she had dared to glance over her shoulder, he had been gazing out at the street below.

Traffic noises drifted up through the window, but there was nothing to distinguish this area—nothing to tell her by the sound where they might be.

When he was not looking out the window, the man came and sat on the edge of the bed. Most of the time when he was sitting there, he watched her. She tried not to make eye contact.

The last thing he had said to her was, "Won't be long now." He hadn't offered an explanation and she hadn't asked. She didn't want the man to talk to her. When he did, it was usually some cruel taunt. After sending the message to Matt, he had asked her, "So, how do you like San Francisco so far?" and laughed again.

What had he meant by, "Won't be long now"? Were they expecting to get what they wanted from Matt sometime soon? But how could he give them what he did not have?

What would they do with her once they found it? Or with Matt? She tried to tell herself they would just let her go if they got they wanted—but her mind held too many questions. She tried not to think about the possibilities.

She did not know how long she had been here. Judging from the slant of light through the window, it must be early afternoon now.

She heard the quiet footfalls in the hallway just before they stopped in front of the door to the room. It was the first time since they had been here that she had heard any sound from outside the door.

The man who was with her had also heard the footsteps; he was already crossing the room when there was a soft knock. "Yeah?" he said.

"Lyle?" answered a voice from the hallway. It was muffled by the door.

So "Lee Waters" is really Lyle Something. Jane stowed that tidbit in the mental file of information she had collected. There wasn't much. She hoped she might have the chance to use the information somehow.

Lyle unfastened the security chain and opened the door.

It would have been hard to imagine a greater contrast to Lyle than the man who entered. Lyle looked seedy beside him. The newcomer was handsome. He had dark hair, a nice tan—not too dark, but healthy looking—dark eyes, and white, even teeth. He wore a navy blazer that appeared to have been tailored and a pair of complementary gray slacks. There was a luster on his black shoes, and they obviously had not come from the neighborhood discount store.

When he smiled at her, she thought he might have been an attractive man if there had been any warmth in his eyes. "Well, Mrs. Randall," he said, "has Lyle been taking good care of you?" He sat down on the end of the bed close to her chair. "Do you mind if I call you Jane?"

"Would it matter if I did?" *Careful, keep your anger in. You don't know how this man might react.*

He seemed to take it calmly enough. "As long as we're going to spend some time together, there's no reason we shouldn't be friendly."

"Is this your idea of being friendly? Putting people in handcuffs while you get on a first-name basis?"

"I'm Greg, by the way, and I'm sorry about the handcuffs, but they're a necessary precaution." He glanced at Lyle. "We thought you might not decide to stay with us if we gave you the choice, and we need you here for a while."

"For what? So you can try to force my husband to give you something he doesn't have?"

"Oh, we're sure he has it. We have our information from a very reliable source."

"He has no idea what you're looking for."

"I hope he does." His smile faded. "For your sake, I hope you're wrong. It could be very painful for both of you if he refuses to give it to us." Greg smiled again, but there was still no warmth in it. "Maybe he *does* know. Maybe he just didn't tell *you*."

"He would have told me. I know my husband."

"Do you? You've been married how long now? Three or four days? How well do you really know this man you married? Do you know all his secrets? Every man has some. Are you really sure you *know* what you think you know about him?" He sat staring into her eyes for several seconds, as though trying to will her to speak, and when she did not respond, he turned to look at Lyle. "How is everything going?"

"Fine. I've been keeping *Mister* Randall off balance—tense, the way you said."

"Do you think he's ready to hear from us again?"

"Sure." Lyle grinned in Jane's direction. "I'm sure he'd love to hear from us."

Greg pulled a cell phone out of his coat pocket, punched in a number on its keypad, and waited. "Room 317," he said. He listened for almost a minute, Jane thought, before he raised his eyebrows and looked at her. "Mr. Randall isn't answering."

* * *

People walking down the stairs to the underground Bay Area Rapid Transit station paid no attention to him. People coming up from the BART station continued along the downtown sidewalks with no more than a glance in his direction. Probably he registered only as one of the street people. If they had looked more closely, they would have seen that he was better dressed—but he probably looked just as lost and alone.

Those people walking past were oblivious to the fact that his world had been taken from him.

On the small plaza at the bottom of the stairs, a few feet below him, people sat at tables under colorful umbrellas, peacefully reading and enjoying coffee or soft drinks or chatting on their cell phones. He and Jane might have been there, enjoying each other's company, if only something cruel—something evil—hadn't intruded into their lives. Matt wished he knew exactly what it was.

How could you fight something if you had no clear picture of it—if you didn't know where to strike?

And he wanted to strike out at something. He struggled with rage. He disliked violent men, men who could not control themselves, and yet right now he wanted to hurt the man who had taunted him on the phone, along with whoever was controlling that small, evil mind. Matt knew it was in his power to hurt people because of his size and strength. But never before had he really *wanted* to hurt someone—not like this. If only he could reach the throat where that voice on the phone—

No! It hadn't done any good to yell at the man when he called. It had only given that man satisfaction, and it had left Matt shaking. It had cost him effort to carefully and deliberately calm himself so he could think clearly again. Anger and fear were his enemies right now, even more than the man on the phone. He had to keep his thinking clear to have any chance of freeing Jane. He had to keep his emotions in control if he wanted to outwit the kidnappers.

He stood with his back against the curving railing of the plaza trying to look relaxed, but he was ready to move quickly left or right. He wanted to leave himself room to move no matter which way a threat might come at him—just in case the kidnappers might have someone watching or following him right now.

He couldn't know who or what to look for, so he kept a careful eye on the people who passed—and the people who didn't pass, who lingered around this plaza for some reason. He wanted to be able to assess anyone who came near. Anyone could be an enemy.

A few minutes ago, a tall man of about 30 had veered toward him suddenly, coming out of the crowd. The man had had a hand in his suit coat pocket, and his eyes fixed suddenly on Matt's face. Matt had planted his feet firmly and tensed his arms, one hand ready to grab and the other ready to strike—face, solar plexus, neck, whatever might be most effective. Then the man had veered away, pulled his cell phone out of his pocket, and moved on down into the BART station. Matt had watched for a couple of minutes to make sure he did not come out again.

Sitting in the hotel room, he had replayed in his mind over and over that message from Jane's phone. The more he had thought about it, the more he had feared the hotel room was a trap. "We'll all get together soon," the message had said. Matt realized that as long as he waited in the hotel, they knew where he was, they knew when he made a move, knew when he made a call—and maybe what he said. They could simply come for him whenever they wanted.

He had managed to calm his mind enough to think out a response to the situation. If they captured both him and Jane, they could take their time trying to find whatever it was they were looking for. Would they punish him—or worse, make him watch while they punished Jane—to try to find out where this elusive thing was? And when they finally understood that he didn't have it, then what? Would they simply dispose of two inconvenient witnesses?

No. He could not let that happen. Both he and Jane would be safer, Matt reasoned, if he did not fall into the hands of the people who had taken her. As long as they believed they needed her in order to control him, they would have to keep her safe—wouldn't they?

Or had they already decided that *she* might have the information they needed? Were they trying to get it out of her right now? Was that why they did not call? The thought made him a little sick at his stomach.

He was hoping he had not made the wrong decision by leaving the hotel—hoping he had not risked her life by disobeying her captors. He had not felt any indication that it was a wrong thing to do—no kind of rational or spiritual stop sign. But had he considered things carefully enough? Was he thinking clearly?

He had put their bags and personal items away in the closet as though he and Jane were simply out of the hotel for the day. He had walked quickly down the stairs and through the hall toward the reception area, skirted around the edges of the lobby behind the pillars and potted plants, and slipped out the front door into the street. Then as he walked away from the hotel, he had waited for the raspy voice to call again and tell him he should not have left his room.

So far no one had called. It had been more than an hour.

And now, because he had not heard from them, he was beginning to wonder if they might have *wanted* him to leave the hotel. Maybe they thought he would lead them to what they were seeking. They might be watching right now. He was trying not to doubt every move he made.

He turned his head quickly in one direction or the other every so often to see if he could spot anyone who looked away suddenly, or suddenly looked down at a mobile phone or tablet, or seemed to be loitering nearby for no reason. So far, the only people loitering nearby were those at the tables on the plaza below, and they were paying no attention to him.

After leaving the hotel, he had satisfied his curiosity about that office window across the street—the one where he had seen the man looking into their room. The building was another older structure, and he had no time to wait for a slow elevator, so he had taken the stairs to the fourth floor two at a time.

The hallways on the fourth floor formed a rectangular passageway around a square inner core made up of smaller offices, the elevator shaft, and the stairwell. Larger offices and suites with windows were on the outside of that square. Matt walked slowly along the hallway that had outside offices facing their hotel. The one he judged to be in the right location had a name lettered on the frosted glass door: MILLS STAFFING SERVICES. He had pushed open the door and stepped inside.

There was only one person in the office suite, a sandy haired middle-aged woman seated at a desk behind a counter. She rose to meet him at the counter. "Can I help you?"

Matt glanced around. There was a waiting area to his right, with a row of several empty chairs. Beyond the woman's desk was a glassed-in office. It was vacant and the door was open. The blinds were raised now. Matt could look through that office and out through its window. He could see their hotel across the street. The hotel room he could see from here had its curtains open, but he could not see the interior of the room—at least not in daylight.

He looked at the woman. "Staffing services? So I would come here if I wanted staffing for what?"

She hesitated a moment before answering, obviously wondering why he had wandered through her door. "Events—conventions, conferences, things like that. Temporary and permanent office staff. Are you looking for a job?"

"No. I came to talk to the man who works in that office," he said, pointing beyond her. "When will he be back?" Matt tried not to sound demanding, but he knew some urgency came through in his tone.

"He won't be in today," the woman answered. "He worked late last night making some final arrangements for staffing a convention."

Matt stared through the office toward the windows of their hotel across the street. He was beginning to see the weakness of his earlier reasoning—

or lack of it. There seemed to be little likelihood that someone could be brought to this office and held prisoner. How would kidnappers force someone in here during the day, or confine a person here, without attracting too much attention? It would take a conspiracy of some kind to cover up the crime, and this woman would have to be part of it. He looked at her again. The woman was small and seemed a bit timid—not like someone who could be part of holding someone by force. "Does Mr. Mills work late very often?" he asked.

She backed away to stand by the edge of the desk, her hand near the phone. She was well out of reach of even Matt's long arms. "I think I've told you as much as you need to know—unless you have some business here."

He glanced again at the building across the street. "Do you have any business dealings with that hotel over there?"

"Information about our clients is privileged." She walked around behind the desk, putting it between the two of them. Her fingers inched closer to the phone.

If she wasn't hiding something, why did she seem to be afraid?

Then Matt understood; he had been so focused on his own pain, his own need, that he had not seen the situation from her viewpoint. She was alone, confronted by a strange man who towered over her and easily outweighed her by more than a hundred pounds—a man asking insistent questions. She could probably feel some of the anger he was trying to suppress. He tried to sound non-threatening: "And when will Mr. Mills be in?"

"Tomorrow." There was relief in her voice.

"Thanks for your help," he said. He took one more quick look at the hotel across the street, then turned and walked out.

Last night what he had seen in the window of this office had seemed suspicious. Now it seemed mundane: a man working late, maybe stretching a bit and relaxing from his work for a couple of minutes by looking out the window. The explanation could be that simple. Any other explanation—some kind of conspiracy—required a stretch of the imagination. He could not afford to spend more time on imaginary dangers constructed in his own fearful mind.

He had to deal with reality. But now that he was outside of the hotel, it was hard to pin that down.

How much, for example could the kidnappers really know? Were they actually able to listen in on his calls, maybe to track him somehow? Or had they simply made lucky guesses?

No. Some of what they knew could not have been guesswork.

But if they could track him, why would they have instructed him to stay in the hotel room? Could that have been some kind of trick to make him want to leave so they could follow him? But follow him where? And for how long? The man who had called him did not seem like a patient person willing to play a waiting game.

Right now, there was too much uncertainty for him to make a plan, to take charge of the situation, to do something to help Jane. Right now, the only thing he could do was wait cautiously himself to see what the kidnappers would do next.

The waiting was torment.

The spot where he stood was within sight of their hotel—close enough to get there quickly or to see people and cars headed in that direction, but far enough away to get an advance look at anyone or any cars coming at him from there.

Fear seemed to be coming at him from every direction, every second. He was working hard to control it.

He could not bear to think about losing Jane. He could not bear to think about what might be happening to her. He wondered whether he should run back to the hotel right now in case the kidnappers had not yet discovered he was missing. But no—something stopped him. He tried to keep his mind on other things. He kept watching the people around him.

He tried not to will the phone to ring.

When it finally did, he almost tore the pocket of his jacket trying to get the telephone out of it. "Hello?"

"Mr. Randall. I believe you were told to stay in your room." It was not the same voice—or at least it was no longer disguised. It sounded polished—but with an edge.

"That didn't seem like a very good idea," Matt answered carefully. He would have to feel his way with the man behind this new voice.

"We need you to go back to your room, Matt. Now."

"I have a problem with that. I started thinking about the message I got with my wife's picture, about how we'd all get together soon, and suddenly the room felt crowded—like a place for you to come pick me up whenever you feel like it."

There was a pause, and then the man said, "Weren't my associate's instructions clear? You realize that Jane could pay the price if you don't do what we tell you?"

So there are at least two of them.

It made him mad to hear this man speak of Jane as though she were some kind of bargaining chip, but Matt struggled to keep his words calm. He needed to keep this man talking. This was the dangerous part—the part where he needed to convince the kidnapper that Jane's safety was an essential part of any negotiation. "We both know that if you do anything to my wife," he said, "you'll lose any hold you have over me. I'll go straight to the police, and you'll never get what you're looking for."

"How do we know you're not with the police now?"

"Hold on," Matt answered. He thrust the cell phone straight out to his left suddenly. The pigeons close by, on the railing above the underground station entrance, cooed in alarm and three of them flapped away noisily. Matt put the phone back to his ear. "Does it sound like I'm with the police?"

The voice on the other end of the line was silent for a moment. Then: "We really don't want to hurt Jane. If we have to do that, you'll be responsible. But we can't negotiate with you unless you go back to your hotel."

"Yes, you can, and you know it. You say I have something you want. Well, you took something very important out of my life—someone who means everything to me. I want her back. In order to get what you want, you're going to have to prove to me she's all right." He paused only a moment. "And I promise you, if you hurt Jane, there will be no place on earth you can hide where I won't find you."

The other man chuckled. "You're in no position to be making threats, Matt."

"Says the man who has to threaten an innocent, defenseless woman to try to get what you want from me. We might have been able to work out something if you had approached me openly instead of hiding."

The knot in Matt's stomach went several twists tighter. It was risky to push these people, but he had thought this out carefully over the past hour. There was no other choice. If he simply gave in to them, he knew there would be no escape for him or Jane. He had to try to force a change in the situation. He didn't breathe while he waited for the other man to respond.

"You're prepared to give up what we're looking for?" the man asked finally.

Yes! There's a way to get to them!

Matt let out his breath slowly. "You can have anything you want that I have if you give my wife back."

There was a pause on the other end of the line. "All right, we can work something out. We'll—"

"No. It's not going to be that easy. You haven't given me any reason to trust you. How do I know my wife is still alive? How do I know you haven't hurt her?"

He could hear muffled conversation, as though someone had covered the phone. Then: "Jane is just fine. You saw the picture. We'll call to tell you where—"

"No." The knot in his stomach twisted even tighter, but he had to be sure. "You could have done something to her since you took the picture. You have to let me talk to her, now—or I'll know you're just stringing me along. I won't take any more calls from you." He closed his eyes, hoping he had not gone too far.

There was silence on the other end of the phone for—five seconds? It seemed like a very long time. He heard someone say faintly, "Talk. Tell him to do what we say." And then he heard his wife's voice. "Matt?"

"J! Are you all right?"

She sounded relieved when she answered. "I'm all right—so far. They tell me if you don't give them what they want, they'll hurt me, but I know you don't—"

Her words stopped suddenly, as though someone had blocked the sound. Then he heard the man's voice again. "Jane will be fine, unless you surprise us again. If you force us, we can do without her and simply come after you. You wouldn't be able to hide from us forever. Keep your phone line open. We'll have to tell you where you'll be making your delivery."

"You can't afford to hurt my wife because you need her to get to me. And I have a feeling you took her because you need what you're looking for *soon*." Matt paused to let the other man absorb his words. "I want Jane back now. So you can tell me where we'll be making the *exchange*. If I don't get my wife back, you don't get anything either. You can name the place, but it will have to be somewhere out in the open."

"You'll hear from us soon." The phone line went dead.

* * *

Greg dropped the cell phone back into the inside pocket of his jacket. He looked speculatively at Lyle. "What was it you said to her husband in that message?"

Lyle's brow furrowed. "Well, I . . . " He was obviously trying to determine what Greg wanted to hear. "I said if he wanted his wife to stay safe, he'd better do what we told him."

"And did you say something about all of us getting together?"

"I, ah . . . I don't remember exactly. I might have."

Greg sat looking Lyle in the eyes for several seconds. Then he looked at Jane. "Does your phone keep copies of messages sent?"

"Yes. You'd be able to read what he wrote." Lyle was behind her so she couldn't see his face when she spoke, but she could almost feel him glaring at her.

Greg looked at Lyle again.

Jane could hear the anger in Lyle's voice as he answered. "I was trying to help him understand he'll see Jane if he does what we say. I told him in the meantime I'd take good care of his wife."

Greg cursed, and his look turned to one of reproach. "There's an art to keeping somebody off balance without pushing him over the edge, Lyle. You knew the plan. Now you've made it harder. Mr. Randall is resisting direction." Greg looked at Jane again. "I just hope Matt understands the importance of cooperating with us. I'd hate to see him a widower so soon." He said it casually, with no sign of emotion.

That fear had been in the back of Jane's mind since Lyle had brought her here. She had never before thought that she might have to face the prospect of death before her life had really begun, or that she might be able to see her own death coming. But she had been dealing with that possibility since Lyle pointed his gun at her this morning.

She had decided that she was not afraid to die—just sad that it might come so soon. There were things she longed to do with Matt, things she wished she had done differently, faults she wished she had conquered. But mostly she had done her best; she had tried to live all the principles she reaffirmed every Sunday when she worshipped and every time she prayed.

Since this morning, she had silently prayed for her own safety a number of times, and she had prayed that Matt would do the right thing, whatever choices he might be forced to make. Beyond prayer, there was little else she could do. She was sad that her time with Matt might be so short—sad for the babies she might never have, sad that she might never see Matt a father, or a grandfather. When she thought of those things, she struggled not to cry.

"Jane, are you with us?" Greg waved a hand in front of her face and moved toward the foot of the bed to sit closer to her chair. He was smiling one of his lifeless smiles. On him, that facial expression was just one more component in some sort of social facade. "Help us out here. You know what Matt is hiding, don't you? Why won't he give it up? Is it more important to him than you are?"

"Matt isn't hiding anything! We don't know what you're talking about!" Jane realized her voice had risen to just below a shout.

Greg looked at her dubiously. "Maybe *you* don't know—maybe. But I have information that tells me your husband knows what we're looking for." He leaned closer and lowered his voice, apparently trying to sound like someone who could keep her secret. "Think about it. Is there something he hasn't wanted to talk about? Some question about his past he wouldn't answer? All men have their secrets. Does he maybe have a place he hides secret stuff? Some little thing like that?"

She looked into his eyes without speaking. It was Greg who finally looked away. "Oh, Jane." He sighed again. "I have a feeling you're not telling us everything. You could make this so much easier for all of us." He paused, apparently waiting for some kind of response. When she gave none, he shook his head slowly. "I think we need to develop a little openness here before we let Matt hear from us again." Greg stood and turned to walk over by the door. He gave Lyle a small nod.

She felt Lyle move close behind her. "I promised your husband I'd take good care of you while you were with us. And I always keep my promises." He chuckled.

Jane felt a small tug at her hair. Lyle was trying to figure out how to undo her braid. She felt another tug. Greg stood in the corner of the room watching, leaning against the door. He smiled as though he were amused by what was happening.

Lyle gave up on trying to deal with the braid and moved his fingers down to caress her cheek. "A man with a beautiful wife like you ought to keep a closer eye on her. He made a serious mistake. He should have given you all his attention every minute of the day. I can take better care of you."

Greg's eyes looked into Jane's as though he were trying to see inside her, trying to determine what she was hiding—trying to will it out of her.

Lyle's hands moved down to rest on her shoulders. "You're tense. You need to relax." He pulled the collar of her jacket open wider and began to massage her shoulders and neck.

Greg's expression did not change. He was studying her like some specimen. How far would he let Lyle go with this, Jane wondered, before stopping him?

And then it occurred to her that maybe he did not intend to stop Lyle at all.

She was afraid of these men. It would not bother them to make things very painful or humiliating for her if they thought it would get them what they wanted.

But right now her anger was stronger than her fear. If she were going to die, she would not be degraded first—treated like something to be used up, then discarded.

Lyle was caught off guard when she sprang up from the chair, her hands grasping its arched frame behind her back. She levered the chair backward into Lyle's shins. He howled in pain. She pushed backward with the chair and drove him toward the corner, where he fell in a heap. Greg had been caught off balance. He straightened up and began to move toward her. She whirled and threw the chair into his path, then took one step to reach the window. Before Greg could get the chair out of his way, Jane had put one leg out the window and was sitting astride the windowsill. "Stay there!" she commanded. Greg froze in place. "I'll jump, and you'll come out of this with nothing."

Lyle scrambled up from the corner screaming curses at her. He drew his gun from his waistband and pointed it at her. "Come back in here right now or I'll shoot you!"

"Go ahead," she answered. "If you're going to kill me anyway, do it right now. Then you'll lose your hold on Matt, and you and your friend can try to figure out why all of this went bad."

"Easy, Lyle," Greg said. He reached out his left hand and pulled Lyle's arm down slowly so the pistol was pointed at the floor. He looked at Jane. "You'd better do what he says."

"Or what?" She eased her torso part of the way out the window.

"You don't want to die, Jane." Greg said in his most soothing voice.

"You're right. That's the last thing I want." She looked down at the street below. "But I'll do that before I'll be your entertainment for the afternoon."

Greg looked at her, seemingly puzzled, for several seconds. "You're really willing to jump? Do women do things like that anymore?" He put on his amused smile again. "It seems so old-fashioned."

"It's a choice I'll make. Why not? You're planning to kill me anyway. I'm not going to let you humiliate me and torture me first."

Greg frowned slightly, then made his face blank again. "Come inside and we'll talk. You don't want to fall accidentally."

"It wouldn't be an accident." She looked down at the street again. The fall would be fifty feet or more. There was an overhang that jutted out from the building just above the ground floor. Her body would probably hit that overhang first and then tumble onto the pavement. Behind her back, she pressed the fingers of one hand hard against the bricks of the hotel's outside wall and the fingers of her other hand against the wall inside the window, helping hold her body in position. Her knee was tight against the inside wall. But if she just let go of her fingerholds and leaned a little to her left, this would be over quickly.

"You're wrong about what we're planning," Greg said, keeping a soothing tone. "You can't know what's in our minds."

"I know what's in *his* mind," she answered, looking at Lyle. "I'm not going to be his toy. I'm not willing to buy a few extra minutes or a couple of extra hours that way."

"You're bluffing," Lyle said. "You'd never jump. You'll come back in here and do exactly what we tell you to do." He started to raise his gun again. Jane shifted to her left so that she was more outside the window than in.

Lyle's eyes went wide in shock when he felt the blade at his throat. Jane had not seen where the knife came from. Greg had moved up behind Lyle, had reached almost casually under the back of his jacket with his left hand, and then Lyle had found the blade touching his neck just above his Adam's apple. Greg reached around with his right hand and pulled Lyle's gun hand down. "Put the gun away," he said. There was a mixture of surprise and fear in Lyle's eyes. When he was slow to respond, Greg increased the pressure of the blade slightly against his throat and repeated the words more forcefully. "Put the gun away, Lyle."

Obediently, Lyle stuck the gun into his waistband. Greg did not take the blade away from his neck. "I'm sure when you told Matt you would take care of his wife, you meant as a guest, didn't you?"

Lyle started to turn his head to look over his shoulder, then thought better of it as the blade moved against his throat. Finally, he said grudgingly, "Yeah, that's what I meant."

Greg reached under his coat again with his left hand. It came back without the knife. "See?" he said, showing Jane his empty hands. "You can come back in now. You'll be safe. I guarantee it."

"For how long?" She looked down at the ground once more. "If I'm dead, Matt will talk to the police, and you'll have nothing to gain by killing him. At least I'll save him."

Greg looked at her with something like wonder. "You'd do that?"

"Yes. There may be no way I can come out of this alive, but I'm not going to let you get him too."

"Jane, you're not thinking clearly about this. We have no reason to kill Matt if he lets us have what we want. And we really don't want to kill you. Scaring him about that is just a way of letting him know he can't take this lightly. It's not right for him to keep something that doesn't belong to him, is it?" He made the words sound earnest. But there was nothing in his eyes—no feeling.

"You'd *have* to kill me. I've seen your faces, I know your names."

Greg shook his head. "First names—and you don't even know if those are real. I don't live in San Francisco and neither does Lyle. Neither do you. After today, our paths will probably never cross again. This business can stay just between us and you and Matt. We don't need to kill you."

"Why don't I find that convincing?"

"Killing you is not my job. If it were, you'd be dead already. I'm just being paid to get something back."

'This is only a *job* to you?"

He nodded. "And when I get what I came for, it's over. Killing Matt, or you, would be a mistake—a messy mistake. Too much publicity, too many questions." He made quote marks in the air with his fingers. "'Young Tourist Plunges from Window.' The people I work for don't want that kind of attention." He shook his head again. "Killing you is not in my best interest."

She looked at Lyle.

"If Lyle touches you, he'll answer to me," Greg responded, looking at Lyle. "Understood?"

Lyle looked at Jane. The hate in his eyes was plain. But he did not dare to defy Greg. "Yeah."

"We're just trying to persuade you to help us," Greg said. "We really don't mean to hurt you." He took one step toward the window. "Come inside. You'll be perfectly safe, and we'll have you and Matt back together as soon as we can persuade him to give us what was stolen. You have my word."

The word of a kidnapper? Does he think his charm is that blinding? Greg was a very practiced liar; Jane knew that much about this man even though they had just met.

She looked around outside once more. About twenty feet away, the fire escape was within reach of another window. But there was no way to get to the fire escape from here. The only way to go from this window was down.

Inside the room were two men who would probably kill her without hesitation if only to protect their identities. But she didn't think they would do it just now. They still needed her. Greg's efforts to persuade her were evidence of that. At least for now, she was an essential part of their plan to manipulate Matt.

And for the moment she had the two men at bay; they did not move, waiting to see what she would do. They did not dare to try grabbing her because her balance in the window was too precarious.

The afternoon sun felt warm on her back. Overhead, there were fluffy white clouds in a blue sky—the kind of sky that delighted her on a summer day. In the distance, over the tops of buildings, she could see a hill with a cable car moving up the middle of a street. They were still in San Francisco. Matt was here, somewhere, and she knew he would never give up on her. Maybe he could find some way to satisfy these men.

Would it be wrong to let her own life end to keep from being victimized by Lyle? To protect Matt? She was not sure of the answer. She had thought about this while she was alone with leering Lyle, and she was ready to make that sacrifice if necessary.

But something made her feel the situation was not that desperate yet.

Just inside the window, dust motes danced in a sunbeam. When she was a girl, she had wondered how God could be aware of every tiny thing in all of His creations. But she had come to understand that somehow He was.

She had come to know that He was aware of her—one individual among billions. Maybe she had not yet given Him enough time to help her.

Whatever happened, she would be in His hands. She would draw strength from that thought.

She leaned her torso into the room. Greg stepped over to the window quickly and took her arm to help her back inside.

Lyle picked up the chair and put it firmly back in place. He glared at Jane.

She looked at Greg. "Can I have my hands free, please?" It couldn't hurt to ask, she thought. "My shoulders are aching with my arms pinned behind me like this."

Greg looked into her eyes for a few seconds, as though trying to judge whether this was some kind of trick. Finally, he said, "I'm sure we can make you more comfortable." He turned to Lyle. "I believe you have the key to the handcuffs?"

Lyle looked at him incredulously. But he fished in his pocket for the key and held it out to Greg, who walked around behind her. She felt him unlock the handcuff on her right wrist. He walked around in front of her. "Hands." She held them out in front of her and he cuffed her hands together in front of her. "I think that's best for now."

He turned to Lyle. "We could use another chair in here. Why don't you see if you can find one in another room?"

Lyle looked at him questioningly once more. But Greg had only to raise his eyebrows and Lyle turned toward the door mechanically. Frowning, he unlocked the door, stepped out into the hallway, and closed the door behind him.

Greg motioned toward the bed. "Why don't you sit down, Jane? I'm sure that will be more comfortable too."

She looked at him doubtfully.

"You'll be perfectly safe. I promise," he assured her.

She was beginning to understand why Greg had studied her while Lyle was fumbling with her hair and massaging her shoulders. That had been a test. He had been trying to gauge her reaction—to see if Lyle would make her afraid. Greg would use her fear to manipulate her. But fear had not achieved the result he wanted. Now he was trying another tactic—pretended kindness, and his version of reason.

Was it only momentary, until he decided on another approach?

This man was a skilled manipulator. She could not allow herself to forget that kindness might be only his tactic of the moment.

She decided to test this new tactic. She looked at the bathroom door. "I, uh, need to go in there."

Greg glanced that way then looked back at her.

"I've been here chained up for hours."

Greg walked to the door and opened it. "Of course." As she stepped inside, he looked at his watch. "Five minutes, and then I'm opening the door."

"You're only thinking about what a *man* would need. And then these handcuffs. . . . ."

He glanced at his watch again. "Okay—seven minutes."

Jane looked at her own watch as she walked through the door. She didn't need the whole seven minutes, but she used it all. She took the opportunity to open the bathroom window and put her head out to see if there might be any way to reach that fire escape. But no—it was too far away, and the window was too small for her to fit through.

The bathroom sink looked like it hadn't been cleaned in years, and there was no soap. But at six minutes and 45 seconds, she turned on the water to rinse her hands as best she could, just before Greg opened the door.

6

Matt was wandering, really—drifting with pedestrian traffic on the city sidewalks. It was more than restlessness. He felt wary of staying too long in one spot, just in case the kidnappers might be looking for him.

He watched faces, trying to notice whether anyone crossed his path more than once. He had changed direction abruptly several times—sometimes in the middle of crossing the street—and tried to check, without being too obvious, whether anyone had stayed with him. So far, no one had.

He tried to copy the aimless, shuffling walk of some of the street people. They seemed almost invisible to other pedestrians. He glanced at his reflection in storefronts a couple of times to see if there was anything that would make people focus on him. He stood out because of his size, but there was nothing about his clothing that might call attention to him, except, perhaps, the baseball cap with the large block A on the front. He kept the cap pulled low over his eyes, partly shielding his face. He kept his head down, looking out from under the bill of the cap at the people who passed. He tried to be alert for people who might stay close to him for too long. No one seemed to do that.

Maybe no one was out here on the streets looking for him—but he could not be sure of anything right now.

So far as he knew, there were two men holding Jane. Were there more people involved in the kidnapping? If not, how could they have known about his calls, or the first time he left the hotel? He had not noticed anyone watching him at the hotel, so how were they able to keep track of what he was doing? Did they have informants he had not spotted?

Or were they using some technology to track him? But everything in his pockets, everything he was wearing had not been out of his sight. How could they have tagged him?

When would they call again?

He carried his jacket slung over his shoulder. It was only warm this afternoon, not really hot, but he was sweating anyway.

When his phone rang, he had it out of his jacket pocket in under five seconds. He ducked into the entryway of a building to answer. "Hello?"

"Matt?" It was a voice he knew instantly—Jane's father.

"Yeah, uh . . . this is a surprise. How are you?" He glanced at his watch. He could not allow his phone to be tied up very long.

"Well, I'm fine," his father-in-law answered—then hesitated. Obviously, this was not simply a social call; Lawrence McDougal had something on his mind. "I, ah . . . I have some bad news I picked up this morning at the courthouse. Have you heard about your boss?"

Cole had mentioned last week that a client was making threats because an investment had gone sour. "Somebody's suing him?" Matt asked. "He told me—"

"No, that's not it. Cole should be so lucky." Lawrence hesitated again. "He's dead."

"*Cole Brewster?*"

"Yes. They say it was an accident. His cleaning lady found him early this morning."

"What happened?"

"He was floating in his pool. He was fully clothed, but there was an injury on the back of his head. The police are saying he may have fallen in accidentally and drowned."

"Drowned? Cole?" He sounded like some mindless echo, Matt thought, but his brain was struggling to absorb what he had just heard. "How?"

"They think he may have been out by the pool a few nights ago and slipped on the deck where it was wet. He could have hit his head before he fell in."

It was a plausible explanation, Matt thought—but unlikely. Cole was not really a pool person; he did not spend much time out there except when he was hosting a party. Matt had been at Cole's home a number of times to drop off or pick up business-related items, and he had never seen the man swim or even stretch out in one of the chaise lounges at poolside. "There was no more to it than that? He just fell in?"

"So far as they know," his father-in-law answered. "There was a broken glass by the pool, and a bottle of whiskey on the deck. He might have had too much to drink."

Not likely either. Cole gathered people around his pool, gave *them* food and liquor, got them relaxed so they would talk, and gleaned information. Gathering information was also part of Matt's job when Cole invited him to social gatherings—keeping his ears open. Sometimes Cole struck business deals at those pool parties, and Matt would be involved in that too. Cole carried a drink in his hand to look sociable, but only occasionally did he take a sip from it. He liked to stay sharp.

"When did it happen?" Matt asked.

"Two or three days ago. Maybe the day after your wedding. Guess you haven't tried to call the office, have you?"

"No. Believe me, Cole and the office haven't been . . . well, I haven't been thinking about work."

His father-in-law chuckled. "Yeah. And even if you'd paid any attention to the news, an item like this from Phoenix probably wouldn't rate a mention over there."

Matt glanced at his watch. They had been talking for almost three minutes. "Is there any more you can tell me?"

"No. I don't know anything else." His father-in-law sounded nonplussed that Matt did not seem more concerned. "I just called because I didn't want you to worry if you found out. I don't know what this will mean for your job, but I was thinking that I know some other financial people here. They might have openings. We can talk about that when you get back."

"Well, I'm shocked about Cole," Matt said, trying to sound that way. "And of course I'd be worried about my job." He could not explain what was worrying him most right now. "But I can't do anything from here."

"Yeah. And I hate being the bearer of more bad news, after the break-in. I hope you can put this out of your mind for now. Things will work out when you get back."

Matt could almost hear his watch ticking. "Well, thanks. I'll try not to worry about it for the next few days."

"Sure. The two of you have a good time." His father-in-law paused. "While I've got you on the phone, can I talk to Jane for a minute?"

"Well, she, ah . . . we're having a short break from sightseeing. She went to the restroom." Technically, he thought, neither of those statements was untrue. But he hated hiding the truth from his father-in-law. The Mc-Dougals had one son and three daughters, of which Jane was the next youngest. Her parents had treated the man Jane loved like another son, and he loved them too. Jane's father was a man of solid, sound judgment. Matt wanted to spill out everything that had happened with Jane and ask him what to do. But . . . but *they* had warned him not to say anything to anyone, and he didn't know just how ruthless they were. What would they do to Jane if he said something to her father and somehow they heard him, or found out?

"Everything's okay there?" his father-in-law asked.

"Yeah—fine." Matt hoped he sounded convincing. Lawrence McDougal had been a successful attorney for many years; he probably could sense when people were lying.

There was silence on the other end of the line for several seconds. "Well, if you get a chance to call again later, we'd love to hear from the two of you."

His father-in-law said good-bye and hung up. Matt started walking again, slowly. He had managed to ignore the knot of fear in the pit of his stomach for a time, but now it was back.

Strange things happen sometimes in life. Cole *could* have fallen and hit his head, then slipped into the pool.

No. "Accident" was an unlikely stretch in this case. What had happened over the past two days seemed to push coincidence beyond its limits. Cole's death, the break-in, Jane's kidnapping—what were the possible connections?

Matt thought back on his work with Cole Brewster for the past nineteen months. Cole was aggressive, and ambitious, but everything he did had seemed legitimate. Matt had wanted to be sure he was working for a company, and a man, that were completely honest. So far, nothing he had seen made him worry about Cole—but maybe there were things he had *not* seen.

He looked again at the telephone in his hand—the thing that Cole had given him.

If Cole had been murdered, and if the same people who killed him had Jane now, was there anything they would not do to get what they wanted? Matt fought to put that thought out of his mind.

He focused his attention on the phone. He had checked its menus and programs this morning, and once more this afternoon after the kidnappers' last call. He could see nothing on the device that anyone might want. There were the few personal phone numbers he had entered into its memory, three or four games that came preloaded, and the financial apps that Cole had put on it for him. But so far there were no files to go with those apps—nothing from the office, no information about the business. Anything that was on the phone could be easily obtained somewhere else.

He stopped in a doorway to run through the phone's files once more. Was it possible he could have missed something?

He was moving through his short address list item by item when the phone rang. He answered before it could ring a second time. "Hello?"

"Matt, we need some further assurance that you're ready to cooperate," the man said. "Are you ready to turn over what you have that belongs to us?"

"How many times do I have to tell you I don't . . . " *No! They have to believe they can still get what they want.* Instantly he regretted letting anger and fear take over. He reminded himself that these people might have killed one person already. "Let my wife go, please!" he pleaded. "Then we can talk."

He held his breath while he waited for an answer to come. Finally, the voice on the phone said patiently, "Wrong answer, Matt. You need to look at your position more carefully. You're holding onto something stolen from someone else. He shouldn't have given it to you—and we *know* he did." There was a pause. Then: "Think of Mom and Pop McDougal back in Phoenix. They trusted you with their beautiful daughter. Would you want to tell her father that you put her in danger for something you wouldn't give up?"

"Tell her father?" Matt sagged against the wall next to him. *How could they know about . . .* Had they somehow been able to listen in on the conversation with his father-in-law a few minutes ago? Or was mentioning the McDougals simply coincidence? How much could they know about what he was doing moment to moment?

"We're going to get what we want," the voice intoned in his ear. "You can give it to us now and get Jane back, or you can force us to take other measures. Think about *all* the other people back home—the things that could happen to them. How high a price are you willing to pay before you have to give us what we want anyway?"

There was nothing veiled about this message, Matt realized: If he kept refusing to cooperate, they would hurt Jane and others too. *They just keep on raising the threat level.* "I've told you I'll give you anything you want if you'll just give me Jane," he said into the phone. "Please."

There was a pause on the other end. "Well. This change in attitude impresses me," the voice said. "So you *do* have what we're looking for?"

Matt weighed his answer carefully. *Why don't these guys say plainly what it is they're after?* He was afraid to ask for specifics. If they realized that he was fishing for information because he really did not know what they were talking about, then Jane might become expendable—a witness they could not afford to leave alive. But if he couldn't satisfy them somehow, and soon, would they start hurting other people—his parents, or hers? There was only one way he could think of to buy time. "Yeah—I'll give you what you want," he answered. *And what if they want it right now? I can't give . . . I need time to think.* "But I'm not carrying it with me," he added. "I'll have to, um—pick it up first."

"That's fine," the voice answered. "We were planning for you to drop it off a little after sundown anyway."

"You mean that's when we'll make the exchange?"

"Yes. You'll receive further instructions closer to the time."

"Wait—don't hang up. Where will the exchange be?"

The man chuckled softly. "Oh, I think I'd like to keep that to myself for now."

"Would you? That's surprising. You seem like a careful planner, but you're overlooking something." Matt was not sure how the idea came to him, but it came so strongly that he followed through without question. "You know I'm in a strange city. I won't know how to get where you want me to go. I'm lost right now—not even sure where *I* am. You've got to give me some time to figure this out."

He could tell by the silence on the other end of the line that the man was thinking about what he had said. Something covered the phone and Matt heard voices indistinctly. Then the man came back on the line. "All right, I'm going to tell you the area where you'll have to come. And Matt, I hope I don't need to remind you that if I see police—if I see *anyone* in the area who looks out of place—Jane will pay the price."

"I *understand*. And if the police were as helpful as the security man at the hotel, you wouldn't have anything to worry about. They probably wouldn't believe me either."

The man chuckled. "Yeah. 'Wife disappeared on your honeymoon? What did you do?' Crazy story." He paused. There was the sound of movement—brushing against something—then what sounded like a breeze blowing over the phone for a moment, and then the same movement again. "Now listen to me. Write this down if you have to. There's a hotel on Sixth Street a block below Market—Hotel Birch. It's on the corner of a nice, quiet side street. That's in the general area where you're going to bring your delivery."

"You'll meet me there with Jane?"

"It's not quite that simple. After I verify that you've given us what we're looking for, then you'll see Jane."

"I want to see her before."

"No. My associate stays with her until I check your delivery. Then you get to see her. You'll have to trust me on that."

"We don't exactly have a relationship of trust. I told you, I have to talk to her before I decide to hand anything over to you. Let me talk to her again."

"Jane is perfectly fine. I certainly wouldn't want to see her harmed, and she won't be if you follow my instructions. You'll get a call 15 minutes before it's time to make your delivery. You can talk to her then. And don't be late with the delivery." The line went dead.

Matt stood looking at his telephone for several seconds, then pushed the button to end the call and dropped the phone into his jacket pocket. He realized his hands felt clammy and his armpits were wet. He held his right arm straight out in front of him; his hand trembled.

He hoped he had not made a mistake promising to make the delivery. He had followed instinct, or inspiration, or whatever that idea was. There had been no time to think things out the way he usually would.

He reviewed the call, trying to fix everything in his mind. He took a ballpoint pen out of the pocket of his jeans and wrote the address on his hand: "Hotel Birch, Sixth Street, block below Market." The man had told him several other things, probably without realizing it. "I'm going to tell you where you have to *come*" probably meant the man was already at that place, or close by. "If I *see* anyone in the area"—he *had* to be where he could watch the delivery point. "My associate stays with her"—it sounded like there were no more than two of them.

The man had not indicated that they—he?—killed Cole. But he had repeated the comment: "He shouldn't have given it to you." Matt reviewed everything Cole had given him at work recently. There were some assignments, and paper files to go with them. Had Cole said something about those files to the person, or people, who had thrown him into his own swimming pool? Was there something hidden in one of the files? But from here, Matt thought, he had no way to check.

Could anyone else do it for him? Darcy, the secretary at the office?

No! He couldn't draw her into this.

At the office! That was probably where they learned how to find him in San Francisco. When he was finalizing arrangements for the honeymoon, he had written the name and telephone number of their hotel in San Francisco on the notepad next to the phone on his desk.

But if they had seen that, they had already searched his office—and they hadn't found what they were looking for.

After this last call he knew some useful things about them too. Now there was something he could do, a way to take action—and that meant he could no longer wander aimlessly. He had to be ready before they called the next time.

He stepped out onto the sidewalk in front of a man hurrying up the street. The man looked up at him in surprise. "Excuse me," Matt said, "can you tell me where to find Sixth Street?"

The man seemed wary—careful not to offend someone Matt's size. "You're on Third. You have to go back up there to Market, then over to Sixth." The man looked more closely at Matt, puzzled. "There's a rescue mission on Sixth, about a block down."

Matt draped his jacket over his shoulder again as he started back toward Market. He felt the phone in the jacket pocket tapping him in the back as he walked, tapping . . . reminding him that it had a GPS program, and maps! Those would work just as well on foot as in his car. He hadn't been thinking carefully again.

The phone could tell him exactly where he was right now, and exactly how to get to that hotel on Sixth. There would be an aerial photo of the place. Maybe even more.

* * *

"I liked the part about 'force us to take other measures,'" Lyle said, chuckling.

"We wouldn't have had to do things this way if he had been handled right in the first place. I could have simply paid Matt a visit at his hotel while you watched Jane to assure his cooperation," Greg answered tersely. "Now we have to make him come to us."

Lyle looked chagrined at this fresh rebuke.

Greg turned to Jane. "Looks like Matt is coming around. I believe he's eager to be reunited with his bride."

Jane's brow furrowed. "What you said about my parents . . . please don't bring them into this. You have me already. That's enough to make Matt give you what you want—if you'll just tell him what it is."

"It sounds like he already knows what it is. Maybe he just didn't tell you."

Greg looked into her eyes for several seconds—trying to read her thoughts?—before he continued. "You don't think Matt would try to fool me about that, do you?"

Jane wasn't sure how to answer. She could not know what Matt had told them, and she did not want to undercut anything he might be planning. She chose her words carefully. "I'm sure if he told you he would bring it, he knows what he's doing."

"I hope you're right. If he cooperates, I don't think there'll be any need to involve other family members." Greg gave her one of his mechanical smiles. If it was meant to put her at ease, it didn't. "And I'm sure he wouldn't gamble with *your* safety, would he?"

Despite Greg's efforts to manipulate her into remaining calm, there was always some background threat of harm if Matt did not cooperate—the little pin prick to keep her fear alive so she would remember who was in control. That, Jane knew, was the real Greg, not the smooth talker. Greg wanted her to be afraid so he could control her, and Lyle wanted it just because he was sadistic. But listening to her fears would do nothing to help her.

She felt like crying in frustration, and because she longed for Matt. She felt sick at her stomach if she stopped to dwell on her situation—alone in a small room with two men with guns, men who would be glad to harm her if it suited their interests. She could not let herself be intimidated by them. She needed to think clearly and not let doubt cloud her judgment. She worked to keep her mind actively focused on other things.

She had been observing small things about both men—personal characteristics, things they did consistently—and trying not to let them realize she was doing it.

Lyle was impatient, liable to make decisions impulsively. But he was Greg's pawn. He did what he thought Greg wanted, responded to what he thought Greg needed, would not do any thinking on his own in this operation—unless he was left alone.

Greg had obviously cultivated sophistication, but his deep roots were stunted. He was amoral; he lived by no standard except self-interest.

She could give a police sketch artist a detailed description of both men. Would she ever have the chance to do it?

Jane sat on the side of the bed, at the head of it. Greg and Lyle's jackets occupied the foot of it. Greg had folded his sport coat neatly; Lyle had tossed his in a heap. Lyle had tucked his pistol into his waistband. Greg did the same, but with the pistol on the opposite side so he could grasp it with his left hand. The clip that held his folding knife in place and a part of the knife itself could be seen above the waistband of his slacks over his left hip pocket. Jane had wondered what would happen if she tried to grab for the knife or one of the guns, but with two armed men in the room, she almost certainly would not survive.

They took turns most of the time gazing out the window. When one was at the window, the other usually sat in the chair opposite her. Lyle tended to leer at her when Greg was not watching him. Greg seemed to study her, as though he were still trying to determine what made her behave the way she did. She tried not to look at them.

She was not sure how long they had been silent when Lyle suddenly straightened at the window. "What's he doing here already?"

Greg stood and stepped to the window to look over Lyle's shoulder. "He just came around that corner," Lyle said, pointing toward the building across the side street from the hotel.

Greg glanced at Jane, then looked back out the window, frowning. "I told him I'd give him a call when it's time."

Matt was out there! Jane rose from the bed and took a step toward the window, hoping she might be able get a glimpse of him. Lyle turned on her, drawing his pistol. He pointed it at her heart. "Sit! Don't even think about opening your mouth."

She sat obediently on the bed again, and Lyle came to stand in front of her, keeping his pistol pointed at her forehead. Greg stood gazing out the window.

"What's he doing out there?" Lyle asked.

"He tried the doors on your car. Now he's looking in the garbage container." Greg took one step back so he would not be framed in the opening if Matt glanced up at the building. "He's straightening something out in there," Greg said, frowning. "It looks like a newspaper. What is he thinking?" He looked at Jane. "Is this some kind of trick?"

She shrugged. "You can see him. I can't. I'm sure he's just trying to figure out how to do what you told him." It was the safest answer that came to mind.

Greg looked puzzled. "Well, it's a crazy thing to do—unless he wants to get you hurt." He flashed one of his smiles. "We wouldn't want that, would we?"

He turned to look out the window again, then changed position and followed something with his gaze. "What's he doing now?" Lyle asked.

"He just went off around the corner again."

* * *

Matt tried to look only casually curious as he shuffled down Sixth Street past the front of the Hotel Birch, but he registered every detail in his mind. The narrow glass entry door had bars over it. Inside the door hung a large bell that would ring if the door were pushed open. The battered registration counter, no more than five feet back from the door, seemed to lean forward at an odd angle as though it had been placed on the grimy carpet without being anchored to the floor. The clerk sitting on a stool behind the counter wore a dirty tee shirt and what looked like a five-day growth of dark beard. There was a large tattoo on his right forearm. He appeared to be dozing, but because of the bell on the door, it would be nearly impossible to slip past him.

Someone stepped into Matt's path as he walked and put a hand out to stop him. Matt looked up at him questioningly.

"Did I see you foolin' around in that garbage container down there next to the hotel? That's mine!"

Matt looked at him in surprise. "Who are you?"

"Everybody calls me Stretch. An' I own that."

The name fit. If this man weren't slouching, he would be tall enough to look Matt in the eye. He was thin—bony. One knee stuck out of a hole in his jeans, and there were holes in the canvas shoes he wore. His beard was salt-and-pepper gray, and his light brown hair was very thin on top. He carried a dirty, nondescript overcoat draped over his arm with a certain air of dignity.

"What do you mean you own that? What do you own?" Matt asked.

Stretch drew himself up to his full height. "That container. That's mine. I live there, an' anything people put in there, that's mine too."

"Well, I'm sorry, Stretch, I didn't know that."

"You take something out of there?" Stretch challenged. "I saw you. I was over by the rescue mission, 'cross the street."

Matt shook his head. "I straightened something out in there—just an old newspaper. I wanted to read the headline."

Stretch looked at him suspiciously. "You can't take nothin' out of there. It's mine."

"I'll remember that," Matt said, and kept walking toward the next corner. When he glanced back, the tall man was watching him go and talking to two other men in front of a building.

Stretch could be a problem later, when it was time to drop off his delivery, Matt thought. Did the people who had Jane know about Stretch, or—

His phone rang just as he reached the corner. He took it out of his jacket pocket and put it to his ear. "Hello?"

"Was there some misunderstanding about the timing of your delivery?" the voice asked curtly.

"I don't think so. Why?"

"You were seen in the neighborhood. You were what—arranging things?—in a garbage container. What's going on?"

"We talked about this already—I don't know San Francisco. I didn't want to risk trying to find the place in the dark and getting lost, especially if the fog rolls in like it did last night."

There was a pause before the answer. "And the newspaper? What was that about?"

"I was checking out the container. The car's locked, so I thought the garbage container might be the place where I would have to leave something. I was trying to figure out how to leave what you want in there so you can find it without digging for it. It isn't the kind of thing you'd expect me to just dump in the garbage, now is it?"

There was a pause. "No." Matt had hoped for more of an answer—some clue as to what he was supposed to bring to them—but the other man had taken his response as only a rhetorical question.

"All right," the man continued, "you've found out what you needed to know about the place. When you bring the package, you can make it easy to find. But don't come back until you hear from me again. I don't even want to see you in the neighborhood—and I don't want to see anyone else who—"

"Looks out of place," Matt finished. "You won't see me until the time is right, but I expect to talk to my wife when—"

The connection was cut off. Matt put his phone away. *You won't see me, but I'll be around.*

He crossed Sixth Street and headed slowly up the other side. He turned his jacket inside out and put it on so the dark lining showed, then took off his cap and stuffed it into one of the pockets out of sight. He shuffled past the rescue mission, deliberately stumbling once, and kept his face toward the building.

He had checked this area out using the satellite photo he found with his phone. He walked just past the rescue mission, turned quickly down the alley on its far side, then stopped in the shadow of a delivery truck. From here, he could look up at the side of the Hotel Birch, across Sixth Street, without being seen by anyone looking out a window.

He could see the corner of Stretch's garbage container on the side street. From this vantage point, he could not see the older Ford sedan parked at the curb behind the garbage container. From here, he could not see the wall of the building that faced the hotel across the side street, but that wall had been decorated with a brightly colored mural depicting the dangers of drink and drugs. One glance at it as he walked away from the garbage container told him that he had seen part of it before—in the window view from the photo of Jane that the kidnapper had sent him.

On the sidewalk next to that mural, a stick of a tree struggled upward from a small, square planter—someone's meager effort at beautification. Broken beer bottles lay at the base of the tree in the planter and on the curb in front of the garbage container. He remembered that just on the other side of the container, in front of the Ford sedan, the pavement had been littered with small squares of shattered safety glass; someone undoubtedly had broken a car window there. The glass had crunched under Matt's feet as he walked through it.

And that was the spot Stretch had called home. Matt hoped the man did not mean he slept there.

He looked up at the windows in the side of the hotel. Again the kidnappers had told him more than they realized. Straightening the newspaper had simply been a ruse to gain time while he looked around the area. But he knew now that they had watched as he spread the paper out inside the container. They could have seen it was a newspaper only if they were looking down from above—from a room in the hotel.

Windows were open in two of the rooms on the fourth floor and one on the fifth. Nothing moved at the windows to give indication that anyone was inside.

But the kidnappers had watched him from one of those rooms.

Jane was up there.

And the kidnappers had made a concession without realizing it. They had allowed him to specify the spot where he would make the delivery.

When they came to pick it up, he would find a way somehow to get to Jane—if there were any possibility, to get her back.

There *would* be a way. He *would* get her back.

7

Greg sat watching Lyle at the window—studying him, Jane thought, the same way he studied her at times. It was as though he were trying to get inside people. Was it a way to learn how to manipulate them more easily?

He glanced at his watch, then turned to speak to her. "We still have some time to wait, Jane. Why don't you lie down on the bed and rest if you want—relax, make yourself comfortable." He smiled at her—one of his smiles that held no warmth.

She looked at him skeptically and shook her head.

He chuckled. "You'll be perfectly safe. I promise you that." He glanced at Lyle. "Go ahead—no one will bother you."

She thought about his suggestion for half a minute or so. At least he was still trying to manipulate her with kindness. Laying down would rest her back, which was beginning to ache from perching stiffly on the edge of the bed. And she would be no more trapped than she was now. Slowly she rotated her body, swung her legs up onto the bed, and lay on her side with her back to Greg. She curled into a fetal position. It was the most comfortable way to lie on this sagging bed. She nestled in the deep dip in the middle, drawing her knees up close and extending her arms so that her hands almost touched her knees, then interlacing the fingers of her hands. It was a defensive position. She could kick out with her legs or strike out with her clenched fists if anyone tried to touch her.

It occurred to her that Greg and Lyle might talk about their plans if they thought she was asleep. Or maybe they wouldn't let their guard down even then. But she lay still and closed her eyes. After a short time she began to breathe more deeply and rhythmically.

Several minutes passed with her laying that way before she heard Greg's chair creak, and then his footsteps. Opening her eyes a slit and looking past her knees, she could see that he had joined Lyle at the window. She closed her eyes in case they turned her way and looked closely at her.

More time passed and neither of the men spoke. Then she heard the floor creak as one of them shifted position, and she sensed that he might be watching her. She hoped she appeared relaxed enough to be asleep.

Finally, Lyle asked softly, "Why wait until after sundown? Aren't we in a hurry?"

"So no one will see us when we leave with two other people," Greg whispered. "And those two people would be easy to identify."

Two *people,* Jane thought. He had said *people,* not *bodies.* That could be a good sign. But he had not said they were going to let her and Matt go free, either.

"Do you think it will be dark enough just after sundown?" Lyle asked.

"It'll do—especially if that fog comes back." Greg paused. "It'll *have* to do. You're right—we've got to get results soon. And I have an appointment later tonight."

Lyle chuckled. "Hot date back at your hotel?" Greg said nothing, but Lyle chuckled once more. There must have been some nonverbal answer.

That hotel was nice—*real* nice—Lyle said, speaking its name almost reverently. The name sounded familiar, and Jane searched her memory trying to recall where she had heard it. *Yesterday—when we were riding the cable car.* They had passed the hotel, across from Union Square. The building was a San Francisco landmark, built before the earthquake of 1906, Matt had explained. The people who stayed there were the kind who didn't mind paying for the finer things of life; three or four nights there could cost a month's rent, Matt had said.

Lyle spoke softly to Greg again. "We're a long way from Leo and Gregori back in high school. Especially you."

High school? These two men went to school together? Lyle—or was it Leo?—looked much older, Jane thought—more worn. Greg had the beginnings of a few wrinkles around his eyes, but that was all.

"You could go farther, Lyle," Greg answered. "You don't have to stay down here on these streets. Sometimes you let the things you want right now or the things you're feeling at the moment take over your thinking. With some discipline, *you* could be one of those people who make all of the things they want come to them."

Lyle didn't give any indication that he was offended by the criticism of his shortcomings. "You've learned how to do it better than I ever could, Greg."

Lyle was close to fawning over his friend, Jane thought, and Greg seemed to feel he deserved the admiration. He answered as though he were the instructor in some warped seminar on managing people. "You learn how to get people to trust you by treating them the way they think they deserve to be treated. You learn to make them believe that what you want them to do is really what *they* want to do. And you have to know how to control them when it's necessary."

"Like telling her husband when he can come here, and he can't see her until we're ready."

"Exactly. That's the way with him. With her, it's moving the handcuffs or letting her get more comfortable when *I* say it's okay. You make them believe that if they do exactly what you say, things might turn out all right for them. They want to believe it. You just help them along."

This was what he had been doing with her, Jane thought—lying to her, stringing her along, trying to let her believe things would be all right if she didn't give them any trouble.

There was silence for a time, and again it was Lyle who broke it. "Are we really going to let them go?" he asked. "Is that what Boris said?"

There was no immediate answer. Jane heard soft footsteps approach the bed. She felt someone leaning over her. She tried to keep her breathing deep and rhythmic, her face completely relaxed. The floor creaked as the person straightened up, and there were soft footsteps again as he walked back to the window. Greg spoke more softly than before: "Boris didn't have to tell me how to handle this. When we're sure Matt has given us what we're looking for, I know Boris wouldn't want them to walk away. Too bad for Matt and Jane. Your job is to make sure they never get the chance to say anything."

So—Greg was not planning to let them live.

Jane shivered involuntarily, and hoped the two men had not seen her.

What Greg had said was hardly a surprise. Each time these two men threatened to kill her, she had no doubt that they meant it. But Greg's manipulative strategy had worked on her to a degree. She had been hoping that if Matt somehow discovered what they wanted and gave it to them, Greg might relent. Obviously, he had no intention of doing so. She struggled to keep tears from coming, afraid they would give away the fact that she had heard the discussion.

Something in her could not—would not—give up. In sports, she had seen the old cliché reinforced again and again—it was never over until it was over. She would keep watching for an opening of some kind, any opportunity to act when Lyle or Greg made a mistake.

The two men were silent for a time, and then Lyle asked, "I can take care of my part any way I want?"

"That'll be up to you. I'll be out of here—leaving tomorrow morning."

"Well, I won't waste any time with the big guy," Lyle said. Jane could hear the leer in his voice as he continued. "But I'll take my time with her."

No. It won't be that way, Jane thought. *Even if you have a gun.*

Greg lowered his voice even more. Jane couldn't make out all of it. " . . . ring has a nice diamond. Keep it for me. . . . engraving on the necklace ruins it. . . . trash."

Jane felt her cheeks burning with anger and fear at the same time. It was all she could do to maintain her pretense of sleeping.

Matt had made a sacrifice, she knew, to buy her a fine diamond through a friend who worked at a jewelry store. The small, gold disk Matt had given her to wear on a chain around her neck was engraved with the letters *M* and *J*, with an infinity sign between. It was a touching symbol of the love they had pledged to each other. Her fear was that she might never be able to have a life together with Matt. But she was furious about the casual way Greg and Lyle talked about using her, stealing from her, then discarding her.

She made an effort not to move, not to frown or let her eyes flutter, not to lose her peaceful, relaxed appearance. But inside she was seething at their cruelty and callousness. *You* won't *have it your way. Every thought I have, every ounce of resolve, every muscle I have will fight you until I'm dead, if it has to be that way.*

"Sometimes it can be good down here on these streets, Greg," Lyle said softly. He chuckled once more. "See that girl who just walked past the mission street? She thinks I'm with the San Francisco P.D. She can be really friendly if I show her my badge and make a little noise about hauling her in on some charge."

Lyle began to describe how he had taken advantage of other women who lived on the streets—destitute, alcoholic, drug addicted. It turned Jane's stomach to hear him.

She had never felt more abandoned, and she was fighting second by second to keep fear from distorting her thoughts. Finally she could no longer stop tears from trickling down her cheeks, She tried to press her face against the threadbare bedspread, hoping the two men would not notice. She tried to focus on some pleasant time out of the past, on some other place, on Matt—anything that took her far away from here. She prayed silently that she would not have to carry Lyle's words burned in memory.

* * *

Matt sat on the steps of the old United States mint studying the map in a tourist brochure. He was little more than a block away from the hotel where they were holding Jane, but it could not be seen from here.

This map of downtown San Francisco showed all the possible approaches to that hotel. He had walked each one of them in the past hour, staying out of sight of those windows in the upper floors on the side.

There seemed to be only two ways into the hotel. One was a side door on the ground level of the building, almost opposite Stretch's garbage container. Matt thought he could walk to this door from the rear of the hotel without being seen if he stayed close to the side of the building; anyone on the upper floors would have to lean out a window and look down to spot him. But then what? Would that side door be locked? Would it make noise and draw attention if he tried to open it?

He could also come to that door from the front of the hotel—the Sixth Street side—without being seen because there was an overhang jutting out from the building that covered the sidewalk. But the problem was the same: would the door be locked? It looked old and rusty. If he could open it, would it be noisy enough to catch someone's attention?

The other way into the hotel was through the front door. That brought a different set of challenges. There was no way the desk clerk would allow him to walk in and simply search the upper floors. The clerk might even be a lookout for the kidnappers.

What were the common ruses someone might use to get past the front desk? A flower delivery? Not in that hotel. Visiting "Mr. Smith"? Not likely. He could try Spanish—looking for "Señor Rodriguez," or "Monica," who used to live here. He could claim he was delivering a check to someone on the fourth floor. But Matt knew he looked so out of place on Sixth Street that the clerk, and probably others, would immediately be suspicious. They might take him for *la migra*—Immigration—or some other agent of the legal system.

If he managed to get inside the hotel, then what? Roam the top two floors of the building listening at doors? He had counted the windows back from the street to the ones that were open on the fourth and fifth floors. He might be able to guess the room by counting the same number of doors in the hallway. In a place like that, a good shoulder to the door would probably get him inside the room. But what if he chose the wrong room and gave his presence away for nothing?

No. Everything that came to mind carried the risk of alerting the kidnappers and causing them to hurt Jane.

He had no idea what kind of weapons they might have. He was unarmed.

It seemed the only option he had was to make them come out to him. The delivery he was supposed to make offered a way to do that—if he could lead them to believe he was giving them what they wanted.

He had begun to wonder seriously over the past hour whether he was a fool for not going to the police despite the kidnappers' warning. Maybe he could do it secretly. Now that he was out of his hotel, they couldn't know where he went—could they?

The police would certainly have the force needed to get into that building. But in this neighborhood any show of police presence would automatically trigger whatever alarm network existed on the street. And the desk clerk might be part of that network.

Matt had tried to put himself in the kidnappers' place. At the first sign of any police operation, they might decide to run. They probably wouldn't allow themselves to be slowed down by a hostage.

He glanced at his watch: 4:55. Time was running out. How long till sunset—maybe three and a half hours? If he went to the police immediately, how long would it take them to set up a rescue operation?

He remembered his experience with Ed Bills, the security chief at the hotel. If he went to the police right now, how long would it take him to convince them that there was a real problem? That he really knew where

Jane was? That he was not some loony-toon, or simply an overwrought husband whose wife had gone shopping and forgotten the time?

Or maybe the police would take him seriously. If they put together some kind of rescue operation immediately, would they be able to surprise the kidnappers? Would there be a shoot-out or a sudden attack in which Jane could be caught in the crossfire?

Any small slip-up in an operation might tip off the people holding Jane, and they did not sound like amateurs at this. The second man sounded detached and dispassionate, like someone who would not be bothered by disposing of an inconvenient witness.

If the two men knew they were trapped by the police, would they choose to shoot it out?

The second man sounded smarter than that. But the first man—the one who had played games with him on the phone—was a question mark. He had a short fuse; he might start shooting. His partner would have some sort of escape route in mind, a Plan B. But it would be an escape for one, and he probably wouldn't leave Jane alive to talk about him or where he had gone. He had already said that he could simply turn his attention to other members of the Randall or McDougal families, if necessary, to force Matt's cooperation.

Matt glanced up from the map he was studying, and it registered in his mind that a man in front of the hotel across the street was staring at him. The same man had been standing there a few minutes ago, and Matt assumed that the man had come out of his hotel to catch a cab or a breath of air. Now he was not sure. *Maybe* the man was only waiting for a taxi— but Matt decided it was time to move on. He shoved the brochure into his jacket pocket, stood, and began walking again.

He stayed always within a two- or three-block radius of the hotel where Jane was.

He weighed the dangers of going to the police against the fact that he was way out of his depth acting alone. He kept trying to think what he could say to convince the police that his story was true. Maybe if he told them about the search of the hotel room last night and had them check with Ed Bills . . . or maybe if he had them check on Cole's death, even though there was no connection he could prove. If they could see the whole picture, they might believe him. If he could just put his finger on a way to convince them immediately that—

His phone rang. He stopped walking and stepped into the doorway of a building, glancing at his watch: 5:20. Maybe the kidnappers wanted to move up the time? Panic gripped him. He wasn't ready to deliver anything yet! Trying to think quickly, he touched the icon to accept the call.

"Matt?"

"Dad? What's going on?"

"I have some . . . " His father's voice broke, and Matt could hear someone sobbing in the background. It sounded like his mother. "I have some bad news," his father continued. "Your brother's gone—kidnapped."

"*Doug?* Someone's got Doug?"

"Yes. And they say you know why. What's going on, Matt?"

"You *talked* to them?"

"They called here, about twenty minutes ago. They let Doug talk to your mother for about fifteen seconds, and then one of them came on and said if we wanted Doug to come home, to tell you. You'd know what they wanted."

"Dad, I don't." He thought for a moment. "I have no idea what they're talking about." That much was true.

"Doug didn't show up for work, so his boss called here, and we didn't know where he was, until . . . "

Matt could hear the hurt in his father's voice. "Dad . . . " he began. But he didn't know what to say after that.

"Matt, are you sure you don't know anything at all about what's going on?"

"There's something I have to tell *you,* Dad. I don't . . . " He stopped himself before saying, "I don't know where Jane is right now either. Someone took her too." They had warned him to tell no one if he wanted her back. And they had seemed to know when his father-in-law called him. He worried that they might be listening in on his calls somehow. It seemed impossible, but still . . .

"What?" his father asked.

"Nothing. It's just . . . nothing. What do you know about them? Did they say who they are? Or where they are?"

"Your mother said she thought the man who talked to her was Hispanic. And there was noise like they were calling from somewhere on the street. That's all."

"Have you . . . what have you done about it?"

"They told us not to let anyone know—but I called the police anyway. The police are coming as soon . . . no, they're here. I hear them at the door. I'm sorry, but I'll have to call you back." His father hung up abruptly.

Matt realized he was holding his breath. Dad had called the police—exactly what the kidnappers had warned *him* not to do if he wanted to see Jane again.

Which one of them had done the right thing?

His mother had been able to have only two children, Matt and Doug, six years younger. Both boys had gone through periods of rebellion in their mid-teens. Mom and Dad and some other good people had loved them through it. Both Matt and Doug had ended up putting their lives on the right path.

Now Doug was at the mercy of people who cared nothing about his life.

First Jane, now Doug. The kidnappers had done what the man on the phone threatened—targeted someone else in the family. What would they do next to ramp up the pressure? Suddenly Matt felt the clock racing even faster.

Were Jane's kidnappers and the kidnappers in Arizona in contact somehow? Would the people holding Doug know immediately if anything happened with Jane?

Matt had assumed the reason for everything that was happening could be traced back to Cole Brewster. Now he wasn't sure. Why would they kidnap Doug when they already had Jane—unless Doug was somehow a threat to them? Was there really something dangerous on that hard drive?

Could there be some connection between Cole Brewster and his brother? So far as Matt knew, the two had never met.

Could Doug really be the key to this puzzle, with Cole's killing only part of some abortive effort to find Doug's brother?

No. That didn't make sense. There had to be some other reason behind what they were doing.

There were too many questions. Matt couldn't keep them all straight in his head.

He tried reviewing the facts he knew once more. The kidnappers were desperate to get something from him. They wanted it badly enough to kill one person and kidnap two more—and still he had no idea what it was they wanted.

If he made the wrong choices now, Jane or Doug might die. Or both of them.

He sagged against the wall of the building, closed his eyes, and tried to keep his knees from buckling. His stomach was empty, but he had to fight back the queasy feeling that something heavy and foul in his belly would force its way out any second now.

He could never have imagined being responsible for another person's survival—much less two people. And he had never realized he could come to need someone so much as he needed Jane right now.

Never in all his life had he felt more alone.

* * *

Matt walked by her side as they cooled down from their run. She enjoyed the feeling of her hand nesting in his. :"Let's sit down," he said as they passed a picnic table in the park. They sat on the bench, and she closed her eyes, enjoying the warmth of the sun. "I've never known any other woman who could look so good after a workout," he said.

She turned to look at him and opened her eyes—to see dirty tan paint on the wall she was facing. The mildew smell in the room brought her back instantly to the cheap hotel.

She had been asleep!

The room was darker now, and quiet. Where were the two men?

She looked down past her feet and saw Greg standing at the window. And then she could almost feel Lyle's eyes watching her. Slowly she moved her gaze upward to the chair facing the bed. Lyle gave her his usual leer. "Sleeping Beauty is awake," he announced.

Greg turned from the window. "Just in time for dinner. Are you hungry, Jane? I was about to ask Lyle to go find something for us to eat."

She sat up on the edge of the bed. There was no way she could be sure what time it was. The sky outside the window had turned from blue to the grey of light fog, but slanting sunlight still filtered weakly into the room. It must be late afternoon.

"What would you like?" Greg asked.

She shrugged. "I'm not really hungry." *And I don't know if I'd dare eat any food you give me.*

"Lyle, why don't you go find something for the three of us to eat. Bring back something you think Jane would like."

It was obvious that Lyle would prefer to have Greg go and leave him to guard Jane. But he shrugged on his coat without saying anything and walked to the door. He stopped and looked back, giving Greg one more chance to change his mind, but Greg only waited expectantly. Lyle opened the door and stepped out into the hallway. There was the scraping of a key in the lock and the deadbolt lever turned in its place on the back of the door.

Jane could not be sure how long she had slept. The thought of having been alone here with these two men, unconscious of what they were doing or saying, was frightening at first. But then some of the conversation she had overheard came back to her and she realized that falling asleep may have been an answer to prayer. She had not had to listen to any more of Lyle's filth.

Greg came to sit on the chair between her and the door. He would have been staring into her eyes if she had let him. Instead, she kept looking around the room, which held nothing she had not already studied in detail.

"I hope you were able to relax," Greg said.

There was no ring of genuine concern in it. The words were more of a tactical statement, an attempt to set the stage for what he wanted her to feel. Let them have some hope, he had advised Lyle. She looked at him as she answered. "How relaxed would you be if people with guns had stolen you away from someone you loved and held you prisoner? Could you relax if they were threatening to kill you?"

Greg did not answer at first, but sat looking into her eyes for several seconds. Finally, he said, "You're a very unusual woman, Jane."

She did not respond.

"Do you know why?" he asked.

"No," she answered, sure he was going to tell her. He seemed determined to have a conversation.

"Most women would have begged me by now to let them go. They would have offered me money, jewels—anything. You haven't tried""

Most women? Had he done this before? How many women had been in this same position with Greg?

"I don't have anything I can offer you," she answered. "Would it help if I begged? I'll do that if it will make a difference."

Slowly, he shook his head. "No. Sorry. I was just saying I think you're a very strong woman." It almost sounded like he was expressing admiration. "Most women would be very afraid."

"I *am* afraid. I'm afraid you're going to kill me, for no good reason, when Matt and I were just getting started together."

"Jane, I've tried to tell you not to be too concerned about the threats. We're only trying to convince Matt that he needs to do the right thing." Greg paused. "I'm surprised your husband was able to keep this secret from you. You really don't know what it's all about, do you? I wonder why he wouldn't tell you."

She did not want to admit there could actually be a secret. Had Matt really withheld something from her? She did not want to believe he could do that, and Greg was undoubtedly trying to plant doubt in her mind—trying to drive a wedge between the two of them.

But it might be dangerous to go on denying that Matt had the thing they wanted.

She wondered if the small sign of admiration Greg had shown for her meant that she might be able to reach him somehow. "Are you ever afraid, Greg? Are there things that make you afraid the way I am right now?"

"No. No, I can't say that there are."

"Nothing? There isn't anything that makes you worry—worry that maybe you could lose something that means everything to you, or worry that you could get hurt because of something out of your control?"

She saw a flicker of recognition in his eyes, and then the mask came down to hide his emotions again. She had been trying to win some sympathy for the position she was in and unexpectedly she had found a weakness: Greg was afraid of losing control.

"No, I don't worry about any of that," he answered, breaking eye contact with her. He got up from the chair and walked over to look out the window.

She tried again. "Are you ever afraid of what God might think about what you're doing?"

He turned to look at her. "You believe in God? A God who loves you?"

"Yes."

He smiled indulgently. "Get real, Jane. How can you believe that—an intelligent woman like you? There is no God. If there were a God who loved you, would he let something like this happen to you?" He shook his head. "We do what we do in life, and if it turns out good, we're happy. If not . . . " He shrugged.

"So are you happy, Greg?"

He glanced at her, then looked away again. He did not answer.

"I believe in a God who wants us to be happy," Jane said, "but He lets us choose. Sometimes bad things happen to people who believe in Him because other people make bad choices. But He promised before we came here that we would be able to choose how we live."

Greg looked at her for several seconds without speaking. Then, slowly, he said, "So the way you see it, I've made a bad choice, and I'm probably going to hell for it."

"It's not up to me where you go." She paused. "But I think it's wrong for you to take away my opportunities to choose."

"And you think I should do what?" He wore the same amused smile she had seen earlier when he watched Lyle trying to humiliate her.

"Let me go right now," she answered. "If Matt has something that belongs to you, I'll see that you get it back. I promise."

Greg laughed. "I don't think so. I've got a job to do, and I can't see things working out very well for me if I try to do it your way."

Killing us is just "a job"? There would be no mercy from this man. She knew it.

He stood with his back to her, looking out the open window.

She was taller than Greg, and he did not appear to be particularly muscular. Could she get close enough while his back was turned to overpower him somehow? Could she perhaps loop the chain from her handcuffs over his neck and choke him? Or perhaps force him out the window?

She could see part of his knife sticking out above his waistband in the back. She could probably pin him against the windowsill with her body so he could not reach the knife to pull it out. Or could she pull the knife out herself, flick it open as he had, and use it on him?

But there was still the pistol stuck in his waistband in front. Could she pin him so the pistol was trapped against the windowsill?

It might be easier to overcome him if she simply clubbed him in the head first with her balled-up fists. Then she could slip the handcuff chain around his neck to choke him.

But she would have to cross the room absolutely silently to avoid warning him before she was within reach.

Jane was horrified momentarily to realize she was actually thinking about attacking—and maybe killing—another human being. She fought the feeling down. That other human being would have no qualms about killing her, and she certainly had the right to protect herself. Attacking wouldn't be wrong in defense of her life, would it? It couldn't be. And she already knew what these two men were planning for her.

Slowly and quietly she stood, trying not to let the bed creak. She was about to take a step toward him when something warned her that this was not the time—that she did not need to attack. The warning was strong enough that she froze in her place.

Greg seemed to sense a change in the room and began to turn toward her. Jane had only an instant to decide what to do. Quickly she stretched her arms above her head.

Greg looked at her suspiciously.

"Stretching," she said. "Sitting there on the edge of the bed like that hurts my back."

Greg turned his back to the window and leaned against the sill. He put his hand on the butt of the pistol in his waistband. "Feel free to make yourself comfortable some other way, Jane. You can lay down again. Or sit on the chair."

She took a step toward the chair—and the floor creaked beneath her foot. That creak would have given her away before she could have begun to get close to Greg.

She sat in the chair and stretched her legs out so she could rest her feet on the bed. Then, to maintain the illusion that she was simply trying to relax her muscles, she stretched her arms out and touched her toes with her fingers. She repeated the exercise three times. Then she stretched her arms above her head and slowly moved them from one side to the other. Her moves were similar to exercises she had done many times beside the volleyball court, warming up for a game.

Greg watched her speculatively, undoubtedly in his trying-to-get-inside-the-mind mode. She hoped his ego would make him believe that his attempts at intimidation had truly been effective with her, that she simply could not be thinking of any kind of resistance.

She felt relief when he took his hand off his pistol, folded his arms across his chest, and stood watching her exercise.

8

"Please put those things in one of the boxes that could hold a dress, or a man's shirt, then wrap it in something bright," Matt asked.

The woman behind the counter examined the items he had handed her. "Is this all? Just these?"

"Yes. I'll pay the service fee. Is there some problem?"

She smiled at him. "No, not all sir." She pulled a large, folded box out from under the counter and began preparing it. She had been trained well in customer service, Matt thought—but people who could afford to shop in this store undoubtedly demanded service. This was the place where Ed Bills, their hotel's security chief, had said a woman might get lost shopping. On the outside, this building looked like most of the other aging gray stone structures in the area. Inside, it was a luxury shopping mall. A wide staircase in the sweeping central atrium led up to several floors of exclusive shops devoted to clothing and personal products. The three top floors were occupied by a well-known upscale department store.

The clerk finished assembling the box and placed his items in it. "I have yellow paper or pink."

"Yellow. I want it to stand out as much as possible. And I'll need a bag to carry it in." Matt tried to smile congenially. "It's a surprise for someone."

Congeniality was not what he felt as he walked out of the shopping center carrying his package. He felt loneliness, frustration, anger—and panic was out there nibbling constantly at the edges of his consciousness.

He knew he had to put the negative emotions aside right now and think clearly. The negative emotions could beat him—and he did not intend to be beaten.

He had spent what seemed like a long time sitting on the steps of that building after the last call, pondering what to do. Or, probably he had been there only a matter of minutes; it had seemed long because he knew time was running out.

When he had stood up and walked away from that spot, the situation had changed in his mind. He still did not know exactly what he was going to do, but he was *not* going to lose Jane to those . . . *jackals*. It was the first description that came to mind—beasts who combined to prey on innocent, unsuspecting victims.. Her kidnappers were vicious and opportunistic animals who had looked for someone they thought they could pick off easily.

They had picked the wrong targets. He could not know what was happening to Jane, but he knew she was strong, and he knew his own strengths. Maybe he wasn't sure what to do right now, but he was through letting the fear in his gut make him weak. He would continue considering all his options, and when he could see the right way to act, he would not hesitate.

Maybe there was still time for him to call the police.

No, not *call*, he reminded himself, just in case the kidnappers were somehow tracing his calls.

Maybe he could still go to the police. He would *make* them understand him. But where was the nearest station?

His problem now was that there were *two* lives depending on the decisions he made. Even if the San Francisco police could get to Jane and successfully rescue her, would Doug's kidnappers find out? How quickly? He could not be sure what effect a San Francisco police operation, no matter how well they pulled it off, might have on the life of his brother far away.

He had prayed for Doug while he sat on the steps of that building, and again for Jane.

Once more he had felt that Jane would be all right in the end. He could not know what that meant. He hoped it meant she would not be harmed. But it could also mean that whatever happened to Jane now, things would be all right in the end because the two of them had promised each other eternity when they married, and she would always belong to him in his heart. He could not bear to think that this was the meaning—that he might lose her so soon. He wanted to belong to her through a long lifetime on earth. He had looked forward to sharing every facet of life with her—happiness, and sadness if it came; babies and grandchildren; struggle, when it was necessary—everything two people who loved each other could experience together.

If any action of his own caused him to lose Jane, he did not know how he could live with that knowledge for the next fifty or sixty years. Tears had come while he was sitting on those steps—and then shame that he was wasting time feeling sorry for himself.

The only clear direction he had received with his prayers was a strong feeling that there was no time to be lost in confusion or indecision, that he had to be up and doing. So he had acted, hoping for direction when he needed to make choices, resolving to follow the positive impressions that came and ignore the fear.

The first step was going to the shopping center and putting together this phony package for his delivery. If he were forced to go along with their demands, at least he was prepared now.

He had realized that prayer was all he could do for Doug at this distance, and his father and mother had already put the matter into the hands of the police. Did the police have any idea where to look for his brother? If they did, he hoped they would be able to pull off the kind of rescue that would keep Doug out of a crossfire—and keep Jane's kidnappers in the dark.

For the moment, he was desperate to get to her, to protect her from the men who held her. He kept thinking that the only way to reach her was to make them come to him.

Was he being a fool? A voice in his head kept telling him to go to the police as his parents had, that he should have done it in the beginning. Now the voice was urging him to hurry, there was almost no time left—and he realized this was in part the voice of panic, the voice of fear.

He walked slowly back toward Sixth Street. Ahead of him, to the west, a bright spot in the fog kept edging lower. He glanced at his watch: 6:21. What time would sundown come officially?

If he could find the police quickly without calling, and then convince them he was telling the truth, would there still be time for them to put together a rescue operation before the kidnappers called him to make his delivery?

It might already be too late.

Until Jane's captors called, he would wait somewhere close by the hotel where he knew she was.

He tried to swallow but his throat was too dry. He had not had anything to eat or drink all day long. He wasn't sure his stomach could handle food right now, knotted up as it was, but he couldn't afford to get dehydrated. Just ahead on Market Street was a small convenience store. He stopped in to buy a bottle of sports drink, chugged the liquid down as he walked, and tossed the plastic bottle into a trash container at the end of the block.

He was waiting for the crossing light at the street corner when his telephone rang. *If this is their idea of sundown, they're early—but I'm glad.*

This voice on the phone was a mystery. "Matt?" He wasn't sure where he had heard this voice before until the man continued: "This is Montie."

Jane's uncle. Montie insisted that everyone in the family call him by his first name. Matt had met him just twice, the last time at the wedding reception a few days ago. He knew only a few things about the man. Montie and his wife had three daughters younger than Jane. Montie taught a Sunday School class on the weekends when he could be at home. Montie worked very hard. He worked for the FBI.

"What's going on, Matt?"

"What do you mean?"

"I mean I'm here with your parents and all of us back home are concerned about the things that have been happening—the break-in, and now your brother's kidnapping." Jane's mother was Montie's older sister; undoubtedly she had called him immediately when she had learned about Doug. "Your boss is dead, in what *may* have been an accident," Montie continued, "so we're wondering—"

"Cole's death was no accident," Matt said.

"How do *you* know that?"

"Cole didn't spend a lot of time around that pool, and he wasn't really a drinker. I hope someone is taking a good look at what happened to him. Have them check out his injury carefully."

"The men who have Doug told your mother that you would know what they want. What did they mean by that?"

"I wish I knew!" Matt answered. It came out with more emotion than he intended. He wanted to say more. In a city this size, the FBI would undoubtedly have people who could respond quickly, and this was a chance to spill the story about Jane to someone who could do something about it. But Matt wondered if he had said too much already.

If only he could be sure there was no one listening to this call.

But he *had* to take advantage of this opportunity if he could.

Maybe if he phrased a question carefully, Montie might tell him whether it was possible for someone to be listening in on his cell phone conversations right now.

Then he remembered that Doug had a cell phone. Could they use its signal to locate him? "Montie, is there a way you could . . . can you trace the signal from someone's cell phone and find out exactly where he is? Could you even listen in on calls?"

There was hesitation before Montie answered. "It's easy to find out where a caller is. With the right technology, you can listen to calls. But there are strict legal limits on when we can do it." He paused. "Why would *you* be worried about that, Matt?"

"I'm not worried. I'm . . . " Montie's response had not told him whether he could speak freely. Matt searched for a way to explain why he needed an answer. "I was wondering if . . . "

He stopped as the significance of Montie's words sank in. Montie had assumed that Matt's question concerned *this* call—and Montie had deliberately hedged in his reply.

Why? What would be going through the mind of an FBI agent right now?

"I'd like to talk to Jane," her uncle said.

"I'm afraid that's not possible right now. She's, uh . . . not available."

"Things look a little strange from here, Matt. The break-in, your boss's death, Doug's kidnapping—all of them seem tied to you somehow. You need to tell us where you are. I'll send some agents to pick you up. We need to talk."

They're wondering if I *did something to bring this on—or if I'm involved!*

The realization stunned him. *No! No, they can't—not now. There's no time.*

No doubt the FBI or the police were recording all the calls in and out of his parents' house. They might be tracing this one right now. A few seconds ago, there had been hope of help. But he still did not know whether he dared talk about what had happened to Jane, and if they wasted effort focusing on him while time was running out for her. . . .

The world was collapsing on top of him. What could he do now? Was there any way to get them to focus on the right things?

"Ah . . . uh, Montie, believe me, I can't tell you what's going on. Are you remembering that Doug has a cell phone too?"

"We're taking everything into account, Matt."

"And Jane. Are you tracing their phones?" Then he pushed the button to end the call. He wasn't sure whether it was panic or prudence that made him act.

If the kidnappers were somehow listening, had he said too much?

His phone rang twice more, in quick succession. When the caller ID showed his parents' number, he did not answer.

How could they possibly think he would be involved in anything that might endanger Jane?

Did his parents believe that? Did her parents? Had Lawrence McDougall become suspicious after talking to him earlier? Or was suspicion simply something that came to Montie's mind based on experience in other kidnapping cases?

Of course the FBI had agents in San Francisco who could be assigned to this case if Montie asked for help. And the bureau undoubtedly would work with local police when there was a need. So if Montie had talked to the FBI office in San Francisco about locating Doug's brother, and if the FBI had passed some kind of bulletin to local law enforcement . . .

Matt's experiences of the day shouted down the logical voice in his head that said he should go to the police right now. *Yeah? And what if they don't believe me—just like Bills this morning? What if they make me wait around in some office while they check out my story? What if they check on* me *and find out the FBI is looking for me?* "There's no way," he muttered. He would be tied up with the police until long after sundown—and time would run out for Jane.

The pedestrian crossing light changed in his favor. He stood still on the curb.

The bright spot in the fog to the west was inching closer to the tops of buildings on the horizon. Matt wanted to wait for sunset right here at the corner of Sixth and Market, in the small café that was no more than a three-minute walk from the hotel where they were holding Jane. He wanted to be close when the call came from the kidnappers.

He looked at the phone in his hand. Mobile phones send signals that ping off of local cell phone towers at regular intervals to establish where they are. The FBI could be using that signal right now to pinpoint his location. He couldn't turn off his phone in case the kidnappers called, but he couldn't sit still and wait to be found. He had to keep moving. He turned around and began walking in the direction from which he had come.

When his telephone rang a couple of minutes later, he glanced over his shoulder at the horizon. Still too early for the kidnappers to call. He looked at the caller ID, recognized the number instantly, and wondered whether to believe what he was seeing. He put the phone to his ear. "Doug?"

"Matt! What's happening? They say you have something they—"

There was the sound of the phone being handled, and Matt could hear Latino music faintly in the background. Then a voice with a Hispanic accent said: "Give it up, man. Do it, or mama don't see her little Dougie no more. And don't be stupid—don't give no information to the police or the feds about this." The line went dead.

Matt stood gazing at his phone. *Did they know when Montie called? Were they listening?* Was that the reason for the last thing the caller had said? Or was his warning just a coincidence—simply the same thing Jane's kidnappers had been telling him?

Quickly Matt dialed his brother's number back. He let it ring for more than a minute, but no one answered.

He felt as though he were in the jaws of a vise with someone gradually tightening it.

No! Focus!

Right now his whole objective had to be freeing Jane. He didn't know whether he might be able to rely on help from the FBI or the police eventually, but winning their help would take time—time he did not have.

* * *

Jane sat on the edge of the bed again, her hands clasped on her knees in front of her. Greg sat opposite her on one of the chairs, eating one of the hamburgers Lyle had brought back. "Here," Greg said, holding one of them out to her. "Eat. You must be hungry."

Jane shook her head. "Not really."

Greg put the hamburger down on the chair beside him with the bags of french fries and drinks Lyle had brought. Lyle stood at the window, glowering while he munched his burger.

When he had returned with the food, he had pulled the second chair into position in front of Jane, intending to sit there while he ate. But Jane had moved farther away immediately, and before Lyle could react, Greg had told him it was his turn to stand guard at the window. Lyle had protested that it was too early for Matt to be in the area, and anyway, Jamal down at the front desk would call if he saw anyone hanging around on the street who did not belong there. In answer, Greg had looked at Lyle as though he had just said something stupid or annoying. Sullenly, Lyle had taken his place at the window.

The window was closed now, against the chill brought by the fog. The light in the room was waning. Jane did not want to ask the time, but sunset must be close.

"Are you sure you don't want anything to eat?" Greg asked, pushing the hamburger closer to her.

She nodded.

He put the hamburger back on the chair and picked up one of the soft drinks. "Thirsty?" he asked, holding it out to her.

She shook her head.

"Jane, you don't have to be afraid. There's nothing wrong with the food. Lyle and I are eating it too." He sucked liquid through the straw in the cup he held, swallowed, then removed the plastic cap and straw from the cup. He held the drink out to her and raised his eyebrows questioningly.

It was more of his pretended kindness. But it was true she was thirsty. Slowly she reached out and took the cup between her hands.

Jane had said very little to the two men for the past couple of hours, speaking only when spoken to and keeping her answers as brief as possible. After Greg had rebuffed her attempt to win his sympathy, she had begun to struggle again with thoughts of what could happen to her. She had cut off the thoughts when they drifted to Lyle's conversation with Greg.

She might not be able to control the outcome of this situation, but she could control her own actions, and she would not wait passively for these two to do whatever they were planning. Her mind was constantly racing, looking for any opportunity to change the situation or any opportunity to act. Greg and Lyle obviously believed they had cowed her into submission. Let them think that; it could help her.

Since Lyle had returned, Greg seemed almost to be playing the genial host, as though this were some kind of social gathering and they were waiting for the last guest to arrive. Greg had been trying to draw her out. Why? Obviously, he was trying to keep her hoping things would turn out all right. He had told Lyle that it was all about control. But was there some other reason he was trying to ingratiate himself with her?

She drank part of the soft drink and reached out for one of the small packages of fries, carefully selecting the one from which Greg had taken a couple of fries already. If he noticed which she chose, he did not mention it.

"That's better," he said. "You've got to keep your strength up."

He looked at Lyle. "I'm sure Matt will be glad to see his bride. This is a woman a man would certainly miss."

Lyle grunted and glanced out the window again.

Greg turned back to smile at her. "You're not like a lot of the women I meet, Jane. You've got something different about you—something real, something . . . " He held his hand out in the air as though reaching for a thing he could not quite grasp. "I don't know—something *solid.* What is that?"

"I don't know." She shrugged, and carefully refrained from asking where he usually met women. What he was doing—toying with her—was a cruel kind of taunting, almost worse than Lyle's vicious goading. But she did not want to make him mad. Let him feel in control.

"You obviously have some sense of fashion," he continued, gesturing at what she was wearing. "This is not the usual tank-top-and-walking-shorts tourist look."

The clothing she had brought was simple and inexpensive, but carefully chosen because she wanted to look good for Matt. The navy pullover and tan chino pants she had put on this morning had been easy choices that required little thought. Now, she noticed, the left leg of her pants was dirty from the side of the building where she had hung out the window, and there was a spot of something on the leg that looked like it might be oil or tar.

"That little gold chain on your neck and those gold studs in your ears are tasteful," Greg said. He looked at her speculatively for a moment, then continued: "A woman like you would look good in diamonds. Or pearls. Small pearl earrings—pearl and gold would look good on you." He turned to the other man. "Don't you think so, Lyle?"

Lyle turned slowly to look at him. "You're right, Greg. You always are." He was obviously still smarting at being exiled to sentry duty. He looked at Jane. "Greg knows fine jewelry," he said with a touch of grudging admiration.

The gold Rolex watch on Greg's right wrist suggested that he knew *expensive* jewelry. "So is jewelry a sideline for you?" she asked, hoping to gather another bit of information about him.

"No," he said, "*this* is a sideline."

Kidnapping and murder are a sideline? His willingness to answer her question was not encouraging; he would not give her information if he thought she would ever have a chance to share it.

"Jane, if you showed up at the symphony or the opening of a play in the right gown and the right jewels . . . " He sat looking at her speculatively again, as though he could see the picture in his mind's eye. It felt creepy. In his own way Greg was leering at her. He was more sophisticated than Lyle, but he was no less corrupt inside.

He reached down and took her left hand, holding it out in front of him so he could inspect her rings. "Your husband must know jewelry, or he shops with someone who does. That's a fine quality stone in your engagement ring—not too large and flashy, but a good diamond."

Jane withdrew her hand. She didn't want these men talking about her or her husband, so she tried to turn the focus of the conversation to Greg. "Jewelry must be your business then."

He smiled and shook his head. "No questions. I told you, we can't let you know too much about us. That could be dangerous for you."

Maintaining the lie: they'll let me go later if I just go along for now.

"Matt is a lucky man," Greg said. "Not many men have a woman of your quality come into their lives." It sounded a bit wistful—even envious. "Does he treat you the way a lovely woman deserves to be treated? Because you would really stand out in the right setting, with the right company." He paused expectantly, as though waiting for her to speak.

It sounded almost like he was hitting on her. Was he hinting at something—maybe some chance for her to live if she would be the kind of "elegant woman" he had in mind? Was he giving her a chance to plead with him? Or was he just finding another way to toy with her?

Jane said nothing.

Greg's fixed smile faded. "I just hope Matt realizes how much he stands to lose."

The not-so-veiled threat—they could hurt me. It's the control factor. He's keeping me in line until they don't need me anymore.

Greg wiped his greasy fingers with one of the napkins Lyle had brought.

He crumpled it up, gathered up his other trash, and dropped it into the bag that had held the food. "Lyle, I can take a turn at the window if you'd like to sit down," he said.

Manners are another part of the lie. He takes them off, then puts them on as needed, she thought.

The two men exchanged places. Lyle came to sit opposite her. He looked down at the food sitting on the other chair. "You gonna eat that burger?"

* * *

Stretch stood out in a group of four men clustered around a doorway. They looked at Matt suspiciously as he approached carrying his package. Then recognition dawned in Stretch's face.

"You gonna be stayin' around here now?" he asked. "Remember what I said—that place up there on the other street is mine." He nodded toward the side street that ran off of Sixth past the Hotel Birch.

"Yeah, I know. I need to talk to you about that place."

"Won't make no difference what you say. It's mine," Stretch asserted.

"I'm not looking to change that. I have a proposition that could make you a little money."

Stretch looked interested. So did the other three men.

"Just you," Matt said. "Let's go up there to talk about it."

One of the other men muttered something Matt couldn't make out. The closest one said to Stretch, "Hey, remember, it's your turn to buy."

Stretch followed as Matt walked up the street. Matt stopped under the overhang at the corner of the Hotel Birch, out of sight of the front door. He pointed at the garbage container just down the side street. "I need to leave something in there for just a little while tonight."

"Anything you put in there, it's mine."

Matt shook his head. "No. I need you to leave it alone." He took his wallet out of his pocket and extracted two twenty-dollar bills. He held one of them out toward Stretch. "This money's yours—if you won't touch the package I put in there. You have to leave the package where I put it. Do you understand me?"

Slowly Stretch reached out his hand to take the twenty dollars.

Matt withdrew it. "No. You can only have it if you promise me you won't touch the package after I put it into the container." He held up both bills together. "You get all of this if you leave the package alone until somebody comes to pick it up."

Stretch looked at the store bag Matt held in his other hand. "What's in it?"

"Nothing that would be worth anything to you. It's nothing to eat or drink or sell." Matt pulled the gift-wrapped box out of the bag and held it out to Stretch. "Here. Feel it. There's nothing in it worth having."

Stretch took the box and hefted it in his hands. "Pretty light." He studied the bright yellow wrapping paper, then handed the box back. "Why you doin' this?"

"It's kind of like a game, or a contest. The other guy is expecting something from me. If I make him believe this is it and he picks up the package, I win. I win really big."

"Whatcha gonna win?"

"Nothing I could share. But you get this." He held up the two bills again. "It's a lot more than you've got right now, isn't it?"

Stretch looked him up and down carefully as though calculating how much Matt might be willing to offer. "It ain't enough. There's somethin' else you got to give me too."

* * *

Greg looked out at the sky and then down at the street below. "Almost time." He lowered the pull-down shade over the window and turned to look at Jane. "It won't be long now and we'll have you and Matt back together. In the meantime, I hope you understand the importance of being cooperative. Maybe you'll be thinking when he's right outside that you could scream and he'd hear you. Maybe you'll think if you try to fight us, he'll hear the commotion. Chances are he wouldn't. But even if he did, there wouldn't be anything he could do—not in time to help you."

He withdrew his pistol from his belt and held it up so she could look at it. He reached into the pocket of his jacket on the bed and drew out what looked like a piece of tubing. He began to fit it onto the front of the pistol. "This muffles the sound of a shot, and there's no one in the next room or close enough to hear anyway. I only need one shot. Do you understand?"

The situation seemed surreal. He wore his fixed social smile while he explained how he could kill her. But he was expecting a response. She nodded.

"Good. I'm glad we're clear on that." He slipped the pistol back into his waistband. "Now, if Matt does what he promised and if you cooperate, everything will come out good for all of us. As soon as I verify that he's brought what we want, we'll be out of this place and we'll have you and Matt back together."

The lie to control me again. "We'll have you and Matt back together." What was Greg seeing when he said that, Jane wondered—their bodies piled together in a heap somewhere?

Lyle grinned at her. "Greg, I've got something to keep her from screaming." He went to the bed and picked up his sport coat. "I brought it out of my car after I went to get the food." He reached into the pocket of the coat and pulled out a small roll of duct tape.

Greg looked at him and nodded. "That's a good idea, Lyle." He turned his smile on Jane again. "But we won't want to make her uncomfortable any longer than necessary. We won't need that until after we call Matt."

9

Matt lingered near the 24-hour café at the corner of Market and Sixth, keeping a wary eye now for any police patrol. The sun was just at the horizon. The kidnappers could be calling soon, and the voice of Kidnapper Number Two had told him he would have fifteen minutes to make his delivery after their call. From here, he could be at the spot in no more than five minutes.

He wanted to wait closer to the hotel, but he stood out too much among the street people loitering in doorways or leaning against the buildings along Sixth. They knew he wasn't one of them, and for all he knew, one of them could be a lookout for the kidnappers. He was as close to Jane as it seemed safe to be right now, and he was ready for the call.

He had walked slowly along Sixth just a few minutes ago and glanced up at the side of the hotel. Through the fog, he could see that two windows up there were lighted, one on the top floor and one on the floor below. The shades were pulled down in both rooms, but there was enough fog now that if the shades had been up and someone had been looking out one of the windows, anyone out on Sixth Street would be no more than a silhouette.

It was a little less than 10 minutes after eight when the sun began to sink behind the buildings on the west.

When his phone rang, he quickly put it to his ear without looking at the number. "Hello?"

"Matt, this is Montie."

Inwardly Matt groaned as he looked at the fading light in the sky. "Yes?" It sounded curt, he knew, but the timing of the call could hardly have been worse.

"We're wondering why we haven't heard anything more from the kidnappers who have your brother," Montie said. "Have you heard anything?"

Matt hesitated. He didn't know what he could say—what wouldn't be dangerous if somehow the kidnappers were listening.

Montie didn't wait for him to answer. "We know you received a call from Doug's cell phone. What did they tell you?" Montie asked.

"The same thing they told my mother."

"And do you have any idea now what they're looking for?"

Matt knew it would sound suspicious if he dodged the question, but he could not say no on the phone—not if there was a chance Jane's kidnappers could be listening right now. Saying no would tell them that he was bluffing. Instead, he asked: "Do you have protection around my parents?"

"Yes."

"And around Jane's family?"

There was a pause before Montie answered. "Is there some reason you think that's a good idea?"

Matt didn't know how to answer this question safely on the phone either, and he was sure Montie hadn't called just to get information from him. They could be using this time to try to pinpoint his location. "Montie, I can't talk right now. I hope you're trying to locate Doug's phone. Text me another number where I could call you back. Please don't call *me* back. *Please.*" He pushed the button to end the call.

The next time his phone rang, he checked its information display. The time read 8:21. The caller number it displayed was Jane's.

When he said hello, the anonymous voice he had come to hate and fear answered: "It's time. You have 15 minutes to make your delivery."

"First, I talk to my wife."

"Your wife is just fine, Matt. I told you we would take good care of her. I've sent you a picture to prove it."

"Yeah, and I know Jane walked away from the hotel this morning because she just couldn't wait to spend a delightful afternoon with you. You could have taken a picture anytime since then. If you want me to believe I should give you what you want, you'll have to let her talk to me."

There was noise of the phone being handled, and then he heard, "Matt?"

"J! Are you all right? Have they, uh . . . are you okay?"

"I'm all right—so far. They just keep threatening me if you don't give them what they want. Please, let them have it."

He listened carefully, thinking he would know if they were forcing her to lie with a gun to her head or a knife at her throat. But he really couldn't be sure. He wished he could think of something smart to say, something to give her confidence that he would help her. And then a movie line came to mind. "As you wish. I love you."

There was a brief pause, and then she answered, "My sweet Matt. I love—"

Her words were cut off, and Kidnapper Number Two's voice came back on the line. "Now that we've established how you feel about each other, we'll get on with things. Your delivery. Fifteen minutes."

"And you'll have my wife there for the exchange."

"You'll make your delivery and walk away. I'll verify that you've given us what we want, and then we'll call to tell you where you can meet us, and Jane."

"No. I told you you'd have to let her go before I give you what you want."

"And I told you we need to make sure first that you're giving us back what's ours."

"You're not getting it unless I get my wife back at the same time."

The man on the other end of the call sighed. "I'm losing patience, Matt. Either make your delivery in the next 14 minutes, or say good-bye to your wife and we'll be in touch later—with you or with someone else in your family. What's it going to be?"

Matt had thought about this. The package itself was a bluff. Now he was trying to run another bluff on top of that one—and he had no real leverage behind it. There was no way he could force them to respond, except with the dummy package he held in his hand.

"Matt? About thirteen minutes now."

"I'll be there sooner," he responded.

The connection was broken.

Hastily, he checked his messages and called up the picture that came with the latest one. It showed Jane sitting on the sagging bed in a room that looked like it belonged inside the decaying Birch Hotel. She gazed at the camera warily, but she appeared unharmed.

"Forgive me, J, if . . . " The words caught in his throat. "If this doesn't go right," he breathed. "I didn't know what else to do."

* * *

"Well, Jane, he's on his way." Greg smiled this time like a game show host who had just announced that someone was about to win the grand prize. "Lyle," he said, and nodded toward the duct tape on the bed.

"You don't have to do that," Jane said. "I won't make any noise."

"Oh, I'd *like* to believe you, but . . . "

Lyle tore a piece of tape off the roll and held it out in front of him as he approached her. She tried to turn her face away and he raised his hand as though he would slap her again. She sat still on the edge of the bed while he stretched the tape over her mouth and pressed it into place. He looked into her eyes and laughed at her. "You'd like to have your hands free, right now, wouldn't you—like to go for my eyes? Not a chance."

Greg walked across the room and turned off the light switch. Then he walked back to the window and raised the shade.

"Can you see it from here?" Lyle asked.

"The streetlight's not much help. But I can see the container. That's enough."

Jane sat on the bed watching them carefully—watching for any opening at all. But she had recognized the movie line Matt had given her—"As you wish," a line spoken by the hero to his long-lost love in *The Princess Bride*. She hoped the answer she had given him in return—"My Sweet," a name used by the heroine of the movie for the man she loved—would let Matt know that she believed in him, that she was counting on him.

* * *

Matt walked quickly down the side street to the garbage container. Then he deliberately slowed, and exaggerated his motions. He turned so the container was on his right and held the gift-wrapped package out in his hand so it could easily be seen. The light of the dying bulb in the street-lamp overhead was filtered through fog; in its anemic glow the color of the package was nearer gray than yellow, but the wrapped box still would stand out from the other items in the container. Matt reached in and laid the box carefully on top of the newspaper he had placed there earlier. Then he walked away rapidly toward Sixth Street.

He had glanced up quickly when he turned by the garbage container.

The light behind the shade on the fourth floor still shone. The light behind the shade on the fifth floor had been turned out. That would be where they were—watching him.

When he rounded the corner onto Sixth Street, out of sight of that window, he broke into a run heading north. Fifty feet up the sidewalk, he veered west, running straight across the street. A car coming out of the fog braked hard for him and the driver honked before continuing on. Matt reached the sidewalk on the other side of the street and headed south again at a quick walk. He could have gone around the hotel block instead and come up the side street behind the Hotel Birch to approach the garbage container, but it would have taken too long. There would have been time for someone to come out of the hotel, retrieve the package from the container, and hurry back inside before he could see what happened. This way, there would be only a few seconds when the garbage container was out of his sight. He could not see much from this distance, but if there had been someone on the street beside the Hotel Birch, he would at least have seen a figure moving in the fog.

When he was out of sight of those upstairs windows once more, he turned and ran straight back across Sixth Street toward the hotel.

* * *

"Did he leave it?" Lyle asked.

Greg stared out the window. "Looked like it. He put something in there—a box, I think."

"Big enough?"

"Could be."

"You going down to check it out?"

Greg was silent for a moment. "I *think* that was him."

"Who else would it be?"

"Hard to tell. But if he brought anybody else into this . . . "

Lyle looked at Jane. "I don't think so. He wants his lady back."

Greg picked up his cell phone off the bed and dialed a number.

* * *

Matt had reached the sidewalk in front of the hotel when his phone rang. He looked at the display, which told him the number was blocked. *What do they want now?* He turned the phone on and put it to his ear. "Hello."

"The deadline's past, Matt."

"And I made the delivery! Are you trying to change the rules on me now? You were going to let Jane go once I dropped it off."

"Can we be sure *you* dropped it off? You know what it would mean for Jane if there's somebody else involved."

"*I* made the delivery, and you know it. Don't tell me you weren't watching that container. You saw me—*me.* I put in a large box, right on top of that newspaper. When you get close, you'll see the box is wrapped in nice yellow paper."

There was silence from the other man for several seconds. Then: "You're right, Matt, we're watching. And we'd better not see you anywhere in the area before I verify that you brought what we want. Then you'll get a call." The connection was broken.

He's coming for it. Now.

Matt dropped his cell phone back into his pocket and looked up to see the desk clerk watching him through the glass front door of the hotel. Their eyes met, and the clerk seemed to be thinking about what to do next. Had the man seen him dashing across the street, Matt wondered?

Slowly the clerk reached out toward the phone on his desk.

If he's a lookout for the kidnappers, I can't let him make that call.

Matt acted on the idea that came to mind without stopping to analyze it. He grabbed the handle of the door and shoved it open. Alarm showed in the clerk's eyes—until Matt pulled his wallet from his pocket and put on a broad smile. "Hey, how much is it to rent a room for the night? I'm, uh—going to bring someone here, and, ah . . . well, how much for two?"

The clerk's expression changed from wariness to a well-practiced smirk. But his hand stayed on the phone.

What happened next was finished in under five seconds. Matt tossed his wallet on the desk. The clerk looked down at it as though wondering how much money might be inside. Matt clamped a hand down on top of the clerk's hand on the phone. The clerk looked up in alarm just in time to meet Matt's right cross to his jaw. The clerk's eyes rolled back and he slumped off his stool. Matt held onto the man's arm long enough to keep him from crashing against the wall, allowing him instead to settle in a heap on the carpet in the corner. He leaned over the man and put two fingers on his neck above the artery there. Strong pulse, and the man was breathing.

"Sorry, guy," he said, picking up his wallet. He hit the switch on the wall behind the desk to turn off the lights, then walked out of the office, letting the door swing closed behind him.

He hurried around the corner and down the sidewalk beside the hotel, keeping under the overhang, then angled toward the hiding place he had already picked out. He struggled to push away fear, but he could feel it knotting his stomach. He would get only one chance at this. His timing would have to be perfect to make it work.

He guessed that Kidnapper Number Two would not send his partner to retrieve this package.

* * *

Greg motioned Lyle to the window. "Think you can keep an eye on her and watch my back at the same time?"

Lyle grinned in Jane's direction as he put a hand on the butt of his pistol. "I'm sure she won't be any trouble."

Greg picked up his tailored blazer from the bed, shrugged it on, and dropped his cell phone into the inside pocket. "Won't be long now, Jane," he said, giving her a smile.

He slipped out the door and walked down the silent, dimly lighted hallway toward the back stairs. Lyle had chosen a room on the top floor because he knew this hotel seldom filled up. They were undoubtedly alone on this floor tonight. There wouldn't be anyone around to see or hear them take Jane out.

Lyle had his uses, Greg thought, as he opened the stairway door and began to descend. The little man could be counted on to do what he was told, then disappear into his personal cesspool until he was needed again.

Unfortunately, Lyle had no appreciation for finer things. He lacked the vision to see Jane for what she was—a truly magnificent creature. Under other circumstances, Greg thought, he would have liked the opportunity to take her out to dinner in a fine restaurant, introduce her to a wine that a connoisseur could appreciate, charm her out of the reserve that kept distance between them. He had dangled the possibility before her to see her reaction. He wasn't sure if she had understood fully what he was offering, but she had definitely turned him down. Too bad. He hated to leave her to Lyle because he hated to see fine things destroyed. Fortunately, he would not be there when it happened.

He had not been seen in Matt and Jane's hotel. When this was over, if they were eventually found, there would be nothing to connect him to them. Nothing except Lyle, and Greg was sure he could rely on greed and a sense of self-preservation to keep Lyle's mouth shut. Lyle was paid well, and he would be hoping for future assignments.

Greg reached the bottom of the stairs and stood just behind the exit door listening. There was no sound except distant, muffled street noises. He took out his pistol, then eased the door open part way. Nothing moved through the fog on this section of the side street. He pushed the door open fully and walked across the street, holding the gun down next to his leg where it would not be seen if anyone happened to turn down this way. But he saw no one. When he reached the garbage container, he slipped the weapon into his waistband and peered over the metal lip of the bin. There was a flat rectangular box sitting on top of the spread-out newspaper.

He put one foot on the projecting base of the container and raised himself up so he could reach the box.

* * *

Lyle leaned casually against the windowsill watching the street below. Jane gauged her chances with him, now that they were alone. Not good. Lyle stood partially turned toward her, and his hand still rested on the butt of his gun. If she moved, there was a good chance Lyle might see her out of the corner of his eye.

Suddenly Jane saw him stiffen. He muttered a curse. "Where did *he* come from?"

Matt! Matt is here.

Lyle yanked at the window frame, trying to pull it up so he could warn Greg. But the window was stuck.

* * *

The man grabbed Greg's right arm, the one that was gripping the top edge of the container to support him. "Hey! You can't—"

Greg reacted instantly, instinctively; he cut the man off with an elbow to the mouth. The big man staggered back. Greg put both feet on the ground and turned, drawing his pistol at the same time. The man was coming at him again, but he stopped when he saw the pistol pointed at his chest. His eyes went wide and he took a long step back. Greg pulled the trigger just as the other man's foot hit the curb behind him and he lost his balance. The man fell backward, and his head hit the curb as he went down.

Greg kept his pistol pointed at the man's chest as he quickly moved toward him, but the other man did not stir. He lay sprawled in the gutter. The baseball cap with the block A on it had fallen off his head. Blood trickled down through his hair to pool on the pavement beneath his head. He was still breathing.

Evidently the bullet had simply grazed him. There was a new hole in the windshield of Lyle's sedan; the bullet was probably buried somewhere in the upholstery of the back seat.

Greg pressed his pistol against the man's chest and tightened his finger on the trigger. Then he thought better of it. Let Lyle take care of this complication. Let him earn his money, and if there was any evidence left behind, let it be tied to him.

Greg turned toward the garbage container again. He had to find out what was in that package.

* * *

She saw Lyle relax at the window and stop yanking at the frame to open it. He strolled across the room to turn on the light and stood smirking at her. She knew that whatever had happened was over.

Lyle stepped closer and watched her face as he narrated it like the play-by-play of a sporting event. "Suddenly the big man in the hat comes out of the shadows. He grabs Greg's arm. Greg hits him and pushes him back. The big man comes at him again. Greg draws his pistol." He smiled as he made a shooting motion with his hand. "And the big man goes down."

Jane felt as though a light had gone out inside of her, as though the part that kept her heart beating had broken. She had to will herself to breathe again. Tears came to her eyes that she could not stop, and she turned away. She would not let Lyle see them fall.

* * *

The garbage container would prevent anyone passing by on Sixth Street from spotting the form lying in the gutter—if they could see this far through the fog. Greg approached the container from the side this time so that his form, too, could not be spotted as he was reaching in to find what he wanted.

He hated it when one of these jobs turned messy. And why did they always bring him to ugly, filthy places like this?

Two or three more jobs like this one and he could retire if he wanted. He would have enough money banked to draw on his investments and live comfortably almost anywhere in the world. He had his eye on a little town in northern Italy, near a mountain lake he had visited once. He could see himself living in a villa there, enjoying the sun and fine wine and the occasional attractive female tourist.

He put his right foot on the base of the container and boosted himself up again to reach for the box.

Absorbed in his own thoughts, Greg missed something he might have caught another time. He heard it at the last second—a small crunching sound in the broken glass on the pavement. His hand was reaching for the pistol again as he stepped down and started to turn—just in time to catch a muscular forearm across his ear. The blow slammed the other side of his head into the garbage container.

* * *

Lyle stood watching her. "Now don't you wish hubby had done what Greg told him?" he smirked.

Jane did not respond.

"Look at me," he demanded. When she did not, he walked over to stand in front of her. "Look at me!" He put his hand under her chin and jerked her head up so she had to look him in the eyes.

She had managed to hold back more tears. She would not let Lyle watch her cry for Matt. It seemed profane somehow—indecent. Lyle was a vicious tormentor who enjoyed her suffering. She would not give him the satisfaction. There would be time to cry later. For the moment, anger dried up the tears in her eyes.

"You'd really like to tell me what you think of me right now, wouldn't you?" he asked. "Well, you'll get your chance—later. I promise you. We'll have plenty of time together, just the two of us . . . to talk." He smirked at her and laughed.

Then he sat down on the bed beside her and put his arm around her shoulders. She pulled away and stood up, moving out of his reach.

Lyle stood too, and took a step toward her, but stopped as his phone rang. He fished the phone out of the pocket of his jacket on the bed. "Hello?" he said cautiously. He listened for several seconds, then said, "Yeah, sure," and turned the phone off. He grinned at Jane. "Sounds like he's got what we were looking for. He says I need to bring you down now. There's something he wants you to identify. What do you suppose that could be?"

He picked up his jacket and shrugged it on, dropped his phone back in the pocket, and withdrew his pistol from his waistband "We're going down the stairs, and you're not going to give me any trouble. We wouldn't want you to get hurt." He grinned at her again. "Not right now."

Lyle opened the door and motioned with the pistol. Jane stepped out into the hallway. He followed her, shut the door, and motioned her forward. She walked down the hallway until she came to a door marked STAIRS. "Stop," he said. Putting the pistol against her ribs, he reached out with his other hand to open the door. "Down," he commanded. "There's nothing hard about stairs. You can do those by yourself. Remember?"

She started down the dimly lighted stairwell wondering what she would do when they reached the street. She wondered if there was any way she could help Matt.

Undoubtedly they did not want to kill her here, although they might shoot her down if she tried to run. She thought that might be preferable to what Lyle had in mind.

Lyle's car would be the final barrier for her. She would not get into his car with him again, no matter what they did to her. She did not care very much at the moment whether she lived or died. One way or another, she would stay right here with the man she loved.

They had gone down two floors when Lyle prodded her in the back with the pistol. "Hurry up!" He shoved her shoulder, making her stumble down several stairs. She ran into the wall on the next landing trying to keep her balance. She turned and glared at him.

He chuckled as he came down to that level. "No use putting things off. Move along." He motioned toward the next flight with his pistol. She started down. He let her take two steps, then shoved her shoulder again. She tripped on the edge of the next step, stumbled down the rest of them, and fell to her knees on the landing.

Lyle grinned again. "Having a problem going down?" He caught up with her and motioned toward the next flight. She stood and started down half sideways, watching him while she tried to keep a solid footing.

His left hand shot out to push her once more. This time she was ready for him; she dodged away and his arm missed her shoulder. When it was just in front of her face, she reached out quickly and wrapped the chain connecting the handcuffs around his wrist. His left forearm was trapped between her hands.

Lyle looked stunned when he realized what had happened. For a moment they gazed into each other's eyes.

He was in danger of losing control of the situation. He outweighed her by at least forty pounds, but she was taller, younger, strong, and athletic. He was none of those things anymore—too many burgers, too much booze, too little exercise. He couldn't allow Jane to fight him. The biggest advantage he held for the moment was in his right hand. He began to raise the gun. She would have to do whatever he said when she was looking down the barrel of his pistol, and if not—well, he could always tell Greg that she forced him to use the gun on her.

With her athletic experience, Jane knew instantly she could not afford to waste the momentary advantage she had. She ducked under Lyle's left arm and whipped it forward, pulling his body past her so that she was shielded from the gun in his other hand. He put out one foot trying to regain his balance, missed the top step, and began to stumble down the stairs. Jane shoved his arm to push him along, but as his arm trailed out behind him, his fingers caught the chain of the handcuffs and pulled her off balance too. She stumbled down the stairs after him.

Lyle fell headlong across the narrow landing and hit his head on the opposite wall. Jane missed a step and was headed for a sprawl beside him on the landing. Instead, she managed to launch herself from the next-to-last stair and land on her knees in the middle of Lyle's back. Air whooshed out of him, and he managed only a small groan of pain. His left arm was crossed under his body and his right arm lay close against his side, the automatic pistol grasped in his fingers. Jane brought her hands down on Lyle's right wrist, pinning it to the floor with her weight. Momentum from her leap carried her into the wall too, but she hardly felt the impact on her shoulder. She yanked Lyle's right arm upward in back as hard as she could, twisting his hand at the same time. He gasped, and the gun slipped out of his fingers. She snatched it off the floor and stood up in one fluid motion.

Grasping the edge of the duct tape across her mouth with her fingernails, she ripped it loose. Her lips and the flesh around her mouth stung, but she was too angry to care.

Lyle lay gasping for breath. He turned his head slowly so he could look at her. "Up!" she commanded.

"I think you broke something," he wheezed. He tried to move his right arm and winced with pain.

She kicked him in the ribs, and realized she wanted to go on kicking him, but stopped herself. "Up! Now." She held the gun pointed at his head.

He groaned again and rolled onto his right side so he could look at her as he maneuvered his left arm out from under him. "Come on, Jane," he said, almost whispering, "you wouldn't want to shoot me. You—"

"Wouldn't I?" She pointed the pistol at his heart.

Lyle shook his head vigorously. "Don't do it. You don't want to go to jail." He stopped to catch his breath. "And anyway, you probably don't even know how to use that gun. You might hurt yourself."

"I have an uncle who's good with these. He thought his daughters and his nieces ought to know how to use guns, just in case. Now, I'm going to count to three. One—"

Lyle held out his hand, palm toward her, in a signal to wait. She retreated to the step just above the landing, looking down on him. Slowly he got to his knees, then stood, keeping his left hand against the wall to steady himself. He glowered at her, looking into her eyes, apparently trying to intimidate her. It took no more than two or three seconds for him to realize that was not going to work with this woman either. He looked away to glance down the stairs.

"I'm coming down right behind you," Jane said. "Don't be stupid enough to try anything. Don't try to surprise me. I'm quicker than you are. In fact, don't do *anything* unless I tell you to do it." She stepped down onto the landing again and motioned with the pistol.

She followed him down staying to the wall side of the stairway, keeping the pistol pointed at his back. He limped slightly. She didn't know whether to believe he was actually hurt, or whether it was a sham to try to put her off guard.

When they reached the bottom and he stepped up to the door, she said, "Stop." She eased up close behind him and put the barrel of the pistol against his back. "Listen, and think carefully about what I say. If the two of you have taken away my reason for living . . . " She stopped, willing herself not to cry. "Why should I care whether you live or die? I haven't used this gun on you because I also want Greg. I want both of you to pay. But if I have to shoot, it will be you first." She paused to let her words sink in. "Put your hands in your coat pockets—carefully."

He did as she had told him.

"Don't move until I say so."

Jane stared at the door in front of them, wishing she could see through it. She had no clear idea of what she was going to do next. Matt was out there, maybe needing help right now. Time could be running out for him, or maybe. . . . *No!* She wanted to push Lyle aside and rush through the door.

But Greg was out there too.

She moved the pistol up Lyle's spine to the base of his skull. "Now, you're going to open that door slowly and we're going to walk out side by side. I'm going to keep the gun covered up, but remember, it will be aimed at your ribs."

He looked over his shoulder at her, trying to appear menacing again. "If you do anything to me, Greg will kill you."

"Really, Lyle? You know Greg. Do you honestly think he would care if I had to shoot you? Would he rush you to the hospital, or even try to stop the bleeding before he left you behind?"

The look on his face told Jane that her question had hit home; Lyle wasn't sure what Greg might do.

She took a deep breath and prodded him in the back with the pistol. "Go."

10

Lyle pushed the door open slowly. "Wider," Jane said. She eased out the door quickly just half a step behind him, her left hand and arm shielding the gun she held pointed at his side.

The fog was thick enough that she could not see Greg clearly across the narrow street. He stood on the opposite curb. The angle of illumination from the streetlight overhead left his face and the front of his body in shadow. She could not see whether he held his gun in his hand.

The figure of a man lay stretched on the pavement to Greg's left. Jane wanted to run to him, to see if she could still help him, but she knew if Greg were holding his gun, she might never make it across the street. She had to get close enough to disarm Greg—or shoot him, if there were no other choice. She wanted to watch his eyes for some sign of what he might do, but she could not see them.

Sweat was running down her back, and there was a growing knot in her stomach.

They were twenty feet from Greg when Lyle suddenly dropped to his knees in the street.

"Take her out, Greg," he screamed. "She's got my gun! Shoot!"

Jane stepped quickly out of Lyle's reach and swung the pistol toward Greg.

"Shoot her!" Lyle screamed again. "She's got my gun."

Jane tightened her finger on the trigger of the pistol almost involuntarily, and that automatic response scared her. As much as she had reason to hate these men, she was revolted by the fact that she was ready to kill another human being. How much of a pull would it take to make the gun in her hand go off?

But Greg did not move. His answer was cutting: "Actually, Lyle, I was hoping you might be able to handle the situation for once. I suppose that was asking too much?"

A tall figure stepped out from behind the garbage container. He held a pistol pointed at Greg's head. "J?" he said.

Jane gasped. "Matt!" She pointed the pistol she held at Lyle again and kept it trained on him as she walked quickly to her husband's side. She did not take her hands off the weapon so she could touch him, but she stood close enough to feel his arm and his leg and his hip against her. "I thought you were . . . " She paused to blink away the tears that wanted to come again, and glanced down at the figure on the ground. "Who is *that?*"

"He called himself Stretch. He said he lives here. I had to pay him off so I could leave the package in that container. He said everything in there is his."

"Is he . . . dead?"

"I don't know. I haven't had time to check. Can you? I'll keep an eye on these two."

Jane knelt beside the man on the ground. His chest seemed to be rising and falling slowly beneath the grimy shirt. She held two fingers to his neck beneath his jaw. "His pulse is strong." She took his arm and shook it, then patted his cheek. There was no response. She looked up at Matt and shrugged.

He glanced at the handcuffs on his wife's wrists. "Who has the key to those?"

She pointed Lyle's pistol in Greg's direction. "He does." Greg shifted uneasily, as though worried about what she might do with the weapon. "That's Greg," she added. "The other one is Lyle."

Matt moved so that Greg could see him from the corner of his eye. "Give—very carefully."

Slowly Greg reached into his left pants pocket, retrieved the key, and held it out at arm's length.

"Drop it," Matt said. "At my feet."

Greg dropped the key and Jane knelt to scoop it up. She held Lyle's pistol out to Matt. "Can you take this while I unlock them?"

"Put it in my jacket pocket," he answered without taking his eyes off of the other two men. He gestured to Greg with the pistol he held. "Face the garbage container. Put your hands behind your head."

Greg's face was expressionless, but Jane knew that behind those empty eyes, he was probably trying to find a way to manipulate the situation somehow to his advantage. He did not respond to Matt's command immediately, but turned to look at him as though to size him up. What he saw evidently convinced him that cooperation was his safest course for now. There was no chance he would win in a physical struggle with Matt Randall. He said nothing as he turned toward the container and put his hands on the back of his head.

Jane started to slip Lyle's pistol into the pocket of Matt's jacket. "Wait," Matt said, "put it on safety first."

"How do I do that?"

Lyle gaped at her. "You said your uncle taught you . . . "

"I said he *wanted* to teach us," Jane answered. "I didn't say I paid close attention. I hate these things."

"Give me Lyle's gun," Matt said. He switched Greg's pistol to his left hand and took Lyle's pistol from her with his right. He glanced down at Greg's weapon long enough to push the SAFETY button, then slipped it into his jacket pocket.

Jane fit the handcuff key into the cuff on her left wrist and opened it. Matt glanced at what she was doing, then spoke to Lyle."Your pistol looks like maybe a 9 millimeter. How many rounds does the magazine hold? I'm guessing nine at least."

"Yeah—nine," Lyle answered sullenly. Greg looked at him disapprovingly.

Matt pointed the gun toward Greg, sure the other man would see the gesture out of the corner of his eye. "Before either of you thinks about trying something, remember that I'll use every one of these if I need to."

"It only takes one," Jane said as she freed her other wrist. "That's what Greg told me when he wanted to help me remember who was in control."

"Are you okay?" Matt asked softly. "Did they hurt you in any way?"

"Not seriously. Greg enjoyed trying to terrify me, and Lyle enjoyed pushing me around. They weren't going to let us live to talk about this. Lyle's job was to make sure we disappeared. He was going to kill you quickly, and then he had special plans for me. He couldn't wait to tell me all about them."

Matt looked at Lyle darkly. "Our room service waiter from last night."

"I figured that out from something he said. Apparently, the wine he brought was drugged—or poisoned."

"Why am I not surprised? And I'll bet Lyle was the one who had so much fun calling me."

"Yes—and making me listen."

Matt gestured toward Greg's back. "I'm guessing he was the one who tried to get into our room with a key card in the middle of the night."

"Last night?" Jane looked surprised. "You didn't tell me."

"I didn't want to worry you. Bad decision on my part to leave you out. It won't happen again." He gestured at Lyle with the pistol. "Move. Over by the container."

Lyle started to stand.

"No. Stay down, and put your hands behind your head," Matt ordered.

"On my knees?" Lyle looked at the pavement in front of him. "There's broken glass! You're out of your . . . " He stopped as Matt took a step closer and aimed the pistol at the center of his chest.

Never before in his life, Matt thought, had he wanted so much to make someone feel pain. It was wrong, it went against everything he tried to live by, but he couldn't deny what he felt. "Lyle, you're lucky I'm trying so hard to control myself. I have your gun in my hand, and I can lift more than you weigh. Do you have any idea what I'd like to do to the man who had plans for my wife?"

"She's lying!" Lyle burst out. "I never said anything . . . " The anger he saw in Matt's eyes and face made him go silent.

"Stay off your feet. Don't think about trying to run."

Lyle winced as he carefully picked his way on his knees through the glass.

"Down, on your face. Jane is going to put the handcuff on your right wrist. Things will work out best for both you and Greg if you cooperate instead of making us handle this another way," Matt said slowly and deliberately. "J, make it as tight as you can."

Jane put one knee down on Lyle's back while she fixed the handcuff in place.

"Now, do you see the shaft that goes down to the metal wheel on the bottom of that container? Wrap the chain of the handcuffs around that shaft."

Jane did as he suggested, then stood and moved away. Lyle was left with little room to move his wrist.

"Since these two like working as a team," Matt said, "we'll keep them close together. Down, Greg. There's room for one more."

"On the *ground?*" Greg said as he turned around. "This is a $350 blazer, and these slacks . . . " He left the sentence unfinished as he saw the same thing Lyle had seen in Matt's eyes. He sat down and stretched out on his back next to Lyle.

Matt kept the pistol pointed at Greg's face as he moved closer. "I'm going to put the other handcuff on you. Do you understand what I said to Lyle about cooperating?"

Greg said nothing, but slowly he extended his right arm up toward Lyle's.

"Lock up his left arm, Matt. He's left-handed," Jane said.

"Good thinking. Roll over, Greg."

"Are you sure you want to handle things this way, Matt? The people who sent us will just take harsher measures next time."

Matt gestured with the pistol. "Roll over."

Slowly, Greg complied. Matt put one knee in the middle of his back and held the pistol behind Greg's head as he locked the man's left wrist tightly in place.

"Matt, I'm suggesting that you consider your own best interests," Greg said. "We need to talk this out and find another solution."

Matt put the pistol on safety, shoved it into his waistband, then took hold of Greg's right arm and pulled it up hard in an arm lock. He bent down close to Greg's face. "Yeah, now that we're all comfortable, we'll talk this out. *Who took my brother? Where is he?*"

Jane gasped. "They took Doug too?"

"They called my parents and told them Doug wouldn't be coming home unless I give up what they want. They called me and let me hear him before they threatened to kill him," Matt answered. "Greg, the look on your face just now made me think this is a surprise to you. But I'm sure you have a good idea who would take my brother. Where would they have him?"

Greg tried to shrug. "I couldn't say, Matt."

"If you didn't know they took my brother, you should be worrying right now about why they left you out. But I think you'll know who did it. Tell me—now!"

"*They* took your brother? *They're* hiding him? Who is this *they* you're talking about, Matt? I don't understand."

Matt increased his upward pressure on Greg's arm. Greg winced, then made his face passive again. Matt leaned even closer. "Try again. Who has him, and where?"

Greg thought for several seconds before he answered. "I might be able to help you, but you'd have to let me go first."

Matt shoved the arm forward sharply Greg moaned and tried to squirm upward to relieve the pain, but Matt's weight would not let him. "*Who, and where?*"

"If somebody's got your brother, I can't do anything about that," Greg answered through gritted teeth. "If you don't do what they say, he's probably history. You have your wife back. Hurting me won't get you anything else."

Matt put his other hand on Greg's neck and pushed down, slowly increasing the pressure. Greg squirmed again and gasped for breath.

Stretch moaned. Matt turned to glance at the homeless man and was struck instead by what he saw in Jane's face—a mixture of fascination and horror as she watched what her husband was doing. Matt looked down at his hand on Greg's neck. It shocked him to realize how much he wanted to make this man suffer too. Slowly he released his hold and sat up straight.

He turned to look at Lyle. "Maybe I should ask your partner what he knows." He stood and stepped over Greg to put one foot on each side of Lyle.

Lyle turned his head trying to look up at Matt. "I'd tell you if I knew anything about your brother, but I don't!"

"If he knew anything," Jane said, "he probably would have spilled it when he was taunting me."

"I only did what Greg told me," Lyle whined. Greg turned his head to look at Lyle threateningly. But it was plain that Lyle was more afraid of the man standing over him at the moment than he was of Greg.

How much, Matt wondered, could he expect to get out of Greg? *If he didn't know about Doug's kidnapping, then he probably doesn't know where they're holding him. But it has to be the same people who sent him after Jane and me.* If a man like Greg had any information, the only way to get it out of him might be to break some of his fingers or an arm, or make him bleed. Matt knew he could not do that, even to these two men—especially after seeing the look on Jane's face.

He tried another tactic. "I guess we'll have to leave this to the police.

Let's see—they'll have Lyle for kidnapping . . . some kind of weapons charge, and—"

"Whatever they call it when you knock someone around," Jane said.

"And Greg," Matt continued. "Kidnapping, and attempted murder, to start. They'll check your gun to see if it's tied to any other crimes. And they'll probably dig into your past to see if you've ever been involved in anything like this before."

"He talked about other women," Jane said. "How many, Greg?"

"They won't find a thing they could use against me," Greg muttered.

"If my brother dies, they'll probably be able to charge you with some kind of kidnapping and murder conspiracy. They've got so much on you that you might want to buy yourself a break. Tell me where my brother is. I'll tell them you helped."

"Let me go and I'll think about it," Greg answered.

"We can't work with a liar, Greg. You don't know where he is, do you? But you know who's behind this."

Greg thought for a moment before answering. "If they don't hear from me that you've given us what we want, then I won't be responsible for what happens to your brother." He paused. "I won't be responsible for what happens to you either."

"You're in no position to make threats. And if I gave you what you're looking for, it wouldn't change anything, would it? They'd still kill Doug—and us." Matt squatted down so he could look Greg in the eyes. "You've blown your assignment. How are they going to feel about that? And if you're not going to help find my brother, there's not much need for me to keep the two of *you* alive."

Lyle craned his neck to look at Matt over Greg's back. "I already said I'll tell you anything I know—but I don't know about your brother!"

The look Greg gave Lyle would have scared him, Jane thought, if both men had been free. But Lyle obviously feared that Matt really would kill him, because that's what Lyle would do if their situations were reversed.

Greg turned his head to look up at Matt. "I don't think you're the kind who could kill someone and just walk away," he said coolly.

Matt looked at Jane and shrugged helplessly. Then he stood suddenly and slammed his hand on the side of the garbage container. Greg and Lyle both flinched at the *bang!*

Stretch moaned once more, and stirred. Jane moved to kneel by his side and patted his cheek again. "Hello?"

Stretch did not answer.

"We'll come back with the police," Matt said to Jane. "But we need to make sure Greg and Lyle can't find any way to get free while they're waiting."

Jane bent down, reached into Lyle's coat pocket, and pulled out his small roll of duct tape. "This could help."

"Good. Now if we had something to tie up their free hands . . . " Matt thought for a moment, then walked around to the front of the garbage container, reached in, and pulled out a discarded broom. "Give me the tape," he said as he walked around beside Greg and knelt on the pavement. He stretched Greg's right arm out behind his back and used the tape to bind the broom handle tightly to Greg's wrist. Then he handed the tape to Jane. "You want to take care of Lyle?"

While she taped Lyle's left wrist to the other end of the broom handle, Matt patted Greg's hip pockets, then reached under his chest. He lifted Greg's right shoulder, found the wallet and cell phone in his inside coat pocket, and pulled them out. "We're going to find out everything we can about Greg before we go to the police, and we're going to see just who he's been calling."

"Going to steal my watch too?" Greg sneered.

"No, we'll leave that," Matt answered. "Looks like you're going to have some time on your hands here."

"Cute," Greg muttered.

"Let's find out all about Lyle too," Jane said. She extracted his wallet from his hip pocket, then tugged the front of his sport coat out from under him so she could reach his cell phone. She found hers also and slipped it back into her pants pocket.

"You keep their phones," Matt said, handing her Greg's. He took Lyle's wallet from her hands. "I'll keep this. I want to find out more about the man who kidnapped my wife."

Lyle's brow furrowed. "Listen, Greg told me—"

"Shut up, Lyle. You're better off if I don't hear *anything* out of your mouth right now."

Jane bent to look down at Greg, who refused to make eye contact. "If we leave them here like this, they may start yelling for help as soon as we're gone." She held up the duct tape. "They put some of this over my mouth so I couldn't scream when you were out here."

Matt nodded. "Yeah—good idea."

"Hey! Who's she?" The voice came from behind them. Matt and Jane turned to look at Stretch. He was up on his elbows watching them. He said to Matt, in a loud stage whisper, "Who's she?"

"My wife."

Stretch struggled to stand. Jane hurried to his side. "Careful. You've been hurt."

Stretch touched his hand to the back of his head. "Yeah." He looked at the dark stain on his fingers. "But I've had worse." He tried again to stand. Jane put her hand on his arm. He brushed it off and struggled to his feet. Then he gave her something like a small bow. "Pleased to meet ya."

He looked up and down the street. "Where's the guy . . . "

Matt pointed wordlessly at the two men lying by the garbage container.

Slowly, trying to be sure he was steady, Stretch walked toward them. He stared down at Greg. "Yeah. That's him." Then his eyes went wide as he remembered, and he stepped back suddenly. "He had a *gun!*"

"Not anymore." Matt took hold of Stretch's arm as he swayed.

Stretch pointed at Greg. "He oughta be in jail."

"We'll take care of that. I promise you, he'll get what he deserves. Right now, we need to get you some help."

Stretch shook his head. "I'll be all right." He touched the back of his head again. "I don't think it's bleedin' anymore."

"You need to see a doctor. You might have a concussion." Matt retrieved the hat with the block A on it and put it back on Stretch's head, explaining to Jane: "I had to give him this so I could use his container. His head gets cold at night."

Stretch grinned ruefully. "Don't have as much hair as I used to."

"Just give us a minute with these two," Matt said, nodding at Greg and Lyle.

Jane knelt next to Greg and stretched a long piece of the duct tape tightly over his mouth. The man's eyes were blank, but she knew what was going on in his mind. He was trying to think of a way to regain control of the situation—and what he would do to them if he could.

When she knelt to put tape over Lyle's mouth, he tried to turn his head away. She took hold of the short hairs on the back of his head and turned it back. "Ow!" he protested. She put the tape on tightly. There was no mistaking the hate in Lyle's eyes, but as he glanced momentarily toward Matt, the hate was mingled with fear. "I know," Jane said, "you'd like to tell me exactly what you think of me right now. Maybe next time we meet—and I hope that won't be until I'm in court testifying against you." She took hold of his handcuffed wrist and tugged at it. The weight of the garbage container kept it from moving.

Stretch shook off Matt's helping hand and took a few tentative steps toward Sixth Street.

Matt walked over to the garbage container, reached in, and took out the wrapped package. He held the package out so Greg could look at it. The package made rustling noises when he shook it. "You'll never know," he said, looking into Greg's eyes.

He gave the garbage container an experimental shove to be sure it wouldn't move, then smiled thinly at the two men handcuffed to it. "Don't go anywhere before we come back."

Matt and Jane began to walk away, past the wall mural, with Stretch following. When they reached the corner by the hotel, Matt turned to Stretch and pointed across the street. "You know the mission over there."

Stretch nodded. "Yeah."

"Go over there and show them your head. Tell them you need help," Matt said. "Think you can make it on your own?"

"Yeah."

Matt and Jane watched as he shuffled past the Hotel Birch and on toward the corner.

They started walking up Sixth Street toward Market, making their way around homeless men clustered in two or three of the doorways. Jane turned to look back. The lights of the rescue mission and the other buildings across the street could be seen only dimly through the dense fog, but she could see a tall figure just arriving at the front door of the mission. She glanced back once more just before they rounded the corner onto Market Street. She could barely see the shape of the hotel where she had been held prisoner.

She pointed to the wrapped package Matt held. "What is it they want so badly that they're willing to kill for it?"

Matt shrugged. "I have no idea. It's still a mystery to me." He handed the box to her.

She was relieved to hear Matt say he did not know what the kidnappers wanted—to know that she had been right about him all along, despite the doubt Greg had tried to plant in her head. She shook the box. "What's in here? It feels so light."

"A couple of tourist brochures. And a note," Matt answered. "The note says if I'm still alive when they read it, I'll do my best to help them find what they want, but only when they bring you to me." He paused. "And if I'm dead, it begs them to let you go because you don't know anything about what they're hunting for."

Jane squeezed his hand. He stopped walking and turned to look into her eyes. "J, I . . . please forgive me. I took a terrible chance. If it had gone wrong . . . but it was the only way I could think of to get to you."

She touched his cheek softly with her fingertips. "I knew you would come for me. It might have been the only chance we had. I don't think anything else would have stopped them from killing both of us."

"I think you're right." He started walking again, holding tightly to her hand. "But they've still got Doug." He paused. "And whatever it is they're looking for, they killed Cole while they were trying to find it."

"*Cole Brewster?* Cole is dead?" Jane had thought there was nothing more about the day's events that could shock her. "How many . . . how far can this go? Do you think Greg could be right—that somebody else might come looking for us?"

"I don't know." He wanted Jane to feel secure right now. "You know Greg's a liar." But Matt still wasn't sure how much the kidnappers might know about them and their movements. "I hope we can find some way to stop them before anyone else gets hurt." He took the package from her, crushed the box in his hands, and stuffed it into a curbside trashcan. Then he pounded his fist on top of the can. Jane looked startled. "They've still got Doug! I was hoping to get information to could help the police find him," Matt explained. "Now I don't know what to do."

She took his hand. "When the police hear what we know, maybe that will help them."

As they neared the convenience store on Market, he asked, "Have you had anything to eat today?"

"A few fries and part of a soft drink. I was afraid to take anything else they offered me."

He led her into the store and bought a package of granola bars and two small bottles of milk. As they walked on down the street, he opened one of the granola bars and handed it to Jane. "Not much, but it'll give you some energy."

"I need to find a restroom too."

"There's one up here in the shopping center."

She gasped in recognition as she looked up at the sign on the building, then pointed across the street. "Our hotel is just over there. I thought we were far away. Lyle drove me around for about an hour."

"Probably trying to confuse you."

"Why don't we just go over to the hotel?"

He looked in that direction, thinking for several seconds before he answered. "I'm not sure that's a good idea. They knew I had talked to Security there. They knew the first time I left the room looking for you. They knew when I made telephone calls, and who I called. They seemed to know everything I did while I was in the hotel."

"Matt, who *are* these people?"

"I don't know. But it sounded like they also knew when I got calls on my cell phone—maybe even what I said."

"How could they know that?"

He shrugged. "After they took Doug, I got a call from Montie wanting to know what's going on with us. I was afraid to tell him anything because I wondered who could be listening. Then right after Montie talked to me, I got a call from the people holding Doug. They told me not to be stupid and give information to the police. So if we call the police right now, I have to wonder if the kidnappers are going to know somehow." He paused. "I've got to think this out—see if there's a safe way we can do something to help my brother. Greg was probably right—Doug's kidnappers will want to hear something out of San Francisco soon. In the meantime, if I do the wrong thing, they may kill him."

Jane took another bite of the granola bar and chewed it as he steered her toward the shopping center. He led her to the bottom level and down a hallway. Ahead of them at the end was a door marked WOMEN, and on the right, a door marked MEN. "I'll be right outside the door when you're through," he said.

Matt waited until she had gone inside, then stepped into the men's room. He was back outside the door to the women's restroom in just over two minutes.

While he waited, he checked for new messages on his phone. There was a text from Montie with a phone number. The message read: "Call ASAP." He still couldn't be sure whether his telephone conversations were secure. But could someone intercept text messages? He thought that was not possible without the kind of sophisticated equipment usually available only to national security or police agencies. Could the kidnappers have anything like that? He weighed the risk of a message against the need to let everyone at home know what was happening. Finally, he sent a short text that he hoped would put Montie on the right track: "Jane freed from kidnappers here. Still don't know what they want. Connections to Doug or Cole?"

He glanced at his watch when he was finished, and estimated that Jane had been gone about six minutes. Then it was seven, then eight, and he began to worry because the last time he had let her out of his sight today, she had disappeared.

At ten minutes, he couldn't wait any longer. He pushed the door of the restroom open slightly, hoping there was no one else inside, and called: "Hello? J?"

No one answered, but he heard a cough, then water running, and then he could hear sobbing. He stepped inside. Jane was standing in front of one of the sinks, her head bowed, crying. He walked quickly to her. "What's wrong?"

She put her arms around him and clung to him without answering, her chest heaving as she tried to catch her breath between sobs. She was shaking. He rubbed her back lightly. "It's all right. Everything's going to be all right." He paused. "I've been worrying all day that I'd do the wrong thing and they'd hurt you, or worse, and if that had happened, I could never have . . . but it's all right. We're together now."

Her sobbing subsided. "I know." She wiped at her eyes, then put her hands on his face and pulled him down to kiss him. "I'm okay, now that I'm with you. It was just—today . . . the stress—everything. I was scared, for both of us. It took everything I had to keep myself together and try to think straight so I could grab the chance to get away if it came. And now—now that I'm away from Greg and Lyle—I started thinking about what *almost* happened. It made me sick—literally. If I had lost you . . . "

"Yeah." He stroked her hair. "Lots of feelings. I can't tell you how happy

I feel right now holding *you*. Then I feel guilty when I remember where Doug is. But so far I can't think of anything we could do—"

They both turned to look as the door creaked open. A female security guard, an African-American woman with graying hair, stared at them from the doorway. "What's going on in here?" She thought for a moment and the expression on her face went from curious to angry. "Out! Both of you."

"I'm sorry," Matt apologized. "My wife wasn't feeling well. I heard her in here, crying, and I, uh . . . "

Jane gestured toward one of the stalls. "I threw up. He was just trying to help me."

"Are you sick?" the woman asked.

"It's tension—stress."

"We're on our honeymoon, and she was, uh . . . just mugged," Matt explained. "Out there." He nodded in the direction of the street.

"Three days ago I was standing in my wedding dress telling everybody thanks for coming to the reception," Jane said. "And today . . . "

The guard walked toward them, looking at Jane closely. "I'm sorry. Are you all right now, hon?"

Jane nodded. "I have a couple of bruises on my knees where I fell."

"Do you want me to call the police? Could you give them a description of the man?"

Matt answered. "He was about five-eight, about 180 pounds, light brown hair. Do you think that would help?"

The woman thought about what Matt had said, then looked at Jane. "I'll have to ask both of you to step out of here. The mall is closing now. But there are some tables around the corner in the food court where you can sit for a few minutes to make sure you're feeling all right. When you're ready, I'll let you out into the BART station."

They sat and ate two of the granola bars from the bag he carried, and she stuffed the others into her jacket pocket. He drank one of the bottles of milk, but she declined the other. "I don't think I could handle it right now."

When they walked to the glass door that led into the underground station, the guard smiled at her. "Okay now?"

"Better," Jane answered. "Thank you for being so kind."

They walked past the BART ticket booth in the nearly silent station. A few homeless men sat or lay on the floor in the passageways leading to the exits. Matt put their spare bottle of milk down on the floor hoping someone who needed it might find it.

One of the homeless men rose from his place and stepped in front of them as they crossed under Market Street. "Hey, buddy," he said to Matt, "could you give a brother some help? Can you spare a little change?"

"Sorry, I'm out," Matt answered.

Jane shrugged. "I'm not carrying any change either. Sorry."

The man inspected them carefully. Slowly, his expression contorted into anger. "People dressed like you got plenty—and you can't help somebody who's got nothin'? You walk around San Francisco droppin' lots of money in places like that fancy mall where a guy like me can't go without some-body followin' him around. You think anybody who can't stay in one of them hotels where you—"

He stopped suddenly and began to back away. "Hey, it's cool, man. We're cool." His gaze was fixed on something at Matt's waist level. "I'm out of here, okay?" He turned and headed for the far exit.

Matt looked down. The bottom of his jacket had hiked up and the butt of Lyle's pistol protruded from underneath it. He quickly pulled the jacket down. "Come on," he said, and led Jane toward the near exit.

They walked out into the small plaza with the tables and sunshades. Pi-geons stirred and cooed along the railing overlooking the plaza as Matt and Jane climbed up the stairs to street level. A block or so away on Powell Street, they could see the lights of their hotel through the fog. Instead of heading that way, he turned down Market.

They were alone in the fog as they walked.

"Where are we going?" Jane asked.

"I don't know." Matt put his arm around her and pulled her close. "But wherever it is, we're going to be together."

11

Greg shoved the broom handle back in Lyle's direction angrily. He was try-ing to learn whether there was a way to free himself from it, but Lyle kept working against him. *Idiot! If you'd stop fighting me, I could get free.*

Painfully, Greg had managed to work his wrist enough to roll down the edge of the duct tape. He could almost curl the fingers of his right hand to touch the broom handle—but not quite. He had tried several times to plant the far end of the broomstick solidly against the pavement on the other side of Lyle so he could wiggle his wrist back and forth against the tape that held it. But each time Greg had thought he had the broomstick planted so it would not move, Lyle had fouled things up by knocking it loose. The one time Greg had been able to twist his wrist against the tape, it had hurt almost more than he could bear. Even so, he had thought he was making progress—until Lyle knocked the broomstick loose again.

It was no use trying to plant his end of the broomstick on the ground because his end held nothing but broken straw.

Finally, he stopped moving and pulled the stick down hard against their backs to get Lyle's attention, then glared at the other man and shook his head vigorously. Lyle got the point at last; he lay still.

Greg tried another idea. He moved onto his right side, facing Lyle as close as he could, with his right arm extending upward from the elbow behind his back. Then, slowly, he drew his legs up into the fetal position and straightened his right arm as far as he could to push the broom handle down toward his ankles. If he could just work the long handle down far enough to slip his left foot over the top of it . . .

Lyle moaned in pain and moved, pulling the stick back up toward his waist. Greg shouted behind the tape, and if Lyle couldn't understand the words, he at least understood the meaning. He stopped struggling and looked at Greg, who glared angrily at him and shook his head once more.

On the third try, Greg managed to get his left foot over the long handle. He stretched out his legs and turned face down again. Now the broomstick passed between his legs. The far end of it lay across the back of Lyle's legs.

Lyle whined again with pain as Greg put downward pressure on the broomstick trying to snap it in two.

* * *

Matt and Jane turned north off of Market Street with no particular destination in mind. They walked silently through the fog, his arm holding her close. They had walked several blocks when an ornate, brightly colored gate loomed out of the fog, arching over the street just ahead of them. "Chinatown," he said. "This morning I was hoping we could come here for some sightseeing."

They had walked half a block past the gate when he glanced over his shoulder at the vehicle coming slowly out of the fog behind them. Quickly, he took Jane's arm and turned her so they were facing a shop window.

Jane looked up at him curiously. "When did you become a connoisseur of Chinese jade art?"

"When I saw the police car that just went by." He glanced to his right to make sure it had continued up the street. "Montie left me wondering if he might have the San Francisco police looking for me. I'm carrying two other men's wallets and two guns that don't belong to me. That would be hard to explain."

She frowned. "Why would Montie have them looking for *you*?"

"He seemed to think I might have done something that brought all this on. *My* boss is killed. *My* brother is kidnapped. *My* wife is kidnapped— even though he didn't know that until I texted him while you were in the restroom. Your mother left a message that someone broke into our apartment and went through our wedding gifts, but they didn't take anything."

"What are they looking for?"

Matt shrugged. "They've kept saying, '*He* shouldn't have given it to you.' I've tried to think of everything some man gave me. If it's one of the wedding presents, I wouldn't know. Cole gave me my new phone—but it's just a phone. Doug gave us that hard drive with the movies he copied. I wondered if he got into something on the Internet he shouldn't have seen. But how would they find him—or us? And why not just grab *him* first?" He stopped talking and looked her in the eyes. "Any ideas?"

She shook her head.

"We've got to focus on what we know. We need to find a place where we can talk things through without being interrupted."

He led her back toward the Chinese gate. "We're wandering. Let's stay in the area we know instead of getting lost. I think Powell Street is that way." He pointed uphill.

They had walked a block when he stopped next to a building, took her in his arms, and kissed her tenderly. He pressed her tightly against him and lingered a long time on the kiss.

She ended it when she felt him trembling. She backed away enough to look up into his face. His eyes were glistening. A tear ran down his cheek.

"Matt, what's wrong?" She reached up to brush away the tear with her fingers.

"I, ah . . . " He stopped to swallow. "A reality moment. I'm feeling what you felt back there at the shopping center. I started thinking about what Greg and Lyle were planning to do with these guns. And then . . . " He stared off into the fog momentarily and swallowed once more before he looked her in the eyes again. "All day long I felt sick inside worrying about you—about what they might do, about losing you. And then when I learned about Doug, it seemed like . . . I couldn't, uh, take the *pressure!* They kept turning it up, every time I was almost ready to go to the police. And I wasn't sure whether the police could actually help. And if I made the wrong decision, I could get one or both of you killed. And then it was too late to find the police, and I just had to—"

She put her fingers to his lips to stop him from talking. "It's okay." She put her arms around him once more and leaned her head against his chest.

"I took a horrible risk with your life. What if—"

"It's all right. What you did worked out fine." She smiled up at him. "I got your message with that movie line. And I believe in you. I knew you would come for me."

"But what if—"

"No ifs! We're here, we're together, and we're going to stay that way."

"J, I need you to understand something. I'm ashamed and afraid of how

I felt back there with Greg and Lyle. I *wanted* to hurt them when I thought about what they planned to do to you. I thought they deserved to feel some of the fear or pain you probably felt. I had to get away from them because . . . because when I was holding that pistol on Greg and Lyle, the thought came into my mind that it would be so easy just to squeeze a little harder . . . and if I said the gun just went off by accident, who could . . . " He held her close to him once more. "Before today, I would never have thought anything like that. It scared me."

"Matt, I felt that way too after I thought Greg had shot you out in that street. When I got Lyle's gun away from him, I told him I would shoot him if he gave me any trouble—but I wanted to get Greg too. I wanted *both* of them to pay for what they had done. And if they somehow killed me instead . . . well, I wouldn't have cared very much. I wanted to be with you." She kissed him lightly. "If I can just have that—being with you—it will always be enough for me."

He stroked her hair softly. "You didn't pull the trigger when you had the chance. Neither did I. They would have—but we can't let this make us like them."

"No. When they had me in that room and I prayed for help, I thought a lot about what I would do if I got out of there alive. I don't want to waste any part of my life hating them, or living in fear of what they could do. Now that I have you back, I'm going to *live* every second I'm with you. *That's* what I want to cling to now. Do you understand what I mean?"

"I understand." Matt kissed her again.

"Come on," she said, pulling him by the hand as she started uphill again. "Let's find someplace we can *sit* and talk—someplace warm."

They turned down Powell Street, in the direction of their hotel again, and walked about a block and a half when he said, "Wait. Look in the window." They were outside a small café with only a few customers left inside, and there was a booth in the corner where two people could be out of sight from the street. "In here."

* * *

Greg dragged the broken broom handle across his back, grabbed the edge of the duct tape covering his mouth, and ripped it away. It hurt. His left thigh was probably bruised where he had pushed against the broomstick to break it, and his jacket was probably ruined now. When he caught up with Matt and Jane, he would make them pay for leaving him like this.

He turned to look at Lyle, who was trying to move his left hand into position to pull the tape off his own mouth. "I don't know whether it got through to you what kind of position we're in," Greg said. "If Boris told somebody else to grab Matt's brother, that means he thinks we're not getting the job done. We'd better prove to him we can do it, and we don't have a lot of time."

Greg maneuvered his right hand under his coat in back. Fortunately, Matt had not discovered the knife he carried, and Jane must have forgotten about it. Greg had looked for an opportunity to pull his knife while Matt was holding the gun, but it seemed too risky.

He managed to slip the knife out and flick open its blade. "As soon as I can get this tape off my wrist, we've got to find a way to get out of these handcuffs. They were *your* idea, so I hope you have a suggestion— something *useful.*"

* * *

The chicken soup was warm, and it helped to settle her stomach. She sipped it eagerly.

Matt sat watching her. "Better?"

"Yes. You need to eat yours."

"I will. I'm just enjoying the fact that I'm having dinner with *you.*" He took a spoonful of his soup. It was good—but anything would have tasted good right now, sitting here with the woman he loved, warm and safe. This day seemed almost unreal.

Almost.

"We've got to decide what to do about Greg and Lyle," he said.

"We've got to make sure they're in prison and can't get out."

"Yeah." His brow furrowed. "I texted Montie about getting you free, and I have a message from him wanting details. No one at home knows what's been going on with us. We ought to call. I told your dad we'd call when we could tonight."

Jane pulled her phone out of her jacket pocket and dialed her parents' number. "Hi, Mom," she said. "Yes, we're all right. But it's been a hard day." She listened for a long time. Then: "Yes, it's awful about Matt's brother.

We're *very* worried. Is there any news?" She listened, then looked at Matt and shook her head. "Okay. If you learn anything, call us right away. If we can't answer for some reason, we'll call you back. You'd better get some rest now. . . . Yes. I love you. 'Bye." She ended the call.

"She doesn't know what happened to you?" Matt asked.

"I guess Montie hasn't talked to my parents yet. She seemed so upset about your brother and the break-in that I couldn't add to her stress right now. We can tell them everything after Doug's free." She handed her phone to Matt.

He held it in his hand looking at it speculatively.

"What?"

"Was Lyle, or Greg, ever out of sight with your phone? Do you think it's possible they could have installed some kind of bug on it?"

"No, they . . . " She stopped and thought. "I don't know."

"I don't want to call home using one of our phones—just in case. I was thinking that under the circumstances Greg couldn't object if I use his."

She pulled her two captors' cell phones out of her jacket pocket. Lyle's was older and beaten up. Greg's looked brand new. It was a cheap, basic flip phone, the kind people buy with prepaid minutes. Matt took it from her and turned it over in his hands. "This can't be the phone that our $350-tailored-sport-coat-guy carries around every day."

Jane frowned. "I thought that too. He wears a gold Rolex watch. Nothing but the finest for Greg."

"Yeah." Matt flipped it open. "I wonder if there's a password? Doesn't look like it."

"I didn't see Greg use one. Lyle's phone has a password—but I know what it is."

Matt looked at her questioningly. "How? He didn't tell you?"

"I watched them, trying to find out all I could about them—trying to find any edge that could help me."

"Being smart is just *one* of the reasons I love you. And by the way, you didn't tell me how you ended up with Lyle's gun."

"He was having fun pushing me around on the stairs and taunting me about what he thought Greg had done to you," she said grimly. "He didn't expect a girl to push back."

Matt smiled. "His mistake. They're going to be sorry they underestimated you."

He punched in his father's mobile number on Greg's phone. The call was answered on the first ring.

"Dad, is there any news about Doug?"

"Matt! No, not yet. We haven't heard a thing. But Montie told us about Jane. Tell us how you . . . oh, wait." The next voice he heard was Montie's. "Matt, what's going on? Why didn't you tell us about Jane immediately?"

"Because they warned me not to tell the police. And they seemed to know every time I made a call and who I was talking to."

"I doubt they could really do that. What happened with Jane's kidnappers? What can you tell us about them?"

"Two guys. One's a street punk, the other's more sophisticated—the brains of the operation. But they're working for somebody else—I think the same people behind Doug's kidnapping."

"Why did they pick on the two of you? Do you have any prior connection with—"

"Montie! Don't even go there! I can't understand why you'd even ask me that question. Do you honestly think I'd do anything to involve Jane in something like this?"

"I'm following procedure, Matt. I have to check everything. In a typical kidnapping case, the victim often has some connection to—"

"Maybe this isn't your typical kidnapping case. And right now you need to be concentrating on finding my brother."

"Take a breath, Matt. We're monitoring his phone number. No calls so far, and we're having a hard time fixing a location. They may be moving around. I need more information from you. Tell me everything you know. Anything could help."

Was Montie trying to keep him on the line? "Am I talking to my wife's uncle, or to Montie the FBI agent? Are you tracing this call?" Could they trace one of these cheap phones, he wondered. How long would it take?

Montie hesitated before answering. "We have to track every call that comes to this number right now, Matt. You should understand that. What else can you give us to go on?"

"Okay, here's everything I know that could help Doug. When his kidnappers called me, the man who spoke sounded Hispanic and I heard Latino music in the background. I still don't know what they're after, but they keep saying someone gave it to me. You need to go over Cole's office and computer files to see what you can find that he might have given to me.

Doug gave us a hard drive with some recorded music and movies, and I think he downloaded a lot of that from the Internet. Check out the drive. It's there at my parents' house. I'll call back later to see if you found anything. And the people who kidnapped Jane said others in the family could be targets if we didn't cooperate. I think that's why they took Doug." He pushed the button to end the call.

Jane sat watching him with her brow furrowed. It was the look he saw when she was worried about something. "You're thinking I did the wrong thing by not telling him more and not letting him know where we are."

"Well, wouldn't Montie and the FBI have a better chance of helping if they knew *everything* we know?"

Matt thought it over for several seconds. "Okay, I guess that *was* a little too edgy. It's just . . . well, everything that's happened today has made me wonder who I can trust. We'll call Montie back in a few minutes." He took the two wallets out of his jacket pocket and handed her Lyle's. "First, let's find out how much we really know about the two guys who were supposed to kill us. Then we'll give Greg and Lyle to the FBI in a nice package."

* * *

Lyle turned on his side so he could extend his arm toward Greg. "Cut the tape off of *my* arm."

Greg had scooted upward, closer to the garbage container, so he could peer at the handcuff that held his left wrist. If he could insert the point of his knife into the key slot, was there a way he could pick the lock? The idea didn't seem promising.

"Cut this tape off my wrist," Lyle repeated.

Greg looked at him. "Do you have any idea how we could get out of these?"

"If I could use my hand, I might be able to come up with something."

"What does that mean?" Greg moved close enough to reach Lyle's left arm, which was stretched behind his back with the broken piece of broomstick still taped to it.

Lyle let Greg slit the tape around his wrist before he answered. "I have another key—in my right pants pocket," he said as he moved the broomstick to where he could grasp it with his handcuffed right hand. He stripped the tape and the broken stick off of his left wrist.

"You've been holding out on me," Greg said accusingly.

"It's one I carry just in case," Lyle said apologetically. "I never needed it before now." With his free hand, he began to tug at his belt. "If I can just turn my pants around far enough to reach into that pocket . . . "

"Wait a minute. I can do it easier than you can. Move this way." Greg lay on his right side, his left hand still tethered above his head, and reached down with his right hand toward Lyle's pocket. "Closer. I can't reach it."

He was concentrating on what he was doing, looking down at the other man's side, when Lyle asked, "Does Boris know who you hire for jobs like this?"

Greg looked into Lyle's eyes. Lyle looked down at his side as though focusing on what Greg was doing, but Greg knew what was going on in the other man's mind. The little weasel was thinking about how to protect himself.

Once they were free, Lyle would be of little use, Greg realized. As soon as Lyle was out of sight, he would probably scurry off to some hole to hide until this blew over. Meanwhile, if Boris looked for someone to blame, Greg's name would be the only one he had. And if the police ever caught up with Lyle somehow, he would probably spill anything he knew in exchange for a break with some prosecutor. He had been ready to tell Matt Randall everything.

Greg tried to look as threatening as possible while lying on a filthy street chained to a garbage bin. "If it weren't for you, we wouldn't be stuck here. And if Matt and Jane come back with the police, you'll be in just as much trouble as I am. You'd better be thinking about what you can do to help get us out of this."

"*You* were the one who let him—"

"Shut up! *You* slipped up because you were thinking too much about Jane. *You* were the one who talked too much when you thought she wasn't listening. You may think you don't have to worry about Boris because I'm the only one that knows who you are. But Matt and Jane know. You'd better worry about them."

* * *

"Not much here," Jane said, laying Lyle's wallet on the table. "Some gasoline discount receipts, a buy-three-get-one-free card from a hamburger place in Oakland, a checking card, a credit card, sixty-three dollars, and a California driver's license for Lyle Walker." She held up the license. "Except that's not his real name. While he thought I was asleep, he talked about the time when the two of them used to be Leo and Grigori, back in high school."

"Those two were in school together?"

"Hard to believe, isn't it?"

"Almost impossible." Matt began to pull items out of Greg's wallet. "Gold credit card. Preferred customer checking card." He riffled through the bills in the wallet and raised his eyebrows. "Nine hundred twenty dollars in cash. A Colorado driver's license in the name of Gregory Alexander, with a home address in Aspen. Do you suppose he skis?" Matt pulled out a small stack of business cards. "And these: 'Greg Alexander, Jewelry Liquidations, Top Dollar for Your Inventory.'"

"Jewelry really *is* his business! He was talking about jewelry this afternoon. He offered an appraisal of my rings." She held out her left hand. "According to Greg, you have excellent taste in diamonds."

"I'll cherish the compliment." He held up a white plastic card from Greg's wallet. "And this—a key card from some anonymous hotel."

"I heard Lyle talking to him about that big hotel we passed on the cable car line yesterday—the one you told me is so historic."

Matt raised an eyebrow. "Very upscale. It fits his pattern." He began putting items back into Greg's wallet. "The strange thing is what's *not* here. I don't know another man alive who isn't carrying old credit card receipts, notes, or some other junk in his wallet. This wallet looks like it belongs to somebody who's very careful not to have a history."

He put the wallet down on the table and picked up Greg's phone. "And this—a plain phone you could buy in any big box store, cheap, no gadgets, no class. Not Greg's style."

Jane thought for a moment and her eyebrows went up. "Of course! It's *not* Greg's style! It's a phone you could smash or toss in the garbage when you're through with it. Nothing left to trace."

"Just like the wallet: no real information, no history." Matt touched the phone's ON button. "Except—I wonder who Greg's been calling, and who's been calling him." He began scrolling through the phone's call records.

Jane took Lyle's phone out of her jacket pocket and did the same. "Lyle got a couple of calls this morning from a number that's blocked," she said.

"I wouldn't be surprised if it was this phone."

"After that, Lyle made several calls to one number, then a call to your cell phone, then another call to the first number."

"The call history on this phone begins with yesterday. Greg has several calls from one number. He made a couple of calls early today to a number with a Los Angeles area code. Then his last several calls were to my phone." He took Lyle's phone from her and held the two side by side. "Let's see if any of the numbers match." He turned the phones so she could see the two lists. "Look—this number that Lyle called several times is the same number that called Greg at 8:30 this morning."

"I wonder if we could find out whose phone that is."

"I think I know—I think it's our hotel. Greg called someone in the hotel this morning, and later Lyle was calling me, in our room." Matt pulled his smartphone out of his jacket pocket. "I can check the hotel's number."

Jane frowned. "Lyle really enjoyed calling you and making me listen. I don't think I've ever known anyone before who did evil things just because he enjoyed it. Malicious little troll! He enjoyed tormenting—"

"Wait! Go back." Matt had stopped with his finger poised over the display screen of his phone. "Troll?"

"Ugly, evil creature. In fairy tales and fantasy stories, with ogres, and goblins, and—"

"Gnomes!" Matt looked down at his phone and his eyes went wide in recognition.

"What?" she asked.

"That pulled out a memory. I think I know where Cole might have hidden something on this phone!" He moved closer to her so she could see the display screen.

"Something he might have disguised?"

Matt nodded, and pointed to the icon labeled GAMES. "Remember when I was fooling around with this on the flight to San Francisco? I was checking out the games that came on the phone. I was looking at a game called *Gnomes* when you distracted me."

"Silly me. I thought you ought to be paying attention to the woman you just married."

"And you were absolutely right. So I forgot all about this."

"What do gnomes have to do with anything that's been happening to us?"

"They could have *everything* to do with it. 'The gnomes of Zurich.' That's a name somebody once gave to the anonymous bankers who handle a lot of those secret accounts in Switzerland. I can't even remember now why we were talking about it, but Cole once said to me that if he wanted to hide money, he'd put it with the gnomes of Zurich."

Matt opened the GAMES file. "Look at this," he said, tapping on the GNOMES icon. What came up on the screen was an invitation: "Find the Treasure of the Gnomes." It was quickly followed by a question: "HB means?"

She looked at him blankly.

"Think football," he prompted.

"Halfback! What you were."

He entered the answer, and a new question popped up: "Tarzan's girl-friend?"

"Jane."

He typed in her name, and one more question came up: "SS#s?"

"*Your* Social Security number?"

"I only got this far on the plane. Let's find out." He quickly entered the nine digits.

"Congratulations! You're a winner!" flashed across the bottom of the screen.

"I was the only one meant to solve this puzzle," Matt said as a new file popped up on the screen.

The new file was a spreadsheet. Two title lines at the top contained a string of numbers and letters, then a series of words in French below them. The spreadsheet below those lines had two columns with broken strings of numbers.

Matt pointed at the second line in the file. "You studied French. What does this mean?"

"'Studied' may be going a little too far. I took a couple of classes. But that looks like the name of a bank or financial institution."

He pointed at the last word in the name: *Suisse.* "A *Swiss* bank?"

Jane could feel his excitement, and she began to sense the reason. She pointed to the first line of the file. "These numbers and letters—an account number? A password?"

"Maybe both," Matt said, pointing. "Look at these letters about two-thirds of the way through it."

She tried to decide how to pronounce ERNMB. "Er . . . Ernembah? They look like random letters."

"Cole and his ex-wife have a nine-year-old daughter—Erin Marie Brewster." Matt frowned. "Cole told me a couple of weeks ago that if anything ever happened to him, his daughter would inherit everything. I wonder if he was afraid of something."

"So this account would be hers now. But we may be the only ones who know that." Jane frowned too as she looked again at the string of characters. "Numbers, then letters for her name, followed by six more numbers. Those numbers must have had some meaning for him. It's a complicated password."

Matt studied the screen for a moment. "I wonder if those last six numbers are a date."

She looked at him skeptically. "Beginning with 19?"

"A date in the European style." He pointed to the third and fourth digits in the string. "Zero four. So, April 19, and the year—"

"Two years ago—maybe when he opened the account?" Jane pointed at the first entry in the left column of the spreadsheet. "Then these six digits could be a date like that one. This date would be April 24—five days after Cole opened the account. Scroll down to the last line."

He moved to the end to the file, and she pointed to the six digits in the last entry of the column. "Nine days ago."

Matt scrolled back up through the file. Each entry in the left column had six digits—a date. Each corresponding entry in the right column was a string of four or five digits.

"If the second number is a dollar amount . . . " Jane suggested.

Matt scrolled slowly back down the file doing the math in his head, then let out a low whistle. "There's nearly six hundred thousand here. There are probably a lot of people who would kill without blinking for that kind of money. And Cole must have thought these amounts were small enough that they might not be noticed! What kind of operation *is* this?"

They sat staring at the screen of the smartphone for several seconds before Matt turned it off. "I don't want to give Montie and friends a signal to trace."

Jane sat looking at the phone for a moment, then slowly smiled, took it out of his hand, and slid it into the breast pocket on his jacket. "They didn't know what they were looking for either! Lyle and Greg. Like in that old suspense movie, *Charade.*"

He looked puzzled. "I don't remember seeing that one."

"My parents rented it for the family once because they liked it. In the movie, everyone's looking for a lot of money that a thief hid after he double-crossed his partners—but they don't know where to look because they don't know what form he hid it in. It could be diamonds, or bonds, or cash—or rare stamps, in the movie. I wondered why Lyle or Greg searched through everything in our room, even my makeup case. They didn't know if they were looking for a key, or diamonds, or numbers on a small piece of paper." She tapped the phone in his pocket. "Or a small file on a phone."

"Or even something on a video recording," Matt said slowly. "Cole must have held out long enough not to tell them about this," he said, pulling the phone out of his pocket. "And there was no evidence of the new phone in our offices, except maybe the phone number. I left the box and all the papers at home." He thought for a moment. "When Greg and Lyle couldn't find what they were looking for on their own, the next step was trying to force one of us to tell them where it was. They were sure I knew."

"They were sure Cole shared the secret with you, and if you wouldn't tell them, then—"

"The way to get to me was through you."

He stared into space without speaking for several seconds.

Jane sat looking at his profile. "You're mad about something," she said. "I can tell."

Matt hammered his fist down on the table harder than he meant to and the man behind the counter turned to look their way, startled. Matt smiled and nodded at him, trying to indicate that everything was fine. The man turned away and Matt lowered his voice. "Cole did this to us! The situation we're in should never have happened, but Cole . . . everything that's happened to us is *his* fault." He turned the phone over in his hands. "What was he thinking when he handed me this? Was he planning to suck me into stealing money with him?"

"You said he promised to show you how to make all the money you could ever want."

"I checked out his business pretty well before I accepted the job offer. I'd never heard of him, and I wanted to be sure it was all legitimate. He asked me if I wanted to learn how to be successful, and I said yes—but I didn't mean I'd do *anything* to get there!"

"Maybe Cole forgot the difference between the right way and the wrong way."

"I remember that conversation now—when Cole told me about his daughter. His ex accused him of trying to hide income so he wouldn't have to share it. He went on a rant about how greedy she was, how she tried to keep him from seeing their daughter, and *then* he told me if he ever did want to hide money, he'd put it with the gnomes of Zurich." He paused and let out a long breath, trying to stifle his anger. "Look what greed did to him—got him killed. Look what it could do to his daughter and her mother if Greg knew what we know." Matt sat staring straight ahead again. "And look what it almost did to us."

"They won't stop, will they?" Jane asked.

"Who?"

"The people who sent Greg and Lyle. For this kind of money, they'll send somebody else, won't they?"

Matt turned to look at her. "Probably." He put his arm around her shoulders and squeezed her closer to him. "I'm so glad they didn't get the chance to hurt you. I kept praying today that you would be protected."

Jane moved away far enough to look into his eyes. "I prayed for that too. And I *was* protected, Matt. The first time, it was Greg. I'm sure he wouldn't believe that he was an answer to prayer, but he protected me from Lyle when I threatened to jump out the window. And the second time—"

"When you *what?*"

"Greg gave Lyle permission to do anything he wanted to try to scare me—and Lyle has a filthy mind. I was sure they planned to kill me anyway, so I threatened to jump instead of letting Lyle do what he was thinking. Greg called him off when he saw I was serious. Then later you saved me, because you were still alive. Lyle could hardly wait for Greg to leave me alone with him after he thought you were dead."

Matt frowned. He picked up the two wallets and put them back in his pocket, then handed the two phones to her. "Come on, let's go."

"Where are we going?"

"To take our lives back. We're going to turn Greg and Lyle over to the FBI and hope Montie and his people can learn where to find Doug. But first

I want to find out from Greg how much the people who sent him know about us, and how to convince them that this . . . this ugly *game* is over."

12

They moved aside for a figure shuffling toward them across Market Street, his eyes fixed on the ground. The man looked up as they neared him, paused in his shuffle as though he were going to speak to them, then shook his head and moved on.

Jane looked back at the man over her shoulder. "How do you suppose they live that way, on the streets?"

Matt shook his head. "I can't understand it. And I felt like one of them for a while today—nowhere to go, trying to drift along without attracting attention, no place I could call safe."

"Claiming a garbage container for a home. It makes me sick to think of human beings having to live that way."

"I'm sorry you've had to see so much of this up close."

Too close, Jane thought. She felt guilty about her own mixed feelings. She had been touched by Stretch's situation, and she had felt pity for some of the homeless men they passed loitering on Sixth Street with no place to go. But she had also felt revulsion about the way some of them looked at her. She would not feel safe there without Matt, and even with him, she wasn't looking forward to walking down that street again.

He surprised her by turning off Market one block before Sixth. "We can come up on Greg and Lyle from behind the hotel. That might be better anyway—less chance of attracting attention." He led her down Fifth Street to the old U.S. mint building, then turned onto the side street that ran toward the Birch Hotel.

They had gone less than half a block toward Sixth when Matt took hold of Jane's arm and slowed her walk. "Wait." Ahead of them, lights pulsed in alternating red and blue smears through the fog. "I think the police are already there."

"Well, then we can just tell them our story."

"But who called them? I wonder if Stretch . . . " Matt frowned. "Right now Greg and Lyle could be making up any kind of story to cover themselves. I'm not sure I want to walk up there carrying the gun that put a bullet into Lyle's car." He thought for a moment. "Let me use Greg's phone."

He dialed 911, and when a dispatcher answered, he said, "It looks like you have officers at the Birch Hotel on Sixth Street. Can I talk to one of them?"

There was a pause while the dispatcher checked out information transmitted with the incoming call. "What is your name, please, and what is your emergency?"

"I have information about what happened at the Birch Hotel. But I'll only give it to an officer on the scene. Can I talk to one of them?"

There was a pause. The dispatcher could probably see the number from Greg's phone. Would they be trying to pinpoint its location? Then: "Just a moment." The line went quiet on the other end. In the distance, from the fog, Matt heard the crackle of a radio transmission, but he could not make out any of the words. After several seconds, the phone line was opened again. "This is Officer Griggs. You have something you want to tell me?"

Matt was sure the conversation would be recorded. "I have information about what happened on the side street next to the Birch Hotel," he said.

"What kind of information?"

"I can tell you about the guys you found, and how they got there."

"'Guys?' You mean the guy by the garbage container?"

"*One* guy?"

"Yeah. You know how he got there?"

Matt was trying to make sense of what he had heard. Jane was watching him apprehensively. "You only have one? What is *he* telling you about how he got there?"

"He isn't up to saying much. You know something about how he got dead?"

"Dead?"

Jane gasped.

Matt turned in a very small circle, staring into the fog, seeing nothing.

His mind was racing. "The, ah . . . the guy you've got there—about five eight, light hair, cheap sport coat?"

The policeman answered his question with another question. "You know him? Maybe you saw what happened?"

The answer told Matt his guess had been right—Greg was gone, and he had left Lyle dead. "Do you have a witness? Do you have anyone in custody?" he asked.

"Is there someone we should be looking for?" the policeman countered.

"Yeah. Good-looking guy, about five ten, dark hair, tailored jacket, expensive gold watch. He and the short guy—"

"Tell them to check Room 510 in the hotel," Jane said.

"The killer and the short guy were kidnappers," Matt continued. "You might find some evidence in Room 510 of the hotel. They kidnapped my . . . they kidnapped a woman to make—" He stopped talking when he heard the police radio crackle again in the distance. A white light began swinging back and forth in the fog near the red and blue ones. Then it began to move in their direction. Matt pushed the button to end the call. "Come on, J." He led her back down the side street quickly.

"Greg had a knife hidden away," Jane whispered. "I forgot about that."

"I don't know how he got loose," Matt answered, "and I can't understand why he'd kill Lyle. But without Greg, we don't have much to show the police or the FBI."

"Maybe he was worried about how eager Lyle was to talk. Greg would get rid of anybody he sees as a threat to him," Jane answered. "We could explain that to the police. We can explain everything."

"Sure—eventually. But there are a couple of things that worry me. First, my brother. If Greg contacts the people who kidnapped Doug, what do you think they'll do? And if *they* can't contact Greg, what will they do?"

"Do you think Greg would risk making contact? He won't want the people who sent him to find out that he didn't finish us."

"Maybe not. But he's probably facing some kind of deadline when he has to show that the problem has been taken care of." Matt stared straight ahead.

Jane thought for a moment. "*They* made Doug part of the problem. If Greg was supposed to kill us, and if Lyle had to be eliminated so he couldn't talk, then they probably, ah . . . they probably won't want to leave Doug as a witness, will they?"

"No. Second question: What do you think Greg is doing now that he's loose?"

She thought for a moment. "He'll be looking for us, won't he? We're unfinished business."

"Yeah. The police or the FBI could protect us, but they can't protect my brother right now. And if we don't go to them for protection, then we have to worry about Greg. I don't know what to do. We've got to think this out."

They were walking slowly back up Fifth Street when a police cruiser came toward them out of the fog. Instantly, Matt turned away from the street, wrapped his arms around Jane, and kissed her. She put her arms around him and held on. They heard the police car slow and stop at the curb. A light played over them. They turned to look at the source, then shielded their eyes as the policemen shined the light in their faces.

"Just out for a walk, officer," Matt called.

The policeman got out of the car and walked around the front of it toward them. "Do you have some identification?"

"In my wallet—in my hip pocket," Matt answered.

"Turn around," the officer said. He played his flashlight over the bulge in Matt's hip pocket. "You can take it out—slowly. And keep your other hand where I can see it."

Matt removed the wallet very carefully so his jacket did not rise up anywhere else. He turned slowly, took out his driver's license, and handed it to the officer. "We're on our honeymoon," he said. "Walking in the fog in San Francisco seemed romantic."

The officer studied the license, then looked up at them. "Mr. and Mrs. Randall?"

"Yes, Mr. and *Mrs.* Randall," Jane repeated, smiling at him. She held out her left hand to show her rings.

The officer smiled fleetingly, then handed the license back to Matt. "Have you seen anyone else out walking in the past few minutes?"

"No, we, uh . . . " Matt took Jane's hand. "Just the two of us."

The officer chuckled. "I'd recommend you folks go back to your hotel to be romantic. There was some trouble a little while ago not far from here." He turned and walked back to his patrol car. They heard his radio crackle as he eased into the car. Matt was walking away with Jane when faint words from the police radio caught his ear: " . . . assault on the clerk at the Birch Hotel. Suspect is a lone white male, over six feet, brown hair."

Jane looked at Matt in alarm. He took her arm and hurried her toward the next corner. "Let's get far away before he realizes he just talked to a guy who fits that description."

They crossed Market and were just past the corner when a plain, dark sedan rolled to a stop at the curb beside them. A small antenna stood up from the trunk lid in the back.

Matt groaned. "They're all over this," he whispered. "Keep walking."

They heard a car door open. "Just a minute, folks," a voice called.

They stopped and turned. A man in a dark, rumpled suit was hurrying toward them around the front of the car. The vehicle sat idling at the curb, the driver's door open. The headlights glaring off the fog illuminated everything for a short distance around the front of the car. For a moment, Jane had the feeling of being part of a tableau in some giant snow globe.

The feeling passed quickly as the man approached them. He stepped to the rear passenger door of the car and opened it. "I'm going to have to ask the two of you to come with me." He stood waiting expectantly.

They did not move. "Is there a reason we should do that?" Matt asked.

"Because I asked you," the man answered. It was obviously meant to sound commanding. He reached into the inside pocket of his suit coat and pulled out a leather case. He flipped it open to show a badge, then started to put it away.

"Wait a minute," Matt said. "I'd like a better look at that."

The man held the badge out at arm's length. "It's real," he said curtly. "And you're coming with me."

Matt peered at the badge. "Detective." He raised his eyebrows. "Marin County Sheriff's office? That's across the bay. It seems you'd be out of your jurisdiction here, wouldn't you, Officer . . . ?"

"Rucker. And we have a duty to enforce the law wherever we are. I heard a San Francisco police broadcast not five minutes ago describing two people they're looking for. Then I stopped at the light back there and the two of you walked right in front of me." He smiled thinly. "Sometimes we get a lucky break."

Matt stood his ground. "And why would the police be looking for us? We're just a couple of tourists, on our honeymoon."

"There's been a murder—a guy involved in a kidnapping. And the lady here"—he nodded toward Jane—"fits the description of the kidnap victim.

She was seen on Sixth Street earlier with the dead guy. We need to talk with the two of you about that."

Matt and Jane glanced at each other. Neither of them moved.

"I can call for backup if I have to," the man said, opening his coat to show a small radio clipped onto his belt above his left hip. Four lights on the front of it blinked in sequence. "I hope we're not going to have to do this the hard way," the man added. He put a hand on the pistol in the holster on his right side, pushed outward by the bulge of his belly.

Matt and Jane looked each other in the eyes for a few seconds. Matt shrugged and moved toward the car. The man held the rear door open.

Matt reached out his right hand as though to put it on the door—but seized the man's right wrist instead. The man looked momentarily shocked, then began to reach across his body for the pistol with his left hand. Jane grabbed his arm to pull it away from the gun. The man shifted his position quickly and grabbed Jane's wrist. The fingernails of her other hand raked his left wrist and the back of his hand. He grimaced in pain—and then Matt's unchecked right to his belly doubled him over.

Matt spun the man into an arm lock and shoved him up against the car. "That's a police scanner on your belt, not a two-way radio. Anyone can get one of those—but you can't call in with it."

"And I was not 'seen on Sixth Street with the dead guy,'" Jane added.

"In fact, the police may not even know there's been a kidnapping. Only the kidnappers could know what the victim looked like. So I'm wondering—how do *you* know?"

The man moved his left hand as though to reach under his coat in back. Matt grabbed his wrist to stop him and put more upward pressure on the arm he held in the arm lock. The man groaned. "You're assaulting an officer," he said through gritted teeth.

"Am I?" Matt answered. He lifted the back of the man's suit jacket and put his hand on the butt of a pistol. He eased it out of the man's waistband. "Small caliber weapon with a silencer. This is the second one of these I've taken away from somebody tonight. Doesn't look like a standard-issue police weapon—more like a killer's gun." Careful not to put his finger on the trigger, Matt touched the barrel of the weapon to the base of the man's skull.

"Hey! Be careful!" the man protested. "That could go off."

Matt let go of the man's arm and stepped back. "Turn around—slowly.

Look at me." When the man turned, he found the pistol Matt had taken from him pointed at his face. Matt pressed the barrel against his forehead. "Now I'm going to take the one that's on your belt. We won't have a problem about that, will we?"

"No," the man said softly, trying not to move.

Matt took the pistol out of the man's holster and put it into his jacket pocket. "Where's your wallet?"

"In my coat."

"Show me. One hand."

Slowly the man opened his suit coat to show the top of a wallet sticking out of the inside pocket.

"My wife's going to take it. You're not going to move, are you?" Matt held the pistol steady against the other man's forehead.

"Wouldn't dream of it," the man answered.

Jane got close enough to slip the wallet out of his pocket, then stepped back and flipped it open. "Now we'll find out if Mr. Rucker is really a sheriff's . . . " She studied something on the inside of the wallet, then turned it so Matt could see it. "Is really Delbert Williams, according to this California driver's license. And there's a card here that says Mr. Williams is a private investigator."

Matt looked steadily into the other man's eyes. "So how does Delbert Williams, private detective, get a badge belonging to a police detective? Steal it? Or did you kill for it?"

"No!" The other man looked away. "I never killed anybody."

"So tonight was going to be a first time? You were going to start with us?"

"I wasn't going to—"

"Shut up and get into the car. Back seat."

Matt slid into the car beside the private detective and prodded him toward the far side. Shutting the door behind them, Matt reached under the back of the man's coat, pulled out the handcuffs that had been hanging out of the detective's waistband, and tossed them on the front seat. "Jane, come around to the driver's side and roll down the windows so Mr. Williams can stick his arms out—one on each side of the doorpost." Jane understood. After the detective stuck his arms out through the two windows, she handcuffed his wrists. "Now get behind the wheel," Matt said to her, "and kill the engine and the lights."

When they were sitting in the dark, Matt put the barrel of the pistol behind the man's ear, careful again not to put a finger on the trigger. "I'm tired of people threatening us and telling us what to do. The only reason we need to spend any time with you is to get answers. You're going to give them to me. Do you understand?"

"Yeah. Okay. Be careful with that gun!"

"You won't get hurt if you tell me what I want to know. Who sent you?"

Jane could see the man's face. Even in the dim glow from the streetlight on the corner, she could see that he was sweating. Maybe it was only the lighting that made him look ashen, but he was afraid the way Lyle had been—afraid Matt might do what he would do if their positions were reversed. "A guy called me—a guy I've done some work for before."

"Name?"

"I don't know. He's just a—"

Matt pushed the pistol's silencer harder against the man's head. "Wrong answer. Name?"

"He's just a voice! I've only talked to him on the phone. I never got a name."

"A mysterious voice on the phone tells you to go out and kill people?"

"I wasn't supposed to kill anybody. It was just like things I've done for him before."

"This gun says you were ready to kill. You do work like that for somebody you've never met? How did you ever get lined up with somebody who pays you to kill people you don't even know?"

"*Not* kill! The voice on the phone said I was just supposed to find the guy who lined me up with him the first time. I was supposed to make sure that guy had gotten what he was told to get from you."

Matt and Jane looked at each other. "The guy you were supposed to find," Jane said, "the one who lined you up with the voice on the phone—what's his name?"

The man licked his lips and looked at her. "I can't. If I tell you . . . "

Matt prodded him in the back of the head with the pistol.

"Please," the man whined.

Jane looked at her husband, then at the detective. "If you're worrying about Greg, he's not going to be able to do anything to you."

The detective looked at her in shock, then at Matt. "You two took out Greg? How . . . "

"Tell us about the man who called you," Matt answered. "Somebody Greg knows?"

"Yeah."

"And you just agreed to do whatever he wanted, regardless of who you might have to hurt?"

"You don't understand! Before he told me what he wanted me to do, he asked about my wife, and my daughter. He knows where I live! He told me he hoped they were well. And *then* he told me what he wanted."

"Which was?"

The detective shrugged. "To be sure Greg did his job—or hold onto you if Greg couldn't. When I heard on the radio about that murder at the hotel, I thought he'd done the job. I was surprised when I saw the two of you in front of me."

"And how did Greg introduce you to this voice?"

"I was doing a job here for Greg one time, and Greg said the boss wanted to talk to me, so I listened while the boss told me what he wanted."

"And that's the only time you've ever talked to him?"

"No. There was another time, when Greg called me down to Los Angeles, and the boss talked to me on the phone that time too."

"But it wasn't Greg who called you this time?"

"No. It was the boss. I didn't know Greg was in town."

"So what else do you know about this voice?"

"Nothing."

Matt prodded him with the pistol.

"Okay! He was, uh . . . he's not . . . I don't know. He doesn't talk like an American. But I don't know what . . . maybe European. I've never been to any of those countries."

Matt took the pistol away from the detective's head. He and Jane sat looking at each other for several seconds. "This is a loose end we can't leave," Matt said.

"Please!" the detective whined again. "For the love of—"

"Be quiet!" Matt snapped. "We're not going to kill you."

He slid out of the backseat of the car and walked around to the driver's side, motioning Jane to join him as he stepped away from the car.

"When they thought I was asleep," Jane whispered, "Greg and Lyle talked about somebody named Boris. Greg said Boris had left this to him to handle."

Matt nodded. "Looks like Boris may have changed his mind," he whispered, and gestured toward the detective. "We've got to turn this guy over to the police right now. But what are we going to tell them? I don't think we should wait around until they show up. If we get taken in for questioning right now, time could run out for Doug."

"I have an idea. But I think I ought to use his phone, if he's got one."

Matt reached into the car, patted the detective's coat pockets until he found a phone, and handed it to Jane.

She inhaled deeply a couple of times, as if she were preparing for physical action, then dialed 911. "Help me!" she said breathlessly into the phone. "There's a man . . . he tried to make me get into his car. He said he's a policeman—but I don't think he is. He's, uh . . . I fought back and he fell, and I put his handcuffs on him. But I'm afraid!" The urgency sounded genuine. Matt heard the dispatcher ask a question. Jane glanced up at the street sign. Even through the fog, they could read FIFTH on the sign. "Wait, I, uh . . . I have to look," Jane said into the phone. "This is Fifth Street, by Market." Matt could hear the dispatcher asking another question. "Just hurry," Jane answered. "The man had a gun, and I get scared just thinking about why he tried to grab me." She cut off the call.

"Nice work," Matt said.

"They'll see through that story the minute they get here," the detective sneered.

"We're going to make sure they check *you* out thoroughly," Matt answered. He took Williams' wallet and the badge and laid them in the footwell in front of the driver's seat. He emptied the cylinder of the revolver he had taken out of the detective's holster, threw the shells into some bushes across the street, then laid the revolver next to the wallet. He pulled the magazine from the .22 automatic, ejected the shell in the chamber, then laid the pistol and the magazine in the footwell next to the revolver. He pulled the car keys from the ignition and flung them into the bushes too.

He took Jane's arm and they began to walk away.

"He'll find you," the detective called after them. "He'll kill you. There's no place you can go that's safe." He screamed a curse at them. "I hope he takes his time and makes it hurt."

Matt and Jane stopped in a doorway up the street and waited until they saw the blinking lights of a police cruiser approaching the detective's car.

Then they rounded the corner and kept moving, away from the vicinity of the Birch Hotel and Sixth Street.

"Do you think he's right?" Jane asked. "There's no place we can go to be safe?"

Matt shrugged. "I don't know." He paused. "But would that be very different from how it is right now? They're already coming after us." He stopped next to a building and pulled her close to him. "Are you getting tired of this? I am. I've had enough of being pushed around. We're going to fight back!"

"Can we do that without being as bad as they are? I know you would never have shot that detective, but can we fight them without guns and knives?"

"We'll have to find a way." He thought for moment. "You're right—we can't fight them the way they've come after us—not without becoming killers ourselves." He took her hand. "We've got to think this out before we decide what to do next, even if that's just calling in Montie and the troops."

She started walking. "Then let's go find a place out of sight where we can think."

* * *

Greg lingered outside Matt and Jane's hotel.

He had been walking down Market when the first police car sped toward him in the fog, lights flashing, headed toward Sixth Street. Greg had ducked into a doorway while it passed, wondering if someone had discovered Lyle already.

Maybe the man who called himself Stretch had talked to the police and told them what he had seen.

Or it might have been the man Greg had met as he came out of the side street next to the hotel. The man had looked at Greg's blazer and the watch on his arm and asked, "Can you help me out, sir? A fiver? Maybe ten?"

Greg had shoved him roughly out of the way, eager to be gone and angry at being seen near the spot where Lyle lay dead.

That homeless man might remember him.

But would the police give serious attention to one of those people who lived on Sixth Street in a haze of alcohol and drugs? Would they pay attention to somebody like Stretch? If the man he had shoved talked to them, would they listen?

Greg did not know, but he couldn't afford to take any more chances. This job had been carefully planned, and the plan was going to pieces because his partner had been stupid. If Lyle had been arrested, he might have spilled everything he knew. That possibility had made him a liability—expendable.

After Greg had freed his left wrist from the handcuffs, he had handed the key back to Lyle, who immediately busied himself with freeing his own wrist. Lyle had not realized what was about to happen when Greg suddenly straddled his body—until the knife blade touched his throat. By then it was too late.

There was yet another loose end, Greg realized—Jamal, the clerk behind the desk at the Birch Hotel. Jamal had seen him come into the hotel this afternoon. The clerk probably had no love for the police, but if they put pressure on him, would he give up anything he might know?

There was no time to deal with Jamal. Greg had to find Matt and Jane and finish with them—quickly. Then he had to get out of San Francisco.

Where were they now? Would they come back to their hotel? Maybe—maybe not. But it was the place to start. And now he would have to risk being seen here, because his contact in the hotel would be gone for the night.

* * *

They sat under an umbrella at one of the tables on the small plaza next to the underground BART station. Matt had chosen a place back in the shadows where they could not be seen by anyone passing on the street level above. He sat with his arm around her. Neither of them had spoken for several minutes. "Fighting back our way, step one," he said finally, "I may be able to do something for Doug now that I know what's going on."

"What could you do from here?"

"Let me use Greg's phone."

He dialed Doug's cell phone wondering whether his brother's kidnappers would answer a call with the incoming number blocked. Would they be wary, or curious?

Evidently someone was curious or did not check the caller ID. The call was answered quickly with a curt, "*Si.*"

Matt responded in Spanish. "*Quiero hablar con el jefe.*"

There was silence on the other end, then, "*¿Quien es?*" It was followed by another pause, and, "Who is this?"

"I said I want to talk to the boss," Matt answered. "Now."

"Yeah? Well, he don't want to talk to you."

"Yeah, he does—and you need to convince him. If he doesn't talk to me, this will all go bad and you'll get the blame. You want that?"

There was noise of the phone being covered, silence for several seconds, and then another voice came on the line. "Is this Doug's big brother?" it taunted.

"Is this the boss?"

"What do you want?"

"To talk to my brother."

The other man laughed. "No chance, dude. Goodbye."

"Don't do something stupid! Listen to me," Matt commanded. "I'll make this simple. If you hurt my brother, I go to the police, the people who are paying you will lose what they want, and they'll take it out on you."

"No way, man. And we haven't hurt little brother—not yet. But there's no way we're going down for him."

This voice also had a Hispanic accent, but not so heavy. Matt had no idea who he was talking to or how many people were involved, but so far he had them listening. "How do I know you're telling the truth? If you don't convince me that Doug's okay, I go to the police. You want to explain to the people who are paying you that you screwed up? I'll make sure they find out I warned you."

The other man hesitated. "Hold on." There was the sound of a door being opened and of the phone being handled. "Talk," he heard the Hispanic voice say in the background. "Your brother."

"Matt?" Doug said. "What's happening? Do you—"

The other voice came back on the line. "Your brother's okay."

"All right," Matt answered. "You make sure he stays that way. You call the people who hired you and tell them I have what they want, but if anything happens to my brother, it's *gone. Acabado. Ya estuvo.*"

"We don't call them, man! They call us."

"So when they call, give them the message. And *you* make sure they understand. *¿Comprendes?*" Matt pushed the button to end the call.

Matt gazed at the far wall for a moment and shook his head. "They're not planning to let him live. We've got to figure out a way to make that their best option."

He handed the phone back to Jane. She put it in her pocket, then took his hand and held it. "I've been thinking too," she said. "Where do you suppose Greg would look for us first?"

"Our hotel."

She nodded. "Uh huh. And where is the last place he would expect to find us?"

Matt frowned. "I don't know. What are you thinking?"

"We need to know more about Greg. The key card for his hotel room is in his wallet, so we do the last thing he would expect—we go there." On the volleyball court, she had been good at this kind of strategic thinking—misdirecting opponents and catching them off guard. Players across the net would jump with her, arms upraised to block her fierce kill shot, only to have her tap the ball lightly across the net into a spot they were not covering.

"Good idea," Matt said. "But how do we find out which room he's in? The hotel isn't going to give us that information."

"I don't know. I haven't figured out that part yet." Jane smiled and batted her eyelashes at him. "Maybe we could try charm."

Matt laughed. "Well, it's worth a try, and if anyone could pull off the charm thing, it would be you. Let's go—and keep that agile mind working."

* * *

Greg glanced at the Rolex on his wrist: 10:24. The reception area wouldn't be busy this time of night; that meant there was a greater chance a clerk behind the desk might notice him when he walked in.

If he had his telephone, he could call the hotel and ask for Matt and Jane's room to learn whether they had come back. But then what if they answered? Polite conversation? No. He had to find out where they were without their knowing that he had found them.

When they had left him and Lyle handcuffed to the garbage container, he had kept listening for sirens or for the approach of some patrolman on foot. But as the minutes passed and it did not happen, he realized that the seeds of doubt he had planted must have had their effect. Matt and Jane had not dared to go directly to the police for fear it would mean death to his brother. Their hesitation gave Greg an edge; the time they spent worrying was time he could use to track them down.

He stood across the street looking at the lighted lobby window of their hotel through the fog. In his mind, he could almost hear the clock ticking. He had promised he would have this problem cleared up by tomorrow morning at the latest. Evidently Boris had decided he was not handling it quickly enough. *I've got to show results—soon. I need to prove I've been in control of the situation.* Boris wouldn't need to know about this temporary setback.

Greg pulled a free newspaper from a nearby rack, then walked quickly across the street, pausing at the hotel's glass door to make sure none of the staff was nearby before stepping inside. The desk clerk did not look up from his work at a computer terminal. Good. Greg skirted quickly around the edge of the lobby behind the pillars and palms, ready to raise the newspaper to partially shield his face if he saw anyone else. He walked down the hallway past the elevators to the stairway door. There was little chance of seeing anyone or being seen on the stairs this time of night.

On the third floor landing, he eased the door open to see if there was anyone in the hallway. No one. He walked quickly toward Matt and Jane's door.

He had not left the searching of this room to Lyle last night. It was a detail he had taken care of himself, slipping into the back entrance from the dock. But tonight that back door had been locked from the inside.

Last night there had not been enough time for a thorough search. He knew he was looking for a great deal of money, in one form or another. It was possible Jane had been telling the truth when she said they did not have it—possible, but not probable. Coleman Brewster said he had given it to Matt, and had promised to get it back. But Brewster could not be trusted, so Greg had taken care of him. Now, Greg knew he had to get the money back on his own—quickly. That was what Boris expected. And any sources of information about the origins of the money—sources like the Randalls—had to be cut off.

Greg paused momentarily at the door of their room to listen. There was no sound. He reached into his jacket pocket for the hotel master key card

Lyle had bought from someone in maintenance here. Fortunately, Matt and Jane had not found it. If there was anything he had missed last night, Greg would take his time now in finding it. And if Matt and Jane came back, he would be here to take them by surprise.

* * *

Everything about the lobby of the historic hotel said elegance. Matt and Jane walked through it silently, holding hands. Passing the elevators and a stairway that led up to meeting and exhibition rooms on the mezzanine, they came to the wood-paneled reception area. "Time to turn on the charm," Matt whispered as they approached the desk.

"Feel free to jump in and help."

The desk clerk stopped his work at a computer terminal and turned his attention to them. He seemed momentarily nonplussed that he had to look up at both of them. "May I help you?"

Jane gave him one of her light-up-the-room smiles. She had his full attention immediately. "We're hoping to surprise a friend of ours, Greg Alexander. He's staying here. Can you tell us where we could find him?"

The clerk looked apologetic. "I'm sorry. We're not allowed to give out guest room numbers."

"Oh. Oh, of course. I'm sorry, I wasn't asking you to do something, uh . . . we wanted to surprise him." Jane put on a look of embarrassment. "This is awkward. We told him we wouldn't be able to come to the class reunion, but we were able to arrange it at the last minute. We were just going to show up for the dinner tonight, but then our flight was delayed. . . . " She shrugged, and smiled again.

The clerk obviously wanted to be responsive to this friendly, attractive woman. "I wish I could help you, but . . . "

Jane had no idea how to draw out useful information; she was making up her end of the conversation as she went along. But she was fairly sure Greg would not have come back to his hotel without searching for them. Could she verify that much? "Maybe you could call him? Just to see if he's here?"

The clerk checked the time on the grandfather clock in the reception lobby, obviously wondering whether it was too late to disturb a guest. Matt made a show of looking at his own watch. "It's not even 11:00, Sweetheart, and this is San Francisco. You know Greg—he's probably still out partying. I'll bet he isn't in his room yet."

The clerk reached for a phone on the desk and dialed four digits. Matt tried to see what they were, but the computer monitor blocked his view. The clerk listened, then looked up at Matt. "You're right. Mister Alexander isn't answering."

"Maybe we'll just have to surprise him in the morning," Matt said, trying to look disappointed. "Would we be able to get a room near his?"

The clerk tapped at the keys on his computer keyboard, then looked up at them and nodded. "On that you're in luck. I can put you just a couple of doors down."

"Perfect," Jane said, and smiled at him again.

Matt reached for his wallet. Jane put a hand on his to stop him. "You charged the plane tickets on your card. Why don't you let me put this on mine?"

He understood. Anyone who had a way to track them would be less likely to look for her maiden name.

The clerk assigned Mr. and Mrs. McDougall to room 619. "Our bags are in Denver, or somewhere," Jane said, "but they'll be delivered in the morning."

On their way up in the elevator, Matt studied the electronic key card the clerk had handed them. "I wonder what happens if you use one of these in the wrong door?"

"I don't think it could work," she said. "Is that what you're asking?"

"I mean they could be programmed to stop working if anyone goes around trying them in other doors. We'd better be sure we know which one is Greg's room before we use his card."

They walked to room 619 and used their card to open it. "Very nice," Jane said as they stepped inside. "The jewelry liquidation business must pay well if Greg makes it a habit to stay in places like this."

They stepped out into the hallway and looked both ways again. "'A couple of doors down,'" Matt repeated. "Which way?"

"I have an idea," Jane said. "You call the hotel on Greg's cell phone, tell them you're Mister Alexander, you'll be back in the hotel in half an hour and you'd like to have a . . . a club sandwich outside your room when you get here. Then we wait to see where they deliver it."

He thought for a moment. "Yeah. That could work. But there might be a quicker way. Hand me Lyle's phone. And back up two doors that way," he said, pointing behind her. He backed up two doors in the other direction. He looked at the small folder that held their key card and dialed the hotel number on the front of it. When the operator answered, he said, "Yes, I need to talk to Greg Alexander. When he left the party a few minutes ago, I forgot to tell him where to meet us for breakfast in the morning, and I need to tell him the time has been changed." Matt covered the phone and whispered, "Listen."

There was no sound for what seemed like several seconds, and then, faintly, they heard the ringing of a telephone. Jane's eyes went wide. She pointed to the door of the room on her left.

Matt walked quickly toward her. "No," he said into the phone, "that's all right." He chuckled. "I guess I'll just have to give him a wake-up call."

He turned off the phone, handed it to her, and pulled Greg's wallet out of his jacket pocket. He took out the key card and held it up. "Show time," he said, and inserted the card into the lock. He pulled it out again quickly, holding his breath—and the light above the handle glowed green. He turned the handle and opened the door. They stepped inside.

Like the room they had rented, this one was elegantly furnished. It looked almost as though no one had stayed here. Nothing was disarranged, and there were no personal items in sight. Matt stepped into the bathroom. A man's shaving kit sat on the counter next to the sink, neatly zipped shut and positioned precisely in the corner next to the wall.

Jane opened the chest of drawers and raised her eyebrows. "Greg can't have been planning to stay here long, but he took time to put his clothes away in the drawer. Not just put them away—he took time to *arrange* them."

"Keep looking," Matt said. "I'll check the closet."

He found clothes—expensive-looking items—neatly hung in the closet, and a wheeled carry-on suitcase on the floor, but it was what he found in the corner that caught his interest immediately. He pulled it out and held it up. "Look—Greg has a computer." He zipped open the case. Inside he found a slim PC notebook and a sophisticated, very-much-in-demand smartphone. "That's our Greg," he said, smiling. "I think I'll search these."

13

Greg stood by the bed looking at the things he had spread out on it.

Nothing. Nothing he could see there held the key to nearly six hundred thousand dollars.

He had even finished ripping apart Matt's shaving kit. Nothing hidden away there. Nothing in the bag except standard man's shaving stuff and a toothbrush, thrown into the case carelessly, he thought—not the way he would do it. But, then, Matt Randall had not handled any of his things as though they held the secret to something important.

There was nothing in Jane's small makeup case either—nothing significant in their closet, nothing in their suitcases, nothing in their clothing. He had even ripped the foot liners out of a pair of Jane's shoes because they looked loose, as though they might have been removed once, but there was nothing underneath. It was just a well-used pair of shoes.

This time he had watched all the scenes recorded in the video camera—fifteen minutes or so of Matt's focusing a lot on Jane. There was nothing that offered a clue as to where the money might be.

Could he have missed something in Matt's office files when he used Cole's key to get in and search there?

No. He knew enough about investments to see that everything in Matt's files dealt with legitimate transactions for people who seemed to be real clients.

Maybe Jane had been telling the truth when she said at first that they didn't have the money.

No! He would not believe that. Cole Brewster said he had given the money to Matt to keep. Matt had to be in on the secret. And Boris was expecting to get his money back—very soon.

Coleman Brewster had been a greedy, arrogant little man. He had tried to deny at first that he knew anything about the missing funds, and then he had asked, smirking, what they could do about the loss. Were they planning to go to the police and report that Cole had taken part of the money he was laundering for them?

Brewster had been Greg's problem because Greg was the one who had made him part of the money laundering pipeline. He and Brewster had met when the little man wandered into a jewelry business Greg was liquidating. Brewster had been looking for a good deal on a diamond pendant for a woman he wanted to impress. Greg had recognized him immediately as the kind of man who loved money and the things it could buy. At the time, Boris had been searching for a way to pour money from his illegal enterprises in the U.S. into investments that looked legitimate. After investigating Brewster quietly, Greg had suggested to Boris that the Phoenix financial consultant was knowledgeable and might be useful. It had been left to Greg to approach Brewster with the offer: launder money on a regular basis in exchange for a small percentage.

Greg regretted now that he had not realized just how greedy Brewster really was. The man had exceeded his percentage almost from the beginning, apparently believing he could hide his skimming from Boris's bookkeepers. It was only when Brewster finally realized his life was in danger that he offered to get the money back.

He hadn't actually said he had given the money to Randall—only that if anything happened to him, his assistant would be the one person who could lay his hands on the money. What did that mean, exactly?

Greg wondered if he had killed Cole too quickly.

Still, it was hard to believe Matt did not know about the money, or where to find it. No one would cache six hundred thousand dollars without providing a key to its retrieval. Somehow Matt Randall held that key.

If the secret to finding the money was not in this hotel room or on paper in Matt's office, then it must be in Matt's head. There might be a clue hidden somewhere in his computer files at the Phoenix office. But if that were true, Matt's cooperation would be needed to find it, and the way to make Matt cooperate was through Jane, or someone else he cared about. That was undoubtedly why Doug Randall had been kidnapped—to put more pressure on Matt. But Greg understood what it meant for him. Boris had grown impatient with the lack of progress in finding his money.

Greg checked his watch. It was just past 11:15, and if Matt and Jane were not here by now, they must have found somewhere else to stay. The best thing to do would be to return to his hotel room, reexamine the information he had compiled about them, and try to determine how he could make them come to him.

He left their room, slipped down the stairs and out the back door this time onto the loading dock. From there he walked quickly through the fog toward his hotel.

He still remembered Matt's phone number, and they had his cell phone too, so maybe he could call them to bait a trap. He could tell them he would help free Matt's brother if they met with him. Or maybe he could threaten to send someone after their parents; if they could not be sure who took Doug, then they could not be sure whether others in their families were vulnerable.

He would have to think of some way to find them and bring them within reach again—before morning.

He walked through the empty lobby of his hotel and approached the desk clerk apologetically. "I'm afraid I've lost my key card," he said. "Actually, it was stolen this evening, with my wallet." He tried to smile ruefully. "Greg Alexander, room 616."

The clerk consulted his computer monitor. "Mr. Alexander? And you, ah . . . you have no other identification with you?" The clerk did not want to offend a legitimate guest—if that's what the man standing in front of him was. But if this man had been out on the town, as Mr. and Mrs. McDougall had guessed, the story about having his wallet stolen was plausible.

"Well, no." Greg thought for a moment. "But you have the imprint of my credit card. I can tell you the number." The clerk opened a file drawer, reached in, and pulled out a piece of paper. Greg recited the sixteen digits of the number slowly from memory.

The clerk raised his eyebrows. It was impressive—but not conclusive. Someone who had stolen a wallet might have that number.

"Alice would remember me," Greg said. "She seemed to appreciate the tip I gave her yesterday when I checked in."

Oh, yes—the Tipper! The story had gotten around among the reception staff. A man in expensive-looking clothes had given Alice Wu five twenty-dollar bills when he checked in, and he had promised her more when he left if the hotel staff took good care of him. He wore expensive jewelry, she had said. The clerk noted the gold Rolex on this man's right wrist.

"And if it helps," Greg added, "I ordered room service last night—the filet mignon and one of your best wines. You'll probably find that on my bill." He recited the dollar amount.

The clerk checked the computer file again. Not only had the man ordered those items on room service, the cost he recited had included a twenty percent tip for the waiter. The clerk smiled at the man across the desk from him. "Yes, Mr. Alexander. Unfortunately, Alice isn't on duty tonight, but I'll do what I can." He quickly found another key card and coded it. "Here you are," he said, handing it across the desk. "And by the way, if you need any other assistance tonight, please feel free to call on me."

"Thanks."

Mr. Alexander's smile seemed almost forced, the clerk thought, as though it were an effort to be sociable. No doubt it had been a tough day for him; maybe he would be cheered by a bit of news. "By the way, two of your friends came looking for you this evening."

Greg was already half turned away from the desk, but he stopped and turned back to speak. "Two people came looking for *me?*"

"Yes." The clerk frowned. He thought this man might be pleasantly surprised by the information; instead, he seemed upset. "Two people—they said they were old friends. A man and a woman." He paused, then plunged onward. "They said they told you they wouldn't be able to make it to the reunion, but at the last second they were able to come."

Greg smiled thinly. "What did they look like? Both of them tall? Gorgeous woman with long auburn hair?"

The clerk smiled in relief. "Yes. You know them?"

Greg's smile broadened, but somehow there seemed to be no humor in it. "Oh, yes. This might be an interesting reunion. Did they say where I could find them?"

"They asked for your room number. Of course, I couldn't give out that information—hotel security. But they took a room here. They said they would surprise you in the morning."

"And of course you can't tell me which room they're in?"

"No, sir. But they asked for one near yours." The clerk paused. "I hope I haven't spoiled anything."

"No. No, you haven't. I appreciate the information. I'll be glad to see them." Greg deliberately widened his smile a degree or two. "It's too bad all my cash was taken. But when I check out, I will remember how helpful you've been"—he peered closely at the desk clerk's nametag—"Robert. And I hope you'll continue to keep information about me confidential."

"Yes, sir." The clerk smiled more broadly. "As always. And thank you, sir."

Matt and Jane deserved points for resourcefulness and daring, Greg thought as he walked to the elevator. He would never have thought to look for them here; he would have expected them to be lying low somewhere.

There could be only one reason they would come here inquiring about him—they had the key to his room.

He got off the elevator on the fifth floor so there was no possibility they could hear a telltale *ding* from its arrival. He walked up the stairs to the next floor, eased cautiously out into the hallway, and walked as quietly as possible to the door of his room. He did not know whether they might have learned his room number somehow, but as clever as they were, he had to consider the possibility. He stood still, listening, but could hear nothing from inside the room. He squatted down carefully and looked at the bottom of the door. The edge of the door met the carpet, so he could not tell whether there was light on the inside.

He had to assume that they could be in there. If they weren't, it would be a relief, but if they were . . .

He needed the pistol. He had bought it yesterday through an off-the-books dealer he knew in San Francisco, and if necessary he could buy another one tomorrow, but there would be no way to get his hands on one tonight. He reached behind him, under his coat, and checked his knife. He started to pull it out so he could have it in his hand, then reconsidered. If he went into the room holding the knife and found Matt waiting with the gun, Greg knew he could be dead before he cleared the doorway. But he did not think Matt would shoot an unarmed man. Greg made sure the clip that held the knife would slide freely from his belt, then let his jacket fall back into place.

He prepared to slip the new key card into its slot with his right hand and reached out slowly with his left to take hold of the door handle, careful not to jiggle it and make a noise. Taking a deep breath, he shoved the key card into its slot quickly, pulled it out instantly, saw the green light, twisted the door handle, and burst into the room.

Jane stood by the window. She turned to look at him, shocked. Matt sat on the bed, working on the notebook computer that had been carefully tucked away in the closet; he too looked up in surprise.

Greg saw the pistol immediately. It lay on the end of the bed, closest to him!

He crossed the space between the doorway and the bed in two quick strides, leaning to reach for the weapon. Matt moved to reach for it too, but he was juggling the computer and he moved far too slowly. Greg snatched the pistol off the bed and pointed it at Matt, grinning. He looked quickly at Jane, to his left, then back at Matt. "Put the computer down," he said, gesturing with the pistol. "On the bed."

Carefully, Matt put the computer on the bed, then stood.

"Don't move," Greg said. He wasn't going to give a man this powerful the chance to take him by surprise again. He glanced at Jane. She had made no attempt to move either. "What were you doing on the computer?" Greg asked.

"Trying to find out who wants that money so badly they'll pay you to kill for it," Matt responded. "Who would that be, Greg?"

Greg did not answer Matt's question. "So you *do* have the money!"

"Not exactly. Whose is it?"

Greg shook his head. "I'm asking the questions. *Where* is it?"

"What are you willing to tell me to find out?"

"You don't seem to understand." Greg pointed the pistol squarely at Matt's heart. "I'm going to find out what I want to know one way or the other." He nodded toward Jane. "She knows too, doesn't she? So I really only need one of you."

"You leave Jane out of this. Don't threaten her!" Matt warned and took a step toward him.

Greg wouldn't make the mistake of killing this man too quickly. He needed to know everything Matt knew about the money. But with the .22 pistol, he could wound Matt and keep him alive long enough to get the information he needed. He could put Jane into Lyle's handcuffs and use her as a bargaining chip if he had to. "Where's the money?" He pointed the pistol at Matt's shoulder. "I never miss, especially at this distance. And no one outside this room will hear a thing."

"Who has my brother, Greg?" Matt took a step closer.

One more, and he would be within reach of the muzzle of the pistol.

Greg took aim at the spot where Matt's upper arm met his shoulder and pulled the trigger. There was a click—and nothing more. Greg looked at the pistol, shocked, then pointed it at Matt and pulled the trigger again. This time there was no sound at all.

"We didn't think it was a good idea to leave that lying around loaded," Matt explained. "Somebody could get hurt." He took one step closer. "We were hoping you'd join us sooner or later. You can help us out here."

Greg tried to stifle the rage that made him want to attack Matt Randall with his fists; it would be futile, maybe suicidal. He could not afford to lose control now. They had tricked him, but he still had a surprise for them. He threw the empty pistol at Matt's head and began to turn toward Jane as Matt ducked away. His left hand snaked under the back of his jacket. Matt would be more cooperative when he saw the knife blade at his wife's throat. Greg turned to face Jane, the knife in his hand, his thumb on the small post to flick the blade open.

For the second time in one night, he had failed to see the danger coming. He stepped forward just in time to meet Jane's clenched fists sweeping upward under his chin in something resembling a volleyball dig shot.

* * *

Jane let cold water from the washcloth drip onto Greg's face. He stirred, and then his eyes opened wide. He started when he saw her and tried to draw away, but found he could not. He tried to jerk his arms toward his chest and roll to the side so he could push himself off the floor, but his arms were held fast by something. He realized he was looking up at the bathroom ceiling. He was lying on the tile floor, his arms stretched above his head encircling the base of the toilet. His wrists were shackled together by Lyle's handcuffs. They had taken his blazer. The tile was cold on his back.

"You forgot that I've already seen your knife trick," Jane said, wiping some of the water off of his face. She touched the cold rag to the left side of his head. "You're going to have a nasty bruise there where your face hit that garbage container by the hotel. Fortunately you didn't hit anything but carpet this time. You've been out for about ten minutes."

"I told you it was a bad idea to threaten my wife," Matt said from where he sat on the foot of the bed, working on the computer again.

Greg's reply was a curse, followed by a demand: "Let me go!"

Matt smiled and shook his head. "No, I don't think so. We need you to give us a little help."

"*Help you?* You're out of your mind. If you don't let me go right now, you'll regret it."

"What? You'll scream and kick your feet?"

"You're in way over your heads—both of you. You have no idea who you're dealing with."

Matt put the computer down on the bed, walked into the bathroom, and knelt on one knee next to Greg. "Let's take a close look at the situation, shall we? You're a prisoner in a very small room with the man whose wife you had kidnapped. You're at the mercy of two people you planned to kill." Matt put his hand on Greg's chest and moved it up toward his neck. "Doesn't it seem like a good idea to cooperate right now?"

Greg glanced at Jane, then looked Matt in the eyes. "You're not the kind who'd hurt me to get what you want."

"How can you be so sure? I'm not. I've never been in this position before."

Greg thought for a moment, and when he spoke it was smoother, the calculating way he had spoken to Jane when he was trying to control her. "I don't really believe you'd do it, Matt. You wouldn't want Jane to see you do anything like that, and it wouldn't get you what you want."

Matt moved his hand up to Greg's Adam's apple. "Whose life do you think is more important to me—yours, or my brother's?"

Greg looked at him uncertainly, then glanced sideways at Jane.

"Don't worry," Matt said, "I'm not going to do what you would do to me. But I've found all the easy stuff in your computer—the stuff that's everyday business. I need to know what's in the files you've got hidden, and you're going to help me find out. I need you to unlock your phone too."

"Those files are hidden because they're private," Greg said coolly. "Anything in them is *my* business. So is everything on my phone. Why should I let you poke around in my personal business?"

"Because *you* made *our* private lives your business. Because I think it might help me find my brother. I'm using your computer right now to run a program I downloaded from the Internet. It will find your password—but I don't know how long it will take. So, you can get points for cooperation if you tell us the password."

Greg smirked at him and said nothing.

"All right. In the meantime, I'm going to explore your phone, so hold still while it gets a good look at you." Matt held the phone in front of Greg's face.

"Forget it!" Greg said and began to move his head from side to side. Matt took hold of his chin to stop him. Greg screwed his face up into an ugly, contorted mask.

Matt sighed. "All right, we can play children's games if you want." He put his hand over Greg's mouth and clamped down tightly. Greg looked surprised. With the fingers of his other hand, Matt pinched Greg's nostrils closed. "When you were a kid, did you ever try to find out how long you could hold your breath?" He glanced at Jane. "Time him. Let's see how good he is at this."

Jane looked down at her watch. "My record was almost two minutes, Greg. I'll bet you can't beat that."

Greg glanced at her in surprise, as though he had expected her to help him.

Jane shook her head. "Remember when we talked about choices, and you said you couldn't let me go because you had a job to do?"

There was a brief flash of guilt in Greg's eyes, and then he looked at Matt again, trying to glare threateningly.

"If you won't cooperate," Matt said, "we'll just wait until you pass out, and then your face will be nice and relaxed."

Greg continued to look at him defiantly. Matt kept the pressure on his mouth and nose. Seconds dragged by. It had been nearly a minute when Greg's brow furrowed. He began to squirm. Matt kept the pressure on. Gradually the expression on Greg's faced changed to one of wonder and then apprehension. His face began to turn red. At about a minute and a half, panic came into Greg's eyes. He gave in and relaxed.

"Much better," Matt said, taking his hands away and holding the phone in front of Greg's face to unlock the device. "We appreciate your cooperation. I'm sure you won't mind if we retrain your phone so we can open it."

Greg took several heaving breaths and coughed. He lay thinking for a moment. Jane knew what he was doing—angling for some advantage in the situation. He proved her right. "If you'll let me go," he said, "I might be able to help find your brother. But don't push me like that again, Matt, or you won't be able to count on *any* cooperation from me."

Matt looked at him in exasperation. "You can't seem to understand what's happened here, Greg. You're still thinking in terms of getting out of this and going on with business as usual."

Matt punched in a number on Greg's phone, then waited for an answer. "Dad? Have you heard anything yet about Doug?" He listened for a moment, then asked, "Is Montie still around? Let me talk to him, please." When Montie came on the line, Matt said: "Here's some more information. You ought to be looking at a man who calls himself Greg Alexander. He lives in Aspen, Colorado, and he runs a jewelry liquidation business that takes him to other parts of the country. Greg takes on extortion and contract killings as a sideline. He was the one who had Jane kidnapped. You'll want to check the phone records for this number. He's connected to the people who took Doug, but I don't know how. Maybe you can find that out." He paused to listen, and glanced at Greg. "Yeah, he's the one who killed the other guy—Lyle. We have the murder weapon with his fingerprints on it, and some of Lyle's blood." He nodded. "We'll take very good care of it for you. I can't talk anymore right now, but if I learn anything else, I'll call again."

Montie was saying, "You need to tell us where you—" when Matt ended the call and turned to face Greg. "That was Jane's uncle. He works for the FBI. *Now* do you understand? You're through—finished, out of business for good. The FBI owns you. If you ever get out of prison, you'll be a very old man. The only thing you've got going for you right now is that you could help free my brother."

Greg struggled to control the hate that burned in his gut. He said nothing.

Matt shook his head, then tapped on the phone for a few seconds and handed it to Jane. "Let Greg's phone learn to recognize your face so *we* can unlock it whenever we want." He looked at the computer on the bed. "I guess I'll have to depend on brute force after all."

"You still don't scare me!" Greg snarled.

"Very macho, Greg—very tough," Jane answered as she positioned the smartphone in front of her face. "In your situation, most people would be at least a little worried. But you're lucky—I don't think Matt means he's going to use brute force on *you*."

Matt gestured toward the laptop on the bed. "I meant the program I've downloaded. It's hitting your hard drive with thousands of combinations of letters and numbers and it won't stop until it finds your password." He picked up the computer and tapped at the keyboard. "How clever are you, Greg? You're a neat freak, and you're a controlling kind of guy, but you're so sure of yourself you didn't even bother with a basic password to lock this computer." He glanced at his watch. "If the password for those private files is only a few letters and numbers, this won't take long." He paused to let Greg think about it. "One more chance to help us out. I'll share that with the FBI."

The answer was another curse.

Matt shook his head. "Try to maintain a positive attitude, Greg. It usually helps when everything's going wrong."

Greg laid his head back on the floor and closed his eyes.

Matt stood watching the computer as the code-cracking program did its work. After half a minute, he gestured for Jane to come close. "There's nothing to do but let this run," he whispered. "Can you keep an eye on Greg for a couple of minutes?"

"Why?" she whispered back.

"This bathroom's a little too crowded. I need to go across the hall. We might as well use the room we rented for something."

"Go ahead," she answered. "I'll be fine."

"Be careful," he said, and stepped out the door, closing it softly behind him.

14

She stood watching the computer and thought momentarily how silly it was to stare at the small clock symbol on the screen as its hands spun around. This program would do its work at its own pace, and watching would not speed it up. Someone like Matt simply accepted the fact that there was an electronic process at work; inside that rectangular case, electrons were racing through circuits at a uniform rate, and when the task was accomplished, the program that someone had designed would report the results. But for most people, who never see the maze of circuits and chips inside those rectangular cases, it might be easy to personify the machine. Inside that flat box there was a little mechanical servant working very hard to do what he had been asked to do. When his job was done, he would eagerly flash—

"Jane?"

She looked into the bathroom. Greg, his arms fully extended, had scooted down far enough to be able to look at her through the door. "I'm cold," he said. "This tile floor is cold."

She walked over to peer at him through the doorway. "What do you want me to do about that?"

"Could you get me something to lay on—something so I'm not touching the tile?"

"You mean you're a little uncomfortable, Greg? You're not used to being in handcuffs, and you wish this nightmare would end so you could just go home?"

"Please," he said pleadingly. "I could have let Lyle hurt you, but I didn't."

There was some truth in what he said, Jane thought, even though his keeping Lyle in check had been self-serving. Mocking him seemed cruel, and she didn't want to be that kind of person.

She glanced at the bath mat draped over the edge of the tub. It might help him. "Stay where you are," she said as she stepped into the bathroom.

Greg was waiting for the opportunity. He whipped his legs toward her ankles, trying to knock her legs out from under her. But like Lyle, he had underestimated the quickness of her athletic reflexes. She was in the air when his legs passed under her, and then she had nowhere to come down but on top of him. He had twisted partly on his side. Her feet hit his rib cage first, and then as her feet slid off of him, her knees hit him in the chest and stomach. He groaned in pain as Jane's knees slid off of him and hit the floor. She fell backwards, striking the doorjamb with her left shoulder and ending with her upper body stretched on the carpet outside the bathroom doorway.

Quickly she drew her legs toward her, away from his body. Greg rolled onto his back, moaning. Jane stretched her legs out straight on the carpeted floor of the bedroom and rubbed her knees, trying to take away the ache. "That was dumb, Greg! Bad thinking. What were you planning to do if you knocked me down—kick me? What were you going to do when Matt comes back—lie there and growl at him?" She massaged her shoulder with her right hand.

Greg didn't answer her. He eased himself backward to relax the pressure on his arms and groaned again.

"Look at me," Jane said, and when he didn't respond, she commanded, "Look at me, Greg!"

He turned his head to look at her. She stared into his eyes as she spoke. "You just used up all the goodwill you had coming. You could make some points with us, and maybe with the police, by cooperating right now. But you're getting desperate because you've lost control of the situation, so you did something stupid. Try to use your head!"

She drew her knees up and was still massaging them when Matt opened the door and stepped into the room.

Matt looked at her on the floor and then at Greg. "What happened?"

"Greg asked me to take pity on him because he was cold, and then he tried to knock me down while I was getting the mat for him to lay on."

"Are you all right?" Matt asked. He scowled at Greg.

"Yes." She held out her hand so Matt could help her up. "But thanks to Lyle and Greg, I'm going to have bruises all over my shins and knees."

"I think I have cracked ribs," Greg said weakly from the bathroom.

Jane and Matt both looked at him. "You think we should believe him?" Matt asked. Jane shook her head. "It could be—but I think Greg forgot how to tell the truth a long time ago. I don't think he knows how to live anything but a lie."

Matt clenched and unclenched his fist. He started toward the bathroom door.

Jane put a hand on his chest to stop him and shook her head slightly when he looked at her. "Loan me the key card for the other room? It's my turn now," she said.

He pulled the card out of his shirt pocket and handed it to her. She took it and held onto his arm as she looked into his eyes. "Remember— we aren't going to be like them."

Matt glanced into the bathroom. "Greg and I are just going to have another little chat."

Jane looked into his eyes for a moment. "Okay. I'll be right back." She turned and walked out of the room.

Matt stepped into the bathroom and knelt next to Greg. "Where did you get hurt?" he asked. "Here?" He put his hand on Greg's ribs and pushed.

Greg squirmed away from him. "Don't touch me!"

He moved too fast to be injured, Matt thought. "I'm sure the police or the FBI will be glad to get you some medical help—if you really need it. Just tell me who's got my brother and where he is, and we'll hand you to the police right now."

The other man turned to glare at him. "Whoever's got your brother will probably kill him—and I wouldn't do a thing to stop them if I could."

Matt leaned close to his face. "Are you a slow learner, Greg? You don't seem to understand how hard I'm trying not to hurt you. You treated somebody I love like trash, and I know you'd kill us if you could. If you were smart, you'd stop pushing me."

"You're all talk," Greg sneered. "You don't scare me."

Matt sighed. He put his hand on Greg's ribs again. The man cringed, obviously expecting Matt to inflict some pain. "If you had someone in this position, you'd hurt him, wouldn't you?" Matt asked. Then: "No—you wouldn't. You don't like to get your hands dirty. You'd rely on somebody like Lyle to do that, wouldn't you?"

Greg did not answer.

Matt eased down the wall and sat leaning back against the doorjamb looking at Greg. The other man looked away, then after several seconds looked back at Matt. "What? Why are you staring at me?"

"Do I make you nervous?"

Greg very deliberately looked away again, as though he were studying the textured ivory covering on the bathroom wall intently. It was more macho attitude—a way to deny that he had any interest in what was going on inside Matt's mind.

"What makes you so sure I couldn't kill you?" Matt asked.

Slowly Greg turned his head toward Matt again. He seemed to be measuring his words carefully when he spoke. "People like you are always afraid. You worry about what would happen if you killed me."

"Why should I worry? You're not telling me what I want to know, so I don't need you. Your pistol with the silencer is over there on the bed, and you said yourself that no one in the next room would hear a thing."

Greg glanced at the bed. "You won't because of Jane. She would know. And the police would know."

"Would they? I could say I was holding the pistol on you while we talked. You tried a move on me, just like you did with Jane, and the gun went off accidentally."

Greg stared in the direction of the bed for several seconds. He looked back at Matt. "If you were the kind who'd do that, you wouldn't be sitting here *talking* about using the gun."

Matt moved as though to stand.

"You don't want to do that because I might still be of some help to you," Greg added hastily. "You never know—we might be able to work out some kind of deal."

Matt smiled slightly. He had put a crack in Greg's shell. "A deal? I don't think so. You're right about me—I try to live by rules that don't let me do some of the things you do. And I'm not going to beat you or make you bleed to get what I want. You think that's weakness, don't you?"

The movement of Greg's shoulders was as close to a shrug as he could get under the circumstances. "I look out for myself. That's what everybody does. Sometimes other people have to get hurt. I don't do it unless it's necessary."

"*Necessary?*"

Greg looked at him as though the question were foolish. Matt returned his stare. Finally, he said, "Just because I'm not going to torture you, don't start feeling comfortable. There's still plenty I can do to you."

Greg raised his eyebrows questioningly.

"I believe people have to live with the results of their own choices. I'm going to see that you face the law for the choices you've made over the past few days."

Greg smirked. "I know some good lawyers."

Matt laughed, and Greg's smile turned into a frown.

"Keep on trying to convince yourself you're in control," Matt said. "But we've got a murder weapon with your fingerprints on it. The story Jane and I tell the police will put you away for kidnapping too." He glanced over his shoulder at the computer on the bed. "And there's more in those files, isn't there?"

"That won't count. You *stole* it. You have no right to look in my files."

"But the police or the FBI will seize all of it as evidence, and they'll know how to mine your files legally."

Greg put on his blank face once more. "We'll see. I'll let my lawyers handle that."

Matt sat watching him, a half smile on his face. Greg tried to look away once more, but somehow he was drawn to look into Matt's eyes. "So—what?" he asked again.

"There are worse things I could do than turning you over to the police."

"Like what?"

"You work for somebody who pays you to kill people," Matt answered. "You've blown this assignment badly. We could leave you at your employer's mercy. I don't think you can expect him to be as good to you as we've been."

The crack in Greg's veneer opened a bit wider; a fleeting look in his eyes said he knew that Matt was right. Then he let his mask fall into place again.

Matt tried to press his advantage. "You could help yourself right now. Help me find my brother. It wouldn't hurt you, and it might look good when you end up facing a jury."

Greg looked into Matt's eyes for several seconds before he spoke. "Some people wouldn't see it that way."

"Who?" When Greg didn't answer, Matt continued, "Are you really more afraid of the people who had Doug kidnapped than you are of the law? The police or the FBI could protect you. All you have to do is give me a name and I'll pass it on to the man I called a few minutes ago."

Greg looked away and said nothing.

Matt sighed. "All right. By the time I get through with your computer, there won't be anything in it that's a secret anymore. Is there evidence that links you to Doug's kidnapping? What will they call that—conspiracy, or accessory? Maybe you've forgotten to pay taxes on income from this little sideline of yours? Income tax evasion. Will I find evidence of other contract killings?" He paused to let Greg absorb that idea. "When the FBI and the police start investigating what I find, it's going to get back to the people you're protecting. Do you think those people will guess where the information came from?"

Greg's face showed surprise, and then anger as he turned to glare at Matt.

"I told you," Matt said, "I'm not going to do anything just because *I* want to make you pay. But don't blame me if you get hurt because of the things I find in your files."

"Sure—I'm supposed to believe you can just say some magic words over my computer and find out anything you want to know?"

Matt glanced over his shoulder at the laptop on the bed. "Cole hired me for my computer skills. He wanted me to protect all his business and private information. But he didn't know everything he was getting because there's part of my background I don't put on my resume—the part about hacking into some government and financial databases when I was seventeen just to prove I could do it. I'm lucky that a good man took time to teach me there were better ways to channel my talents."

"You haven't told Jane about all that, have you?" Greg managed a lop-sided smirk. "I told Jane you were keeping secrets from her. I said—"

"Greg, the part you need to worry about is that I've got a side gig too. I'm a computer security consultant. I hack into computer systems to show where their weaknesses are. You think you've protected your computer against someone like me?"

Greg didn't answer, but his expression had changed. There was apprehension in it.

"Worried?" Matt got to his feet and walked over to look at the computer. "This program tells me you've only got a six-letter password—and it already has four of them. It won't take much longer." He sat down on the bed to watch.

* * *

Jane was washing her hands at the bathroom sink when she glanced up at herself in the mirror. She looked as tired and worn as she felt—not the way she had hoped to look on her honeymoon with the man she loved.

She sighed; at least she was with him. Things could have been different tonight.

Right now, she would like to use this hotel room to actually rest, maybe sleep a little, but there was no time. She splashed cold water on her face, then toweled it off.

She was drying her hands when one of the telephones in her jacket pocket began to ring. She pulled them out to check the caller ID. Greg's cheap, disposable phone showed a local number. She couldn't be certain, but the number didn't look like one of those she had seen earlier on his record of calls.

Who would be calling Greg at this time of night? The people who hired him?

She wanted badly to know who was behind this, and any little bit of information could be useful. This phone number would be added automatically to the record of calls on his phone, and it might be of some help, but if she answered the call now, maybe she could . . .

No! It was a crazy idea—possibly dangerous. What if it *were* the people who hired Greg, and they learned that he hadn't finished his job?

The phone had already rung three times. How quickly would it go to voice mail?

There might be a way to find out who was calling without giving away her own identity. She punched the TALK button, held the phone at arm's length, and said what came to mind. "No, *I'm* going to answer it. I want to know who's calling you this late." She giggled and added, "You enjoy your cocktail. I'll be right back." Then she put the phone to her ear and said, "Hello?"

The woman who spoke sounded shocked. "Is Grigori there?"

What could she say, Jane wondered, that would get more information? She hesitated, and when nothing better came to her, she said, "I'm afraid he's tied up right now. May I tell him who called?"

There was silence for four or five seconds and then a click on the other end. The line went dead.

A *woman*? Could it have been a woman who hired Greg to eliminate them? Or was this person simply a go-between for someone else?

Lyle had talked to Greg about a "hot date" tonight. This woman?

Whoever she was, Jane hoped she did not know enough about Greg's activities to guess who had answered the phone. Or if the caller knew Greg's real errand in San Francisco, Jane hoped she would assume that he had already completed the job and was relaxing somewhere.

Jane put the phone back into her jacket pocket, then left their rented room and walked back up the hall to Greg's. She knocked softly on the door and after a few seconds Matt opened it to let her in.

He pointed at the monitor screen of the notebook computer on the bed. "We have his password." He glanced at his watch. "Fourteen minutes."

Jane looked at the characters highlighted on the computer's monitor screen: *Lqd8tr*. "'Liquidator.' Very clever, Greg—in a twisted sort of way." She looked at Matt. "Greg just had a phone call. It was a woman—a local number."

"You *answered* it?" Matt frowned.

"Don't worry, I didn't give anything away. I hope I made her believe that Greg is out partying with someone."

Matt grinned. "You devil. You're good at this intrigue stuff. What did she say?"

"Nothing, really. She just asked for Grigori. I told her he was tied up and couldn't come to the phone. I offered to tell him who called, but she hung up."

"'Tied up'? Cute!" Greg said sourly from the bathroom.

"Where's your sense of humor?" Jane replied. "Lyle thought that line was hilarious when he said it to Matt about me."

"Nothing else?" Matt asked.

Jane shook her head. "I wondered if it was the woman Greg stood up tonight. He told Lyle he had a date for this evening, after he planned to be finished with us."

Matt thought for a moment. "But she knows his real name and his throwaway number. She's not a casual acquaintance he picked up somewhere." He looked at Greg. "Care to share?"

Greg stared at him impassively.

Matt sat down on the end of the bed and picked up the computer. "You might be more clever than I think, Greg, but I won't be surprised if this one password opens up everything in your files." Greg tried to mask his apprehension as he glanced at the computer. "I'll give you one more chance to save us some time by telling us who has my brother."

Again, Greg did not answer him. Instead, he looked at Jane. "Talk to your husband. Tell him he's going to get both of you killed. The two of you don't want to get involved with the people who, uh . . . "

"The people who hired you?" Matt responded. "Why? Would they kill us deader than you were going to?"

"You ought to worry about what they'll do to you—and her—*before* they kill you!"

Jane thought it was the first time she had seen Greg show fear. "Are you really concerned about us? Or are you worried about what they'll do to you when they find out you failed?"

Greg looked away and said nothing more.

"Okay," Matt said, "let's see what we can find." He hunched over the computer working at the keys. Jane sat in a chair watching him. Greg watched too, with the fascination of someone who knows something bad is about to happen and can't turn away. Minutes passed as Matt worked, his expression unchanging. His fingers tapped the keys rapidly, he paused to scan the screen, then tap-tapped again. "All kinds of personal and business stuff here. Interesting, but not what we're looking for," he muttered, then glanced at the man lying on the floor in the bathroom. "Some of it looks like Greg could have been skimming profits from his clients—the same thing Cole Brewster was doing."

Matt continued browsing in the files for two or three more minutes, then stopped to stare at the screen. He looked up at Greg. "This file labeled C.B.—notes all about Cole Brewster. You've got our names in here too." He pushed the arrow key to scroll the file down the monitor screen. "And our families—our parents . . . my brother . . . my wife's younger sister."

Jane looked at Greg in surprise. "Kristy? She's only seventeen, and she couldn't know anything about Cole's business, or . . ." Jane's face went pale. "Could you get any *more* evil?"

Greg's only response was a small smirk.

"Easy, J, I've already asked Montie to protect our families," Matt said. "Greg, are you the only one who has this information, or have you shared it with anyone else?"

Greg looked away, and made Matt wait before he answered. "That's something you won't be able to find out from my computer. But I might be willing to tell you—if you let me go."

"Nice try, Greg, but it won't fly," Matt answered grimly. "You're staying right where we have you."

"Want to know what I think?" Jane asked. "I think Greg has too big an ego to share everything he knows." She walked over and squatted down by the door where Greg couldn't avoid seeing her as she spoke. "You still believe you can play us. If you pretend you're holding something back, you might be able to negotiate." She looked at Matt. "But he told Lyle this operation is in his hands. Greg wouldn't share any more of his information than he has to because it's his power—it helps keep him in control." She turned to speak to the man on the floor again. "Isn't that right?"

Greg retreated behind his blank mask.

Matt went back to exploring files in the computer. "Information is an interesting commodity, Greg," he said. "It can give you power—or it can be used against you if it falls into the wrong hands."

He scrolled farther down the list of files in the computer. "Very neatly alphabetized." He opened one. "Let's look in Liquidations, Estates." He scanned the information in the file. "Looks like you have some clients who are fairly wealthy. You collected some nice commissions—from the sellers and buyers too. Is that ethical—or were you watching out for yourself again?"

Matt closed the file and moved to the next one. "Liquidations, Family Trusts. . . . Looks like you made out okay here too."

Close, open. "Liquidations, Personal . . ." Matt suddenly sat up straight and glanced at Jane. "This one isn't business as usual. It's names and phone numbers, with a file for every name." He double-clicked the first file to open it. "Alberto—and the phone number is in Colombia. You sell a lot of jewelry in Colombia?"

Matt began to scroll through the file. "Hmm. Lots of information here about Alberto—address, wife's name, children's names and ages and schools, girlfriend's name, clubs where he hangs out . . . and second in command." He stopped scrolling. "Personal info about another name. Looks like a lawyer, from his title, or maybe a judge. Then there are two figures followed by dates—fifty thousand dollars, then another fifty. The last date was three and a half months ago." Matt looked down at Greg. "Was that when this man died? This is your sideline business, isn't it? *Very* personal liquidations."

Greg ignored the question.

Matt scanned the file again. "Even the places where Alberto's kids like to hang out. Was Alberto the man who hired you to liquidate the judge? What would Alberto do if he knew you'd collected this kind of information about him?" When Greg went on ignoring him, Matt continued. "Maybe we should give Alberto a call and chat about this. What do you think, Greg? We'll just—"

"*Don't!*" Greg had turned to look Matt in the eyes. "Don't do that. You don't want to talk to that man. You won't like what happens."

"Or *you* won't." Matt tapped the keys on the computer to close the file. "Let's see who else you've got on your list. We might want to call all of these people. Antoine . . . Becker . . . Boris!"

"*Boris?*" Jane stood quickly and walked over to sit by Matt on the bed. "*There's* a name we know. Let's see what Greg has on Boris."

Matt opened the file and the two of them scanned it together. "*Very* thorough, Greg. Boris must be someone *really* important," Matt said, scrolling to the next screen.

Jane pointed to the three lines at the bottom of the page. "There—Cole's name again." She looked at Greg. "And ours."

"Fifty thousand next to Cole's name—but that's all," Matt said. "Because you haven't finished the job you were supposed to do. And there's nothing next to our names. Does that mean you were offering a group rate this time—two extra for free?" His voice rose on the last sentence.

The anger radiating from her husband could almost raise the reading on the thermostat in the room, Jane thought. The tone of his voice and the look he gave the other man had brought fear into Greg's eyes again. Maybe Greg was beginning to realize how vulnerable he was.

Jane put a hand on Matt's arm. "You stopped him. You're stronger. Remember that."

Matt glanced at Greg once more, then turned back to the computer.

Greg opened his mouth and started to speak, then thought better of it when he looked at Jane's face. She shook her head slightly.

"I don't think Greg does anything for free," she said to Matt. "I think Cole was supposed to be the only target, but Greg messed things up with him."

Matt looked at Greg. "Did you kill Cole before you found out everything you needed to know? Were you too cocky about this from the beginning?"

"Cole said *you* had the money!" The words seemed to come out of Greg almost involuntarily. "And you lied when you said you didn't know anything about it!"

Matt ignored the assertion. He had drawn a response from Greg. Maybe they were wearing him down. "Boris probably wasn't happy when you didn't get the money back from Cole. Was my brother kidnapped because Boris thought you needed help doing your job?"

"You can ask him when you meet him! I'm sure you'll have the chance—unless you let me go."

"Oh, I don't think we ought to wait," Matt replied. "I think we ought to ask Boris right now."

"No! Don't call him! Trust me, you don't want to do that."

"Why?" Jane asked. "Because he'll know you opened the door for us to find him?"

"No, it's uh . . . there has to be a better way."

"Yeah, there is," Matt answered. "Tell me where to find my brother, if you know."

"Look, I, uh . . . I know some places. Maybe if you let me think about it . . . "

"No good, Greg." Matt looked at his watch. It was 1:30 A.M., approximately two and one-half hours since he had talked to Doug's kidnappers. "The clock is ticking on my brother's life. It's ticking for you, too, and you probably don't even realize how fast. Three hours ago, we met another guy who was looking for us—somebody else sent by Boris. But I'll bet you didn't know you had help on this job, did you?"

Greg looked surprised. "What are you talking about?"

"A man named Dexter Williams," Jane answered. "Boris called him and told him to help you out. It doesn't sound like Boris thinks you can handle this by yourself."

Greg blanched.

"Do you want to reconsider helping us find Doug?" she asked.

Greg thought before answering. He had a tie to Boris that they did not know about, and he hoped that would protect him. If he could get just one break, he still might be able to deliver Matt and Jane. But he needed to regain some control of the situation. "I don't see how I can help you when I'm a prisoner. Let me loose and we can talk."

"No chance," Matt answered. "We don't have time to play games with you." He scrolled backward in the computer file to a list of telephone numbers he had seen. "Hmm—here's one with a Los Angeles area code. J, let me borrow Greg's flip phone. I think this was a number he called yesterday." Again, Greg seemed to watch with morbid fascination while Matt checked the list of calls in the cheap telephone's log. Matt looked up at him. "Yeah—first thing yesterday morning."

Matt punched the CALL button and waited, hoping Boris, or someone close to him, would answer at this time of night.

The phone rang three times without going to voicemail, so Matt knew it must be turned on. But would anyone pick it up? It rang once more and someone did. "*Slushayu*," a deep male voice said.

Matt did not know what the word meant, but the tone sounded commanding. The voice did not sound sleepy. Apparently the man on the other end of the line had not been surprised by a ringing phone at this time of night; it seemed he might have been expecting a call, from someone who spoke his language. "Boris?" Matt asked.

There was silence for several seconds. Finally, the man said, "You have wrong number."

"No, I don't think so. If this is Boris, you and I need to talk."

"I have no reason to talk to man I do not know who calls in middle of night."

"Yes, you do—almost six hundred thousand reasons. I'm sure you could find something to say about those. I want some answers from you. I want to know where my brother is."

The pause on the other end was longer this time. In the background, Matt heard a woman speak. He could not make out the words, but Boris replied to her softly in what sounded like Russian. Then he came back on the line. "Your brother? I know nothing of brother."

"Greg—Grigori—seems to believe you do." Matt was watching the face of the man on the bathroom floor. It might have been only the lighting reflected off the white tile and bathroom walls, but Greg seemed to be pale. "You're smart enough to guess who this is," Matt continued on the phone. "You had my brother kidnapped so you could get something back. There's absolutely no way you'll ever get it unless my brother goes free."

The man paused again. "Who is Grigori?"

"The man you sent to get the money, and playing dumb with me isn't going to get it for you. If Greg had asked nicely, I might have given it to him. But he didn't—he wanted to take it and kill us. That's the job you gave him, isn't it?"

"You have my money?"

Progress, Matt thought. He had forced Boris to drop the pretense. "I know where it is. Where is my brother?"

The other man ignored Matt's question. "Money was stolen from me. You will give it back."

"*I* didn't steal it, and I don't want it. But unless my brother goes free, you'll never see it again."

"*You* do not say what will happen. *I* say."

"Not this time." Matt hoped he was not pushing his—or Doug's—luck too far. But this man did not sound like one who would consider a polite request. He was used to commanding, and commanding was probably the only approach that would hold his attention. "If you want your money, you'll let my brother go. It's that simple. If anything happens to my brother, or to anyone else in my family or my wife's family, you lose the money—and more. I'll use the information I have to make your life impossible."

"You know nothing. You are—how you say, *bluffing*."

"Bluffing you would be like bluffing a shark, and I'm not stupid. I don't believe you're stupid either. Think about it—I have your private number. And was that Yelena you were talking to, or someone else?"

The man said something harsh in Russian. When he spoke in English again, he was obviously trying to keep his anger under control. "Maybe you learned some little things from Grigori, but—"

Matt laughed. "There's a lot more information where that came from. You would find yourself in deep trouble if it got out."

"You will not tell police. They will not find your brother in time. If you talk to police, your brother—"

"My brother had better stay well and safe. Otherwise, I'll use the information I got from Greg to tie your life in knots you can't even dream about."

"I do not believe you could do this. You would have to prove to me. You would have to prove to me you can get my money."

"Fine. We'll meet later today and I'll show you—in some public place. One o'clock. That should give you time to get to San Francisco. I'll tell you where we're going to meet after I get a call from my brother saying he's free and at home. I'd better get that call by eleven o'clock this morning. Eleven—no later. You can find me at Greg's telephone number, but don't call unless you're going to tell me my brother is on his way home." Matt turned off the phone.

Greg lay staring at him with something like amazement. "You just signed your own death warrants!"

"Or yours," Matt answered. "But don't worry—we need you alive. We're going to make sure the police get you so Boris can't."

Greg looked up at the ceiling. "You don't know him." He shook his head slowly. "He'll never stop coming after you. *Never.*"

"Does the woman who called know where you are?" Jane asked.

"I didn't tell her," Greg said.

It was another of his non-answers, Jane thought. Was he telling the truth, or trying to find some way to hide it? "If no one else knows where you're staying," Jane said, "you'll be perfectly safe. But if you're lying to us . . . "

* * *

The man drummed his fingers slowly on the night table next to the bed.

Grigori was a disappointment. The boy had shown great promise in the business when he was younger, but he had been enjoying the good things of America for too long. His love of fine clothes, fine wine, fine women had made him soft—and careless. He no longer had the edge needed to do the jobs for which he was paid. That was a shame. But it was truth. Grigori had failed on this assignment—twice.

The Russian turned on his telephone again and dialed a number. When the call was answered, he spoke rapidly in his native language. After he ended the call, the woman beside him asked sleepily what was so important in the middle of the night. Just business, the Russian explained. It would take him away for a day, but then it would be over.

He dialed another number, and when a voice finally answered, he said, "We must go to San Francisco, soonest possible. We will meet you at airport—one hour."

"*Now?*" the voice on the other end protested. "Tonight?"

"Yes, tonight," Boris said coldly. "You will be paid well, as usual. Is problem?"

"No, no," the other man said hastily. "At airport, one hour."

15

Matt leaned close to her and whispered. "We can't stay here. We have to go somewhere else."

"I know," Jane whispered back. "There may be somebody out there who knows where he is, and they might come looking for him."

"I've just scratched the surface in his computer files. I'm sure Boris has no idea how much information Greg collected. I need time to do something with it."

"We could go to the room across the hall."

Matt frowned. "Yeah." He nodded in Greg's direction. "But he knows about it. If someone finds him, he'll give us up in a second."

Jane thought for a moment, then nodded. "Okay. We need to look for another place—one where no one is likely to find us."

"We'll need an Internet connection so I can—"

"Matt? Jane?"

They moved so they could see Greg in the bathroom.

"You have to let me out of here."

"Actually, we don't," Matt answered. "Why would we do that?"

"Because . . . because you just dared Boris to come after you. And if he comes after you, he'll, uh . . . "

"Find you first?"

Greg's voice rose as he spoke. "You haven't seen what he does to people who cross him. What was the idea of letting him think I *gave* you the information about him?"

"You mean how dare I make *my* problem *your* problem? Where could I have gotten the idea of doing something like that?"

Jane studied Greg's face. "Why are you so afraid of having Boris find you?"

"I'm not afraid!"

The fear in his eyes told her it was a lie. "What will he do to you if he finds you?" When Greg did not answer, Jane asked, "*Will* he find you? Does he know where you are?"

"No."

"Does anyone else know where you are?"

Greg did not look at her as he answered. "No."

"Not the woman who called?"

"I said I didn't tell her!"

The non-answer again. "Is there *anything* you'd tell us that we can believe?"

"Believe me when I tell you you've made more trouble for yourselves than you could possibly understand. But I can help you. I think I could still get Boris to leave you alone." Greg's eyes darted from Matt to Jane and back. His words came out in a rush. "If you'll tell me where the money is— I could call him, I could . . . if you gave it to him, maybe we could all walk away and forget this. Maybe—"

"Greg!" Matt cut him off. He put the computer on the bed and walked over to stand in the bathroom doorway. "You're losing it. Take a deep breath."

Matt sat down in the bathroom doorway again. "Think. You were already in trouble with Boris when he had my brother kidnapped. Then he hired Williams. The way he probably sees it, you've botched this so badly that—well, do you really believe you can fix everything up with him somehow?" Matt paused to let Greg consider the question. "Right now, the solution to our problem is the solution to your problem. The best thing you could do for yourself is tell us where to find Doug. How about you tell us where to find Boris too? That way, you're safe from him and the courts will see you cooperated."

The two men looked into each other's eyes for several seconds without speaking. Finally, Greg looked up at the ceiling. He relaxed his neck and let his head lay back on the floor for several seconds, until he slowly shook his head from side to side. "I'd never be safe."

Matt exhaled in a sigh. "I can't understand why you're not getting this. The next best thing that could happen to you is that we turn you over to the police later today as a murderer, a kidnapper, and an accessory to everything Boris may have done to my brother. Or, there's door number three: you've been lying to us about nobody knowing where you are, and Boris finds you somehow before this afternoon. Do you think he's going to say, 'That's okay, Greg, everybody's entitled to a little foul-up now and then'?"

Greg raised his head and looked at Matt again. But he did not speak. Boris would be angry—Greg knew that. But Boris could not treat him like just some hired help.

Matt waited for several seconds, giving the other man a chance to change his mind. But finally he stood. "Jane and I will be leaving you here by yourself." He walked over to the bed where Jane sat and leaned down to whisper to her again. "We can't leave him free to create a commotion. I'm going to look for something we can use to tie him so he can't move so much. It would help if we could think of a good way to keep him quiet."

"I have the rest of Lyle's tape in my jacket pocket."

"That'll probably do it."

Matt opened the closet and examined the clothing on the hangers. There was another pair of Greg's tailored slacks, a monogrammed dress shirt, and a knit pullover that was color coordinated with the slacks. There were two silk ties. Matt tossed them on the bed; they might be useful if he could find nothing else to tie Greg's legs together.

Jane walked into the bathroom. "Are you willing to behave this time if I get you a drink of water?"

Greg looked up at her as though he suspected some trick.

She took the glass off the counter, filled it with water, and knelt down beside him.

He looked at her curiously. "Why are you doing . . . I mean, after everything?"

"I don't know. Sometimes I even surprise myself," she answered. "Think you can drink that way?"

Greg opened his mouth. She poured water between his lips. He swallowed, and Jane tilted the glass to pour again. Greg shook his head. "No." He looked into her eyes. "Thanks. That was enough."

"You're welcome." She reached for the bathmat hanging over the edge of the tub and placed it on the floor beside him. "Lift up," she said. Greg arched his back and she slid the bathmat underneath him. "That will keep you a little warmer."

He looked at her in wonder. "Thank you."

It was the first thing she had heard him say that sounded like he genuinely meant it.

"J, look at this."

She turned to see Matt holding a length of nylon rope in his hand. He had taken it from a compartment inside Greg's suitcase, which was open on the bed. "I doubt that Greg uses this for a clothesline after he washes his clothes at night." He reached into the suitcase and pulled out several narrow strips of plastic.

Jane's brow furrowed. "What are those?"

"Plastic handcuffs. They're used to restrain prisoners." He reached into the suitcase again. "And this." He held up what looked like a black drawstring bag.

Jane frowned and shook her head. "I don't . . . "

"My guess is it's a hood to keep someone from seeing where she's going, or where she is."

Jane looked down at the man on the floor. "How cruel!" Greg couldn't meet her eyes.

"I think we can use a couple of these things," Matt said. He walked into the bathroom carrying the rope and some of the plastic strips.

"What are you going to do?" Greg asked apprehensively.

"I'm going to make sure you can't move around so much that you wiggle off that mat onto the cold tile floor," Matt answered. He handed Jane the plastic handcuffs. "Use two of these strips to tie the links in the handcuff chain together so Greg doesn't have any slack to move his arms. Greg, I'm going to use the rope to tie your legs. It will be better for both of us if you don't fight me—but it will especially be better for you."

Matt wound one end of the rope around Greg's ankles and tied them together firmly. "Ow!" Greg complained. "That's too tight. It's cutting off the circulation."

"The last time we left you restrained, you managed to get loose somehow and killed somebody. That's not going to happen again."

When Jane had finished with the handcuffs, Matt checked to make sure they were as tight as possible. Greg couldn't pull his wrists apart more than an inch. "Good job, J. Now help me move Greg over a bit."

They moved his body so his legs stretched out on an angle toward the king-sized bed. Matt passed the rope between Greg's calves twice, twisting it around the rope circling his ankles to tighten that loop. Then he stretched the remainder of the rope toward the heavy frame that supported the bed. He wound the rope over and under the steel arms of the frame at its corner and tied the end of the rope tightly to the leg of the frame. When he finished, Greg was stretched out with both his arms and his legs tightly secured. He could do little more than arch his body a bit.

Jane knelt beside him, took the duct tape out of her jacket pocket, and began to pull a strip of it away from the roll.

"You don't have to do that, Jane. I won't make any noise," Greg said.

She noticed that his eyes did not look distant or vacant now. Maybe this was finally the real Greg at the level of his heart. But how long would his meekness last once they were out the door? "I'd like to believe you, Greg. I really would," she said sadly. She put the tape across his mouth, lifted up his head and passed the roll of tape underneath, then brought the tape around tightly from the other side until it overlapped before she tore it free from the roll. Greg looked at her with the same fierce hate she had seen earlier when she pointed out how his ego had left him vulnerable. His meekness had not lasted very long.

Matt put Greg's computer back into its bag. He took the plastic liner bag out of the ice bucket, carefully stowed Greg's pistol and knife in it to preserve the fingerprints, and slipped that package into the outer pocket on the computer bag. He found a plastic hotel laundry bag in the closet, put Lyle's pistol into it, and stowed that item in the computer case as well.

He stepped into the bathroom and looked at Greg, trussed on the floor. "One last chance: would you like to tell us where the FBI could find Boris?" Greg simply glared at him. Matt turned out the light in the bathroom. "We'll come back for you later, after we finish with him."

They glanced around the hotel room just before opening the door to be sure they had left nothing behind. Matt turned off the light, they stepped into the hallway, and Jane hung the DO NOT DISTURB sign on the door handle as it shut. They took the elevator to the hotel's mezzanine level, then walked down the stairs into the front lobby so that they were out of sight of anyone at the registration desk. There was no one to see them as they stepped out onto Powell Street.

In the distance to their right, they could see dimly through the fog the headlights of a car coming uphill from the direction of Market. Matt pointed across the street. "Let's head that way." They walked to the corner, pushed the button for the crossing light, and waited, even though the car was still a block away.

Jane laughed lightly.

"What?" Matt asked, looking at her.

"I've been kidnapped and held captive most of the day, we escaped getting shot, we just left the man who was responsible tied up in his hotel room, and after all that, in my head right now I can hear my mother saying, 'Always wait till the light says WALK. That's when it's safe to cross.'"

Matt laughed too and put an arm around her to draw her close. The car passed them and the pedestrian crossing light turned into a symbol of a man walking. They crossed the street and walked up a set of stone steps into deserted Union Square.

The column of the war memorial rose above the center of the square, and metal benches along the edge formed a border. The fronts of exclusive stores faced the square on the south and east. At the northeast corner, the mostly dark shape of a high-rise hotel towered above the square. Matt and Jane strolled toward the hotel holding hands.

On the east side of the square, they passed a sidewalk cafe. Its small tables and the metal chairs that went with them had been gathered inside the building. Matt stopped, looking through the glass front of the café at the tables and chairs. "This could make a good spot for a meeting in public." He turned and surveyed the square, then looked up at the high-rise hotel. "A really good spot. At midday, there'd be a lot of people here. Don't you think Boris would be afraid to try something with so many people around?"

Jane's brow furrowed. "Are we really going to meet him? Do we still *need* to do that?"

Matt frowned. "What do you mean?"

"Well, what will we gain by meeting with him? We're not going to give the money back, are we? Even if you were to give the money back, he still probably would want to kill us—and Doug—because of what we know. If we gave all the information we have to Montie and the FBI right now"—she glanced at her watch—"they'd have more than an eight-hour head start on finding Doug, in case Boris decides not to cooperate."

"And if we gave them Greg," Matt said slowly, "he wouldn't have any choice but to cooperate, would he? Just by being in the hands of the FBI, he'd probably be compromised in Boris's eyes." He stood looking at her for

several seconds while he considered the possibilities. "That's good thinking, J. It's probably the best thing we could do for Doug right now."

He put his arm around her again and led her toward the steps on the
east side of the square to sit down. He put Greg's computer on his knees.
"Let me use Greg's disposable phone. I hope Montie's still there. I hate to
wake my parents in the middle of the night."

"I doubt they've had any sleep."

They heard the ring tone even before he turned on Greg's phone. It
took a few seconds for them to realize where it was coming from—the
computer bag. Matt quickly fished out Greg's smartphone. He glanced at
the caller ID display and raised his eyebrows in a question: "No number.
Boris?" He put the phone to his ear. "Yeah?"

"You called people who are with your brother."

There was no mistaking the deep voice. Its tone was accusatory. Matt
didn't like the sound of it. "I wanted to make sure Doug was all right," he
answered. It was an explanation, not an apology. "Have you called to tell
me that they're letting him go?"

"You will not talk with him again unless I get money."

"No. If I give you the money first, you'll kill him—and probably us too. I
told you before, when I know my brother is free, then we'll talk about your
money. That's the way it has to be."

"I tell *you* before, you do not say what will happen. *I* say."

The man obviously was trying to assert control over the situation. Matt
did not want to have this confrontation with his brother's life at stake, but
he saw no way to back down without leaving Doug in more danger. "You
don't seem to understand your situation," he said slowly. "Right now I'm
the most dangerous man you know. If I go to the police with the information I have, you're through. Your business is over—finished. That's what I
will do if you hurt my brother. There's only one way you can keep it from
happening—let my brother go."

"I do not believe you."

"Now you're trying to bluff *me*. Or maybe you're not as smart as I
thought you were. But I promise, if you hurt my brother, it will cost you
much more than you can imagine right now."

The Russian did not answer for several seconds. Matt wondered what
was going on in his mind. Finally, the other man said, "You say eleven in
morning. It will not be possible before."

"I had better hear from him by then. If I don't . . . well, you won't like what happens. I'll do as much damage to you as I can."

"Brother will die if you lie to me about this!" It was obvious the Russian was having difficulty controlling his fury. "He is not in same place. Other people are with him. If you tell police—if they *think* police are close—they will start fire and leave him. Do you know what I tell you?"

"You'd better not let that happen. The next time I hear anything about my brother, it had better be from him. When I hear from him, then I'll call you and tell you where we'll meet." He turned off Greg's phone.

"What did he say to you?" Jane asked.

Matt did not answer. He sat staring straight ahead for several seconds, then slowly bent forward until his head touched his knees. He groaned.

"What is it?" Jane put a hand on his back. She could feel him trembling. "Matt—what's wrong?"

Matt sat up again. "He's moved Doug. If the people who have him see the police or even think they're close, they'll start a fire and leave him to burn to death." Pain showed in his face when he looked at her. "I've put my brother's life on the line. If Boris believes I can't make good on what I told him, Doug will die—maybe before Montie and the troops could ever find him. But if I give Boris what he wants, all three of us are on his hit list after that. What are we going to do?"

She put an arm around him and moved close. "I don't know. But you handled things pretty well today. You saved me. Go with what you feel. I'm with you."

"All day long I was afraid if I did the wrong thing it might get you killed, because Greg made it clear they wouldn't mind sacrificing you. Now I think Doug has even less of a chance with this man." He paused. "I *could* call Montie, but even if we knew where Doug is, would the FBI be able to get to him before . . . could they do it without alerting the guys who are holding him?" Matt's voice trailed off as he thought for a moment. "And Doug might not even be in this country. I can't give the FBI a single clue from Greg's files about where he is."

"Are you sure? You didn't get much of a chance to work on his files."

"Well . . . no, I didn't."

"Maybe you ought to dig deeper before we decide about calling Montie. There could be something in there." She took hold of his hand and stood.

"Come on." She nodded toward the high-rise hotel. "Let's find a warm, safe place to work."

The lobby of this hotel was meant to suggest elegance too, but not in an understated way, like the hotel Greg had chosen. This one had a large atrium that seemed almost cavernous because it was empty. The contemporary furniture was obviously expensive. The planters, ash stands, and trash receptacles were shiny brass. The floor in the reception area was marble, and the long oak reception desk made the lone night clerk appear even smaller than he was.

He had to look up at both of them. He seemed to be assessing Matt, as though trying to determine what kind of person would wander in at almost 2:00 in the morning. Then he looked at Jane, and smiled. "May I help you?"

"We'd like a room," Matt said.

"We had to leave our last hotel," Jane added.

The clerk's brow furrowed slightly. Then he began to tap at the computer keyboard. "I'll see if we have a room available right now."

The clerk had just added their sudden appearance at this time of night with Jane's comment, Matt realized, and gotten the wrong answer: These two were "problem" guests. Matt glanced at the name badge on the man's jacket. "Rafael, you looked at my wife like you thought you recognized her face. Am I right about that?"

Rafael looked up at him, then at Jane, studying her, obviously trying to decide how to answer. No man would want to admit he did not recognize a beautiful woman whose face he ought to know—especially a man in Rafael's line of work.

"She has a face you'd see in a magazine or in paparazzi photos, doesn't she?" Matt suggested.

Rafael smiled slightly. "Well, yes, she does look familiar." There was relief in his voice.

"Do you have guests sometimes who have to ask you to protect their identity because there are people out there"—Matt jerked his thumb toward the street—"who just won't leave them alone?"

"It's horrible," Jane added. "There were people who came right into our hotel after us. One of them even pretended to be associated with the hotel. He showed me a phony I.D. just to get me to open the door so he could talk to me."

Rafael drew himself up to his full height before answering. "We're very careful to protect our guests' privacy in this hotel."

"We were hoping to find a place like that," Matt answered. "Would you happen to have a room overlooking Union Square—one that's not too high up?"

The clerk checked his computer listings. "Yes." He looked at Matt as he continued. "Would the fourth floor be all right? That room would be three hundred forty-nine dollars."

"We'll take it."

The clerk poised his fingers over the computer keyboard. "Will you be paying by credit card?"

"We used our credit card at the last hotel," Matt answered. "We wondered if that was how they tracked us." He took Greg's wallet out of his pocket, opened it casually so the clerk could see the bills stuffed inside, took out four 100s and laid them on the counter. "I hope you can take cash."

The clerk glanced at the money and his face took on a pained look. "Yes, sir. But I'm afraid we might not have any change. We don't keep much cash on hand at night."

"There won't be any need for change, Rafael. The rest is in appreciation for hotel staff members who can keep our presence here confidential."

Rafael brightened. "Certainly, sir. Now, if you'll just fill in your name and information on the registration form." He handed the form and a ballpoint pen across the desk. "I can file the form where only our management will have access to your names."

Matt took his time with the form, thinking that if the FBI or the police had sent out any kind of bulletin about them, their real names might raise a flag, and there was no way of knowing what feelers Boris might have sent out. How many people in "management" would be able to see the information? Matt searched his mind quickly for other names, and the first surname that came up was Powell—the street where their first hotel was located. He filled in the name Grant Powell, and the street address where he had lived while he was in college.

The clerk handed him two key cards. "Your room is 432."

"Thanks for your, ah, special attention to protecting our privacy, Rafael. We'll have our luggage sent over tomorrow."

Rafael smiled at him. "Thank *you*, sir."

As they walked across the lobby, Matt said softly, "We'll have to pay Greg back. But I didn't want to leave tracks online with a credit card."

They rode up in the elevator holding tightly to each other. Matt chuckled, and she looked up at him questioningly. "Rafael will be trying to remember where he's seen your face," he explained.

"That was fast thinking. You're getting onto this game too," Jane answered.

When the door of the room closed behind them, Matt put the computer bag down on the floor, took Jane in his arms, and kissed her. "I haven't been able to do that the way I really wanted since this morning—I mean yesterday morning."

She pressed him up against the door and kissed him back. "I need you— more than I could have ever understood just yesterday morning."

She laid her head on his chest and he stroked her hair lightly. She wrinkled her nose as she looked up at him. "Can you smell that?"

"What?" he asked.

"I can still smell that cheap hotel room where they took me—on my hair, on my clothes. Ever since Lyle touched my hair, I've felt like I need to wash it." She backed away from him and pointed to a stain on her left hip. "Something from Lyle's car. And these dirty spots on my legs are from when I hung out the window and when Lyle pushed me down the stairs." She glanced at the bathroom door. "I don't suppose there's much I can do to help you on the computer. Would you mind if I took a quick shower? I'll have to put on the same dirty clothes, but at least I'll *feel* cleaner."

"Go ahead. I'll be checking in Greg's files to see if there's any clue about where Doug might be."

When she came out of the bathroom after her shower, he was sitting on the bed working. "Any luck?" she asked.

He shook his head. "Not really. It looks like Boris has a Mexican connection—bringing drugs across the border. But I can't pin that down to a particular spot in this country." Matt paused. "For some reason, Greg seemed to concentrate more on Boris than on the others in his files. There's so much here I hardly know where to start." He looked up and smiled slowly, almost mischievously. "But I have some things in mind. There are a lot of doors here I can open."

Jane dried her hair with the dryer in the bathroom, then came to lay on the bed beside him. She curled toward him and pulled the bedspread over her. "I'll be right here if you need me," she said, closing her eyes.

Matt shut the top of the computer, putting it in sleep mode, and laid it on the nightstand. He stretched out beside her and began to stroke her hair lightly. He moved closer and kissed her lips. She responded quickly and put an arm across his shoulders, drawing herself closer to him. "I wish I weren't so tired. But right now all I could do is sleep. And anyway . . . "

"You're still feeling a little too vulnerable?"

She nodded. "With Boris—and who knows who else—out there. I have a feeling he may be playing for more time. If you weren't here beside me, I wouldn't feel safe enough to rest." She stroked his cheek. "Aren't you tired too? Do you need to rest for a little while?"

He shook his head. "Can't. I'm running on adrenaline. My head is full of things I could do to him. Close your eyes and sleep. I have a lot to do."

She was asleep in under five minutes. Matt eased off the bed and took the computer with him. He turned off the overhead light and turned on the small lamp on the desk so he would have enough light to work.

He had not told Jane, but after their experiences of the past several hours, he also felt uneasy not knowing what Boris was doing. Once while he was working over the computer at the desk, Matt stopped to listen to footsteps in the hall and wondered who it could be at this time of morning. The footsteps passed, faded, and then he heard nothing more, but he could not stop feeling vulnerable too.

Finally, he sat on the floor, his back against the desk, partially blocking the door with his legs. He took the plastic bag containing Lyle's pistol out of the computer case and laid the pistol on the floor beside him. Now, even with a key card, no one would be able to take him by surprise coming into this room, and to get to Jane, they would have to get past him.

Feeling as prepared as he could be for anything, he lost himself in putting the information from Greg's files to good use.

* * *

The two men behind the pilot conversed steadily in Russian. It was animated, and occasionally it seemed heated. But the pilot kept his eyes forward and concentrated on his flying.

The man who was paying him—in cash—had definitely been angry when he got on the plane. He had talked with someone in English on his cell phone during the pilot's preflight checks, and the conversation had obviously not been congenial. The pilot had been too busy to pay attention to what was being said, but when the conversation ended, the Russian had muttered a few emphatic words in his own language, then dropped the phone into his pocket and paced back and forth in agitation.

His only words to the pilot when they boarded the plane had been, "How long?" and his reply when the pilot answered had been simply, "Faster!"

Now the man punctuated his words to his companion by stabbing at the air with his finger or chopping at it with his hand. He had mentioned one name—Grigori—several times. The pilot thought he had heard an English name too—Randall. Or was it some Russian word that sounded similar?

The pilot knew nothing about this man's business, and he thought it best to leave things that way.

The Russian interrupted the conversation with his associate long enough to ask the pilot, "What are best hotels in San Francisco?"

The pilot thought for a moment, then mentioned a couple of hotels overlooking the bay and the landmark building on Union Square. "I can check some out on my phone when we land. I might be able to find a few more."

The two Russians continued talking, and the name Grigori was mentioned again. In a few minutes, the man in charge spoke to the pilot once more. "In San Francisco, you wait. We come back afternoon. How long now?"

"We'll be on the ground in just under an hour," the pilot replied.

16

Matt woke with a start. Was that the *ding* of an elevator down the hall? The sound of footsteps was soft, but someone was approaching the door. Instantly Matt's hand was on the pistol at his side. The footsteps passed and moved away down the hall. Matt waited until he could hear no other sound outside the door, then took his hand off the weapon.

He realized that his left leg was partially numb. Jane lay asleep with her head pillowed on his left thigh, her body stretched out on the floor with the bedspread covering her. The computer had slipped off his lap and lay propped against his right thigh. It had put itself into sleep mode.

The last time he had looked at his watch, it was 6:58. Now it was 7:39. Sometime in the past forty minutes, he had dropped off to sleep and Jane had come to lie by him.

He stroked her hair. "J?" She stirred and opened her eyes to look at him. "That can't be very comfortable," he said.

She smiled. "It felt good to me because I was closer to you. Time to get up?"

"Probably. There are a couple of things we need to pick up this morning. We need to try to sneak back into our hotel room and get the video camera."

"Why?'

'We're going to take advantage of the window in this room while we're meeting with Boris out there on the square." He held up his hand with his fingers crossed. "If the fog burns off like it did yesterday."

She sat up. 'Did you get a lot done?"

"Not everything I wanted. Enough for now, and there's more I can do later this morning. He's in for some nasty surprises. But right now I need you to help me with something."

He turned on the computer and hunched over it working for several seconds, then handed it to her. "You fill in that last part—up to 20 characters—and when you're done click EXIT."

She studied the screen for a moment. "Do you want to see what I put in here?"

"No. You have to remember it, but don't tell me." Matt walked into the bathroom, turned on the faucet, and splashed cold water on his face to help him wake up. He toweled it off and stared at himself in the mirror. His eyelids were puffy, his hair was mussed, and a wiry stubble of whiskers darkened the lower half of his face. "I look like I belong on a 'Wanted' poster," he muttered.

Jane put the computer down on the floor and walked into the bathroom to stand beside him. "We're a pair," she said, looking at their reflection. "No makeup, and I need to do something with my hair." She ran her fingers through it. "I look like one of those 'morning after' arrest photos."

"You're beautiful without makeup. I've told you that." He kissed her cheek. "You're always beautiful to me. You always will be."

Jane smiled indulgently at him. "You say that just because you know I love to hear it."

"I say it because it's true." He glanced at his watch and grinned at her. "We need to be on our way in about ten minutes, Beautiful."

* * *

Greg was dozing on the bathroom floor when he was awakened by the sound of the hotel room door opening.

Was it Matt and Jane coming back—or someone else, coming to help him?

Greg had tried to make Matt and Jane believe that he never told the woman who called where he was staying. Technically that was true—but he had called her twice from this room, and he knew that if she wanted, she could track him down using the telephone number. She was resourceful, and well connected. He had been hoping she would come to help him, or would send someone.

He had exhausted himself trying to break free. Matt and Jane had left him trussed too tightly. His shoulders ached from struggling to budge the toilet without any leverage. He was wiry, but he did not have the strength of a man like Matt, who might have been able to move the heavy bed by tugging on the rope tied around his ankles.

If only he could get free, there still might be an opportunity to redeem himself by finding Matt and Jane and finishing with them. And then he would have to get out—out of the country. He had thought about his situation early this morning as he lay worn out on the floor. The Randalls had ruined things for him. He would spend his life in prison if he stayed in the United States. If he could drop out of sight for a time in Latin America or Asia or one of the eastern European countries, the money he had put away in foreign banks still might keep him well. But before he went away, he wanted to make Matt and Jane pay for what they had done to him.

He could hear someone moving about quietly in his hotel room. Then a pair of legs appeared in the bathroom doorway. There were western boots on the lower part of them, with the boot tops covered by jeans. Greg's gaze moved upward to the face of the man standing there.

Yuri! Help came in the form of Boris's enforcer. Greg's mind worked rapidly as he thought of the hard explaining he would have to do very soon—but in the meantime he and Yuri might be able to track down Matt and Jane to stop them from doing any more damage.

Yuri squatted beside him and looked into Greg's pleading eyes. Yuri reached behind him, under his jacket, pulled out a folding knife and flicked it open in one smooth motion. He laid the blade of the knife next to Greg's ear, slipped the tip of the blade into a small crease where the duct tape was not tight against Greg's skin, and carefully slit open the tape. With his fingers, Yuri grasped the end of the tape and ripped it forcefully off of Greg's mouth.

Greg winced, but took care to thank Yuri as politely as he could, in Russian.

The man's face showed no acknowledgment of the thanks. He was good at keeping that face expressionless. Greg had never seen him show pain, and rarely pleasure, except when he was enjoying a bottle of vodka or when he was about to hurt someone.

Yuri balanced the knife between his thumb and fingers, casually waggling it back and forth as if it were a pencil or a pen. Where were the two Americans, he asked in Russian. Where would they go?

"Probably to their hotel." Truthfully, Greg doubted they would be there—but it would be the place to take Yuri to start a search. "It doesn't matter where they are right now. I know how they think. I can make them come to me, and then the two of us together can find out where the money is." What he said was partly true. For the moment, Greg could not come up with details of a plan for getting the Randalls to come to him, but he thought he had in his head enough information to make Jane believe her younger sister was in danger. Yuri's presence could help him sell that idea. "Cut me loose and I'll call them right now to make them come to us. Then you can get the information out of them." He knew Yuri would enjoy that part.

"Where is hotel?"

"Down the street. New Palace Hotel, room 317. Cut me loose and we can be there in 10 minutes. If my contact is at work now, we can find out if the Randalls have come back."

"Contact? Who?"

* * *

Matt slipped Lyle and Greg's wallets into the plastic bags with the pistols and knife and stowed those in the small safe in the closet. He situated the computer bag behind some pillows on a shelf so the bag could not be seen. As they left the room, Jane hung the DO NOT DISTURB sign on the door handle.

In the lobby, Matt said, "We'll need to pay for another day." Of the three clerks at the reception desk, only one was unoccupied—a young blonde woman. "If she asks any questions about why we're paying cash, I hope we can make her buy the fleeing-from-paparrazzi story."

Jane studied the young woman as they approached her. Every hair was in place, and her makeup was perfect. That might be the key to winning this woman's confidence.

"How may I help you?" the woman asked brightly.

"The Powells, in room 432," Matt replied as pleasantly as he could. "We'll be staying another day." He laid four hundred-dollar bills on the counter.

The woman's eyebrows went up ever so slightly. Her smile did not waver, but the question in her eyes as she reached for the money was apparent.

"We told Rafael last night that we didn't want to leave a credit card trail because somehow the wrong people seem to find out where we're staying," Matt explained. "You know—people with cameras who follow others around trying to make a buck by harassing them. If they recognize my wife. . . . " He shrugged. "We had to leave another hotel last night to lose them."

Jane wrinkled her nose as she leaned closer and whispered, "Those people are vultures! But they probably wouldn't know me today. I'm sure I must look awful without my makeup. You look just perfect. Do you know a good place where I could buy some makeup—and maybe a new outfit that nobody's seen?"

"Yes, of course," the clerk replied, blushing slightly. "Many of our guests shop at that exclusive store across Union Square. There's also another one across the street from it." She paused to smile at Jane. "And you really look quite good"

It was exactly the right thing to say to a guest, Matt thought—and this woman seemed to be buying their reason for wanting anonymity.

"Thank you! That's sweet," Jane answered. "And do you think they'd have that shade of nail polish?" She pointed to the woman's fingers. "It looks so good on you!"

The clerk smiled again, obviously pleased that a woman like Jane would ask her the question. "At the store across the square. It's my favorite 'Crimson Allure'."

Jane looked at Matt. "Ooh, I know where I want to *start* sightseeing today."

Matt lowered his voice confidentially to speak to the clerk. "Have you, ah, seen anyone hanging around outside this morning with a camera—or just hanging around?"

"Not on our plaza," the woman answered. "But they could be out there on the street." She nodded toward a hallway at the far end of the desk. "You can go that way, if you want. It leads to the exit at the rear of the hotel." She laid the change from the $400 on the counter in front of him.

He glanced at her name badge as he pushed the money back toward her. "Alicia, we told Rafael last night that we appreciate the help of the hotel staff in protecting our privacy. If anyone comes in asking about two people who fit our description, we'd hope you wouldn't remember seeing anyone like that today."

She smiled slightly. "We see *so* many people here. It would impossible to remember just one couple. Enjoy your sightseeing."

'Thank you. We won't forget your help."

As they walked away from the desk, he whispered to Jane, "Nice work, J. Just the right touch. She and Rafael may compare notes, trying to remember where they've seen you."

"Well, she went to a lot of trouble to look good today. Somebody ought to let her know it was noticed."

"I'll remember that next time I need to impress a clerk in a hotel or a store."

Jane took hold of his arm. "You already make an impression, Mr. Tall Hunk. What you need to remember is who's trying to look good just for you."

Matt laughed. "You don't have to try very hard."

They visited the continental breakfast bar in the hotel's restaurant long enough to down a couple of glasses of orange juice and pick up two sweet rolls. Then they exited the hotel through the back entrance the clerk had pointed out. "What will we do if we need to stay here tomorrow night too?" Jane asked as they reached the street.

Matt shook his head. "I'm afraid today will be the only shot we have. If what I've set up doesn't convince the Russian to let Doug go, there won't be anything more we can do." He shook his head once more. "I wish we could get some information about where they're holding him. I hope Montie and company are having better luck."

"You didn't find anything to help them?"

He shook his head. "I think Greg doesn't really have a clue about where Doug might be. He was lying to us. Are we surprised?"

They walked one street past Powell, then turned downhill toward their hotel so they could approach it from the rear. "Let's hope the back door is unlocked again," he said as they stepped up on the loading dock.

It was. He opened the door a crack to be sure the hallway that led toward the lobby was clear. They eased inside quickly, opened the stairway door on their right, and walked up to the third floor. Once more Matt checked to see if the hallway was clear. They waited while a couple strolled down the hall and turned the corner toward the elevator. Matt and Jane walked as quickly and quietly as they could to their room. He had the key card ready in his hand, and he had the door open in under five seconds. They stepped inside and shut it behind them.

Everything in the room seemed at first to be as he had left it yesterday. The bed was mussed as though someone had sat on the edge of it. Had he done that? He looked around slowly, then stepped to the side of the bed and glanced into the closet. It appeared that everything was in its place. "I'll get the camera," he said, reaching into the closet for his carry-on bag.

"Do we have a couple of minutes—long enough for me to fix my hair a little?"

He smiled over his shoulder at his wife, who was already headed for the bathroom. "I think so. No one could know we're here."

As he turned back to his bag, the blinking message light on the telephone caught his eye. Who would have called here? His dad or mom? Jane's parents? Montie?

No, not Montie—he knew Matt was not spending time in this room. And his parents would have called his cell phone. So would Jane's.

Then who?

Slowly he lifted the telephone receiver to his ear, pushed the message button, and followed the instructions to retrieve the messages. There were two of them, both left this morning. The first one was brief: "Mr. Randall, would you please contact the registration desk? There is a question about your bill." The voice sounded familiar, but he couldn't quite place it.

What problem could there be with the bill? He had charged the room on his credit card.

He punched the code to retrieve the second message. It was only slightly longer. "Mr. Randall, the hotel security chief would like to get more information about the trouble you reported yesterday. Please contact Mr. Bills." The same woman's voice.

He hung up the phone. Ed Bills and the break-in here were yesterday's problems.

Matt opened his carry-on bag to take out the video camera. Had he left it out of its carrying case? He slipped the camera into its case and put his carry-on bag back into the closet. He frowned as he walked over to the bathroom door. Had he simply forgotten to put the camera away yesterday?

Jane was putting a bit of mascara on her eyelashes. She smiled at him, but the smile faded as she saw his frown. "I know this seems silly. But I wanted to look my best for my husband on our honeymoon. I'm hurrying."

"No problem. It's okay."

But it wasn't, really—and he wasn't sure why. Something was nagging at his mind.

He glanced at his shaving kit. It was not in the spot where he had left it on the bathroom counter. It had been placed neatly in the corner under the edge of the mirror.

Greg had come here last night. He had searched their room again.

The phone messages! There was no reason for any difficulty with the hotel bill, and Ed Bills had dismissed his problem yesterday, so why would the security man want more information now? There was no real need for either of those two messages—unless . . .

"J, we've got to get out of here—now!"

She looked at him in surprise. "Why?"

"The phone—there were messages. I shouldn't have listened to them. I think they were a trick—a way for someone in the hotel to find out if we came back to this room."

Jane frowned as she closed the mascara container and put it down on the counter. "I didn't think there was any possible way Greg could get loose this time. But if not him, then who?" She stepped past Matt and picked up her jacket she had left on the bed. "Let's go."

Matt put the strap of the camera bag over his head as they crossed the room, tucking the small camera bag in between his arm and his body. Jane shrugged on her jacket. He opened the door and stood back to let his wife pass through.

The doorway was filled immediately by a large, black-haired man in jeans and a leather jacket. He seemed surprised momentarily that Jane could look him in the eyes and that Matt was several inches taller. But surprise didn't keep him from acting. His left hand snaked out and grabbed Jane's right wrist. "You come," he said to Matt, leering triumphantly. He began to raise his right hand, which he had been keeping close to his leg. It held a knife.

The man was obviously used to intimidating people. He was unprepared for the instant reaction he got from these two. Matt's left hand shot out to grab the man's right wrist. Matt hammered the man's wrist and hand against the doorjamb. Jane, instead of resisting the pull of his other hand, stepped toward him, ducked under his arm, and ended up on his left side stretching his twisted arm out away from his body. She dug the fingernails of her free hand into the soft flesh on the underside of his wrist. His response was to fling her away from him, against the wall.

The man managed to turn the knife enough to jab the point of the blade into the back of Matt's hand. Matt battered the man's right wrist and knuckles against the doorjamb again, then a third time. The man's hand opened and he released the knife. As it was falling to the floor outside their door, Matt's fist drove into the man's stomach. Matt gave him a right to the stomach again, and again, driving the man across the hall and up against the wall. The impact of Matt's fist left the man partly doubled over. He swung wildly with his left hand. His fist connected solidly with Matt's chin. Matt went down and lay still against the wall in the hallway.

The man straightened up at the same time Jane was getting to her feet. He took one step across the hallway and bent down to reach for the knife lying on the floor. "*No!*" Jane said, rushing him. She brought her knee up into his chest with as much force as she could, throwing him against the doorjamb. But with his left arm, he caught her legs below the knees and pulled them out from under her. She fell on her back in the doorway. He was on her before she could get away. He sat astride her waist and put his right hand on her throat, clamping down on her windpipe. He leered at her again as he began to press harder. She clawed at his arm with her left hand while she tried to reach his eyes with her right, but he slapped her hand away from his face. When she sunk her fingernails into the underside of his right wrist, he let go of her windpipe, but immediately his left hand lashed her across the face. She tried to buck him off of her, but he probably outweighed her by seventy or eighty pounds. He smiled at her as he slowly raised his right hand. She tried to deflect the blow, but still his open hand hit her hard across the face. She did not see his left coming; the fist struck her full on her right cheek. Jane's head snapped to the side and she lay still, her eyes closed. The man raised his right hand again, realized she was no longer resisting, thought for a second, and made a fist to hit her anyway.

Before he could swing, his right wrist was seized from behind. The man reached behind him with his left arm trying to get some hold on Matt, and Matt took advantage of the man's movement to twist his right arm into an arm lock, jerking the arm up tightly behind the man's back. At the same time, he grabbed the man's left wrist. The man strained against Matt's grip, and when he realized that Matt was too strong for him, began to thrash around, trying to break free. He threw himself to the left, trying to pull Matt off balance. Instead, Matt pushed the man down to the carpet on his face and quickly moved on top of him. Straddling his back, Matt held the man's right arm in the arm lock and pinned his left arm against the floor. The man tried to buck Matt to the left and at the same time tried to tug his left arm free so he could roll, but he was not strong enough to break Matt's grip. Struggling to free his left arm, the man relaxed his right momentarily and Matt's powerful leverage pushed that arm sharply upward, beyond its limits. There was an audible cracking sound. The man moaned with pain and stopped resisting.

Matt moved off from him and rolled him over. The man lay looking at him with wonder in his eyes, as though he were amazed at being bested. Matt grabbed him by the shoulders. The man winced, and moved to relieve the pressure on his right shoulder. "Who are you?" Matt asked. "Boris? No, he would't come to do this himself, would he? Are you Yuri?" The man looked surprised that Matt knew his name. "Where can I find Boris?" Matt demanded.

Suddenly the man swung at Matt with his undamaged left arm. Matt dodged the blow, grabbed the man's wrist with his left hand, and swung with his right. His fist caught the man full in the face. Matt drew back and hit him again, and was preparing to do it once more when he realized that Yuri was lying limp, unresisting, his eyes closed. Matt was not sure how hard he had hit the man, but he had held nothing back either time. The man's nose was flattened to the side and blood was running from it. Slowly Matt opened his hand and flexed his fingers.

Then he remembered Jane. He scrambled off the Russian and crawled to Jane on all fours. She almost looked like she was asleep, but blood trickled from her nose. "J?" He touched her cheek, but she didn't move. Could she be seriously hurt? Worse than unconscious? He saw no other blood. He patted her face with his fingers and started to turn her head, but thought better of it in case her neck had been injured. "J, are you—"

Her eyes popped open and she came up swinging. He caught her hand just before her fist connected with his face. She looked wild-eyed for half a second, then focused on him. "Matt! What happened? Where . . . "

"Over there," he answered, pointing at the man lying in the hallway.

She raised up on her elbow to look at the other man. "Who *is* that?"

"Yuri, I believe—Boris's right-hand man He recognized his name."

She sat up and started to stand, reaching for the door handle to support herself.

"Wait." He put a hand on her knee to stop her. "Wait a minute. Are you all right?" He looked into her eyes as though trying to see if she might be hurt anywhere inside.

She patted his hand. "I'm all right, Matt. I've been belted like that a couple of times before, in a game. I'm okay." She put her hand to her right cheek and winced. "I'll probably have a black eye." She looked at his left hand. "You're bleeding. What . . . "

"He got me with the point of his knife."

Matt pulled his handkerchief out of his back pocket and carefully dabbed the blood away from Jane's nose. Then he wrapped the handkerchief around his left hand to stop the bleeding from the shallow cut on the back of it.

Jane stood and walked over to look down at the man on the carpet, then reached out with the toe of her shoe and pushed tentatively at his outstretched arm. "I want to kick him," she said angrily. "I want to hurt him."

"He wouldn't feel a thing right now." He reached down to grab Yuri's feet. "Help me get him inside." He dragged the Russian by his legs while Jane helped maneuver his body through the door into their room. "What's wrong with his arm?" she asked when she noticed that it was trailing at an odd angle.

"We wrestled. He lost. I heard something break."

He positioned Yuri at the foot of the bed, then took a quick look around the room. "We'll leave him here. There's nothing else—" He stopped when he noticed the tears running down Jane's cheeks as she stood looking at Yuri. "What's wrong?" he said, alarmed.

"What I said—about wanting to hurt him." She looked up at Matt. "I want to cause *him* pain. It's so *hard* not to hate them. I don't like feeling this way. I feel ugly—bad."

He put his arms around her and held her to him tightly. "It's all right. I understand. Just remember what you told me—we're stronger than they are. We're going to beat them—on our terms. The pain they'll feel will be what they bring on themselves."

She nodded against his chest. Then she backed away from him and wiped the tears from her eyes with her fingers. "I'm tired of being slapped around by these *animals*. I'd like to meet Boris so I can see what kind of man surrounds himself with people like this."

He grinned at her. "Kind of like looking into somebody's eyes across the net?"

She smiled weakly. "Something like that." Slowly her smile broadened. "When I get them in that position, I know I can beat them."

"We'll get him there—in due time. Right now we have to be on our way." He paused to look into her eyes again, peering into one, then the other. "Are you *sure* you're all right?"

She touched her cheek and grimaced. "I'll be sore tomorrow—but I'll get over it. I'm *not* letting them beat *me*. If I start to feel strange, I'll let you know."

Matt picked up the knife, which lay just inside the door, holding the end of the handle carefully between two fingers. They closed the door of the room and walked down the hall toward the stairway.

"I'm surprised no one else heard any of that," Jane said.

"I think the people across the hall left yesterday. I saw them with their luggage." He shrugged. "I don't know about the other rooms. Maybe everybody's gone to breakfast."

They walked quickly down the stairs. He paused at the bottom to push the door open carefully. There was no one in the hallway but Irina, the telephone operator he had met yesterday.

As Matt and Jane stepped into the hallway, Irina looked their way and gasped. When she saw the knife Matt held in his hand, her eyes went wide. The papers she had been holding in her hands fluttered to the floor and she began to back away slowly from the door of the telephone office. Then she turned and walked quickly into the lobby.

"Irina!" Matt said. "*She's* the insider!"

Jane's brow furrowed. "Who is she?"

"One of the telephone operators. *She* was their eyes and ears in the hotel."

Irina paused at the front door to look over her shoulder at them. She stepped outside and began to run down the street past the front of the hotel.

"She could find out what numbers I called on their phone and when," Matt explained. "She saw me once when I went out while Lyle had you. It was her voice on the phone messages. She must have been the one who let Yuri know we were here."

Jane thought for a moment. "The woman who called Greg last night sounded like she could be European—maybe Russian."

"Yeah. I wonder if she was just trying to find out whether Greg stood her up—or if she was supposed to get information from him and report it to somebody else."

He turned toward the door of the hotel security office. "Come on. I need to introduce you to someone."

Matt pushed the door open. Ed Bills sat at his desk with a file spread out in front of him. Recognition showed in his face as he looked at Matt. He glanced at Jane and smiled. "Well, I see you found your wife. Is everything all—"

"Not 'found'—rescued," Jane corrected firmly. "I was kidnapped, right out of this hotel, Mr.—" she glanced at the sign on his desk—"Bills. And I understand you weren't very much help. You really should take your guests' safety more seriously."

Bills pushed back his chair and started to stand, then sat back down as Matt stepped closer. Bills' face showed alarm when Matt laid the knife on the desk in front of him. "I took this away from the man who's upstairs in our room. He attacked us," Matt explained. "Big guy, leather jacket, cowboy boots—you can't miss him." He held up his left hand with the handkerchief wrapped around it. A spot of blood showed on the handkerchief. "You'll probably find some of my blood on the blade, so this knife is evidence of a crime. I assume you still remember how to take care of evidence?"

Bills sat staring at the knife as Matt opened the door and checked the hallway. It was empty. "By the way," he said to the security man, "I'm wondering how well you checked Irina's background. She was helping the kidnappers."

Bills looked up at him. "There's some dried blood on the heel of this knife blade. Do you know—"

"No. But this man has obviously used a knife before, so watch yourself."

They left Bills looking after them as Matt pulled the door shut.

"Let's take the back way again," he said, opening the door to the loading dock, "just in case Yuri brought friends."

17

They turned downhill toward Market Street.

"Where are we going now?" she asked.

"There's a camera store down here. I need a cable to use with the video camera. If they don't have it, I saw an electronics store a couple of blocks over." He walked five or six yards farther, then stopped. "But . . . "

"What's wrong?"

"I was thinking about what just happened to us." He turned to look at her. "What's wrong with this picture?"

Jane thought for a moment. "Yuri *didn't* bring a friend. I wondered about that too. Where's Greg?"

"Yeah. I assumed that Yuri knew where to look for us because he found Greg. But why wasn't Greg here to gloat? Maybe Yuri didn't talk to him after all. Maybe Yuri already knew about Irina and worked directly with her." He thought for a moment. "We've got to find out if Greg's loose again. We still need him to testify—to tell what he knows about Boris."

"You don't think what you found on the computer will be enough to put Boris away?"

"Yes, on money laundering or drug charges. But Greg could tie him directly to your kidnapping and Cole's killing." He turned uphill. "Let's go. I think we'd better find out if Greg is still resting comfortably."

They had walked half a block when she asked, "Do you think Greg was right to be worried about what they might do to him? After all, he's *their* man."

"I don't know, J. You were with him longer than I was. What do you think?"

"I know his fear was real. That was one of the few *real* things he showed me all day."

They approached Greg's hotel on the side street and walked in through the garage entrance. Pausing at the glass doors to the registration area, they quickly scanned the people near the desk inside. There were couples and one group of women—guests going about normal business. A man in a dark suit stood alone by a pillar watching the people who came and went. He wore a hotel name badge on the pocket of his charcoal gray suit. "I hope he's really hotel security," Jane said, "and not someone else."

"Looks like he's official," Matt answered, "but we'll keep an eye on him."

Matt pushed the door open and they strolled unhurriedly through the registration area. The man in the suit looked them over as soon as they stepped inside—it was the kind of attention the two of them were used to receiving—then shifted his gaze to another couple that was just entering. Jane made it a point to glance at his name badge as they passed him; it appeared to be genuine. They walked into the front lobby and took the stairs up to the mezzanine level, where Matt stopped her. They stood waiting at the top of the stairs for several seconds to see if anyone from the lobby might follow them, but no one did. They walked up one more floor. Alone in the hallway, they called the elevator.

On the sixth floor, they moved quickly down the hall to Greg's room. Matt fished in his pocket for the key card.

Jane's brow furrowed. "If Yuri came here first, Greg might not be tied up anymore. We have no idea where he is. He could be out there somewhere looking for us—or he could be in here waiting. This could be a trap."

"Yeah—but if Boris is planning to do anything to Greg because he fouled up, I want to turn Greg over to the police before that happens." Matt paused before inserting the key card. "If anything seems wrong when I open this door, run for those stairs." He pointed at the EXIT sign down the hall. "I'll be right behind you." He pushed her backward gently so she would not be seen from inside the room when the door was opened.

She knew Matt wouldn't run away from anything before doing his best to protect her. There was no way she would run. She would not be separated from him again. She would stay and fight by his side if she had to.

Matt took hold of the door handle firmly, ready to resist if there was any sudden downward pressure from inside. He inserted the key card slowly, then withdrew it quickly. There was a soft click and the small light above the handle turned green. Matt pushed the handle down carefully and held it in that position for a few seconds, then slowly shoved the door open a crack and waited to see if there was any response from inside.

Nothing happened. He could hear no sound from inside the room. Motioning to Jane to hold her place, he slowly pushed the door open farther. The room seemed empty. He moved so he could see the bathroom doorway. The rope still stretched tightly from the leg of the bed to Greg's lower legs, protruding out the bathroom door. Matt stepped inside, drew Jane in with him, and shut the door most of the way. "Hold it open just a crack while I check the bathroom," he whispered.

She stood with one hand holding the door handle while he walked as quickly and quietly as possible across the carpet to the bathroom door. He peered quickly around the doorjamb then drew back. She could see shock registered on his face as he stepped slowly into the bathroom doorway again and stared down at the floor, transfixed.

"What? What is it?" She left her post by the door and walked toward the bathroom.

Matt put out a hand to stop her. "No! Stay there. You don't want to see . . . " He took a step into the bathroom. "Just stay there," he said over his shoulder. He stepped out of sight and she started to follow him into the bathroom, but he came out again quickly and stopped her before she reached the doorway. "No," he whispered. "Let's go. Let's get out of here!" He turned her and pushed her toward the door, his hand in the small of her back. He followed one step behind.

They stepped into the hallway and he shut the door softly behind them.

"What? Is he . . . ?" Jane asked.

"Dead, I think. He has to be." Matt took her hand and led her to the door of the room across the hall that they had rented. "His, uh . . . his throat was. . . . "

"They *killed* him?" she asked incredulously. "Did you check to be sure?"

Matt shook his head as he fumbled in his shirt pocket for their key card.

"I didn't want to touch the body. But with that much blood, I don't think there's any way . . . We can call for help just in case." He opened the door of their room quickly, pulled her inside, then rushed to the bathroom and bent over the toilet with his head hanging over the bowl.

She followed him to the bathroom door. "Are you okay?"

"Not sure," he answered hoarsely. Slowly he knelt on the floor by the toilet. He pulled the small paper folder for their key card out of his pocket and held it out to her. "Call . . . hotel security."

Jane used Greg's throw-away phone and dialed the hotel number while Matt leaned over the toilet again. He retched, but nothing came.

Someone answered the phone with the name of the hotel. Jane said, "Could you connect me to the hotel security office, please. It's urgent." She waited, watching Matt with concern. When she heard someone on the telephone say "Security," she made up a story as it came to her. "I, ah . . . my fiancé is staying at your hotel—Greg Alexander. He was going to meet me at the wedding planner's this morning, and he, uh . . . well, I talked to him earlier, and he said he wasn't feeling well, and now he's more than an hour late. I'm worried about him."

Her mind was on Matt. She watched as he retched over the toilet once more with no result. She only heard the last half of what the man on the other end of the line said to her: " . . . think there's something wrong?"

"Yes. With Greg. He must be sick. It would have to be serious. He hasn't even called. Could you, um . . . would you please check his room?"

"And what is your name?" the man on the other end asked.

"Please, just ask him to call me so I'll know he's okay." She ended the call.

Matt pushed himself up slowly to sit on the edge of the tub. Jane sat beside him. "Are you going to be all right?"

Slowly, he nodded. "I think so." He shook his head as though to clear it. "Somebody did a thorough knife job on Greg." He put his hand to his throat.

"Yuri?"

"Must have been. He pulled off the tape that covered Greg's mouth, then put it back—probably so Greg couldn't scream." Matt paused to swallow. "Greg would have looked like he was lying there asleep . . . except for the deep cut on his neck—and the blood. The bath mat, and the floor . . . "

Jane tried not to think about the man lying on the floor in the other room. She focused on her husband's face. It was ashen.

He closed his eyes and leaned over to put his head between his knees for several seconds. Then he sat up to look at her again. He put his hand on the edge of the tub and pushed himself up. "We've got to get out of here."

"Are you sure *you* feel up to it?" she said, standing and taking hold of his arm.

"Yes. Yes, I'll be fine."

She searched his eyes, saying nothing. His expression softened. "All right, not fine. But I'll manage."

He took Greg's phone out of her hand. "There's something we have to do first." He found the phone's list of recent calls, looked for the Los Angeles number, and punched the CALL button. The phone on the other end rang only twice before he got the same gruff answer he had heard a few hours earlier: "*Slushayu.*"

"I hope that means you're listening carefully," Matt said, "because you'd better pay close attention to this. Your man Yuri blew his assignment, and it was a mistake you're going to regret." Obviously, the Russian had been expecting to hear another voice; there was no immediate answer, so Matt continued. "You killed Greg for nothing. I have all the information he had, and more. Right now you have one hour and fifty-seven minutes to get my brother home safely. You're going to do it, or I'm going to take your world apart piece by piece."

"Is bluff," the Russian answered angrily. "You cannot do this."

"I thought you might say something like that, so I prepared a little demonstration for you," Matt answered. "You have accounts at four financial institutions in the Los Angeles area. Pick one—*any* one—and check the status of your account right now. You have ten minutes to call me back. And *don't* give me another reason to show you what I could do to you. Don't try pushing me again." He ended the call.

His hand was trembling as he handed Jane the phone.

"Matt, what's wrong?" she asked.

"It's today—the past twenty-four hours. It's them . . . *him.*" His hands were clenched into fists. Slowly he opened them and made a helpless gesture with his hands. "It's being forced to play rough just to get through to them. You know how I hate it when people push other people around just because they can. But with him . . . " He let out a long breath. "That man's not going to give in unless he gets hit where it hurts him most. And there's no way we can back off now."

Jane understood. What showed in Matt's eyes was pain, not anger. For all his size, her husband was a gentle man. Treating people kindly seemed to come naturally to him. The way he treated children was one of the things that endeared him to her, and outside of a hard game of neighborhood football, she had never seen him use his size and strength against another person—until an hour ago. She touched Matt's cheek. "I know.

You're not that kind of person. But neither one of us has ever been in this kind of situation before, and saying 'Please' to someone like him doesn't work."

Matt nodded, and sighed. "Force is the only thing that seems to make an impression. Strength. Power."

"What's he going to find when he checks his bank account?"

Matt smiled slightly. "Nothing. That's the point. All the money has been transferred, to the same place Cole put the rest of it."

"You have every right to be angry." She put her arms around him. "It's hard not to be. You know I'm fighting it too. I was struggling not to hate Lyle and Greg—and now that they're gone I can see it would have been useless. But now there's Yuri, and this man, and I'm trying hard not to let *them* make me hate. I could even hate them because of what they did to Greg—and that doesn't make any sense to me at all." She laid her head against his chest.

Matt put his arms around her and squeezed her closer. "There isn't very much about any of this that makes sense." He paused. "But we're not going to let him get away with what he's done. Let's go."

As they stepped out into the hallway and shut the door, three men came toward them from the direction of the elevator. One was tall and thin and wore the same kind of hotel name badge on his charcoal suit that the man downstairs had been wearing. The other two men wore dark suits without identification. Matt nodded at them as they passed. He stopped at the elevator and punched the DOWN button.

Jane turned to look back down the hall. The three men had stopped in front of Greg's door. "This is his room," the one with the hotel badge said as he pulled out a key card. He unlocked the door and stepped inside, followed by one of the other men, but the second man stood watching Matt and Jane. She turned toward Matt and mouthed, "FBI."

"How do you know?" he whispered.

"It's a guess, but I've seen Montie with some of his friends—coworkers."

A *ding* announced the arrival of their elevator. The man who had been watching them began to walk toward them. They stepped into the elevator and stood with their backs against the wall. The man stopped in front of the elevator just as the doors began to close and put out a hand to stop them. He opened his mouth to speak—and then someone called from the direction of Greg's room, "Selden! In here! Now!" The man took his hand away from the door and stood looking at them as it closed.

On the ground floor, they hurried out of the hotel as quickly as they could to mingle with pedestrians on the sidewalk. They had almost reached the street corner when Greg's phone rang. Matt glanced at his watch. "Very good—only seven minutes."

Jane took the phone out of her jacket pocket, but instead of handing it to Matt, she touched the TALK button and put it to her ear. He watched with curiosity as she spoke: "I keep wondering what kind of man sends other people to beat up and kill women and men who just happen to get in his way. Do you ever think about *talking* first?"

There was silence in her ear for several seconds, but finally a deep male voice said coldly, "I will talk—to husband."

"Have it your way—but if I were you, I'd be nice to him." She handed the phone to Matt.

"Where is money?" the Russian demanded as Matt put the phone to his ear.

"Out of your reach. And now I think you have at least eighty-seven thousand more reasons to let my brother go."

"You will give back—*all* back."

"Maybe. But not before my brother is safe. And if anything happens to him, believe me, it will cost you much more than money."

"You cannot—"

"*Don't* tell me what I can do! You should be smart enough to take a lesson from what just happened. And by the way, if you're still thinking you'd like to kill us, trust me, the last thing you want is for something to happen to my wife or me."

"What is mean—what do you mean?"

"Don't try to find out—you'll regret it. And don't call me again. The next voice I want to hear is my brother's telling me he's at home, safe. When that happens, I'll call you." He ended the call and handed the telephone back to Jane.

She smiled as she put it into her pocket. "For a guy who doesn't like to play tough, you do all right."

He shrugged. "What else could I do?"

The morning fog was beginning to burn off as they walked downhill toward Market Street.

At the camera store, Matt bought a small collapsible tripod and the cable he needed. When they came out of the store onto Market again, they were little more than a block and a half from the hotel where she had been kidnapped twenty-four hours earlier. Matt headed down Market Street. "Let's find another way back to Union Square," he said. "And if you see anyone around us who looks like someone you've seen before, tell me."

Jane nodded, and glanced over her shoulder. She had not thought of the possibility that there might be others watching the area of their hotel.

When they came to the small sunken plaza on Market with its entrance to the underground BART station, Matt led her down the stairs to the umbrella-canopied tables. A few people sat in the shade of the umbrellas with cups of coffee from a small snack bar on the plaza. Matt led Jane to a table against the wall that had vacant tables on either side of it. "I've been thinking that we probably need to talk to Montie," he said as he pulled out a chair for her.

"Why?"

"Well, our fingerprints will be all over Greg's room, and those agents saw us in the hall. I'd like to find out if they've got a full-scale manhunt going for us. I'd also like to know if they've heard anything about Doug."

He borrowed Greg's burner phone from her and dialed his parents' number. His mother answered very tentatively. "Hello?"

"Mom, is there any news about Doug?"

She gasped. "Matthew! Where are you? Montie said they haven't been able to find you, and I was afraid—" She stopped abruptly as though someone had cut her off. When she spoke again, it was more guarded. "Where are you? We've been worried about you."

"We're both fine, Mom. We're in San Francisco." The FBI already knew that much. "Nothing more about Doug?"

"No. No, not yet." He could hear the apprehension in her voice. "Do you—" Apparently someone cut her off again. After a pause, she continued. "Matt, Montie wanted to talk to you, but he's not here now. They're going to send your call to him. They say it's really important. I love you. Please be careful."

"We will, Mom. Tell Dad—" But the line had gone dead. Then the phone began to ring somewhere else. The voice that answered was Montie's: "Carver." It was very businesslike.

"Have you heard anything more about Doug today?"

"Matt! No, we haven't. Have you?"

"No. What did you learn about Greg Alexander?" Matt asked, trying to make it sound casual.

Montie's response was carefully phrased: "Have you seen him this morning?"

"We were too late," Matt said. "Your people were too."

"Who left him tied up so neatly?"

"We did—last night. We tried to talk him into telling you everything he knew, but he wouldn't, so we left him tied up for safekeeping while we went somewhere else to work with the information we found on his computer."

"Who killed him, Matt?"

"Probably the guy who attacked us this morning at our hotel. I took a knife away from that man. I wouldn't be surprised if it turns out to be the weapon that killed Greg. I left it with Ed Bills, the head of security at our hotel."

"These are dangerous people you're playing with. They wouldn't think anything of killing you just like they did Greg."

"I know. And we're not *playing* with them, Montie. We're trying to stay alive. They can't do anything to us now without paying a very, very high price."

"You said *you* have some information?"

"Greg had extensive files on the people he worked for."

"Give them to us. Maybe there's information on them that will help us find out where Doug is."

"I couldn't find anything. So you still don't have a clue where Doug is?"

"We're working on it."

"Be straight with me," Matt said. "I'm trying to be straight with you."

"No, we don't have much. Give us the files. We may be able to get things out of them that you can't. We have *teams* of people to handle these kinds of puzzles."

"One way or another, you'll have everything I have before the afternoon is over."

"What does that mean?"

"It means I know my limits."

"Do you? You're playing a risky game. You could get yourself killed, and Jane too. Think about *her*. I know you love her."

"Yeah. They took her away from me once. They're not going to do it again."

"Are you really that sure of yourself, Matt? These are very clever people, and they're ruthless."

"I'm sure the FBI would like to take this decision out of my hands. I expect that you're still tracing my calls. You'd pick us up right now if you could, wouldn't you?" Montie did not answer immediately, so Matt continued: "I asked you to be honest with me. I'm being honest with you."

"We know you're in downtown San Francisco. It's not easy to pinpoint a location because you have a cell phone and you move around. But with a little time, we can do it. You're a material witness to a crime, and we need to talk about what you know. It would be better for everyone if you'd tell us where to find you. You'd be doing your brother a favor."

"If you find out where he is, please be careful. They told me they'd leave him to burn to death if they even thought they saw law enforcement."

"We know what we're doing, Matt. Tell us where you are. You'd be protecting your wife—and yourself."

Matt thought for a moment. "You could be right—but I'm not going to make the decision by myself. J and I are in this together. Talk to her. I'll go along with what she decides." He handed the phone to Jane.

"Montie," she said, "have you learned anything about the people who hired Greg?"

"We know he has ties with some pretty nasty Russian mafia types. They ought to give you nightmares. They would me."

"I've met some of Greg's friends already. Right now I want to know if you have any idea how to stop them."

"We can protect you. Janie, you've got to talk Matt into letting us know where you are." He had always called her Janie when she was small and he was the favorite uncle treating her like one of his own; he had only quit calling her by the diminutive of her name after she grew tall enough that he had to look up into her eyes.

"Can you stop the people who are after us?" she asked. "They just keep coming. They don't give up."

"We'll put the two of you under guard. We'll hide you where they—"

"For how long? Until you know all those people are dead? Or until the government decides it's not paying off and tells us we're on our own? I can't stand the idea of taking a chance—maybe coming home someday and finding one of these guys in our apartment. Or maybe they'd try to snatch me out of the parking lot at the supermarket so we can start this game all over again. Can you guarantee it would never happen? Because I *won't* live in fear. I refuse. This has got to end."

"Jane! Sometimes you're as stubborn as your mother," Montie exploded. "Have you thought about what those people would do to you if they find you before we do? Do you have any idea how—"

"Montie! I've been kidnapped and slapped around, I've been threatened with death several times. One of the Russians has tried to kill me already this morning. Yes, I have a pretty good idea what they might do to us. Can you promise me the government will be there to protect us until these people forget all about us? Do you think you can wait them out? Because if you can't, I think we have a better chance of stopping them right now than you do."

"Jane, nobody can completely guarantee the future." Montie sounded like he was trying to be patient; he seemed to realize he was not talking to his little niece anymore. "But you know me. Do you think I'd let anyone throw you to the wolves?"

"No—*you* wouldn't. But priorities change for the government, and sometimes people fall through the cracks." She paused. "Tell Mom and Dad we love them, and we're okay. We'll call you later."

"Jane—"

She cut off the call and put the phone back in her pocket. "I know he'd try to do the right thing. But I want this over." She stared off into space, frowning. "Do you think Greg was right? That the Russian will never give up?"

"What do you think, J?"

She looked back at him. "Greg was scared of this man. I believed him about that much."

"Yeah. Me too." He sighed. "I'd really like to believe the FBI could pick him up right away. But if they don't . . . "

She took his hand. "Come on. Let's go get ready for a meeting."

Matt frowned. "Or not, if the Russian decides to gamble."

They walked down into the BART station and followed the long underground hallway to the other end of it, farther down on Market. As they climbed the stairs and came above ground again, he pointed back at the area of the small plaza where they had been sitting. "Look." A man in a suit was walking slowly past it on the street level, gazing down at the plaza, scanning the area where the tables were located. As they watched, he raised his hand to his mouth and spoke into the small radio he carried. "They were closer than Montie wanted us to know. We'd better keep moving." It occurred to him that by now the San Francisco police might have made a connection between last night's call about the killing near the Birch Hotel and Greg Alexander's death, so the local police might also be looking for him and Jane as possible witnesses—or suspects.

They rounded a corner and walked rapidly toward Union Square. Neither of them spoke until they had walked a block. Then he stopped and drew her into a doorway. "This is a risk, J. I don't know how big. It might not stop him, and I don't have the right to risk your life as well as mine. He could be evil or hard-headed enough to take his chances anyway trying to kill us."

She looked up into his eyes. "Yes, he could. But the way you've set things up—well, he'd have to be crazy not to see he'll lose in the end. I have faith in what you've planned. And if we don't do this, I think there's a 100 percent chance he'll go on trying to kill us. Don't you?"

He looked into her eyes for several seconds. "I keep on discovering reasons why asking you to marry me was the best choice I've ever made." He took her hand and started walking again. "If we can stop him from hurting anyone else, that would be good too."

* * *

His instructions had been terse, and the Russian knew that the Mexicans had not liked them. Doug Randall could identify them, and if they let him go free, they would have to stay out of sight in Mexico, at least for a time. They would lose some of the new business they had been building in Arizona and California. They reminded him that he had told him they could collect a ransom for the younger Randall in the end, and now they would not get that either. The Russian had answered angrily that he didn't care about *their* problems, they would do what he said because he was paying them.

But he knew he needed those people. He would have to move some extra business their way to help make up their losses. The inconvenience could not be helped. He had to humor the American—for now.

He would do only as much as he was forced to do. And in the end, when he was through dealing with Matt Randall, the man would pay—and his wife would pay, and his brother, and maybe others in his family. The Randalls would learn that Boris—as he chose to be known outside his small circle of close associates—could not be taken lightly.

He was still wondering just how he would handle the meeting today. He would have to come up with a firm plan in the next hour or two, but he was sure he had not yet lost his touch in dealing with situations like this.

In the days after the end of the Cold War, he had clawed his way upward in the streets of Moscow. Anyone who knew him then had known better than to give him cause to be angry. As his operations grew and he was able to afford it, he had hired more people like himself. Yuri had been the first, and Yuri had been the best—a good enforcer. Everyone who knew the big man feared him. The two of them were middle-aged now, but still no one dared to defy them. A few of the younger up-and-comers had casually mocked Yuri, with gray in his beard now, and lived to regret it. In fact, one of Yuri's more persistent and bold challengers had *not* lived, and this won Yuri the grudging respect of younger thugs on the street. Boris had always been able to count on Yuri to make problems go away.

Except this time. Boris wondered what had gone wrong. Yuri was almost never taken by surprise. Matt Randall must be a very lucky man—or he must be much stronger and more clever than Greg had realized. Had the young American left Yuri dead, or seriously injured? If so, Randall was indeed a dangerous man—a far more serious problem than they had thought.

Without Yuri, it was going to be harder to handle the Randalls today. Boris needed Yuri's experience combined with his own right now. But in the beginning, he had operated alone, and he could do it again if necessary.

People he knew in Moscow—some of the younger, more sophisticated operators involved in laundering money and stealing it online—said he was behind the times. He knew what they said about him behind his back—he was a fossil from the frozen tundra of Siberia. Cowards and weaklings, all of them. He would prove them wrong.

He reached into the inside pocket of his suit jacket and pulled out the pistol he carried, a small .22 automatic with a silencer. It was quiet but deadly at close range—and he had made it a habit to come close enough to see the terror in people's eyes. But it had been some time since he himself had been the one to use the gun; ordinarily, he left that part to Yuri. He pulled the magazine out of his pistol to be certain it was fully loaded, and then tried the action of the weapon to be sure it would not jam.

Undoubtedly Matt Randall would insist on meeting in public. The Russian knew he would have to lure them into a more private place, alone with him—perhaps the back seat of a rented limousine—before he showed the gun. He would call to see if there might be a limousine available.

If he were able to separate the man and woman, they would be much easier to handle. Each would worry about what was happening to the other; separated and anxious, they might give in on things that they would resist together.

But without Yuri, it would be impossible to separate the Randalls.

After calling to arrange for a limo, the Russian stretched out on the bed in his hotel room to wait. This place was cheap and dirty—not the kind of accommodations he usually demanded. But early this morning it had been the only thing they could find near the center of the city.

It was 10:23 when his cell phone rang.

Who would be calling him here, at this hour? Matt Randall with more instructions? He frowned. Eventually, this American would pay dearly for his insolence. "Yes," he said into the phone, trying to make it sound intimidating.

The response was in his native language—a voice he had not expected to hear.

The Russian smiled. He would not be alone after all.

18

Jane looked up from her writing and glanced at her watch. "It's 11:00 o'clock," she said gently, wondering if he had not noticed the time.

Matt nodded. "Yeah." He continued adjusting the camera pointed down at the plaza below their room in the high-rise hotel. "The Russian will push us as far as he thinks he can because he doesn't like being told what to do. But I'm going to wait fifteen minutes more, just in case something went wrong that no one could foresee."

His phone rang at 11:09. Quickly he crossed the room (to the desk where his jacket hung over the back of the chair, pulled his phone out of the jacket pocket, and accepted the call. "Hello?"

"Matt?"

"Doug! Are you all right?"

"Yeah—thanks to you, I think. How did you pull that off?"

"I convinced the man behind all this that it would be in his best interests to let you go. I tried to make sure they wouldn't hurt you. Did they do anything to you at all?"

"Shoved me around. Threatened me with a gun. They talked between themselves about killing me. You know I didn't get a lot out of Mrs. Guerra's Spanish class, but it was enough to understand that part. They decided for some reason that they couldn't do it. I think they were afraid of the man who gave them their orders—or they were afraid you could find them somehow. Matt, what's going on?"

"The man who's behind this believes Cole gave me some money that belongs to him. He's been trying to force me to give it back, but I don't have it. I can explain all that later. Right now I need you to do something for me on the computer. Are you up for it?"

"On the computer? Sure—but the FBI has other plans for me. They want to know everything that's happened to me since yesterday, so . . . "

"When they hear what I want you to do, I hope they'll go along with it. Here's what I need."

Doug asked questions as Matt explained, and it was clear that the idea fired his imagination. "Yeah. Yeah, I could do that. Even more," he said when Matt finished. "Do you mind if I add a few little touches of my own?"

"Go for it. But you've only got an hour and a half."

"That's enough. You'll have this guy right where you want him—and I can't tell you how much I'd like to see that happen."

"Great. Ten minutes to 1:00 is our deadline."

"It'll be ready." Doug paused, and Matt could hear another voice in the background. "If the FBI will let me do it," he added.

"Tell them if they'll stand back and let you do what I'm asking, they'll be able to—" Matt stopped talking when he heard the sound of the phone being handled. The voice that came on the line was a new one. "This is Agent Schuyler, Matt. What you're doing is very dangerous, and you're impeding an official investigation. We need to talk."

"Yeah, we probably do—but not right now. This isn't just a simple case of kidnapping for ransom, and you know that. If you'll let my brother do what I asked him to do, you'll have a chance to reel in a very twisted bad guy. You'd like that, wouldn't you?"

"It's not up to you to decide how this investigation is going to go, Matt. You don't have the expertise or the authority to—"

"So far your expertise and your authority haven't gotten the Russian off our backs. Can we expect that to happen sometime in the next hour or so?" He paused momentarily to wait for an answer, and when there was none, he continued: "I didn't think so. Now listen to me: what we're doing is a way to bring Boris out into the open. If we back out on this, he'll never stop coming after us, so we're going to do what we can to stop him now. If you let Doug do what I asked, you'll have a chance to take him down." He pushed the button to end the call.

Matt stared out the window, frowning. Jane looked up from her writing. "Do you think they'll let him do it?" she asked.

"I hope so." He held up his hand with the fingers crossed. "J, it's still not too late to turn things over to the FBI, if *you* think that's what we should do. We're in this together. But they're right; this guy really is dangerous—maybe uncontrollable. If I call him now, we're committed."

Jane thought for a moment. Her brow furrowed. "And what if we turn things over to the FBI, but they don't get him?" She shook her head. "He'll keep coming after us—or someone in our families. I'd rather face him now than wonder for months or years if he's still out there biding his time. I think your plan is the only way to make him go away." She paused. "Are you afraid it won't work?"

"The only thing I'd really be afraid of right now is the thing that had me in knots all day yesterday—losing you."

Jane shook her head. "That's not going to happen. You said it—we're in this together. I have faith in you, and I have faith in us. We're going to beat him, remember?" She put the pen to paper again. "I'm almost done writing this up. I'm adding the things I heard while Greg and Lyle thought I was asleep. It might help the police solve some other crimes too."

Matt picked Greg's phone up from the bed and dialed the Russian's number. The man answered on the first ring. "Yes?"

"One o'clock. It will be near Greg's hotel. I assume you know where that is. You'll get another call 15 minutes ahead of time telling you exactly where to meet us. Don't be late, and don't bring a weapon. If you force us to protect ourselves, you will regret that."

"No police. If I see police, you will be one who regrets."

"Just be there." Matt turned off the phone.

The Russian had seemed calmer, less belligerent this time. Why? It didn't seem to be the man's nature.

But there was no time to think about that now. There was still a little over an hour to work with the information from Greg's files.

* * *

The limousine cruised smoothly up Powell Street from Market. It slowed while it passed the hotel where Matt and Jane had stayed, and then again a few blocks farther on in front of Greg's hotel across from Union Square. The Russian looked to his right and studied the square. As the car moved forward and the open square gave way to street-front businesses, the Russian spoke to the limo driver: "Turn right at corner." A couple of minutes later, they approached Union Square once more on the opposite side, passing in front of the high-rise hotel with its small plaza and gleaming facade. The limousine cruised slowly down Stockton Street while Boris looked across the open square toward Greg's hotel. At the corner, Boris directed the limo driver to turn right once more and go around the block again. Boris kept his gaze fixed on the square to their right, studying it.

This space was open, completely public, with many people passing through it. It was exactly the kind of place a man like Matt Randall would pick, the Russian explained to his companion. People like the Randalls would feel safer in the open, sitting on one of the benches in the square or at a table outside the small cafe. They would think no one could dare do something to them in public.

But this place would not be so safe as they thought. They had underestimated him.

* * *

Matt opened the small safe in the closet of their hotel room and looked at the package he had put there earlier. If someone else had to retrieve it, there would undoubtedly be a question as to why a bag labeled LAUN-DRY was inside the safe. What would they think, he wondered, when they opened it and found two pistols, two men's wallets, and Greg's knife?

The papers he laid on top of the package would explain. The seven sheets of hotel stationery contained Jane's hand-written account of everything that had happened to them over the past forty hours or so. He closed the safe and made sure it was locked. Then he placed another sheet of paper on the desk in the room. On this one, he had written in large letters: "In case of our deaths, open safe." Both of them had signed this sheet. He read again the way she had signed her name: *Jane M. Randall.* That thought was comforting; no matter what happened today, their two lives were inextricably bound together.

He took her hand. "Let's go, Mrs. Randall."

* * *

The tall agent looked again at the display screen of his mobile phone, studying the two photos that he had received from Phoenix. He had seen the man and woman in the sixth-floor hallway for less than a minute, but he was almost certain these were the same faces.

The photos had come with a request that they be given also to the San Francisco Police Department; there was a possibility that the woman had been the victim of a kidnapping. That detail did not fit with what he had seen here in the hotel, Agent Selden thought. She had seemed to be going with the man willingly, holding onto his arm. But it *was* this woman.

What connection, if any, did these two people have with the dead man?

Crime scene technicians were still examining the man's bag and the room. Selden was not needed at the moment, so he took the elevator down to the registration lobby. He approached the dark-suited man who was watching people pass through the registration area, flashed his badge, then showed the two photos on his phone. "Do you remember seeing these two people in the hotel today?"

The man started to shake his head, then stopped and studied the pictures. "Yes. They were both very tall. They came in from the parking area." He nodded toward the door.

"They came *in* this morning? Did they stop at the registration desk?"

"No." The man lowered his voice. "Is this about the dead man on the sixth floor?"

"It might be."

Selden walked to the registration desk and showed his badge to a clerk. "I need the names of guests who registered last night or early this morning and were assigned to the sixth floor."

* * *

Jane followed the car with her eyes as it slowly drove along the edge of Union Square, but she did not turn her head. She sat with her back toward Greg's hotel, across the square. When the vehicle turned at the corner and started along the south side of the square, she glanced that way as though she were looking toward the big department store across the street. The car kept moving slowly. "That black limousine . . . "

"Yeah," Matt answered, "second time around. I'm wondering if that could be our man." He glanced at his watch: twelve minutes since he had called the Russian from the store where they bought the bottle of sparkling cider that sat on the table in front of them. "If that's him, he enjoys going in style—just like Greg."

The limo drove slowly around the square and out of sight, but at almost exactly fifteen minutes from the time Matt had called, it was back, passing on the east side of the square again.

The car turned the corner south of them once more, then slowed and stopped at the curb. The rear passenger door opened and a thin, balding man of about Greg's height stepped out. He wore a gray suit and a dark blue shirt with no tie. Matt and Jane watched as he strode directly across the square, keeping his eyes on them. "This would be Boris," Matt said. "Not exactly what I expected." He had envisioned a large, barrel-chested Boris with thick black hair—a Russian bear of a man. He reminded himself that this gaunt, gray-eyed man would be equally dangerous.

"I hope you're not expecting me to play the obedient little wife and sit quietly while this man threatens us," Jane said.

Matt gave her a quick smile and squeezed her hand. "I don't think I married that kind of woman."

The Russian stopped in front of their table, staring into Matt's eyes, ignoring Jane. "Randall?" he asked. It was obviously meant to sound firm, even menacing.

"I'm sure you already knew that," Matt said affably. He picked up his phone, tapped an icon on the front a couple of times, then gestured toward the chair across the table. "Sit down."

Jane laid her own phone on the table in front of her and watched Boris, waiting expectantly to see what he would do. He ignored her as he took the chair facing Matt. "Now we will talk about what you have that is mine."

"Now we'll talk about the way you've treated my wife and my brother and what's going to happen to you because of it."

Jane glanced at something behind her husband, then gasped, and stared. Matt felt something hard touch the middle of his back. He swiveled his head to look over his shoulder.

Yuri! The Russian who had attacked them this morning stood close behind him. The man's right arm was in a makeshift sling. Was he on some kind of painkiller? Matt couldn't tell, but if not, Matt thought, he must have a very high tolerance for pain. His left hand was out of sight behind Matt's back, but Matt had no doubt about the object he felt touching him next to his spine—the barrel of a pistol. He turned to look at the Russian across the table.

The man's scowl was obviously meant to intimidate. "We will talk about how people pay who steal from me."

* * *

Agent Selden drummed his fingers on the arm of the couch in the lobby as he waited for the Phoenix office to put his call through. It was no more than seconds before a voice answered: "Selden, this is Montie Carver. You saw the two people we're looking for?"

"Yes—on the same floor in the hotel where we found Greg Alexander, the man you were asking about. Alexander's dead. His throat was cut. Is there a connection between him and the two people you're looking for?

"You've been briefed about Alexander's ties to the Russian Mafia?"

"Yes."

"There's something on the Internet you need to be watching right now. Can you access it on your phone?"

* * *

"There's no chance you're going to get that money back," Matt said, "except maybe if you cooperate with us." He paused. "I said *maybe.*"

The Russian looked up at the man standing behind Matt and nodded toward Jane. Yuri moved behind her. Matt could see the .22 automatic with a suppressor that Yuri held in his left hand, shielded from the view of others on the square by his body. Yuri pressed the end of the suppressor against Jane's lower back, then smiled as he ran it slowly up her spine, almost as though he were caressing her with it. The man's smile was chilling. Matt turned to the Russian across the table and tried to maintain his commanding tone. "I said no weapons. Tell him to put that away before you regret it."

The Russian shook his head. "She will go with Yuri, for ride in car. Then we will talk."

"*She* will not go anywhere," Jane answered coolly. If she was afraid, she did not show it.

The Russian across the table seemed taken back momentarily. Then he smiled thinly as he spoke to Matt. "Both will do as I say, or I will kill you. I can kill families."

Matt glanced at Jane. She nodded slightly. Matt looked into the Russian's eyes again. "The secret of finding your money would die with us—and if he pulls that trigger, he'll be killing *you*."

The Russian glanced uncertainly from one to the other, then resumed his threatening scowl. He was obviously determined not to make even small concessions.

Matt felt his gut tighten more. Yuri was a variable he had not taken into account; he had planned to have Boris facing the two of them alone. His mind raced. Mentally he calculated the distance between himself and Yuri. The odds were against him; if he moved suddenly, Jane might die. The man standing behind his wife was unpredictable and proud—still smarting from the fact that he had been beaten earlier. Pain in his shoulder was probably a reminder. He would undoubtedly enjoy killing them both.

Jane was not cowed. Glancing over her shoulder at Yuri, she said to Boris. "You need to keep him under control—for your own good." She paused just a beat before throwing out what she knew would be a challenge. "He *is* under your control, isn't he?"

The Russian looked shocked. He stared momentarily at Jane, then turned to Matt questioningly. Matt nodded toward his wife.

Jane tapped her finger on the table in front of the Russian. "Here. Look at *me*," she said evenly. "*I'm* talking to you."

He glared at her.

She looked steadily into his eyes. "I'm *not* going anywhere with Yuri. If you're going to have him kill me, he'll have to do it right here in public, but that will be just one more of your bad decisions." The Russian's eyes narrowed and his scowl became more menacing. Jane ignored it. "Anyway, too many people are watching you right now."

Boris glanced around them. "No one is looking. Bullet would go into heart. You would just . . . " He made a gesture with his right hand indicating someone falling forward. "We would walk away and no one would stop us, or we would shoot someone else. Mr. Randall would come with us. If not, we would talk with him again very soon—or with someone in family."

Matt shook his head. "You're not paying attention. This is really simple: You can't do *anything* to us without cutting your own throat. And it's not the people around us you have to worry about. You're on camera. Everyone who's watching can see that gun Yuri is holding."

The Russian glanced to each side quickly. "No. Not true."

"It *is* true. Tell Yuri to put the gun away and sit down. Then I'll show you."

"I do not believe you."

"After this morning, you still want me to *prove* things to you?" This was the moment when he needed to convince the Russian that caution was the best choice. But in case it didn't work, Matt wanted to divert Yuri's attention from Jane. "First, get your trained monkey under control. Tell him to sit down. He's good at pushing *women* around, but that won't help you this time."

Anger flashed in Yuri's eyes. Keeping the pistol low in front of his body, he pointed it toward Matt.

Slowly Matt stood, stretched elaborately, and took a step toward Yuri. The man smiled thinly and raised the gun a bit, pointing it at Matt's belly. Matt took another step, keeping his eyes on Yuri's. He was within arm's reach. He was fairly sure—but not certain—that Yuri would do nothing without a command from his boss. What happened next would depend on the man who liked to be known as Boris.

Boris was puzzled and trying not to show it. These people should be afraid, and if the man did not fear him, at least he should be angry. An angry man was a man who made mistakes. Boris had expected this meeting to end in one of two ways: Randall would watch helplessly, fearfully as Yuri took Jane away, or, less preferable, Randall would be angrily defiant and Boris would give Yuri the signal to put a bullet through Jane's heart. The latter course would be messier, and much riskier here; it could be dangerous in the unlikely event that some of these Americans, unused to intimidation, decided to get involved. But either way, this young fool Randall would learn who was in control, and he would pay for his boldness.

The situation wasn't working out the way Boris had planned. Randall seemed completely in control of himself, too sure of what he was doing—like a man with something hidden in reserve, perhaps a trap that could not be seen. Had he taken this young American too lightly? Eventually, Boris knew, he would exact retribution from these people for defying him, but right now that didn't seem to be the smartest choice. He snapped his fingers to get Yuri's attention, and when the other man looked at him, Boris stared into his associate's eyes and nodded toward the other chair at the table.

Yuri's leer faded, and he looked at his boss quizzically. Boris's brows knitted as he nodded toward the chair again, more emphatically. There could be no mistaking his meaning.

Matt took advantage of Yuri's momentary inattention to reach out quickly and put his right hand on top of the pistol in Yuri's left, forcing the barrel of the gun downward and to the side. Almost instinctively, Yuri's finger tightened on the trigger, but he felt Matt's fingers behind his, keeping the trigger from moving. At the same time, Matt reached out to put his left hand on Yuri's right shoulder and squeeze hard. To anyone watching, it might have seemed like a friendly gesture. But Yuri winced in pain and his knees buckled slightly. He looked almost helplessly at his boss. Matt bore down harder on his shoulder. Yuri gritted his teeth trying not to show the pain he felt. Matt forced the pistol down even farther so it was pointed at the concrete patio.

Boris nodded toward the chair once more, glowering now, and said something softly in Russian. Yuri looked into Matt's eyes again and sneered. But he relaxed his grip on the pistol and let Matt take it out of his hand. Matt turned the weapon upward so it rested against the inside of his own arm and couldn't be seen by others as he slipped it into his jacket pocket. He waited for Yuri to take the chair opposite Jane, then sat down between them.

He picked up a paper napkin that lay on the table next to the bottle of cider, took his pen out of his shirt pocket, and wrote: *www.colecash.org.* "If you want to see what we look like on camera, call someone you trust and have them check out this website, right now." He pulled his own telephone out of his pocket, opened his list of contacts and scrolled down it, then wrote a Manhattan telephone number underneath the web address. "Try your imports office in New York. It's too late in Moscow—almost midnight." He shoved the napkin across the table.

The Russian read the URL, then the phone number and looked at Matt in surprise. He took out his own telephone and dialed the number. While he was waiting for someone to answer, he glanced impatiently at the time, 1:15 P.M. now—4:15 in Manhattan.

Jane noted that the wristwatch he wore was a gold Rolex, just like Greg's. Had it been a gift, in better times, from Greg to a favored client?

After several seconds, Boris scowled as he turned off the phone and shrugged.

"Maybe everybody in the Manhattan office took an hour off at your expense?" Matt was prepared for this possibility. "Check the site out for yourself. You can sign in as Boris if that's the name you like."

The Russian tapped in the URL on his phone and waited. His eyes narrowed suddenly as an image came on its screen. He raised his eyes to scan the windows of the hotel he was facing. Matt smiled slightly. Boris would not be able to see the camera; only the front of its lens protruded through a small opening in the blinds.

Jane looked into the eyes of the man to her right as she raised her left arm and waved cheerily in the direction of the hotel. The Russian watched on his phone, then looked at her and spoke angrily in his native language. When he turned to glare at Matt, there was fury in his face again.

Matt smiled congenially. "My brother invited a lot of people on Facebook and Twitter and some other sites to join us for the little celebration we've arranged for our friend Boris. Doug asked them to spread the word. He's good at social networking; you might even have your own Facebook page or Instagram account by now. I have no idea how many people are watching, or where. But we promised them a show."

He reached for the bottle of sparkling cider and twisted the top open. Jane separated the three paper cups next to the bottle so Matt could pour cider into them. He glanced at Yuri as he poured. "Sorry there aren't enough cups. We weren't expecting extra guests."

Matt reached across the table to place a cup of cider in front of the Russian, then Matt and Jane stood and raised their cups as though toasting him. When they began to sing "Happy Birthday" loudly, people at the nearest tables turned to look. Matt and Jane drew out the name "B-o-r-r-i-s-s" as they sang. People around them smiled, and after the song was over, several applauded. Matt and Jane each took a sip of cider before they sat down.

The Russian looked as though he couldn't decide whether to be bewildered or angry. Matt smiled again. "You're a star on the Internet now. I think a lot of people will remember seeing *you* here today, with us. I think Doug may even be recording this moment."

Slowly a deep red flush crept up the other man's neck. He shoved his chair back and stood. Yuri followed suit, but it was plain he had given up trying to determine what might happen next. His boss pointed a finger at Matt. "We will talk another time," he hissed, keeping his voice low so his words would not be heard by people at other tables. "Next time we talk, will not be time for *singing*."

"You mean you'd walk away from more than six hundred thousand dollars?" Matt asked.

The Russian reached into an inside jacket pocket, pulled out a wad of bills, and waved them toward Matt and Jane contemptuously. "I make back in two months," he hissed. "You will not live that long." He stuffed the bills back into his pocket, then moved as though he would turn and walk away.

"Sit down, Sergei Alexandreyev," Matt said firmly. "We haven't finished talking."

The Russian's eyebrows went up in surprise.

"You're surprised we know your real name?" Matt asked. "We know a lot more than that. Sit down and we'll talk about it." He nodded toward the chair facing him.

The Russian hesitated.

Matt held up his phone. On its face was a countdown timer. The timer ticked past 24:00 . . . 23:59 . . . 23:58. "We both know you can't afford to walk away without knowing what we could do to you, and you don't have a lot of time to think about it," Matt said. "Sit. Down. Now."

The Russian looked at Matt with contempt. It was obvious he wanted badly to turn his back and walk away, to maintain an appearance of control. He looked at Matt's phone again, and it was equally obvious that the countdown timer worried him. The truth hung in the air: The information Matt and Jane had could be dangerous to him. Sergei stood looking into the distance for a few seconds, then glanced at Yuri. Slowly, he turned and sat down at the table again, motioning Yuri back to his chair.

Yuri looked at his boss in disbelief; clearly, he was not used to seeing this man obey someone else.

Sergei looked at the numbers ticking down on Matt's phone. "What is . . . ?"

Matt ignored his question. "Tell me, do you have a lot of security around number 9 Prospekt Place in Kaliningrad?"

The Russian's eyes went wide.

"That's where you go when things get a little too hot in Moscow, isn't it?

Close to the border with Poland, and just across the Baltic from Sweden." Matt paused. "What about the apartment in Marseilles? Or the place on Central Park West in New York City?"

Jane leaned closer and asked: "What about the girls' school in Connecticut?"

Sergei turned to look at her sharply. Anger came back into his eyes.

"Oh, you're upset? You mean it would make you mad if someone threatened to hurt a person close to you—a person you loved? You mean you'd be tempted to hurt *them?*"

The implication of her question was not lost on him. Sergei struggled to regain his composure. "Only Brewster had to hurt. This did not have to include others. Everything was business—only business."

"*Business?*" Matt could feel the flush come into his face. He wanted to leap across the table and take this man by the throat. "You call kidnapping my wife and my brother *business?*" He struggled to keep his voice controlled, but he knew the other man could feel the rage in it. "You call killing Cole and Greg *business?*"

The Russian did not answer; Matt's anger did not seem to touch him. He glared as though he did not like to be lectured.

"Don't worry," Jane said softly, "your wife, and your daughter in Connecticut, are safe. *We're* not going to bring harm to innocent people." She paused. "But nothing else you care about is safe right now."

"Greg was a great collector of information—especially about you," Matt added. "The places you live, the women you live with, the people you hire, the shipments you make—and where you put your money." He paused. "I can touch all of the financial accounts you have in America, and all of the ones Greg found in other countries. I can touch just about everything you *think* you own." It wasn't completely true; there had not been enough time to make a tie with all the accounts. But he had probably compromised enough of them to make the Russian a believer.

"Impossible!" Sergei snorted.

Matt chuckled. "You still want me to prove it to you?" He picked up his phone, tapped in a number, and watched the display screen. When he got an answering message, he typed in several keystrokes, then put his phone back on the table.

Sergei had been watching him apprehensively. "What?" he asked again, nodding toward the phone.

Again, Matt ignored his question. "Greg had big files on several clients who paid him to eliminate problems like Cole. There were a couple of men in South America, a Ukrainian, a man in Hong Kong, somebody in New York, and a few more. But Greg seemed to concentrate on you. Why?"

The Russian did not answer the question. He looked at Matt speculatively for several seconds. "Files on people?" he asked.

Matt nodded. "All involved in the same businesses you are."

"I will give one hundred thousand dollars for files."

Matt studied the Russian's face. "Are you making us an offer, Sergei? You want a deal?"

Sergei looked at Jane. Ordinarily, he thought he could tell what women were thinking—but if not, it didn't matter to him. This time, though, he sensed that he had underestimated the woman. And the man. He looked at Matt once more and realized that this time he would not be able to dictate the terms under which he would negotiate with them. He nodded once. "Yes—deal."

Matt smiled slightly. "Information on the operations of some of your biggest competitors—and it's only worth a hundred thousand dollars to you?"

Sergei returned his gaze, as though trying to measure the level of his opponent's greed. Finally, he said, "You keep money you have. We will call it deal."

"And if we give you the information," Jane said, "how much of that money will we get to spend before something unfortunate happens to us and we're dead?"

Sergei looked at her coldly. It was plain he did not like having to negotiate with a woman. "You have my word."

"I had Greg's word that nothing would happen to us if we gave him what you want. But it just didn't seem we could trust him."

Sergei's phone beeped with an incoming text message. He glanced at its display, frowned, and tapped a button on the screen so he could read the text.

"That will be an urgent message from Philadelphia," Matt said. "It's probably telling you they just lost control of their computers. All their data disappeared and they can't get it back."

The Russian seemed skeptical. He gazed down at his phone and began reading the message. Then he looked up at Matt, stunned.

"You thought only your people knew how to do something like this?" Matt chuckled. He waved his hand dismissively. "It's no big deal. Philadelphia was one of your smaller operations—not much of a loss."

"My people will fix," the Russian said slowly, trying to sound authoritative.

"No, they won't. They'll have to start over—probably with new computers after the bug I sent them does its job, and you'll never get that money back either. If your computer people told you they had you well-protected, they lied. Your security was outdated. They were lazy."

Sergei shook his head as though he were trying to clear it, or to reassure himself.

Matt leaned forward, putting his elbows on the table. "What would you be willing to give up to get Greg's computer files?" He pointed at Yuri. "Him?"

Yuri looked at Matt in surprise. He turned to his boss waiting expectantly for some reply and seemed nonplussed when none came. Sergei maintained his poker face as he stared at Matt.

"Think about it," Matt said. "The knife I took away from him is in the hands of the police. It will have his fingerprints all over it, and I'm sure they'll find it was the weapon that killed Greg. Yuri stands out, so he'll be easy to spot, and if you get caught with him, you're an accomplice to murder at least."

"Police would have to prove this," Sergei said slowly.

"They will." Matt nodded toward Yuri. "He's your weak point. Spilling everything he knows about you would probably be the only way he could save himself."

The big man at his left was glowering at the turn this conversation had taken. Matt ignored him. "We have a deal to offer you. *Just* you." He glanced at Yuri, then pointed toward the tables at the far side of the cafe. "Tell him to go sit over there."

Yuri looked at Matt in shock, then looked questioningly at Sergei.

"Tell him. Now," Matt said firmly.

Sergei continued to look into Matt Randall's eyes for several seconds trying to assess him. Finally he looked at Yuri and nodded. Yuri scowled and held his position. Sergei spoke one word in Russian, sharply. Slowly, Yuri stood.

"Tell him he can wait over there where we can see him until we're through talking to you," Matt said.

Yuri looked to his boss once more. There was a red flush in Sergei's face as he nodded. Slowly, Yuri looked at Jane, then Matt. There was no mistaking the hatred in his eyes. Matt gestured toward the far end of the café. Yuri turned contemptuously and walked away. Matt and Jane watched him until he took a seat at an empty table.

Matt frowned as he looked at Sergei. "In the past 12 hours, I've taken three .22 automatic pistols away from people who work for you. Do you get some kind of bulk discount on those things?"

Sergei sat rigidly without answering. It was clear that he was simmering about being humiliated in front of his enforcer, obviously struggling to sit passively without reacting.

"We don't want your money," Jane said to him. "We never did. What we want won't cost you anything at all—but if we don't get what we want, that will cost you *everything*." She stopped to let him think about her words. "All we want is peace."

"We want to be left alone," Matt said. "If anything happens to either one of us, all the information we have about you will go to law enforcement agencies in the U.S., Canada, England, France, Russia, China—everywhere you have operations. It will also go to some of your competitors—people Greg had in his files. It's set up to happen automatically. It can only be stopped by entering a password phrase—and I only know half the password." He glanced at Jane. "She knows the other half. It will take both of us to keep the information about you from going out on the Internet. And there's a deadline." He held up his phone. The countdown clock ticked past 19:15 . . . 19:14.

Sergei seemed to be weighing what Matt had said. "How to know you are telling me—"

Matt laughed, and shook his head. "We both have to check in before this timer hits zero."

"I can pay more for information from files," Sergei said. "How much?"

"It's not for sale," Jane said. "Money seems to be the only thing you care about, so we used money to get you here. There's just one thing *we* really want—to be protected from you—and you may be the only one in the world who can give us that. On the other hand, if you do anything to either of us, you'll be on the run for the rest of your short life."

Sergei looked at her as he had at Matt, seemingly trying to assess her. "If I give what you ask," he said to Jane, "information will not go out on Internet?"

"It won't go public and it won't fall into the hands of your competitors," Jane answered.

"We're not going to protect you from justice," Matt added. "So if you think the police will find any evidence to convict you in Greg's computer files, you might want to consider getting out of this country—and staying out."

There was a momentary flash of hatred in Sergei's eyes as he considered what Matt had said, and then the hate disappeared, masked again by the man's poker face. Jane studied him as he weighed his options. He had been maneuvered into this position because he was greedy. She knew he would not simply give up his current lifestyle. How long, she wondered, would it take a man like this to build up new networks and new enterprises they might not know about?

Finally he spoke to Matt. "We have what is called in chess stalemate." He spread his hands in a gesture of helplessness.

"No," Matt said. "What we have is a clear win for our side, and a history lesson for you. You need to understand it. What we have is Mutually Assured Destruction—the same balance that existed between our two countries during the Cold War. We can destroy you, and now you know it. We wouldn't enjoy it—not even after you've treated us like human garbage. But if you attack us, you'll be killing yourself. We think you're smart enough not to commit suicide."

Matt leaned forward in his chair. "Don't think you can block me or build up defenses on your computers. You're wrong. I can see into them. If anything—*anything*—makes me believe you're trying to come after us— well, you haven't even begun to think of all the things that could go wrong for you. Maybe information about your competitors will go public or go to the police—and your competitors will find out it came from you. Or how about this: Your competitor in Marseilles would receive proof that you had Greg eliminate his son-in-law. What would he do about that?"

Sergei looked shocked, as though Matt had surprised him again when he didn't believe more surprises were possible.

"You know those stolen personal banking files you just sold to your client in China? He's not going to like it when he finds out the files are corrupted. I wonder if he's connected to the Chinese government—maybe the military? How do you think he's going to feel about you?"

Sergei seemed to pale a bit, Jane thought.

"Remember that Facebook page I mentioned?" Matt said. "Maybe all your personal information will end up on it for the whole world to see. Use your imagination when you think about all the bad things that could happen to you. That's what I did." He pointed at Yuri. "And people like him would never be able to protect you. They can't kill information."

Yuri had been pretending not to pay attention. He turned when he saw Matt point and looked uneasily at Sergei's back, obviously concerned about what was happening in this negotiation.

Sergei studied Matt speculatively. His gut burned for having to show deference to this man, but he was trying to keep the anger he felt under control—out of sight. He could not remember a time when an adversary had so clearly outmaneuvered him.

"We didn't create this situation," Jane said. "You did. But we *will* protect ourselves."

Sergei turned to look at her. "Lady, you have luck. You married man with much guts." He said it with something that sounded almost like admiration.

"You made a mistake about us. *Both* of us," Matt said. "You can blame your own choices for anything that happens to you now. If you'd just left us alone, you could have—"

Matt stopped as his telephone rang. The number on the caller ID panel was blocked. He frowned at Sergei. "This better not be some kind of surprise you've arranged. I wouldn't react well to any surprises right now."

The Russian looked at him blankly and shrugged.

Matt picked up his phone and tapped the button to accept the call. "Hello?" he said cautiously.

"Matt, this is Montie. *Don't* hang up this time. You're in a great deal of danger."

Matt phrased his answer carefully. "Yeah—since yesterday. And how are you?"

"I take it you can't talk freely?"

"That's right. But we're fine here." Matt tried to sound cheerful.

"The man you're sitting with is Sergei Alexandreyev. He's into drugs, arms sales, all kinds of rackets, and he doesn't hesitate to kill anyone who gets in his way. Did you know that?"

"Yes, that's right." Matt smiled disarmingly in Sergei's direction. The Russian looked at him questioningly, but Matt gave him nothing more.

Montie went on. "Greg Alexander, the man you said we should check on—we believe Sergei killed him, or had him killed. Greg was family—Sergei's nephew. Did you know that?"

"That's . . . interesting," Matt answered slowly. He couldn't fake a smile again, remembering the last time he had seen Greg.

"We want Sergei, and believe me, you want us to get him," Montie said. "Why don't you pass the phone to Jane and let her talk to me while you keep him occupied. We need a couple of minutes to close in on your location."

"Yeah. See you soon." Matt handed the phone to Jane. Then he forced another smile at Sergei. "Family. They were wondering why they haven't heard from us in the past couple of days."

The Russian looked doubtfully at the telephone in Jane's hand.

"Hello?" Jane said cheerfully. "Oh, Montie. How are things there?"

The Russian looked back at Matt. His eyes narrowed.

"You don't talk to your family very often?" Matt asked. "When it comes right down to it, family is everything, Sergei. You've got to put family above anything else." He looked at Jane. "I'll do anything I need to do to keep my family safe."

Sergei looked at Jane too and realized that she was not speaking into the phone, only holding it to her ear. "Is trap! You set up me!" He looked like he had experienced yet another shock.

Matt shook his head. "This is nothing we planned. My wife's Uncle Montie called."

The hate was in Sergei's eyes again. "Uncle?" He shook his head. "No. Police." He pushed his chair back and stood.

Matt reached into his jacket pocket and put his hand on the pistol.

Sergei looked down at the jacket and then looked Matt in the eyes again. "You would not shoot. *You* are not killer. Your police would put *you* in prison."

"Yuri *is* a killer. Leave him behind. He'll only slow you down anyway."

Sergei shook his head. "I will not leave friend."

"A friend? Or someone who knows too much about you?"

A flicker of response in Sergei's eyes told Matt he had been right. Then the other man's face went blank again. Sergei started to turn slowly, tentatively. Matt slid the pistol out of his pocket and held it under the table. Sergei looked down at the table as though trying to see through it, then looked into Matt's eyes once more and smiled slightly. "You will not. I know. You know."

Matt knew it was true.

Jane held the phone so Sergei could see the timer: 11:47 . . . 11:46. . . .

Matt realized he was sweating, and not because the day was warm. No matter what advantages they had on their side, this man was still dangerous and unpredictable. Was there a way to stall him a little longer? Matt couldn't think of one. He let go of the pistol and put both hands on the table. "You know what we want. Peace—or everything you care about is gone right now and you're history. Are you going to force our hand?"

Sergei frowned and opened his mouth as though he were going to argue. He stood looking from Matt to Jane and back.

Matt took the phone from Jane's hand and laid it on the table facing Sergei. The timer counted down 11:22 . . 11:21 . . . 11:20. . . . Sergei thought for a moment longer, then nodded once. "Peace."

He turned, and strode rapidly away between the tables, motioning to Yuri as he passed. Yuri rose and followed him to the black limousine across the square. Yuri held the car door shut and spoke angrily to his boss, looking back toward Matt and Jane. Sergei answered with equal force, but his words were inaudible. He slapped Yuri's hand away from the door of the limousine, jerked it open, and climbed inside. He tugged on Yuri's belt so that Yuri had to follow. The limo began to pull away while the door was still open. The last thing Matt and Jane saw before it closed was Yuri glaring out at them.

Matt slid the pistol back into his pocket.

He could hear Montie's voice coming through on the telephone, but he couldn't make out the words. "Yes," Jane said into the phone, "the open-air café on the far side of the square." She paused, then added, "I wish you were here, Montie. It would be easier to explain all of this to you instead of someone we don't know." She listened again, then smiled and handed the phone back to Matt. "He was already on his way. Touchdown at the San Francisco airport is in seven minutes."

Matt put the phone to his ear. All he could hear was Montie issuing instructions to someone in the background. He ended the call.

Jane picked up her phone and tapped on its face two or three times. Their conversation with Sergei began to play back from the phone. "Out of his own mouth—words to convict him," she said.

She looked around the square. With the fog burned off, it was a beautiful summer day in San Francisco. The sun felt warm on her face.

Two days ago, she would have enjoyed a leisurely exploration of this part of the city. Now she wasn't sure she would ever be able to come here again.

She reached for Matt's hand and intertwined her fingers with his.

He sighed as he looked at her. "I'm sorry our honeymoon had to turn out this way."

"Considering the way things looked yesterday at this time, I think it's turning out wonderfully well."

Matt noticed two men in suits moving toward them across the square from behind her—the two FBI agents she had pointed out earlier in the hotel. Each had a hand under his jacket. Their eyes swept the square carefully as they moved.

"Look," Jane said. He followed her gaze toward the other side of the square, on the east. A man and a woman were getting out of a dark sedan parked at the curb. The woman also had a hand under her jacket, and her eyes also scanned the square as she and the man moved forward. The man spoke into a small radio, his eyes fixed on Matt and Jane.

Matt looked at his wife. "I promise I'll make all of this up to you someday."

Jane gave him one of her smiles that made everything else go away. He hadn't seen one of those since early yesterday morning. "Right now," she said, "if I know we have tomorrow, I'll be happy."

Epilogue

Matt handed Jane her plate, then selected a steak off the grill for himself. They were celebrating his first paycheck from a new job. Cole Brewster's company was in the process of liquidation, but fortunately, Jane's father had been able to give Matt the name of some contacts, and one of those men had decided that his company needed Matt's skills.

Jane and Matt sat on their balcony overlooking the small patch of green lawn next to the play area for children in their apartment complex. A man sitting on a bench next to the play area looked up at their balcony, then turned away when he saw Matt watching him. He gazed instead at the children on the swings.

He might have been a father watching over a small son or daughter.

"Today's security detail?" Jane asked, looking at the man on the bench.

Matt nodded. "That would be my guess. I think I've seen him before."

They had not asked for protection from the FBI, but Montie had told them it would be there—unobtrusively. They had gotten used to seeing someone at the edge of the nearby park in the mornings when they went jogging, or in an unmarked vehicle two cars behind when they went somewhere together. Jane knew a car would be following her at a discreet distance when she drove to work in the morning now that school had started again. The car would be there in the rearview mirror later when she came home. Matt could not be sure whether he was followed, but they had gotten used to seeing someone around the apartment complex who could blend in with the surroundings—sometimes a man, like today, or sometimes a woman who might be a young mother watching her child on the playground. One tip-off was the longer, loose shirt the agents usually wore, even in the Arizona heat. Presumably, it covered a weapon worn in a holster at waist level.

Matt and Jane wondered if the security detail was more for their protection or because the FBI wanted to grab Sergei if he came close to them again.

Jane pointed across the play area toward the other side of the complex. "Montie." Her uncle strode toward their building. He confirmed their speculation about the man on the bench by sitting down to talk with him.

Montie had been almost livid about Sergei's escape.

"You had Sergei Alexandreyev sitting across the table from you, and you let him walk! I can't believe you did that!" Montie fumed.

"Would you have been happier if I'd shot him—maybe killed him?" Matt flared. "That was the only other choice. He said if I did that you'd have to put me *in jail. Would you?"*

Montie pointed a finger at Matt's face and lowered his voice as though the other agents in the 12-by-15-foot hotel room might not hear his words. "I put my job on the line by allowing you to carry out your little plan. And for what?"

Jane stepped up to look her uncle in the eye. "Montie, our lives *were on the line. We risked everything to bring Sergei into the open—but we couldn't arrest him for you. Now he's gone and our lives may still be on the line."*

Montie stood in silence looking up at her for a moment, hands on his hips, then turned to Matt. "Officially, I have to let the two of you know the FBI is very unhappy about how this turned out. You should have shared any information you had with the bureau right from the beginning and let us take over. I'm supposed to let you know officially that you might be charged with obstructing an investigation."

"Tell the bureau it has a bad attitude," Matt answered. "Officially, how would the bureau feel if I could give you information on all of Sergei's financial operations in North America? Officially, how would the bureau like to have leads on some of his competitors too?"

Montie's eyebrows went up. "You could do that?"

Matt glanced at Greg's computer sitting on the desk by the window, next to the video camera on its tripod. "Yeah—and more. If you'll let me—""

"The bureau will take over from here." Montie looked into Matt's eyes for several seconds. His face did not give away anything about what he was thinking. "Based on my training and experience, I have to say you did a lot

that looks pretty dumb. You should have let us step in from the beginning. We could have—"

"Rescued Jane? But what if they—"

Montie held up a hand to stop him and shook his head. "Things could have gone sour on you anytime, and Jane might not be here right now—or you. You were extremely lucky—or blessed."

"You think I haven't told myself that? I was dying inside while they had Jane, but I had to do something. *I did what impressed me as the right thing at the time."*

"I think in this case we have to agree you were blessed." Slowly, Montie let himself smile. "Unofficially, I have to say I'm glad you were here for my niece. I knew you were smart, or Janie—Jane—wouldn't have picked you out. But I had no idea you were sharp enough to take down somebody like Sergei. I underestimated you." He put out his hand.

Slowly, Matt smiled as he shook it.

"These agents will debrief you," Montie said as he glanced at the men examining the computer, "but I'll be sitting in on it. I'm sorry, Jane, but this will take some time."

"I've already written out everything that happened up to our meeting out there on the square." She pointed at the papers on top of the bagged items they had taken from the hotel room's safe.

"That'll be a big help. But right now we need both of you to tell us everything you heard from Sergei."

"Would you like a recording?"

The mystery about Sergei was what happened after he left the café in Union Square.

Nothing.

After he had walked away from them seven weeks ago, he had simply vanished. Agents had caught up with the black limousine creeping through downtown San Francisco traffic—but only the driver was inside. The FBI had learned the identity of Sergei's charter pilot from Los Angeles and sent agents to meet the plane when it returned to the airport where it was based. But Sergei had paid the pilot several hundred dollars cash to change the flight plan and land first at a different airport. Sergei and Yuri had rented a car and had not been seen by anyone since then. The car had been found abandoned near the border a little southwest of Yuma, Arizona, two days later.

All of Sergei's business operations in North America seemed to cease within two or three days. In Europe, they went on for almost two weeks, then tapered off. Matt wondered what the FBI made of it, but he was in no position to ask. He had turned Greg's computer and all of its files over to the bureau and its experts. But he had quietly retrieved copies of the files, links, and information from one of the sites where he had stored them for safekeeping; he wanted to monitor Sergei's activities on his own in case the Russian did anything that seemed threatening.

There had been no new activity of any kind in Sergei's North American accounts or operations since the third day after their meeting—no money in or out, no shipments recorded. It was puzzling. Matt was almost certain Sergei did not have enough money stashed somewhere else to fund all of his operations, nor did he believe the Russian would abandon the amounts of money sitting idle in his accounts in the United States. Was he laying low somewhere?

Matt felt no great fear for their safety day to day, but still, he maintained the protective Internet shield he had established, and he and Jane kept their two-part password phrase updated.

On the green area in front of their building, Montie and the other man stood, shared a few final words, and walked in opposite directions. Montie came toward their building. He looked up at their balcony and waved.

"Come up and join us," Jane called. "We have enough for one more." While he climbed the stairs to the door of their apartment, she rose from her chair and walked across the living room to let him in. Matt brought another chair to the balcony.

"Thanks for the invitation, but I'll have to pass on dinner. Kathy will have it waiting when I get home," Montie said.

"Are you sure?" Matt asked, holding out a plate. "We have an extra steak, and you don't want to miss out on this potato salad."

Montie glanced at Jane. "Your mother's recipe? I never could pass up her potato salad." He took off the coat of his lightweight suit and draped it over the back of a chair. As he sat down, he adjusted the holster on his belt so his weapon could clear the holster quickly if he needed it. The gesture seemed automatic.

Jane dished up a large helping of the potato salad. "I've added a couple of secret ingredients of my own."

Matt and Jane exchanged looks as Montie took a bite and savored it. Matt's look was questioning; Jane simply shrugged.

"Oh, Matt, you don't know how lucky you are. She cooks as well as her mother," Montie said, savoring another bite. "I'd love to enjoy more of this. But I can't stay long. I just came to share some news with the two of you."

Jane frowned as she glanced down at the empty bench on the play area. "No more security?" she asked.

Montie smiled slightly. "You won't need it." He pulled his phone out of his pocket, tapped its touch screen a couple of times, and showed them the photo on the display. "Does this look familiar?"

The photo showed a gold Rolex watch and a folding knife in separate plastic bags.

Jane's eyes widened. "That watch looks like the one Sergei was wearing."

"The knife is the same kind I took away from Greg and Yuri," Matt added.

Montie nodded. "Yesterday border agents nabbed a *coyote* who's been near the top of their want list. He's trying to make a deal, so he offered to tell them about a dead terrorist who attacked him in the desert."

"You're talking about a people smuggler—one of those men who bring people across the border?" Jane asked.

Montie nodded again. "The government's looking at prosecuting the guy for murder because a couple of months ago he left some people in the desert to die while he got away. He wanted to make points with the prosecutors, maybe get them to drop some of the charges, so he offered to show them the spot where this terrorist was planning to cross the border."

Matt raised his eyebrows. "Going *south*?"

"The smuggler said maybe this man was running from some crime up north. His story was that the guy suddenly came at him out of the dark speaking Arabic. The man had a knife, so the smuggler shot him. He led the sheriff to where he left the body."

"Speaking Arabic?" Matt asked.

"Our smuggler understands English fairly well—when he wants to. He claims he wouldn't know the difference between Arabic and Russian."

Jane's brow furrowed. "And the 'terrorist' was Sergei?"

Montie called up another photo on his phone, looked at it for a moment, then put the phone down. "I don't think you want to see this one. When deputies found the body, the buzzards had—" He stopped, catching the pained look in Jane's eyes. "It would be hard to identify the remains from a photograph. But the man was wearing this watch. The smuggler who shot him took his knife after he died, and there are still traces of blood on the blade. The blood is a DNA match to his enforcer, Yuri."

Matt and Jane looked at each other, then back at Montie. "Where was Yuri?" Matt asked.

Montie pulled up another photo on his phone. It showed a man's western boots with jeans covering the tops. The man apparently was lying down somewhere in a shallow trench; dirt partially covered his lower leg above the boot. Matt and Jane studied the photo for several seconds. "Yuri was wearing boots like those," she said.

"We want to be completely sure about the first body. We've contacted Sergei's daughter in Connecticut to try to get a DNA match."

"How horrible for her! Imagine finding out about her father that way."

Montie frowned. "Yeah. The agents who talked to her said she was broken up about it—but she wasn't surprised. She knew what her father was. We think he was grooming her to help in his businesses in this country. He used to interrogate her for information about her rich classmates' families—information he could use somehow. There was no one he wouldn't use if he could. The two of you probably didn't know this, but Irina was Greg's cousin—Sergei's niece. Sergei sent both of them to America when they were young teenagers so they could be educated here and he could use them later."

Montie took another bite of the salad and savored it.

"Can you show me that knife again?" Matt asked.

Montie called up the photo and held out his phone.

Matt studied the knife in the plastic bag. "Sergei was probably carrying that when he met with us. After I took the pistol away from Yuri, he still had the knife in reserve." He looked up at Montie. "What happened out there in the desert? Does anyone have any idea?"

Montie shrugged. "There were fingerprints from two people on the knife—the smuggler, and Sergei, we think. It looks like Sergei might have used the knife on Yuri. The big guy had a couple of defensive wounds on his forearm and his good hand. Hard to tell now, but it looks like he was stabbed and then his throat was cut. We don't know why they would have had a falling out. Our best guess is that the two of them were trying to cross the border to reach Sergei's contacts in Mexico."

Matt and Jane looked at each other again. Matt nodded.

Montie raised an eyebrow. "You know something I don't?"

"They didn't agree on what to do about us," Jane answered. "Yuri still wanted to kill us. I think Sergei saw the logic in cutting his losses and getting out of the country."

"Yuri would have held him back," Matt said. "I tried to convince Sergei to leave him behind, but Sergei said he wouldn't give up a friend. When I asked if he was afraid to let Yuri be captured because he knew too much. I could tell that hit home."

Montie thought for a moment. "You mean if we had Yuri, we could have charged him for murder, and his only hope would have been to flip on Sergei."

"Yeah."

"So maybe there was an argument and Sergei decided you were right about Yuri," Montie said, thinking.

"Do you believe the coyote's story?" Jane asked.

Montie smiled slightly. "Tell me, why shouldn't we?"

"Well, doesn't it seem a little too—I don't know, convenient, or weird? The smuggler is out in the desert at night all by himself and suddenly this terrorist comes at him out of the dark?"

"Sergei had some Mexican contacts," Matt said. "Maybe he was running to them for help."

"You're thinking the way we did," Montie answered. "From what your brother told us, the kidnappers were expecting to collect some ransom before they let him go. They went away empty handed. Sergei tended to push people around, and those cartel guys don't like to be pushed. Maybe they decided to get rid of a problem. Sergei was shot at very close range."

"What happened to Irina?"

"She's back in Russia. She chose to be deported rather than face prosecution as an accessory to Jane's kidnapping. Yuri put real fear into her by telling what he'd done to Greg and threatening her if she didn't help him locate you. After you were able to take down Yuri, she was afraid she might be on *your* radar."

"I could almost feel sorry for her," Matt said, frowning. "Almost."

"Our contacts in Europe say Sergei's operations are being taken over by others little by little. So far, based on the information you gave us, we've been able to arrest 27 of his people in this country." Montie gazed at Matt speculatively. "The bureau's tech experts tell me they think somebody's been quietly checking on Sergei's operations—somebody who covers his tracks pretty well."

The comment had been carefully worded; it was not a direct question. Matt chose the words of his reply with equal care. "Unless someone was obstructing their investigation, they wouldn't need to do anything about that, would they?"

Montie smiled slightly. "Probably not. By the way, our tech people were impressed with the way you got into Sergei's computers and his files—the way you tied him up. Some of them were so impressed that they wouldn't mind seeing a job application from you."

Matt's eyebrows went up. "Me?" He glanced at the weapon on Montie's belt. "I don't think so. I don't think I'm cut out for your kind of work."

"My 'kind of work'?" Montie chuckled. "Actually, the FBI has a lot of tech people and analysts too. It could be a good career." He stood. "I've got to go. But you might give that some thought."

Montie put his empty plate on the table, stood, and slipped on his suit coat. Matt walked him to the door and saw him out, locking the deadbolt afterward—a habit he and Jane had cultivated since San Francisco. Then he walked back to sit by his wife on their balcony. They ate in silence, thinking about the news Montie had brought.

Matt felt some of the constant underlying stress—the fear he had tried not to acknowledge—beginning to drain away.

These past seven weeks, they had tried to begin building a normal life—but there had been tension just under the surface. More than once Jane had awakened sobbing from nightmares—variations on being threatened and tormented by Lyle and Greg in that filthy hotel. Each time Matt had held her close and comforted her until she calmed down and was able to sleep again. He had not told her about his own nightmares. Each time in his dream he had been back in their hotel room on Powell Street, awakened by that small noise from the door, and when he had looked there had been a dark figure silhouetted in the doorway holding a knife. Then he had come awake in his own bed in Phoenix, sweating, fists clenched, ready to fight. Who was the dark figure—Greg? Yuri? Sergei? He had not been able to decide.

Lyle and Greg and Sergei had each been surprised when Jane held her own against them so well, and Matt admired her emotional and physical strength. But he still worried that he had let her down. It was a husband's duty to protect the woman he loved, and he still regretted leaving her alone in their hotel room that morning. Logic told him he could not have predicted what would happen, but he had not been able to let himself off the hook completely. He was grateful for a release from the undercurrent of tension.

After San Francisco, he had felt certain that Sergei was neutralized—and yet every day when he had said good-bye to his wife, there had been a twinge of uncertainty, a desire to linger and hold onto her a little longer. He had continued to struggle with anger and hate for the men who had threatened the woman he loved. Today's news might help him let go.

He looked at Jane. She was gazing out toward the playground, where two mothers were watching their children play on the swings. Tears were sliding down her cheeks.

"J? What is it?"

She smiled at him. "I was just thinking I could be one of those mommies out there by the playground." She reached for his hand and squeezed it. "We can have a baby now."

"You mean *Sergei* was why you've been feeling we should wait?"

She nodded. "I knew we put him in a box—at least my head knew. But my heart worried. What if he decided to come back sometime and we had a child who could be a target?"

Matt took her hand between both of his and tugged her gently toward him. "Come here."

She came to sit on his lap. "Want to know what I learned in San Francisco?" she said.

"What?"

"That I married a man I can rely on completely." She leaned over to kiss him lightly. "Totally." She kissed him again. "With all my heart." She kissed him once more.

"Want to know what I learned?" he asked.

"What?"

"That nothing else will ever mean as much to me as what we have between the two of us—not while I'm breathing, and even after that. For always."

"Always. I'll hold you to that." She kissed him again, and lingered on his lips this time. Then she laid her head on his shoulder. "But let's try to go on breathing for a long, long time."